An author of more than ninety ~~novels for~~ adults with more than seventy ~~more for Mills & Boon,~~ **Janice Kay Johnson** writes about love and family and pens books of gripping romantic suspense. A *USA Today* bestselling author and an eight-time finalist for the Romance Writers of America *RITA®* Award, she won a *RITA®* Award in 2008. A former librarian, Janice raised two daughters in a small town north of Seattle, Washington.

Lisa Dodson is a nationally bestselling author and an Amazon number one bestselling author of over nineteen novels in multiple genres. Lisa writes positive, realistic characters that she hopes readers can connect with while enjoying her novels. Lisa works as a business development manager at a technology consulting firm, is the mother of two adult children and a Maltipoo, Brinkley, and lives in Raleigh, North Carolina.

Also by Janice Kay Johnson

Hide the Child
Trusting the Sheriff
Within Range
Brace for Impact
The Hunting Season
The Last Resort
Cold Case Flashbacks
Dead in the Water
Mustang Creek Manhunt
Crime Scene Connection
High Mountain Terror

Also by Lisa Dodson

Six Days to Live

Discover more at millsandboon.co.uk

THE SHERIFF'S
TO PROTECT

VG

JANICE KAY JOHNSON

THE BODYGUARD'S
DEADLY MISSION

VG

LISA DODSON

MILLS & BOON

First Published in Great Britain 2024
by Mills & Boon, an imprint of HarperCollins*Publishers* Ltd
1 London Bridge Street, London, SE1 9GF

www.harpercollins.co.uk

HarperCollins*Publishers*
Macken House, 39/40 Mayor Street Upper,
Dublin 1, D01 C9W8, Ireland

ISBN: 978-0-263-32215-6

0124

MIX
Paper | Supporting responsible forestry
FSC™ C007454

This book is produced from independently certified FSC™ paper
to ensure responsible forest management.

For more information visit: www.harpercollins.co.uk/green

Printed and Bound in the UK using 100% Renewable Electricity at
CPI Group (UK) Ltd, Croydon, CR0 4YY

THE SHERIFF'S
TO PROTECT

JANICE KAY JOHNSON

Chapter One

The phone call came out of the blue, as Jared's always did. About to start work, Savannah Baird had just turned off her ringer, so it was pure chance she saw his name come up before she stowed the phone in the pocket of her fleece vest. The timing was lousy, but since she heard from her brother only a couple of times a year, she never sent him to voice mail. She wasn't all that sure he'd *leave* a message.

She accepted the call, said, "Hey, Jared," and then to the groom on the other side of the fence holding the young Arabian horse's reins, "I have to take this. Can you walk him?"

He nodded.

Jared said, "You there?"

"Yes." Savannah turned away from the fence and headed into the cavernous covered arena, currently empty, where she could sit at the foot of the bleachers. "How are you?"

"Uh...tell you the truth, I'm in some trouble."

His hushed voice scared her right away. She pictured him hunched over his phone, his head turning to be sure he was still alone. The picture wasn't well formed, since she hadn't seen him since he was a skinny sixteen-year-old. The couple of photos she'd coaxed out of him via text refused to supplant in her head the image of the boy she'd known and loved so much.

"What kind of trouble?" she asked.

"Better if I don't tell you that, except..." Now he sounded raw. "I'll try to run, but I think they're suspicious."

They had something to do with illegal drugs. That was all she knew, except a couple of years ago he'd said something about redeeming himself. She thought Jared really had gotten clean, but too late; he'd been caught up in a shady business and not been allowed to escape. Or maybe he didn't want to. Unless he was attempting to bring down his employer? Savannah had never dared ask, afraid if she did, he'd quit calling at all.

Now he said with unmistakable urgency, "I should have told you this before. I have a daughter. Almost five. Her mother has problems and got so she couldn't take care of her. I'm all she has." He made a sound she couldn't identify. "Vannah, will you take Molly, at least until I straighten things out? I have her stuff packed. She's a good kid."

Staggered, all Savannah could get out was "A daughter? In five *years*, you couldn't tell me?"

"I lost touch with her mother. I kept thinking…" He huffed. "It doesn't matter. She's mine, and I don't know what they'd do to her. At best, she'd end up in the foster care system."

Savannah knew who was at the root of his problems: their parents. Specifically, their father, who hadn't just been hard on Jared, he'd seemed actively to dislike him, while their mother's efforts to protect her brother had been ineffectual. Meanwhile, *she'd* been Daddy's little princess. The contrast had been painful, and nothing she'd been able to do had ever made any difference. The astonishing part was that he mostly hadn't blamed her.

Now there was only one thing she could say.

"Of course I'll take her. Can you bring her to me? Or… where are you?"

"Still in San Francisco. Can you come here?"

"Today?"

"Yeah." The tension in his voice raised prickles on her arms.

She glanced at the phone. "Yes. Okay. It's early enough. I should be able to drive to Albuquerque and get an afternoon flight. When and where shall we meet?"

"Call me when you get in." He paused. "No. If things go

bad… Ah, come to Bayview. It's not the best part of the city, but we can make the handoff fast." He gave her an address.

Never having been to the City by the Bay, she had no way of envisioning the neighborhood. Thank goodness for GPS.

"Yes, sure. I'll rent a car."

"Thank you. Molly is everything to me." His voice roughened. "Make sure she knows I love her. I'd have done anything for her. I just wish I'd done it sooner."

"Don't sound like that! You're smart. You'll get yourself out of…of whatever mess this is. In fact, why don't *you* come with me, too? You know I'm working in really remote country in New Mexico."

"Maybe I'll try."

He didn't believe himself. She could hear it in his voice. Now even more scared, she clung to the phone. "Jared?"

"I love you," he said and was gone.

The beginning of a sob shook her, but she didn't have time for fear. She had to talk to her boss, the owner of this ranch dedicated primarily to breeding Arabians and training them for show as well as cutting, barrel racing, roping and the like. A stallion that stood stud here had been a national champion four years ago. Ed Loewen had made his money in software, using it to follow his dream. He wouldn't be happy that she had to take off with no notice, but he had kids and grandkids of his own. He'd understand.

Not that it mattered. She would go no matter what.

In fact…she hustled back to the outdoor arena and let the groom know she wouldn't be riding Chopaka after all. Then she jogged for the house.

SAVANNAH'S FIRST STOP after picking up the rental car was a corner convenience store to buy a can of soda and a few snacks. She added extras in case Molly was hungry. Then, the afternoon waning, she followed the voice coming from her phone. Take this exit onto another freeway. Stay in the second lane from the right. Exit. Left onto a major thoroughfare. Traffic grew steadily heavier.

Once she broke free of it, she was winding through the city itself. Another time, she would have paid more attention to the Victorian homes or tried to catch glimpses of the bay or the graceful arches of the Golden Gate Bridge. But the light was going, and fog rolled in off the ocean, making visibility increasingly poor. She couldn't have said when she realized that she'd entered an area of a very wealthy city that "isn't the best." Vacant storefronts and graffiti were the first clue. Small groups of young men with the waistbands of their pants sagging below their butts clustered in groups at corners. None of them would get far slinging a leg over the back of a horse, she couldn't help thinking. Or running. When she slowed for lights, she didn't like the way heads turned and she was watched.

Why here? Did Jared live in the neighborhood? If this was his home address, why hadn't he said? But her gut told her this was nowhere near his usual stomping grounds. He wouldn't want anybody he knew to see him transferring his darling daughter to another person.

The daughter, she thought uneasily, who could be used to apply pressure on him. Probably not his sister; whoever lurked in his secretive world had no reason even to know he had a sister.

I'm imagining things, she tried telling herself stoutly, but it didn't help much as night closed in, muffled by the thick, low fog. She could see lights on porches and lit windows in the few businesses still open as if through a filter. She imagined Jack the Ripper's London had looked rather like this.

Oh, for Pete's sake—her real problem was that she'd never spent time in a major city. The buildings crowding in, the sense she was wandering a maze, made her feel claustrophobic.

GPS instructed her to make another turn. Without the guidance, she might have passed the street. The next storefront she saw had Gone Out of Business spray-painted on plywood nailed up to cover a window.

GPS was telling her she'd reached her destination. Not the store that had gone out of business, but two doors down. A dry cleaner's, closed for the day. No other car waited for her at the curb.

With a shiver, she signaled and pulled over, her eyes on her rearview mirror. She seemed to be completely alone on this block. Had Jared been held up? If only there was a streetlight closer; the recess in front of the door was awfully dark. Except…something huddled there.

Oh, God. Savannah was out of her car without having conscious thought, rushing across the sidewalk toward the child who crouched in the door well, hugging her knees and peering up at Savannah.

A small, shaking voice said, "Are you Auntie Vannah?"

Savannah choked back something like a sob. "Yes. Oh, honey. You must be Molly."

The head bobbed.

"Where is your daddy? I thought he'd be here."

The face she could see was thin and pinched. "He…he had to go. He promised you'd come. He said I shouldn't move *at all*. And I didn't, but I was *scared*."

"I don't blame you for being scared, but I did come." Tears wanted to burn her eyes, but she blinked them back. "Once we're in the car—" *locked* in the car "—I'll call him." She summoned a smile. "The pink suitcase must be yours."

"Uh-huh," her niece said in her childish voice. "Daddy left this for you."

This was a duffel bag that didn't appear to have much in it. Did it contain a few changes of clothes for himself in the hopes he could wait and hop into Savannah's car for a getaway? Or was it really packed with more for this little girl? She'd look later. Her priority now was Molly and getting her safely away.

Savannah helped her up and, without releasing her hand, led her to the car. At Molly's age, she should probably sit in the back, but Savannah lifted her into the front seat anyway. She wanted to be able to see her face, to hold her hand. Then she popped the trunk and stowed the two bags before rushing to get in behind the wheel and hit the lock button.

Just as she did, a car with lights that seemed to be on high beam approached, hesitated, then passed.

Savannah started the car. "Let me drive a little ways."

A few blocks later, she found a small grocery store with several cars parked in a small lot. Feeling a bit safer, she joined them, set the emergency brake and said, "Okay, let's call your daddy."

Molly watched anxiously, listening to the multiple rings, then the abrupt message.

"Jared. I'll call you when I can."

Savannah said, "I have Molly. Will you *please* call? As soon as you can?"

She waited for a moment, as if he'd magically hear and rush to answer. Since it wasn't as if he was listening to messages in real time, she set her phone down and focused on this child who had just become her responsibility.

A little girl who had no one else.

It was chilly enough this evening that she wore a pink knit hat pulled over her ears, but Savannah could see that she had long blond hair. It must be Jared who'd braided it into pigtails, although strands were escaping. She couldn't be sure, but thought Molly had blue eyes, like he had. Savannah's had been blue when she was young, but eventually turned more hazel, just as her pale blond hair had darkened.

Otherwise, she couldn't see Jared in the scared face looking back at her, but that was hardly surprising with the inadequate light and the stress they were both feeling.

"Your daddy is my big brother. He probably told you that."

Molly nodded.

"He wants you to come home with me, at least for now. Until we hear from him." When, not if. "So right now, we're going to get a room at a hotel near the airport, and I'll buy us tickets to fly in the morning back to New Mexico, where I live."

What would she do with a child this age while she worked? she wondered in sudden panic, but that worry could wait.

"Okay?"

"Daddy said to do what you told me," Molly said as if by rote.

Savannah smiled. "Are you hungry?"

"Uh-huh."

She reached to the floorboards on the passenger side and produced the grocery sack. "I have some snacks in here to hold you. Once we find a hotel, we'll get dinner." There had to be some restaurants open late in the vicinity of the airport.

Molly peered into the bag and tentatively reached in, producing a bag of Skittles. Savannah's stomach grumbled, but she decided to wait until they were out of this neighborhood, at least. She felt as if eyes watched them.

Paranoid, but…why had Jared had to go so urgently he'd leave the little girl who was his "everything" alone in a dark doorway in a sketchy part of the city?

As soon as he called, she'd demand answers. In the meantime, she entered the address for a hotel she'd noticed by the airport into the maps app on her phone. She gratefully followed instructions even as she flickered her gaze from one mirror to another as well as to the road ahead, watching for… she didn't know what.

MY NIECE.

Unable to sleep yet, Savannah had left the one nightstand lamp on. They had a room with a single queen-size bed because she'd asked Molly whether she wanted her own bed.

She'd shaken her head hard.

So there she lay, a small lump almost touching Savannah, as if she wanted the reassurance of cuddling, but wasn't quite brave enough to commit to it. After eating a tiny portion of her cheeseburger and fries at a Denny's, she had changed from saggy pink leggings and a sweatshirt that was too big for her into a nightgown Savannah found in the pink suitcase. Her toothbrush and toothpaste were in there, too, as well as a pink hairbrush with long blond strands caught in the bristles. Jared had packed several days' worth of clothes, but no alternative to the worn sneakers his daughter had worn, and only one toy, a stuffed rabbit that Molly had latched right on to, and now held squeezed in her arms as she surrendered to sleep.

Savannah knew she should go through the duffel bag, but she felt deep reluctance. When they got home was soon enough, right?

Except…it wasn't, and she wouldn't be able to sleep until she saw what he'd left for her. There had to be a message, right?

She eased herself carefully off the bed so she didn't awaken Molly. The bag felt absurdly light when she picked it up and carried it to the comfortable chair by the window. The zipper sounded loud to her ears, but the child didn't stir.

Most of what she pulled out initially was Molly's: more clothes, a pair of sandals, a couple of games in boxes and a yellow-haired doll with…yes, a shoebox full of doll-size changes of clothes. Something bumped her hand, and she immediately recognized the shape and smooth texture of a cell phone. If this was Jared's, that meant it had been ringing in the trunk of her rental car when she called him.

It opened right away to her touch, and she explored to find that, indeed, a missed call from her showed at the top of a very limited list of other calls. There was the one he'd made *to* her, as well. The realization that he had abandoned his phone chilled her and made plain that he'd never even considered fleeing with her and Molly.

The fact that the phone wasn't password-protected had to be out of character for her brother. This was part of his plan, she assumed—the plan he hadn't confided to her. He'd cleared away any passwords he'd used to give her complete access to his phone. Why? What was she supposed to glean from the numbers and messages? His contacts list…was empty.

She looked down to see that her knuckles were white, she

gripped the damn phone so tightly. It felt like her only connection to her brother.

I can pick it up again, she reminded herself. *Search it for any hidden messages.*

At the very bottom of the duffel bag lay a manila envelope. Savannah opened it apprehensively. The first words that caught her eye were *last will and trust*. Dear God, he'd expected to die. Or disappear and eventually be declared dead? She hoped it was the second alternative.

He'd left an investment account and the contents of a savings account to his daughter, Molly Elizabeth Baird. He named his sister, Savannah Louise Baird, to assume guardianship of Molly, giving her complete control over the money until his daughter reached the age of twenty-one.

Swallowing, Savannah flipped through the few other pages. The bank account contained fifty-two thousand dollars and change. The investments handled by a brokerage firm added up to over a hundred thousand more. Not a fortune, but enough to put Molly through college, say, or pay expenses in the intervening years.

No, Savannah decided right away; she didn't need to draw on his money. She didn't want to use money she was horribly afraid had been earned in the illegal drug trade. She'd honor Jared's trust, though, and invest it as well as she could for his daughter's sake.

After repacking the duffel, she sat staring at it. Jared had said goodbye. She refused to believe he meant to kill himself, which led her back to the two alternatives: he hoped to vanish…or he'd known before calling her that he was a dead man.

After a minute, Savannah walked silently to the hotel room door and checked to be absolutely certain she'd put on the probably useless chain as well as the dead bolt lock.

She felt even less sleepy than she had when she slipped from the bed.

Chapter Two

"What the hell are you doing?"

Logan Quade had hoped to be done mucking out the stalls before his father caught him in the act, but no such luck. Dad had undoubtedly heard his truck even though he'd parked at the barn instead of the house when he'd driven up at the end of the day. He straightened, leaning on the shovel. Weather was really turning. He was glad for his sheepskin-lined coat and leather gloves.

"Same thing you made me do every day growing up, football practice or no. Same thing I did yesterday." And would do tomorrow. He couldn't take over running his father's ranch; Dad wouldn't stand for it. But Logan had moved back to Sage Creek in eastern Oregon three months ago to help out his father whether he wanted help or not, and Logan fully intended to keep assuming as many of the heavy tasks as he could.

"You *have* a damn job!" His father scowled at him.

Yes, he did. Logan had agreed to take over as county sheriff for the remainder of the previous sheriff's term. That had given him an excuse to come home that Dad accepted, and something to do besides ranch work. He'd never wanted to follow in his father's footsteps and someday take over the ranch, which was a sore point between them since his sister was even less interested. Knowing the land would be sold after he was gone didn't sit well with Brian Quade. That knowledge would fester even if Logan's mother had still been alive, but he felt sure his dad would have listened to Mom and been more reasonable about taking it easier.

"I did my job," Logan said briefly. "I've made as plain as I can that I'll be lending a hand here. Your doctor says you can't do heavy labor, and I'm here to make sure you follow Dr. Lancaster's orders."

"Blasted doctor doesn't know what he's talking about," Dad scoffed. "I feel just fine! A little cough is nothing."

Not to mention obvious shortness of breath on any exertion. "Because you quit smoking and because I'm riding you about doing your exercises." How many times did they need to have the same argument that hadn't been laid to rest in the months since he'd moved back into his childhood home? "They don't restore your lungs to working order, and you know it!"

His father snorted. "What am I supposed to do, sit on my ass and watch soap operas so I can live a few months longer?"

Logan's spurt of temper died. He did understand. This was the life his father had chosen. He had zero interest in retiring to a senior community in Arizona, or taking up hobbies that didn't include any real physical activity. That didn't mean he could accept his son's help with reasonable grace, even though Dad had to know that COPD was a progressive disease.

"Dad," he said quietly, "I came home to help." The progression could be slowed, but, always stubborn, Brian Quade resisted dealing with the depression that was part of his problem. "I want to spend time with you, not know you're working yourself to death—literally—while I'm on the other side of the state hanging out with friends when I'm not on the job."

The job, for him, was being a cop. Specifically, he'd been a detective with the city of Portland police bureau. Just last year, he'd been promoted to sergeant, so that he not only worked investigations directly, he supervised ones conducted by other detectives. That experience, along with his hometown boy, star athlete status, had been why the county council had named him sheriff in the absence of any other good options. Logan's captain had promised to rehire him when the time came.

Unless, of course, he became addicted to the power of being in ultimate charge. He might have snorted himself if he hadn't been facing down his father.

Who grunted dismissively. "Shovel manure if you want. Mrs. Sanders says dinner will be on the table in forty-five minutes."

Dad had been subsisting on microwavable meals until Logan hired a housekeeper-slash-cook first thing. They'd fought about that, too, but Dad had quieted down about it once he became accustomed to decent food on the table most evenings again.

"I'm nearly done," Logan said. "Just have to empty this wheelbarrow." He'd drop hay into the mangers, too, and let the horses back into their stalls, but that was no secret from his father, who gave him a last flinty stare before he turned and stalked off back toward the house.

Logan watched him go.

At times he thought his father hadn't changed one iota in the past twenty years except for a deepening of the creases on his leathery face and the white that had gradually come to dominate dark brown hair. Then there were moments, like now, when he couldn't help noticing weight loss, frailty and a slowness in every movement, never mind the rasp of his breath. His stride wasn't the same.

A stab of pain felt too much like a knife inserted between Logan's ribs. He'd been happy enough with his job, his friends, the women he'd hooked up with for a few months at a time, but he hadn't realized how important it was to know that Dad was still here, that *home* was still here. His complacency had taken a serious jolt when his father grumblingly admitted to his diagnosis after he'd seen the doctor assuming he might have some bronchitis that could be cured with an antibiotic. A lifelong smoker, he'd hated giving up the cigarettes but had done it, and that took real guts.

Yeah, Logan understood. Dad had lost his wife, his kids had taken off into the world with no intentions of coming home permanently, and then he'd had to quit smoking. He'd never been much of a drinker, so what was left?

The indignity of having to admit he was failing, that was what. And worse yet, it was his son to whom he had to make that admission. The son who had the strength he'd lost, who was a decorated cop and now the county sheriff.

Maybe humility didn't come easily to either of them, Logan thought ruefully.

"OH, HONEY." Savannah sank down on her niece's twin bed. "Another nightmare?"

Two night-lights in the bedroom and the overhead light left on in the bathroom across the hall weren't enough to make Molly feel safe. Many nights, Savannah ended up letting Molly get in bed with her. Even then, as often as not she awakened every couple of hours gasping or sobbing or, once, screaming. She could never quite verbalize who or what those terrible dreams were about. Savannah was getting madder and madder at her brother, even though she reminded herself regularly that the little girl had spent much of her short life with her mother, not her daddy.

The mother who couldn't take care of her child. Jared *had* stepped in, but had he been any more able to offer a sense of real security? Savannah wished she knew, but Molly wasn't even able to tell her how long she'd lived with her father versus her mother.

Now she rocked this little girl who felt too thin, just skin covering fragile bones, offering her warmth and murmured words. "You're safe, Molly. I won't let anything happen to you. I promise. I know the dreams are scary, but they'll quit coming eventually. Why don't you think about riding Toto again tomorrow?"

Toto was a fat gray pony living an easy life here on the ranch for the benefit of the frequently visiting grandkids. Molly had been entranced at first sight. Not surprisingly, she'd never even petted a horse before, never mind ridden one. Her upbringing presumably hadn't been the kind that included sunny Sundays at the zoo, where there might be pony rides, or friends' birthday parties that included ponies as well as cake. Savannah had been spending more time than she should leading the pony around and around the arena with Molly clutching the saddle horn for dear life but also looking thrilled.

"Can I get in your bed?" she whispered.

"Of course you can." Savannah gave her a big hug, scooped her up and carried her to the full-size bed in her own room.

"Will you sing 'Sunshine' to me?" Molly asked.

Savannah did almost every night. Apparently Jared had told his little girl that "You Are My Sunshine" had been Auntie Vannah's favorite song when *she* was a little girl. Of course, she knew the tune well enough to hum it. Who didn't? The truth was, though, she didn't remember her mother ever singing it and had had to look up the lyrics. She stuck to the chorus, since there was too much else in the song that was sad.

Now Savannah murmured, "You don't even have to ask," and softly began as she cuddled her niece under the covers. The stiff little body gradually relaxed.

Child behavioral experts would probably disapprove of her letting Molly sleep with her so often, but they dealt with kids whose night terrors weren't associated with a seamy underworld of drug dealing, a mother with unknown "problems" and a daddy who'd dropped her off at a dark strip mall to wait for an aunt Molly had never met before disappearing.

The two of them were getting by. Savannah thought her niece was starting to trust her, but both of them were waiting, too, for a call from Jared that might change everything. The bigger problem was her own exhaustion. She'd been shocked last night when she looked at herself in the mirror after brushing her teeth. The blue circles under her eyes more closely resembled a pair of black eyes. She felt dull, too, her brain foggy. A young mare had kicked her yesterday, something that wouldn't have happened if she weren't all but sleepwalking. Now she had a livid bruise on her lower thigh and a knee that hurt.

Savannah's boss hadn't said anything yet, but he'd been spending more time than usual watching her work, one boot propped on the bottom rail, arms crossed on the top one, face shaded by a dark Stetson. He had to know she wasn't giving the horses her best. She needed that almost-magical connection she'd always felt with horses, but her tiredness and indecision were interfering.

So far, she'd been lucky that the wife of one of the ranch hands was willing to take care of Molly during the day along with her own children, but Brenda was noticeably distressed every morning when Savannah had to pry Molly's hands off her and hand her over, crying quietly. Once Auntie Vannah was out of sight, Molly was good, Brenda reported; too good, too obedient, too anxious. If she napped at all, her nightmares came even more frequently than they did at night.

Jared, where are you? Savannah begged, her cheek pressed to the little girl's head. *What were you* thinking? *Can't you call and let us know what's going on?*

And then, *What am I going to do?*

There was an obvious answer, one she had been reluctant to even consider. She could go home. Take Molly to meet her grandparents. And, oh, she didn't want to confess she needed her parents.

Her own horribly mixed emotions concerning them weren't what worried her. The question was how her father would respond to the granddaughter they hadn't known about. If Savannah had been bringing home her own child, she had no doubt both her parents would welcome her with open arms and set about spoiling her. No matter what, she knew Mom would adore Molly from the minute she set eyes on her. Savannah *wanted* that for this fragile child.

But Molly was Jared's child. Even Mom had seemed to slump in relief when he ran away. Tension in their house kept anyone from talking about him. Over time, Savannah had the impression even Mom had shrugged off his existence and the dangers he faced as an unprotected teenager out in the world as if he was nothing to them. Would Molly be tainted by association with the unwanted son?

But Savannah knew she was going to have to find out. She needed help, and Molly needed more family. People who loved her and were willing to do anything to protect her. Savannah's parents had been begging her to come home for years, promising to expand the horse breeding and training part of their business since that was what interested her most, reminding her that the ranch would someday be hers.

Lying there in the dark, aware her young charge had fallen asleep, Savannah let out a long sigh. She'd call Mom and Dad tomorrow. If she was ever dissatisfied with how Dad treated Molly, well, she would up and move again. She wouldn't let herself be turned into a coward the way Mom had been. She had a reputation as a trainer; she could get another job.

She just had to shake off her fear that a return to Sage Creek was the last thing Jared would have wanted for his daughter. Well, too bad; he'd given up any right to make decisions for Molly, hadn't he?

STILL WEARING HIS UNIFORM, Logan stopped at the pharmacy to pick up prescription refills for his father. He could have asked Mrs. Sanders to do it—she had taken over grocery shopping—but Logan wanted to keep an eye on how well Dad was taking his medications, and short of stealing into Dad's bathroom to count pills, staying on top of when they needed refilling seemed like the best option.

He was cutting through the store toward the pharmacy counter at the back when he saw a woman pushing a cart in the toy aisle. A kid sat in the cart. His stride checked. There was something about—

At that moment, the woman lifted a boxed toy from the shelf and, smiling softly, showed it to the little girl. Logan felt a warning flare in the region of his heart.

Damn. Savannah Baird was back in town. She always had left him feeling conflicted. Not that the reasons mattered anymore, he realized, since she obviously had a daughter. Probably there was a husband, too, who just didn't happen to be with them right now. He was surprised his father hadn't mentioned that she'd married.

He started to back up, which caught her attention. She stared, too, then said, "Logan?"

"Yeah, it's me." He sounded gruff for a reason. Jared Baird had been his best friend growing up. After Jared had run away—or just plain disappeared—Logan hadn't tried to hide how he felt about Jared's sister, the little princess in that household. The one who shone so brightly, no one seemed to see Jared. Logan had hurt her feelings and refused to care. He was solidly in Jared's corner.

"Are you…visiting your dad?" she asked tentatively.

They were adults now, and there was no reason not to be civil. He walked down the aisle toward her, evaluating how a beautiful, spoiled-rotten young woman, a rodeo queen and homecoming princess, had matured.

Really well, was his conclusion. She was still slim, maybe a little curvier in the right places, and her gray-green eyes were as pretty as he remembered. Her hair had darkened some, but he'd still call her blonde, pale streaks mixed with light brown. Maybe the streaks were courtesy of a hairdresser.

Refocusing on her question, Logan made himself say, "Dad's having health problems. COPD."

Her nod meant she knew what that meant. "I'm sorry."

"I quit my job and came home to help out on the ranch. If I weren't here, he'd keep on the way he always has, even if that cut years off his life." He shook his head. "He's fighting me the whole way."

She smiled. "As stubborn as ever, then."

"Yeah." He studied the kid, who watched him warily with big blue eyes. "What about you? This must be your daughter."

Some emotion crossed Savannah's face like a shadow. He might have read it better if he'd been looking right at her. He did know that she was hesitating.

"No," she finally said. "Molly is Jared's daughter." She smiled at the girl. "Molly, this is Logan. I'll bet your daddy talked about him, didn't he? They were best friends when they were boys."

What the hell? The shock rocketed through him. He'd assumed Jared was dead—in fact, had wondered if Jared had died during a confrontation with his own father and been buried all this time somewhere on the family ranch. Had he come home and not bothered to call?

The girl still wasn't sure about Logan, but she gave a timid nod. "Daddy said you went riding together all the time. That you lived near him."

"That's right. My father's ranch is on the same road as your grandmother and grandfather's ranch is."

She hardly blinked, finally shifting that slightly unnerving stare to her...aunt?

"Is Jared home, too?" Logan asked.

"No," Savannah said quietly. "He...asked me to take care of Molly. We're...waiting to hear from him."

What did that mean? Nothing as simple as Jared having to take a business trip, Logan guessed.

"I always assumed he was..." Logan glanced again at the little girl and amended what he'd been about to say. "Gone."

"Did you?" The tilt of Savannah's head and the sharp tone in her voice were a challenge.

One that irritated him. "You mean, you've known what he was up to all these years? You didn't think to say, by the way, Logan, *your best friend is fine*?"

"Why would I?" she responded coolly. "Now, if you'll excuse us, we need to pick up a few things."

As if he wasn't still there, Savannah turned her back on him, added the toy, whatever it was, to the cart and then wheeled cart and niece away from him.

Logan stood stock-still, stunned in some way he didn't entirely understand.

The girl who'd had a crush on him had grown to be a woman who looked at him with open dislike. And, damn it, she was even more beautiful than she'd been. Back then, he had tried hard not to analyze his intense reaction to her, but now…yeah, he'd been attracted to her. Nothing he'd have acted on even if he hadn't detested her, too; she'd been too young. Three years mattered then.

His mind jumped, as if he was playing hopscotch.

Jared was alive. Logan had had other friends, but there'd never been anyone he felt closer to than Jared. They'd been brothers at heart. Even after he started giving Jared a hard time about his drinking, the parties he went to, the experimentation with drugs, opening a distance between them, he'd have still sworn the bond was there. Until Jared took off without telling him, and then a year went by, followed by another and another.

Why would Jared have stayed in touch with the little sister whom Daddy had adored, the sister Jared had resented so much, and not with his best friend?

Maybe he hadn't, it occurred to Logan; maybe he hadn't contacted Savannah until he needed help with his little girl.

Logan shook his head, confused and, yeah, hurt. He had to pull himself together. He was a cop, and situational awareness wasn't optional. He didn't like knowing someone could have walked right up behind him without him noticing. Sure, he was home in Sage Creek. He hadn't personally made an arrest yet and had no reason to think he'd acquired any enemies.

Unless Savannah fell into that category.

A minute later, as he waited at the pharmacy counter for the guy to retrieve his dad's prescriptions that were ready, Logan had another thought. Only one person could give him answers to any of his questions—if he could convince her to talk to him.

He'd have been happy never to run into either of Jared's parents again, but he thought he might drop by the Circle B ranch in the next few days.

Chapter Three

That evening over dinner, Savannah paused in the act of dishing up a small serving of potato salad for Molly. They were still negotiating what foods Molly would and wouldn't eat—or, in some cases, had never seen before. Savannah wasn't sure about this one. Fortunately, her parents were patient with this new granddaughter who'd unexpectedly appeared on their doorstep. In fact, they doted on her, as they'd done on Savannah. They'd apparently dismissed the reality that Molly was actually Jared's child.

"I saw Logan Quade today," she said, going for casual. "Apparently his father is having health problems."

Dad said, "The county council appointed the Quade boy to be interim sheriff. Sheriff Brady had a heart attack and had to retire." He took a bite. "Carried quite a gut around with him these past ten years or so."

"Logan is hardly a boy," Savannah protested. She knew exactly how old Logan was—still remembered his birthday—but went with, "I'm thirty-one, so he must be...thirty-four."

Just like Jared, as they all knew.

"Young to take over the sheriff's department."

"You disapprove?"

He grunted and took the serving bowl from her to dish up a hefty helping of the potato salad for himself. "No reason to. Heard he was a sergeant with the Portland police department, so he must know what he's doing."

"Did Logan say what's wrong with his father?" Savannah's mother asked. She'd had lunch today with friends, so she wore her prettiest snap-front shirt and makeup, and had styled her hair in a smooth bob. The blond shade had to be courtesy of her hairdresser. Savannah remembered Mom's natural color as a light brown that had started graying as much as ten years ago.

"COPD."

Mom gave her husband a minatory look. "That's what comes of smoking."

Sounding irritable, he shot back, "You know I've never smoked over a pack a day."

Savannah was tempted to comment on how many cigarettes a year that added up to, but refrained. Because...she didn't care? No, that wasn't true; she loved her father. But she also knew nothing she could say would sway him. It never had before.

"I take it you haven't stayed friends with Mr. Quade?"

Dad looked surprised. "Sure we have. We see him regularly at the Elks Club and the Cattlemen's Association get-togethers. Noticed he'd quit smoking. He hasn't said a word about his health."

"Pride."

"It's not the kind of thing you want everyone talking about. Could be he likes his privacy."

She had to concede the argument. "Except if he'd let people know, they might have offered to help him out so Logan didn't have to come home so soon."

Her father grunted his opinion of that. "Ranch is going to be his."

The idea that Logan might not want the ranch was apparently inconceivable to Dad.

"Is he married?" her mother asked. "Does he have kids? I don't think Brian ever said."

"I didn't ask, and Logan didn't say."

In his usual blunt fashion, Dad put in, "Well, he was Jared's friend, not yours."

Savannah didn't need anyone to tell her that. Logan had always made that reality plenty clear.

Later that evening, after she'd tucked Molly into bed, knowing full well she'd wake up sobbing in a couple of hours, Savannah debated going back downstairs and pretending to watch TV with her parents.

Tonight, she couldn't make herself, and she knew why she felt so on edge.

The encounter with Logan bothered her more than she wanted to acknowledge. From the time she was a little girl, she'd adored her big brother—*and* his best friend. They had included her in activities sometimes, less often as the years went on and they thought they were big, tough boys and she was a nuisance who wore too much pink. Both boys were athletes; they'd played Little League baseball together, Pop Warner football, then naturally become stars of the high school baseball and football teams.

Until Jared had been suspended from both, Savannah reminded herself. By then, it wasn't that he was too busy for her. Nope, he was too angry, too secretive, too sullen.

Too resentful?

She'd convinced herself that he still loved her, that he didn't blame her for Dad's obvious bias or Mom's weak efforts to intervene. He'd seldom been around to hear Mom and Dad's low-voiced fights, as if they thought Savannah wouldn't hear what was being said. But she'd quit kidding herself that Jared still loved her when she saw the way Logan's lip curled at the sight of her, the way he shook off any attempt by Jared to include her in whatever they were doing, and later, after Jared was gone, by the way Logan pretended not to even *see* her once she was in high school, too. Jared had to have complained to his best buddy about his *perfect*, walks-on-water little sister. Why else would Logan's attitude toward her have curdled?

So even before Jared had taken off, she knew he must have come to hate her. Who could blame him?

She'd tried so hard to head off Dad's vicious swipes, to talk

Jared down after Mom begged him to avoid aggravating his father. To pretend the near-violence that thickened the air when father and son were forced to share a dinner table or conversation didn't exist.

When Savannah pressed her, her mother had eventually admitted to her fear that Jared would be damaged by his father's treatment of him. Dad refused to see what he was doing to Jared and got increasingly angry when his wife pushed him.

"What can I do?" Mom had said helplessly. "I have no working history. If I leave your father, how could I support the three of us? Child support wouldn't be anywhere near enough. Grandma and Granddad wouldn't help. They didn't want me to marry Gene in the first place."

Savannah hadn't known that.

"I don't see how poverty would help Jared. If he would just... step lightly, quit baiting his father, he'd be fine! The tension isn't one-sided, you know! It's not *that* long until he graduates from high school. If only he'd listen to me."

As an adult, Savannah understood her mother's decision better than she had then, but the hot coals of anger still burned. Yes, the idea of leaving her husband must have been terrifying, but the choice she'd made had essentially been to sacrifice one of her two children. Although, really, by the time of that conversation, it had been too late to change Jared's increasing alienation and anger.

Savannah had kept trying. She'd rolled her eyes when either of her parents bragged about her achievements. She'd gone to every one of Jared's games that she could. She'd confronted her father, for what good that did. Later, she'd read enough to know that instinct had led her to play the role of peacekeeper in their family dynamic, except nothing she did was ever good enough.

What Mom had never understood was how that failure had damaged Savannah's confidence, too.

When Jared called her the first time, almost a year after he took off, she'd almost fallen to her knees in relief. She'd had a secret fear that her own father had killed Jared when a fight escalated into violence. She still remembered clutching the phone, tears pouring down her face, because he was alive. He wanted to talk to *her*. He hadn't called to mine her for news about what was happening at home. *I just wanted to hear your voice*, he'd said, sounding sad in a way that haunted her still.

But what good did it do to brood about a past she couldn't change? She was in the middle of a book she was enjoying. She'd curl up in the easy chair squeezed into her bedroom that had been her refuge as a teenager when she couldn't take her family for another minute. She found the book and had just sunk into the chair, curling her legs under her, when her phone rang. Surprised, she reached for it. The number was unfamiliar. Her heart jumped. *Please let it be Jared.*

She answered cautiously.

"I'm hoping to reach Jared Baird's sister," a man said. "Would that be you?"

Her heartbeat picked up. "Who is asking?"

"I'm sorry." He sounded sincere. "I'm Detective Alan Trenowski, San Francisco Police Department."

Should she deny any relationship with Jared? No, that ship had sailed. And…she needed to find out why a detective was calling. Except… Oh, God. How would she know if this was a lie, if *he* was one of the men Jared was fleeing? Or…had Jared been running from law enforcement? He wouldn't have wanted to tell her that.

"I…" She swallowed. "I'm Savannah Baird. Jared is my brother."

"Ah. Then I'm sorry to have to deliver bad news." The voice became gentle. "Your brother's body was pulled from the bay by a boater late this afternoon. He'd been shot."

Oh, Jared.

THERE WAS MORE, of course. Police assumed whoever had murdered Jared had dumped his body in the bay hoping tides would pull it out to sea, where it might never be found. They'd identified him from his wallet, left in the back pocket of his jeans.

He'd also carried a cheap phone—the officer had started to say "a burner" before correcting himself—with only one person in the contacts: her. He'd labeled her as "sister" along with her name.

Plainly, he'd wanted to be sure she was informed if he was killed. In a way, that was the bad news: his killers had left the wallet and phone on his body so he would be identified and she'd learn of Jared's death.

Why?

Scary question.

She answered more questions from Detective Trenowski and also agreed to speak with him again in the morning. She told him which of Jared's possessions she had, including the phone—and how the phone lacked any real information. She explained how little she knew about her brother's life, but revealed her belief that in the past he'd been involved in the illegal drug trade in some way. She told the detective about that last phone call, how Jared had admitted to being in trouble. She remembered word for word what he'd said: *I'll try to run, but I think they're suspicious.*

Yes, of course she'd asked for an explanation, and all he'd say was *It's better if I don't tell you.*

There would be an autopsy, of course. Someone would be in touch when the body was freed for burial.

Savannah's hand shook as she set down the phone. She hunched in on herself, almost shocked at the power of her grief. She'd imagined a call just like this so many times, why was she even surprised? And yet she was. She'd *talked* to Jared only a few weeks ago. Found out she had a niece, now asleep in Jared's old bedroom.

I'll have to tell them, she thought. Would Dad care at all? Pretend to care? How would the news hit Mom, who must have spent years trying to convince herself that somewhere out there, Jared was doing fine? That someday he'd call.

Worse yet, she'd have to tell Molly that her father would never be coming back for her.

Shuddering, she curled forward and let herself cry.

That meant, of course, bloodshot, swollen eyes when she went downstairs. The stop in the bathroom to splash her face with cold water hadn't helped at all.

Only her mother glanced her way when she appeared in the opening leading to the living room. Dad's gaze didn't leave the TV until Savannah's mother sat up so fast, her recliner squealed in protest. Then they both looked at her.

"Can you...turn that off?" Savannah asked, gesturing toward the TV.

Her father used the remote, plunging the living room into silence.

Until her mother almost whispered, "Is something wrong?"

Is something wrong? The absurdity quelled renewed tears.

"Yes. A police detective in San Francisco just called to let me know that Jared is dead. His body...was found today."

Her parents just stared.

"Why did they call you and not us?" her father asked, sounding a little huffy.

Was he really offended?

"He had my name in his phone contacts."

"Oh, no," her mother murmured.

Suddenly nauseated, Savannah almost turned to go back upstairs. She had to think about Molly, though. Unless she wanted to make a permanent break from her parents, she couldn't tell them how angry she was.

"Do they know how he died?" her father asked.

Her throat wanted to close. It was hard to get the next words out. "He was shot, his body thrown in San Francisco Bay."

Dad grunted. "I suppose it was the drugs." Because his death had to be solely Jared's fault, having nothing to do with the childhood tensions. Only...her father's voice carried a heaviness she didn't recognize.

"I...think he'd been straight for some years now," she said. "I'm sure he was when he called. He said something about 'them' being suspicious. He might have been, well, working undercover to bring them down."

Her mother stood up, cheeks already wet, and rushed past her, hurrying up the stairs. Dad half stood, then sank back down. "I thought she'd shed her last tears for that boy."

"Did you ever shed any tears for him?" Savannah asked quietly, not waiting for an answer.

A PLUME OF dust trailed Logan's department-issue SUV as he drove down the Bairds' long drive. A minute ago, Logan had passed a couple of ranch hands stretching barbed wire on the rough-hewn posts alongside the road. Both had glanced up and nodded. He didn't recognize either, but they were too young to have been around when he spent half his time at the Circle B. He couldn't tell if the work was routine or if a section of fence had gone down. This was the season, though; it was the kind of job that got done in late fall and winter, when other business slowed down. Last weekend Logan had helped replace sagging sections of fence on Dad's place. He had a long scratch on his left arm to prove it.

When he first reached the two-story white ranch house, so much like the one he'd grown up in, he didn't see anybody. The broad double doors at the barn stood open, the interior shadowed. Not a soul seemed to be around.

He hesitated between going to the house or walking around first, choosing the look-see. He'd rather not have to be polite to Jared's parents.

Just as he rounded a corner of the barn, he heard a woman say, "It's a long ways down, isn't it?"

He had no idea if Savannah could sing; she hadn't been in the school choir, as far as he knew. But her voice had always had a musical quality that triggered a reaction in him. He could close his eyes and imagine her in his bed, talking to him, that voice as sensual as her touch.

Irritated anew at any reaction to Jared's sister, he followed her voice anyway. Sure enough, there she was in an outdoor arena, her back to him as she gazed up at the girl, sitting atop a sorrel mare who looked downright somnolent. He kind of doubted this was a top-notch cutting prospect, although appearances could be deceptive. The girl—Molly—clutched the saddle horn in a death grip.

"I promise you Checkers won't take a step unless I'm leading her or you nudge her with your heels. Okay?"

The blonde head bobbed. The kid was nervous, then, but not terrified.

"Let me lead you around for a few minutes. Then I'll get on and we can ride double."

Unnoticed, Logan stayed where he was while Savannah led the ambling mare along the fence of the oblong arena. After a moment, he walked up to a spot beside the gate, crossed his arms on the top rail and watched as Jared's little girl noticeably relaxed. Her back straightened and she held her head up.

Not until they rounded the far end of the arena and faced him did they notice him—at the same moment he saw the remnants of tears on both their faces. What the hell?

He straightened, too, waiting for them to reach him. Then he tipped the brim of his gray Stetson. "Savannah. Molly."

Savannah's gaze took in his dark green uniform and the star pinned to his shirt, and probably the heavy belt holding the holster and other implements. "Sheriff. Are you looking for my father?"

"No, you. Happened to be nearby—" *happened* not being quite the right word "—thought maybe we could talk a little more."

Strain on her fine-boned face made her less obviously pretty than when he'd seen her in the pharmacy, but now he knew he wasn't viewing a careful facade.

"I was going to call you later," she said stiffly. "Um…give me a minute." She turned back to her niece. "I need to talk to the sheriff. I'll just tether Checkers, and we can ride some more in a little bit. In the meantime, why don't you go see if that first batch of cookies is out of the oven yet?"

The kid was a cutie, even scowling at him, and she lifted her arms so Savannah could swing her off the horse's back. Logan opened the gate, although only the girl came through it. Savannah looped the reins around a rail, then walked along the fence, Logan doing the same on the other side of it, until she could watch as Molly plodded toward the house, finally disappearing inside.

Then she looked at him, devastation in her eyes. "Jared is dead."

"What?" he said, almost soundlessly. Hadn't she told him, just yesterday, that—

"I got a call last night, from a San Francisco PD detective. Jared's body was pulled out of the bay. He'd been shot. They don't seem to know much yet, even where he was tossed in. Whoever killed him didn't take his wallet or phone. The phone was one of those cheap ones, you know."

Logan nodded. He seemed to be numb, but didn't know how long that would last.

"Which means—"

"They wanted him to be identified."

"Or…or at least didn't care if he was."

Considerate of a killer, he thought, but didn't say.

"Does this have anything to do with why he asked you to take Molly?" he asked.

She closed her eyes for a moment and took a deep breath before fixing that anguished gaze back on him. "I know it does. I don't remember what I told you—"

"Almost nothing," he said, more harshly than he'd intended.

She took a half step back, making him feel like a bastard.

"He's called me, oh, once or twice a year ever since he took off."

A slow burn of anger ignited. "He stayed in touch all that time?"

Her chin rose. "You think I should have told you?"

"You had to know I worried about him."

"How would I know that? Did you ever speak a word to me again?" Oh, she was steamed, too.

And in the right, he was ashamed to admit to himself. He hadn't even been civil. "I...regret that," he said roughly. "Too little, too late, I know, but I am sorry."

She searched his face, then sagged. "I didn't know that Jared wasn't calling you, too. And... I suppose I was being petty."

"You had reason," he said wryly.

She let that go. "Anyway, for the first few years, he was mostly stoned or maybe drunk when he called. Not falling-down plastered, but I could tell. Then... I think he was trying to get clean. He'd sound great a couple of times, then—" Her shoulders moved. "I'm pretty sure at some point he got involved in the drug trade. I don't know if he worked for a cartel doing business in this country or just a distributor. A couple of years ago, he said something about trying to atone. That worried me, because I wondered if he was endangering himself."

No question now that was what Jared had done.

"When he called a few weeks ago, he said he was in trouble. That they were suspicious. That's when he told me about Molly—I had no idea he had a child. I guess she'd been with her mother, but he said she couldn't take care of Molly anymore. I don't know how long ago it was that he took her. He begged me to meet him, to take Molly until he got in touch."

"You *met* with him?"

She told him about flying to San Francisco, reaching the address her brother had given her and finding only the little girl and a couple of bags.

"I think he knew all along that he didn't dare meet me. He just didn't want me to know—" her face contorted "—that he was really saying goodbye."

"Savannah." He put his hands on the rail with the intention of vaulting the fence, but she backed up again.

"No. I'm okay. I've expected this for years. It's just...harder when I really thought I'd see him again. And because of Molly. Telling her this morning—" A shudder passed over her, but her eyes met his again. "Now I'm wondering whether whoever killed Jared has any reason to track *me* down."

After years of being a cop, Logan had already leaped to wondering the same thing. What drug traffickers would want with Jared's sister was a mystery, but why else had they all but handed the SFPD a handwritten note saying *Here's who to contact to claim this body*?

And maybe answer a few questions?

Logan cursed, but silently.

Chapter Four

Savannah walked Logan to his car, a marked police SUV with a light bar and bristling with tall antennae. At five foot nine, she wasn't short for a woman, but he'd always been taller. Now she'd guess him to be six foot two or so, all of him lean and athletic, made bulkier by his coat.

And, heavens, she'd let herself forget—or was that *made* herself forget?—how striking he was. His dark brown hair was short enough to tame the waves she remembered. Icy gray eyes were as startling as ever in a thin, tanned face with sharp cheekbones and a mouth that had provoked her hormone-ridden teenage fantasies.

Her gaze slid to his left hand. No wedding ring, but maybe he chose not to wear one.

As if his marital status mattered.

Frowning, he said, "Have your parents accepted Molly?"

"Yes. I wasn't sure Dad would, but... I needed help. She's pretty traumatized. She clings to me, which made it hard to leave her when I had to work, and she has constant nightmares."

His big hand drew her to a stop. "That's why you look so tired."

She must look really bad. "Sleep is an issue," she admitted. "I think Mom would get up with her, but so far that isn't an option. Molly wants me. Apparently, only my singing will put her to sleep. I'm actually thinking—" Whoa. Why would she confide in *him*?

But with those pale eyes intent on her face, he prodded, "Thinking?"

"Oh, we have an empty cabin. Dad's cut back a little on the size of the herd and didn't hire as many hands this past year. This cabin was meant to house a worker with a family, but Joe Haskins—do you remember him?—is the only employee here right now fitting that criteria, and he's had his place ever since he started with us. I don't really want to keep living in my childhood bedroom and feeling like a guest in the rest of the house. Molly and I could be more of a family if we had our own place, but I could still rely on Mom to watch her during the day."

"I always thought you'd stay, since it was obvious the ranch would be yours." His tone was careful, but his opinion obvious.

"Whatever you think, I was mad at both of my parents. I wouldn't be here now if it weren't for Molly." Savannah took a step back. "Thanks for stopping by. I need to keep my promise and give her a longer ride before I start work."

"You're training for your dad?"

"Yes." She kept backing up.

He continued to watch her, his gaze unnerving. "Savannah." She stopped.

"I'm the law around here. If you hear anything more about Jared, and especially from the people who decided he was a threat, you need to let me know."

The steel in his low, resonant voice irritated her, but Savannah also understood that if she or Molly were threatened, he'd be their ally. No question. Who else could she turn to?

"I'll do that."

Their conversation over, she turned and walked toward the house, not once looking back even after she heard the powerful engine start or the SUV recede down the ranch lane.

HER FATHER CLEARED his throat. "Your mother and I have been talking."

Bent over as she loaded the dishwasher, Savannah looked up in surprise. Her mother was putting away leftovers in the refrigerator, but turned a hesitant smile on her. So they'd planned this. Was it ominous that they'd waited for whatever discussion this was meant to be until they had separated her from Molly? Savannah could hear a song from *Aladdin*, the Disney movie the four-year-old was watching right now.

"What's that?" Savannah asked, straightening.

"There's no reason for you to put your life on hold because of your brother's whims," Dad said brusquely. "I don't know why he'd think he could put the burden of raising his child on you when you're not married or settled."

"I always thought Jared would come home again. Having his daughter here…" Mom choked up. "She's a sweetheart. She reminds me so much of you at that age, except for her being so…timid."

"Molly has reason for that."

"We know she does." Dad again. "If you keep moving, maybe meet someone, start your own family, that'll be hard on her. Would have made more sense for Jared to give us custody."

"We'd be really glad to have her," Savannah's mother said with quiet fervency. "We've missed you so much. It would almost be like starting over with you."

That stung. "Would you be hoping for a better result?"

Mom gasped. "How can you say that? Have we ever been less than proud of you?"

No. Her parents had glowed with pride in her, even as any praise for Jared was handed out grudgingly.

"I was…sort of kidding."

"Oh," her mother said, mollified. "We don't mean any kind of criticism of you. You're wonderful with Molly, but our offer is sincerely meant. You must have noticed that she has even your father wrapped around her little finger."

Dad's face did soften whenever his gaze rested on his granddaughter. Thank goodness Jared had had a daughter instead of a son, a girl who looked enough like Savannah to be *her* daughter. Her parents had been good to Molly, relieving Savannah of a major worry. Molly seemed less reluctant to be left in her grandmother's care than she had Brenda's. That didn't mean Savannah was going to say—what?—*Oh, great, she's all yours.* And then take off, free as a bird?

"That's generous of you," she said carefully. "You know I moved home because she needs more family. Having her grandma and granddad here to give her what she needs is really important. But I love her. Jared entrusted her to me, and I plan to live up to that. As far as I'm concerned, Molly *is* my daughter now."

"Oh, well." Mom was clearly disappointed, but also nodding approval. "Just know, if you ever change your mind—"

"That won't happen, but thank you." She took a couple of steps so she could hug her mother, then smiled at her father. "It's been good to be home."

In some ways, but there was nothing to be gained anymore in reminding them of how they'd treated Jared, or even in pursuing the *why*.

Maybe this was the wrong time, but she took a deep breath. "Actually, I've been thinking I'd like to move with Molly into that empty cabin. Unless you have plans for it?" She looked to her father.

He frowned. "No, but why would you want to do that? This house is plenty big for all of us. We're family, for God's sake!"

"I know. But I'm thirty-one." Thirty-two in March. "I haven't lived at home since I left for college. In one way these last two weeks have been good, but…finding myself back in my old bedroom, mostly just helping around the house like I did when I was a teenager, I feel as if I've gone backward, you know? I guess I'd like a little more sense of independence, but staying here on the ranch would let Molly and me lean on you, too."

Her parents exchanged a glance. She could tell they didn't

like her idea, but if pressed, they'd probably both have to admit they understood how she felt, too.

Wanting to let the concept of her and Molly moving out settle a little, she asked, "Dad, did you get a look at Akil? He's gorgeous."

The Arabian gelding had been sent here by an owner she'd trained for in the past. They wanted him for cutting, but so far he wasn't patient enough. It was possible that, in the end, she'd have to give them a dose of reality and suggest they find another focus for him, but it was equally possible that the trainer who had worked with him was the one lacking in patience.

Her father grunted. "Pretty enough, but you know I like quarter horses."

"Big butts," she teased, and he grinned.

"Damn right. You can *see* the power."

They had had nothing but quarter horses on the Circle B, but part of the deal they'd made before she came home was that she could take in other horses to train as a side business, as long as she had time for the animals bred and raised here at the ranch.

"Okay," he said abruptly. "No reason you can't have the cabin. I'll have Jeff look it over, make sure there are no problems before you move in."

"Oh, good." Now she hugged him. "I can probably buy beds and some of the furniture in town—"

"You don't have any in storage?" her mother asked, sounding startled.

"No, I always had furnished apartments. It'll be good to change that."

"Well, we certainly have more beds and dressers and the like than we need, so you can start with that," Mom said firmly. "Although it might be fun for Molly to make decisions for her own bedroom."

Savannah wrinkled her nose. "Expect pink. I guess that won't surprise you. You're lucky I never went through that stage."

"No, you didn't," her mother agreed. "You were a tomboy

from the get-go. After having a boy, I was so looking forward to buying you cute clothes, and what did you insist on wearing?"

"Jeans and cowboy boots."

Mom sighed. "Even when you were chosen as the rodeo princess, you balked at being too girlie. Your words."

Savannah laughed. "Although there were homecoming and prom dresses."

"Except you hated shopping, and picked out the first thing that fit."

"Well, just think." Sound had quit coming from the living room, and she saw the little girl appear in the doorway. "You-know-who will *love* cute clothes."

Mom looked…hopeful. And clothes shopping was one task that Savannah would be delighted to leave in her mother's hands.

"PINK COWBOY BOOTS?"

Those were the first words out of Logan's mouth, partly because he didn't have any real excuse for having stopped by the ranch for the third time in four days.

After seeing him, Savannah had reined a glossy bay gelding to a stop at the arena fence where Logan hooked a boot on the lowest rung and crossed his arms on the highest so he could watch her in action. Her mount had the classic dished face of an Arabian.

A small herd of steers bellowed and shoved in a narrow holding pen to one side. Usually they'd be raising dust, too, but the temp last night had dropped well below freezing, and the ground was still crisp. Logan had felt ice that wasn't visible cracking under his boots as he walked from where he'd parked closer to the house. Ugh. The time to start throwing out hay for the herd was upon them, and Logan foresaw new arguments with his father.

Savannah laughed about his last comment. "You saw those, huh? Mom took her shopping yesterday."

"Doesn't bode well for her to want to grow up to be a rancher."

"No reason she can't herd cattle wearing pink boots and shirt, is there?"

"No, but they wouldn't end up near as pretty after roping calves or getting down to wrestle with them."

He liked that Savannah laughed again. "She'll have to learn that the hard way." She waved to a ranch hand who had been waiting for the command, and he lifted a bar to allow the cattle to jostle each other through the chute and into the arena. In typical fashion, they circled the arena at a trot a couple of times, searching for a way to make a break.

Savannah's horse quivered with his desire to take charge as the steers lumbered by, continuing to bawl their displeasure, but she kept him still with legs, hands on the rein and a quiet word.

Also as usual, the small herd finally clumped together at one end.

"Did you have a question?" Savannah asked him. "Otherwise, I need to get to work."

Logan shook his head. "Just checking on the two of you. I don't mind watching you in action. It's always a pleasure."

He'd swear she blushed, but she turned the gelding away before he could be sure. What he'd said was the honest truth. He was good on a horse, as were most ranchers in these parts and their children. Sure, ATMs were used for a lot of the jobs once handled by men on horseback, but they all spent plenty of time in the saddle, too. From the time Savannah was eight or nine, though, she'd taken his breath away when she rode.

As he watched, she reined the gelding right into the middle of the small herd, ambling along so as not to alarm the cattle. No, not as relaxed as he'd initially thought; the horse hunched his back once, skittered a couple of feet sideways a minute later, causing restlessness around him. Savannah had him cut through the herd, circle out, then do it again, over and over again, until he decided he didn't have to get excited.

Logan knew he should get back to work; with ice lurking in shaded stretches of the roads, there were bound to be more accidents than usual. This time of year, even locals forgot to be cautious. A long skid was a wake-up call that seemed to be necessary every winter. Those same locals couldn't seem to get through their heads that pickup trucks, bearing most of the weight in the cab, didn't handle well in icy or snowy conditions unless some weight was added to the bed. Sandbags, say, or bales of hay.

He'd planned to patrol this morning, since his deputies were spread too thin, but he couldn't seem to take his eyes off Savannah. She had that high-strung horse meandering along as if he had nothing more on his mind than finding a sunny spot to graze.

The gelding was momentarily startled when she set him to work cutting a single steer out of the middle of the herd. He moved a little too sharply, stirring up the herd. Once he'd edged the one steer into the open arena, though, horse and rider were a treat to watch when it came to preventing the steer from rejoining the others. Each attempt to break free was blocked, the Arabian spinning on his haunches, Savannah moving as one with him, hardly seeming to do a thing.

At last, she gave an invisible signal to her mount, and they stayed still and allowed the steer to rush back to the safety of the herd.

Waiting a couple of minutes, she started all over again, choosing a different steer, again from the center of the herd. In a cutting competition, taking one from the edge would result in poorer scores; what was called a "deep cut" was rewarded. Still a little too much movement from the cattle; riders were downgraded if the herd was stirred up.

He stayed to watch her repeat one more time, then made himself leave. Logan was frowning when he fired up the engine. His current fascination with this woman wasn't compatible with the disdain, even dislike, he'd felt for her all these years.

Having been burned so recently by another woman made his interest even more nonsensical. No, he hadn't been to the point of asking Laura to marry him, but they had been living together for a few months and he'd considered that the relationship might be going somewhere. He'd debated before asking her to move with him, and been stunned when she dismissed the idea as if it were a complete absurdity.

She'd been really peeved when he hadn't been in the mood a few hours later to hop into bed and have some presplit sex.

No, he hadn't been brokenhearted, but he hadn't enjoyed the experience of finding out how low he was on her scale of importance. You might say he was a little off women right now.

Which made more inexplicable this compulsion to keep a close eye on Jared's sister.

OF COURSE, the San Francisco police detective kept calling. She would have given a lot to be able to share anything the slightest bit helpful to his investigation into her brother's death. Clearly, he'd like to get his hands on Jared's phone, but hadn't pushed the issue yet.

He seemed surprised when he admitted that the autopsy tests hadn't found any illegal substances in Jared's blood. In fact, he'd appeared surprisingly healthy and fit for a man with a history of drug addiction. The pathologist agreed with Savannah's guess that Jared had been clean for a number of years now.

What she didn't know was why her brother hadn't cut himself free of the dark underworld of drug dealing. He'd given her hints, but stayed closemouthed during their phone conversations. Had he thought someone might be listening?

She did remind Detective Trenowski that she'd wondered whether Jared wasn't working undercover, although she had no idea who he was reporting to, if so.

"Was he going by his own name?" the detective asked.

Of course she had to say, for at least the dozenth time, "I don't know. Except, well, his driver's license was in his name, wasn't it?" Why hadn't she pushed for more answers? But she knew. She'd been afraid Jared would quit calling her at all.

"I might check with the DEA in case they've been pulling his strings," Trenowski said thoughtfully.

"Will you let me know?" she asked. Or was that begged?

"If I can," he said. "Ah, your brother's body has been released. Have you come up with a plan?"

She took a deep breath. There was something awful about choosing a funeral home from Yelp reviews, but that was what she'd done. She hadn't even discussed this with her parents. Mom had fretted that "those police" wouldn't let the family bury her son, but she'd also never asked when Jared's body would be released.

Ultimately, Savannah had decided on cremation. Jared's ashes would be mailed to her. She couldn't imagine shipping his body home to be buried in Sage Creek, not after he'd run away and never returned in all these years. Anyway, who would go to the funeral, if she'd arranged one? Logan and her. Oh, maybe there'd be a few friends from school or teachers who'd attend. Her parents undoubtedly would, but Savannah couldn't stomach any hypocrisy from her father.

No, it was better this way. Eventually, she and Molly together could decide what to do with Jared's ashes. Savannah wished she'd known the adult Jared well enough to guess whether he'd want his ashes spread in the ocean, the mountains... Not in the dry, sagebrush-and-juniper country where he'd grown up, she felt sure.

Logan asked about Jared's body, during his fifth or sixth stop by the ranch, and frowned when she told him what she'd decided. To her relief, though, after a minute he only nodded and said, "He wouldn't have wanted to be buried here."

"No."

They let the subject drop.

He asked, as he had every time he came by, whether she'd had any phone calls that made her uneasy, any hang-ups, any hint at all that somebody might be looking for her and Molly, but she shook her head at that.

Savannah hated the fact that she had started looking forward to seeing him, and that his crooked smile made her heart squeeze every bit as much as it had during the height of her teenage crush on him. The truth was, Logan might be presenting himself as an old friend, but he was a cop whose interest had been piqued, and who maybe was outraged on behalf of his old friend. When he stopped by here, he was Sheriff Quade, and she shouldn't kid herself otherwise.

Chapter Five

Her father's voice always had carried. Savannah was hanging towels in the bathroom after slinging the new matching bath mat over the tub curtain rod when she heard him snap, "This is a damn fool thing for her to be doing! But try to talk to her?" He snorted. "She's too independent for her own good." Logan and Dad had carried in her new sofa a few minutes ago.

Logan answered, his voice as calm and deep as always. "I don't know, Gene. I've got to sympathize, since I've moved back into my old bedroom, too. It's not just that my feet hang off the bed. It's having Dad keeping an eye on me, ready to jump on me if he's not happy with the way I do something. This seems like a good compromise for Savannah to me."

Bless him! She hadn't been sure how she felt about his appearance a couple of hours earlier to help her move in. She hadn't invited Logan, but he'd known which day they planned for the great move, and shown up bright and early. He'd even brought a completely unexpected housewarming present.

Shoving a big item in a sack at her, he'd said, "You may not need this. If not, the receipt is in the bag. I just thought…" Sounding embarrassed, he'd trailed off.

He'd bought a high-end coffee maker for her. Way to a woman's heart. She hugged the gift.

"I haven't bought one yet. Thank you, Logan. This is…really nice of you."

He'd given one nod and then said, "What can I do?"

Really, there wasn't that much, but he had helped Dad dismantle a couple of beds at her parents' house and carry frames, springs and mattresses downstairs and the quarter mile or so to the cabin. Mom had helped Savannah make up the beds once they were in place. Molly had brand-new bedding with purple unicorns galloping over rainbows along with matching curtains. She hadn't left her bedroom since. Savannah could hear her across the hall singing tunelessly to herself.

Didn't Dad know *everyone* could hear what he was saying?

Savannah had been doing well restraining herself where her father was concerned, but his attitude was rubbing her the wrong way. Now that she was home, he wanted his wayward daughter under his thumb, day and night.

Logan's low-key explanation of how she felt might be more effective than her efforts, though. Both men's voices had gone quieter, and she let herself relax and look around the bathroom. She'd gone with peach and rust in here, and thought she might paint the walls if it looked like she and Molly would be staying. The kitchen, too. Maybe a lemon yellow, she thought.

The scuff of a footstep had her turning sharply to find Logan filling the doorway with those broad shoulders. As always, she was hyperaware of his very presence.

"Looking good."

"Thanks."

He eyed the towels. "Is that color close enough to pink to please your little cutie?"

Savannah laughed. "We had a minor argument, but she's satisfied because she got to pick out her own bedding. Have you seen it?"

His grin was even sexier in such close quarters. "Yeah. She's singing 'Over the Rainbow,' except I don't think she knows most of the lines."

"I noticed. I've already looked it up on the internet so I can sing it for her. I bet it's now on her favorites list along with 'You Are My Sunshine.'" Her own answering smile wobbled. "I love seeing her so happy."

"Yeah." He could sound remarkably gentle. He glanced over his shoulder and lowered his voice. "Maybe this isn't the time, but I've been meaning to ask, ah, whether you've considered looking for her mother. Just to be sure she won't pop up someday wanting her daughter back."

"I haven't yet, but I should, shouldn't I?"

Creases deepened on his forehead. "I think so."

"The thing is… I don't want to trigger her interest."

He gripped the door frame on each side of him. "I can do the looking, if you want."

Savannah tried to decide how she felt about that. "I thought about hiring a private investigator. The trouble is, all I know is the woman's name from Molly's birth certificate. I have absolutely no idea whether she stayed on in San Francisco or moved to Chicago or anywhere else. Or how long it's been since she gave up Molly."

"I'll be glad to conduct a search," he said. "Law enforcement databases give me access to a lot of information."

"I…" She hesitated for only a moment. "Yes, thank you. Let me try talking to Molly again first, in case she can tell me anything at all. You'd think she'd remember whether she had to travel when Jared took her, for example."

"You would. I'm no expert on kids her age, but she seems pretty verbal to me."

"I think she is, too, except she clams up when it comes to talking about her mother or anything except the recent past. I think she'll need counseling, but maybe not yet when so much change has been piled on her."

"Understandable."

He just stood there, a big man who effortlessly dominated this small space. He had a way of watching her from those unnervingly pale eyes that awakened an awareness that she was a woman who hadn't been involved with a man for an awfully long time. Blame the crush she'd had on him as a boy, she told herself desperately. Yes, he'd grown up to be as sexy as she'd imagined he would, but this was the guy who'd looked at her with contempt when he happened to notice her in the high school halls, remember?

"Do you know where my mom is?" she asked briskly.

His gaze lingered on her for a minute longer before his arms dropped to his sides and he stepped back. "Up at the house. She says lunch should be ready in about ten minutes."

Savannah managed to offer a smile that was no more than pleasant. "I trust she invited you?"

"She did."

"Well, let me take a peek at the living room, and then we can head over to the house." She hesitated. "Thank you for what you said to Dad. He isn't happy about us moving out of the house."

"Not hard to tell."

She walked past him and into the small living room, which at present held only her new sofa, a new wall-hung television, and a small bookcase and antique rocking chair Mom had dredged up from the house. The curtains were ugly, but she planned to have blinds installed to replace them, and for her bedroom window and the kitchen and bathroom windows, too. Every once in a while, she had an uneasy remembrance of how she'd felt watched that night when she picked up Molly, about the car that had slowed and pinned hers in bright lights. The crime level in a rural county like this was nothing compared to a rough neighborhood in a big city, but she would still be happiest to know that nobody could peek in the windows.

"Auntie Vannah?" The high voice came from behind her. "Where's Grandma and Granddaddy?"

"Getting lunch ready." Savannah scooped her up, twirled once, smacked a kiss on her cheek and said, "But you're not hungry, are you? Not even for mac and cheese. Or cookies."

Molly giggled as she hadn't been able to do in her first weeks with Savannah. "I'm always hungry!" she declared.

Logan grinned at her. "Then how come you aren't bigger? You should be at least this high." He held a hand a foot over the top of her head.

She sniffed. "I will be. When I'm five. Or maybe six."

"Five is coming up pretty soon, isn't it?"

"Uh-*huh*."

"January," Savannah said. "That really isn't far away."

"'Cept Christmas comes first," Molly informed them. "I want my own pony for Christmas."

They kept talking as they walked along a white-painted fence bordering a pasture where brood mares were kept. Not as many as Savannah would like to see in the future, but she was looking forward to foaling season anyway.

Molly would love seeing newborn foals.

Savannah smiled and turned her head to meet Logan's compelling gaze. After a moment, his mouth curved, too.

LOGAN HAD EXPECTED to find himself bristling when he had to spend any time with either of Jared's parents, but today had felt surprisingly comfortable. Or maybe he shouldn't be surprised. He'd spent a lot of time here as a kid, just as Jared had at his house. Things weren't as bad in the early years. Except for the irritation Savannah had let him see once, she seemed to be getting along fine with her parents, too—who showed signs of worshipping this new granddaughter as much as they had their daughter.

After an excellent lunch, Savannah walked him out to the porch to thank him again for his help. Looking down at this beautiful woman, no longer glaring at him, he did something out of the ordinary for him.

He let impulse seize him.

"Any chance I could take you to dinner one of these evenings?" he asked.

She looked startled.

Since he was undecided about his own motivation, he added, "I've been hoping to hear more about Jared. Sounds like you talked to him pretty regularly over the years. I've spent a lot of time wondering."

Her face softened again. "I can imagine. Why he didn't call you, I can't imagine."

His jaw tightened. "I can." As annoyed as he'd been to find out that his old friend *had* called Savannah on a regular basis, Logan tried not to lie to himself. "That last year, he was getting into things I didn't approve of. The drugs, especially, but heavy drinking, too. He developed a flash temper. You probably knew that. He was involved in a lot of fights."

She nodded. The principal would have been calling her parents to pick Jared up after a teacher or the vice principal in charge of discipline had broken up those fights. How could she help but hear about it, and see her brother's black eyes and raw knuckles?

"I came down hard on him." This was hard to say. "Told him if he was using or drunk, I didn't want to see him. I didn't think of it as tough love, but I guess that's what I was going for."

"Only, it didn't work," she said, pain in her voice.

For the first time, it occurred to him that she might have used a similar tactic with Jared.

"No. By the time he took off, we were hardly speaking, not spending any time together. I was probably the last person he'd have confided in."

She offered a twisted smile. "I tried to stand up for him with Mom and Dad, but…he wasn't exactly confiding in me, either."

"Dinner?"

The smile became more natural. "That sounds good. I guess you can tell Mom will be thrilled to have Molly to herself."

"It's obvious she's besotted. I think that's the word."

Savannah chuckled. "Dad, too, even though he's not much into hugs or explaining what's happening in the NFL games to her."

"And sometimes the Seahawks are especially hard to explain," Logan muttered. "Assuming your dad's a fan." The Seattle team wasn't having a good year.

She laughed again. "He is, and I really doubt that Molly would understand why he's yelling at the TV. Um." She nibbled on her lower lip. "I'm free any evening."

"Tomorrow?"

"That's fine. Shall I meet you in town, or...?"

She probably realized how silly that sounded, given that he lived just down the road. She didn't argue when he said a little dryly, "Why don't I just pick you up?"

Logan left after a moment that felt awkward to him. He wanted to kiss her, even just on the cheek, as if they'd always parted that way. But, no, they hadn't, and he still had some serious ground to make up...if he decided he wanted to upend a relationship that had him uneasy.

He'd have to see how it went.

A HALF HOUR into the evening, Logan discovered how good it felt to talk to Savannah and how much he liked having her confide in him.

They'd decided on an Italian restaurant, which had excellent food even by his tastes, altered by years spent in a cosmopolitan city. This had been a pizza parlor when he was a teenager, but clearly someone had bought it out and upgraded in the intervening years.

They did talk about Jared initially, Savannah showing him the few photos she had of an older Jared. Logan looked at them for a long time.

"I can email them to you, if you want," she offered.

"Yeah." He cleared his voice. "I'd like that."

She shared some of what her brother had told her over the years.

"The worst part was knowing that his addiction drove him into... I don't know exactly, whether he was selling illegal drugs or helping run them or what. Or maybe that was part of his rebellion, knowing how much it would offend Dad." She made no effort to hide how hard it had been to continue to love someone whose lifestyle she utterly opposed. "If I hadn't known the causes of his depression so well, I'd have been angrier at him. As it was, we never talked for long, and I tried not to say anything that might make him quit calling. At least I knew—" She shrugged.

"He was alive."

"If not well. Except sometimes he sounded really good. Another thing I never knew was whether he was fighting the addiction on his own, or whether he went through rehab once or a dozen times, but I would let myself hope. And I'd swear he *had* been completely straight the last few years."

Being a cop, Logan wasn't big on excuses for not doing the right thing. "Then why didn't he walk away?"

She was quiet for a minute, turning her wineglass in her hand, but finally lifted her gaze to Logan's. "I was never sure, but...he hinted a few times that he might be working undercover. He used the word *atone*."

"They were getting suspicious. Isn't that what he said?"

"Yes." Expression troubled, Savannah said, "Wouldn't you think he'd have told me? Or left something in the duffel that I could have taken to authorities?"

Instincts sharpening, Logan said, "Are you so sure he didn't?"

"He left a will naming me guardian and some paperwork about investments for Molly. His personal phone, too, but it has so little on it. There are the numbers of people he called, but...not many. No messages or texts. I wonder if he had any friends at all. I searched in hopes of finding more about Molly's mother, but failed unless one of those numbers is hers. Otherwise, nothing."

"Maybe he wanted to keep you and Molly out of the dark side of his life," Logan said slowly. That would have been his own inclination. "He wouldn't have liked the idea of endangering you."

"No." Savannah tried to smile. "That's what I tell myself."

"I suppose in coming home, you've dropped off the radar. Who'd know?"

"My former boss. I guess the IRS will when I file next year's taxes."

"The IRS knows all," Logan intoned.

He loved her laugh. From then on, as if by mutual agreement, they let the subject of her troubled brother go, instead talking about what had changed—notably, this restaurant—and what hadn't in Sage Creek. Which wasn't much.

"Well, I noticed they did finally build a new elementary school," Savannah conceded. "Do you remember what a *pit* that place was? The one building got condemned, so we weren't allowed in it, and everyone started to think it was haunted."

Logan's turn to laugh. "I hadn't heard that. Who was supposed to be doing the haunting?"

"Mostly teachers who'd moved away or died. Do you remember Mr. Barrick?"

"PE? God, yes."

"You know, the gym was in that building. It made sense he'd still be there terrorizing students." Humor brightened the color in Savannah's eyes.

"Him, I'd believe in. Except I think he just retired. He's probably terrorizing neighbors in Arizona or Florida, wherever he and his wife moved to."

She giggled. "Can't you picture him ruling over a homeowners' association? He could ride a golf cart around the neighborhood making notes about any landscaping violations."

He suggested a few teachers he could picture choosing to hang around as ghosts, and she added a couple more. Small as the school district was, they'd had many of the same teachers, from kindergarten up through high school, despite being three years apart.

From there, they moved on to mutual acquaintances—who was still around, who'd died, who'd gotten divorced, taken over a parents' business and so on. Since he'd been back in town longer, and stayed in closer touch with his dad than she had with her parents, mostly he updated her on the local scandals. They were both laughing when the check arrived.

He unlocked his truck and held the door open for her, only going around to get in behind the wheel once she was fastening her seat belt. As he steered the truck out of the parking lot onto the main street here in town, he was surprised at how busy Sage Creek was this evening. Dad had always claimed the town rolled up the carpet by eight o'clock, and it was mostly true. Restaurants, a few taverns, a bowling alley and something going on at the Elks Club provided the only evening entertainment.

Once they left town behind, darkness surrounded them. Only a few passing headlights intruded. Logan tried to retreat from the sense of intimacy he felt in this cocoon by starting a conversation again—and not the first-date kind they'd had in the restaurant.

"Jared was expecting a lot from you, asking you to take on his daughter," he said. "Given that you'd never met Molly."

"Didn't know she existed," Savannah said dryly.

"Yeah."

"He had to be so desperate he didn't think about it. What else could he do with her?"

"It must have been a shocker for you."

"That's an understatement." She was quiet for a minute. "Especially when we didn't hear from him, and it sank in that I was all she had. I had to quit my job. Molly was too traumatized to settle into the only day care available, and she had so many nightmares, I started feeling like a zombie. There were moments—" She broke off.

"Moments?"

"Oh, it doesn't matter. I'm lucky she's such a sweetheart."

"It's a surprise she is," he said, "given how much change *she's* suffered." Damn, they were almost to the ranch. He didn't like having such mixed emotions about this woman. Wanting to see her, get to know her again, lay his hands on her, while also having the equal and opposite reaction, thinking that the way she presented herself now could be a facade.

"We might be in the honeymoon phase," Savannah commented. "Her wanting to please me because she's scared of what will happen if she makes me mad. After all, she's been abandoned twice already in her life."

He'd read that was common behavior for foster kids in a new home, or new adoptees. The suggestion made sense.

That led to him speculating on how Savannah *would* react if that cute little blonde girl started throwing screaming temper tantrums and yelling, *I want Daddy! I don't want* you!

With no experience at being a mother, did she even know?

He couldn't forget that the girl he knew had been the unfailing center of her parents' lives. If Jared was to be believed, she'd always gotten what she wanted when she wanted it. That hadn't changed; even though her father hadn't liked her moving into the cabin, she got her way. Went without saying she'd also been popular at school. Had she ever faced the slightest bump in her belief that *her* life would be one of sunshine and rainbows?

Look at her now. The minute she felt burdened, she'd run home to Mommy and Daddy.

She was good with Molly. He'd yet to see her be anything but patient. But how long would that last? How long before she needed to be the center of attention again, no matter who that hurt?

Chapter Six

Savannah was chagrined to realize how much she wished Logan had done more than kiss her lightly on the cheek before he left her on her parents' porch. As he looked down at her, his eyes had narrowed with the kind of purpose she recognized. His gaze had flickered to her mouth, she'd swear it had, and her pulse quickened. She might even have started to push up onto her tiptoes when his expression changed and he brushed his lips on her cheek. Then he'd said gruffly, "Good night, Savannah. I'm glad we did this." And darned if he didn't bound down the porch steps, walk to his truck, get in and drive away without more than a casual lift of the hand.

She stood there on the doorstep long enough that if her parents had been listening for her, they'd be wondering what she was doing. Or not wondering. She puffed out a breath.

She'd wanted Logan to kiss her, all right, but because it would be a fulfillment of her youthful crush, not because she liked and trusted him down to the bone. So...it was just as well they hadn't gone there.

She made a face. Uh-huh. Sure.

Her phone rang, distracting her. The number was blocked. She never answered calls that looked like spam. If it turned out to be anyone she wanted to talk to, she'd return the call after she heard the message. If she was lucky, it would be someone tracking her down to train a problem horse.

Blocked, though. That seemed strange. Especially after telling Logan her speculation that Jared might have been trying to bring down an organization with ruthless employee relations. As in: *you betray us, you're dead.*

Which Jared was.

Stepping into the house, hearing the TV in the living room and her mother's light voice, she realized there'd been no follow-up *ding* indicating the caller had left a message.

Well, who didn't get junk phone calls?

She almost dismissed her worry.

Still, after she and Molly walked back to the cabin and she tucked her niece into bed, Savannah was left restless, feeling a warm curl low in her belly, a sense of anticipation she hadn't had in a long time. Or ever? She hadn't had a steady boyfriend while she was in high school. None of the guys could compare to Logan, even after he'd left for college.

Truth to tell, her couple of later relationships that had gone far enough for her to share her bed had been a form of *settling*. Funny that she hadn't seen that, but the ranches where she'd worked were typically remote, and she had never been a big fan of hanging out in taverns. That left the pickings sparse, and she'd never been sure what kind of man she wanted. Some of the ranchers reminded her too much of her father, gruff, single-minded, not given to tenderness and lacking any sense of fun. Many of the hands seemed to have no ambition. Probably because of Jared, Savannah recoiled from heavy drinkers.

Somewhere in the back of her mind, she'd believed that, someday, she'd meet the right guy. It was more than a little disquieting to discover that Logan had been there all that time in the back of her head, too. He'd only been eighteen the last time she saw him except from a distance during his visits home, but no one she'd met since measured up.

Wonderful. She still had a thing for a man she deeply suspected hadn't gotten over despising her. Chances were really good that he'd been dropping by regularly out of loyalty to Jared, thinking that she and Jared's daughter might need his protection. He might have been briefly tempted to kiss her tonight, but he'd easily resisted that temptation, hadn't he?

Well, despite her occasional unease, she thought it unlikely that they'd need him. He'd pointed out himself that she'd effectively disappeared, right? Her phone number was out there, but not her whereabouts. And why would anyone think she'd know anything about Jared's business?

Despite her perturbation when she went to bed, Savannah slept well. So well, she didn't wake up until her mattress started bouncing, as if she was in a boat in rough water.

She pried open her eyes to find Molly jumping up and down and giggling.

"Aargh!" Savannah lunged up, snatched her niece into a hug and growled into her ear. "You're making me seasick."

Molly beamed at her. "Grandma said maybe we could get a trampoline. That would be even *more* fun!"

"Yes, it would." Except Savannah had qualms about how safe they were. She'd definitely vet anything her mother considered.

And then she had a thought. "You didn't have a nightmare! Not even one!" Unless she'd slept through it, but she couldn't imagine.

"Uh-uh. I didn't wet the bed, either."

That had happened only a few times, but embarrassed Molly terribly.

Savannah hugged her even harder, then set her aside. "I don't know about you, but *I* need the bathroom."

"I already went, and I washed my hands, too," Molly told her.

"Good for you."

This move home had been the right thing to do, she thought as she got out the cereal, bowls, milk and a banana. Molly really was thriving, not only because she was gaining confidence that Auntie Vannah was solidly in her corner, but also because of her grandparents.

Even Jared might forgive them if he could see how good they were for his daughter.

And, yes, things wouldn't always go so smoothly, but they'd get through them.

She'd sent Molly off to get dressed and was loading the dishwasher when her phone rang again. The call looked just like last night's: *No Number,* her phone told her. That was weird, but she didn't want to lose a good training opportunity because she refused to listen to a sales spiel or whatever.

So this time, she answered with a "Hello."

"Have I reached Ms. Baird?" The voice was a man's and unfamiliar.

Could it be the police again?

"Yes," she said cautiously.

"I understand your brother died recently."

Her skin prickled. "That's true."

"He worked for me. Having him vanish was…a shock." He paused. "I'm sure it was worse for you."

"Yes."

"I don't know how much he's told you—"

"About his work? Nothing," she said quickly. "We were mostly estranged."

"I see. Well, he was undertaking some critical work for us that should have remained confidential. Unfortunately, it's clear that when he took off, he had information that should never have left, er, the company offices. It's my understanding that he met with you before his death."

Why would he have thought that? Did they have an informant on the police force who'd implied that she had lied to the detective and might really have seen Jared?

Scared, she shook her head hard at Molly, who appeared in the kitchen doorway.

To the man, she said, "I wish that was true. I'd have loved the chance to see him, but…he didn't show up."

"He gave something to you." On the surface, the tone was still civil, but somehow darker.

"His daughter. She's just a little girl. That's all he left for me—Molly and a pink suitcase with her clothes and toys." She immediately regretted telling him Molly's name.

"I'm having trouble believing that," he remarked coldly. The gloves were off.

"I can't help that," she said, going for offended in hopes of hiding her fear. "I hadn't seen Jared in eighteen years. That's a long time. We only occasionally spoke on the phone. I have no idea what he did for a living. I'm glad he felt he could trust me enough to raise the daughter he loved. I don't even know where Jared lived. I can't help you find whatever you're looking for."

"If you expect me to buy that—"

"I'm sorry. This has been difficult enough. I have nothing else to say." She ended the call, and silenced her phone with a quick flick of her fingernail.

Oh, dear God. Could she hope Jared's boss—and his minions—couldn't find her and Molly?

BY CHANCE, Detective Trenowski called an hour later to let her know Jared's cremated remains should arrive on her doorstep within the next day or two. He sounded alarmed when she told him about the phone call.

"I hope you planned to let me know about this," he said sternly.

She agreed hastily that she had, which was true. In fact, she'd just left Molly with Grandma and had sought the quiet and relative warmth of the tack room in the barn to hold this conversation. The soft sounds that reached her, rustles as horses moved around in their stalls or nosed hay in mangers, an occasional clomp of a hoof or a nicker, should have been familiar and comforting.

"You might want to consider getting in touch with local law enforcement," the detective suggested. "Just...let them know about the call and why it's worrisome. If you give them my phone number, I'll be glad to talk to them."

"Thank you," she said. "I'll do that." In fact, she'd intended to call Logan first. Why she'd been standing here waffling, she didn't know.

Logan answered his cell phone on the first ring. She could hear a vehicle engine and assumed he was on the road. "Savannah?"

"Yes. Um, after you dropped me off last night, a blocked call came in on my phone. I ignored it, but this morning, when it came up again, I answered. It was a man, saying he'd been Jared's boss."

"Damn it."

He already disapproved? "You think I should have kept ignoring whoever was calling?"

"No, I didn't mean that," he said quickly. "I'm annoyed at myself. I should have thought about having you download a recording app onto your phone."

"Oh. That would have been good. Except the guy didn't come out and say anything direct enough for you to act on."

"No, and technically you're supposed to tell someone they're being recorded, but at this point I don't care."

Law-abiding to a fault, she didn't, either.

"We'll do that as soon as I can get away," he added.

"Why would he call back?" she had to ask. "I said, no, I hadn't seen Jared, that he'd never talked to me about his work, we were mostly estranged, and I apologized for not being able to help."

"Tell me what he said."

She reported the conversation the best she could and didn't like the silence when she was done.

"You didn't get the impression this guy was satisfied?"

"No," she said reluctantly. "The last thing he said was that he didn't buy what I was saying."

Logan swore. "I really wish I could have heard the conversation." He let out a long breath. "I can't do anything right now. I'm on my way to a vehicular accident. A head-on."

"Oh, no."

"I'll see if I can arrange some drive-bys, but you're pretty remote. You have a bunch of hands living on the ranch as well as your parents, right?"

"Yes."

"There's probably no reason to worry." He didn't sound as confident as she'd have liked, but he was right. It would be too obvious for anyone with hostile intentions to drive as far as the house and barns, and it would be a long, dark walk otherwise. Any unusual noise would arouse curiosity. Loud curiosity, when it came to the ranch dogs.

"Oh—the detective I've been talking to in San Francisco suggested I give you his number."

"Can you text it? I'm driving right now."

"No problem. I should let you go."

"Yeah." Logan's voice had changed, and she knew he'd arrived at the site of what might be a gruesome accident.

"Thank you for listening," she said.

He was gone without another word.

LOGAN DID MAKE a quick stop at the Circle B the next day to talk Savannah through downloading the app to record conversations, even though he leaned toward thinking that a repeat call was an unlikely next step—if there would be any. Jared must have had friends, even a girlfriend. It sounded like Savannah had been as clear as she could be in telling the caller she'd had no appreciable relationship with her brother in many years. What else could they do on the phone except issue threats, and why would they expect that to do any good?

He'd interrupted her in the middle of a working day. In fact, she was taking a quarter horse around some bright painted barrels in the arena when he arrived. Not yet at full speed, but even so, each turn around the barrel would look hair-raising to someone not accustomed to sticking on a quarter horse's back when he used those powerful hindquarters to spin. On the dime, as the saying went.

Logan was just as glad to have no reason to linger when they were done. He hadn't resolved his confusion where she was concerned and had decided avoidance was the smartest tactic until he did. He was damn glad he hadn't kissed her the way he'd wanted to; he still harbored plenty of doubts about this woman.

He had a particularly busy week at work, too. The head-on collision had taken place on a county road rather than a state highway, unfortunately, so the responsibility for measuring distances and more, so that he could determine speed and trajectory for each vehicle, was his. He made the immediate decision to send someone else in his small department for training in accident reconstruction.

As was all too common, the speeder had been a seventeen-year-old boy, probably trying to impress his girlfriend. She survived; he didn't. If it had been the reverse, there would have been legal consequences, but beyond that, Logan doubted the kid would have ever gotten over his culpability in such a tragedy. The car had hit a pickup truck, severely damaged it, but it had been solid enough to keep the driver from serious injury. Since the kids were locals, a pall had swept over the entire county. The funeral was planned for next week, although the girlfriend would still be in the hospital.

Local residents were also facing a rash of thefts from mailboxes—hard to combat, given the vast number of miles of road in a rural county like this one versus the number of deputies Logan could deploy. And, yeah, that was a federal crime, but no federal law enforcement agency had time for an isolated, little-populated area like this.

To top it off, there'd been a break-in at the farm-and-ranch store. The list of items taken was long enough that the thief had spent as much as an hour "shopping" and probably had a pickup truck backed up to the loading dock in back. The lock showed some damage, but not enough. The camera aimed at the loading dock had been mysteriously disabled. That added up to a guilty employee or, conceivably, ex-employee who'd copied a key.

Not that he managed to put thoughts of Savannah aside. She

was always there, for several reasons. Coming face-to-face with her in the pharmacy, not to mention their dinner together, had brought a whole lot back to him. Jared was tangled up in so many of Logan's memories of growing up. He'd turn his head and remember taking that trail on their horses, or when he went by the high school he would grimace at the memory of the two of them sharing a six-pack sitting on the bleachers late at night.

That was the first time he'd gotten drunk, although now he wondered if that was so for Jared, even though they'd been only...fourteen, Logan thought.

Dad mentioned Jared now and again, too. He went so far as to drive over to the Circle B to say howdy and meet the little girl who had Jared's eyes.

"Wouldn't mind a grandchild," he remarked after that.

Logan grinned at him. "Call Mary and nag her." He happened to know that his sister and her husband intended to have children but weren't yet ready.

His dad laughed.

This evening, he'd checked for a last time on his father, showered and stretched out in bed. Now he let his thoughts wander.

He'd contended with equally mixed feelings about Jared's younger sister back when they were kids and then teenagers. She had dogged their steps whenever they allowed it, and he'd secretly admired her determination and toughness on the occasions when she took on more than she should have and got dumped from a horse or banged up in some other way. Of course, if her parents were around, they'd rush to her side to fuss over her, and if Jared was around, he'd be chewed out for letting his sister get hurt.

Logan had been acutely aware of her later, when she developed a figure and he'd see her sashaying down the hall at school, her butt really fine in tight jeans, her honey-blond hair rippling down to midback.

By then he'd blocked any memories of fondness. He heard and saw Jared's hurt every time Mr. Baird made plain how worthless he thought his son was in comparison to his beautiful, smart, talented daughter. Logan convinced himself that she gloried in the praise and didn't care about the brother she'd pushed aside.

Now he thought he knew better. Mostly, Jared had been neutral about her. Loved her, even if he couldn't help resenting her, too. Logan just hadn't read it that way, still felt suspicious of Savannah's character.

Maybe because here she was, home again, to her parents' open delight. Why wouldn't she be eating it up? No sullen brother to get in the way.

That was probably unfair, but he couldn't seem to shake an opinion of her that had solidified by the time he was thirteen or fourteen years old.

No wonder his attraction to her disturbed him.

And yet…considering she was the first woman who'd seriously caught his eye since his return to Sage Creek, he wondered if he wasn't a fool to hesitate making a move on her. She had to have done a lot of growing up since he'd last seen her.

Maybe he'd stop by the ranch tomorrow, he thought. Why not get to know Savannah as a woman instead of a girl? A few dates didn't equal any kind of commitment, after all. Satisfied, he sought sleep.

SAVANNAH'S EYES POPPED open to near-complete darkness. She lay stiff, peering toward where she knew her bedroom doorway was. Was Molly having a nightmare? She'd made it without one last night, for the second time this week. But she wasn't screaming, and Savannah was sure she'd have heard even quiet crying.

She focused immediately on the heavy tread of feet on the front porch, a sound that was familiar but didn't belong in the middle of the night. Something must be wrong. That had to be Dad or one of the ranch hands—

She sat up and swung her feet to the floor, surprised to have heard no knock. Barefoot, she slipped out of her room into the hall. She could peek out through a crack in the blinds.

But when she reached the living room, she saw the doorknob turning and heard a thump when an attempt to open the door failed because of the dead bolt lock. Silence followed.

Heart racing, she tiptoed forward.

Rap, rap, rap.

It came from the window, not the door. Seconds later, she heard another thud that might be someone jumping off the porch. Not ten seconds later came another *rap, rap, rap*, this time from the kitchen window. The back door rattled but the lock held.

Pulse racing, she yanked open a drawer and put her hand right away on the butcher knife. Maybe the cast-iron skillet would be better... No, she'd take both.

The next raps came from the bathroom, followed by Molly's bedroom. Terrified by this time, Savannah hovered in the doorway. Thank God, Molly was either still asleep or huddled in a small ball under her covers pretending nothing was happening.

Savannah dashed for the window, desperate to see out, but already her tormentor was knocking on *her* bedroom window. Was whoever this was trying to lure her out? Or was the message quite different?

We're right here, only a few feet away. We could break the glass and come in, and you couldn't stop us.

She should have gone for her phone instead of inadequate weapons, she realized suddenly. But the ranch dogs had started to bark, deep and threatening, and they were coming this way.

Chapter Seven

Savannah would have waited until morning to call Logan, but she couldn't stop her father. She was so shaken, so unnerved, she'd rather not have to describe every minute once again, but apparently she had no choice. Dad was even more upset than she was, if such a thing were possible. He'd always been protective of her, one reason he'd hated her moving away for work.

She sat at her kitchen table, Molly on her lap clutching her tight, face buried against the one person she evidently trusted. Dad had suggested Molly go back to bed, and since then she'd held on even tighter.

"I could have reported this in the morning," Savannah repeated. "You shouldn't have dragged Logan out of bed. What can he do? Whoever was out there is long gone."

"You know that for a fact?"

"Of course not!" She breathed deep a few times and regulated her voice. Dad meant well. "How could I? But after rousing the whole ranch, nobody but a crazy man would come back tonight."

Dad turned his head. "That must be Logan now." His relief was obvious.

Rocking slightly to comfort herself as much as the little girl she held, she wanted Logan; she did. But she'd have rather felt more together before she talked to him.

He knocked on the front door and then walked in without

waiting for anyone to open it for him. His eyes went straight to her and Molly before turning to her father.

"What happened?"

Savannah opened her mouth to answer, but Dad didn't let her.

"Savannah says someone circled the house, trying the doors and then tapping on the windows. Dogs started barking, who-ever he was ran. Back when the kids were teenagers, I'd have thought it was some kind of prank. Jared might have thought it was funny to scare his sister. But now? If those drug dealers know she and Molly moved into this cabin…" Face choleric, he didn't finish.

Logan's brows drew together. She met his eyes and was dismayed to see doubt. Maybe it was even valid. If this had anything to do with that phone call, how *had* the creeps who thought she had something Jared had stolen known she'd moved home in the first place, and then which cabin she and Molly lived in? But who else would set out to terrify her?

Feeling Molly trembling, Savannah said, "I woke up to heavy footsteps on the porch. At first I thought Dad had come over be-cause something was wrong, or maybe one of the ranch hands, but…whoever it was tried the door, but didn't knock. Then he rapped three or four times on every window as he walked around the house. He tried the back door, too."

"Him?"

"I can't be sure. The footsteps sounded like a man's."

"You didn't try to get a look at him?"

"I…was going to peek out at the porch, you know, just through a slit in the blinds, but by then he'd moved on. I wasn't fast enough. Anyway, I didn't think finding myself face-to-face with him was a good idea. I ran to the kitchen so I'd have *some* kind of weapon in case—"

Logan's gaze lowered to the heavy skillet and the knife that sat on the kitchen table, then met hers again. Those icy eyes were intense. "Why do you think he ran?"

"Because he'd done what he meant to do? Or maybe because the dogs had started barking and were tearing this way?"

He didn't say anything for a long time. The distinctive lines on his face seemed to deepen. Finally, he said, "You think this has to do with Jared."

"What else could it be?"

"It...seems strange."

She wished she could feel numb. "You think I'm imagining things."

"Imagining?" The pause left a lot unspoken. "No."

Then what?

She licked dry lips. "The message seemed pretty clear to me. 'We know where you are. We can get to you anytime.'"

"Isn't that unnecessarily dramatic, when they could just call and tell you the same thing?"

"This had...a lot more impact." She hoped her voice wasn't shaking.

He grunted, pushed back his chair and said, "I'm going outside to take a look around."

"Why are you bothering?" she said to his back.

He ignored her and went outside.

"He'd damn well better take you seriously and do his job," her father snapped. "Meantime, why don't you take Molly up to the house? With your mother there, at least she can get some sleep."

"She's scared. I think she'll do better here. She can sleep with me."

"You sure she wouldn't feel more secure with us?" His idea of gentle fell short, but he was trying.

"I don't believe whoever this was will come back tonight."

He scowled, of course. Her father wanted to believe he could handle anything. Calling in law enforcement would normally be a last resort, in his view.

He didn't argue, though, and they sat in frigid silence until the front door opened and closed again, and Logan walked back into the kitchen.

"Too bad there's no frost tonight," he said. "I don't see any footprints."

Of course there weren't any.

"I'll talk to the employees," her father said. "You'd think someone would have heard a part of this. If anyone working here was drunk and thought this was a joke, it'll be his last laugh."

She'd been getting to know the half dozen men. The ones Dad kept on through the winter were all long-term employees. The odds weren't good any of them had been wandering around on a dark night, but considering the vibe Logan was giving off, another witness would be good.

"With cold weather, you ever had a vagrant break into one of your cabins?" Logan asked.

"Never. We're too far out of town."

Logan focused again on Savannah. "Would have been better if you'd gotten on the phone right away," he commented, his lean face unreadable. "When we might have had a chance to catch the guy."

"Tell me," she said acidly. "How many deputies do you actually have patrolling in the middle of the night? One? Two? What are the chances one would have been anywhere nearby?"

His jaw tightened. "Why'd it take the dogs so long to get worked up?"

Molly burrowed more deeply into Savannah. *Had* she heard any of the noise? If so, she was too afraid to say anything.

Savannah stared at him expressionlessly. "Because there was nothing to hear, of course." She shook her head. "Tell me why I'd do this. For attention?"

Dad scowled at Logan. "You questioning my daughter's word?"

"I didn't say that."

But he was wondering. She could tell. *This* was the Logan who'd long despised her.

Nauseated and feeling more alone than she had since the

night she'd found Molly abandoned in a frightening situation, Savannah squared her shoulders.

"I think it's time Molly and I go back to bed. Mom will be worrying," she added to her father. "Tell her we're fine."

"If someone was here, he won't be back tonight," Logan conceded.

Her father's face was set in deep lines, but he nodded and pushed himself to his feet. "We can talk more in the morning."

She held out a hand and squeezed his. "Thank you for coming, Dad. Good night."

Dark color ran over his cheeks. "Would I ever not come running if you needed me?" Obviously embarrassed, he let himself out the back door.

Unfortunately, Logan didn't follow him.

She reverted to her deep-breathing exercise.

"Sometimes it's my job to ask hard questions," he said. "Always had the impression you thrived on attention."

Her laugh had to be one of the least pleasant sounds she'd ever made. "You're wrong, but you've always thought the worst of me. I've never forgotten the way you curled your lip every time you saw me." There. He'd done it now. She shook her head and looked down.

"Savannah. I'm just trying to figure out how an intruder knew where you were staying. You don't get much traffic out here at the ranch. How could someone have been watching without being noticed? Are you sure your imagination wasn't at play here?"

"Please leave," she said tonelessly, bending her neck so she could press her cheek to Molly's head. "And... I'd rather you didn't come back, even if you are the sheriff. You'll never get over despising me because of Jared. We both know that."

"You're talking nonsense—" he snapped.

She raised her head again to look directly at him. "Is it?"

He took just a moment too long before saying, "It is, but we'll settle that later. What do you plan to do tomorrow?"

"Buy a gun, and maybe throw out feelers for a new job."

"Savannah…"

Stone-faced, she stared him down.

He muttered a curse. "You're misunderstanding me."

She didn't let even a faint crack show on her face. Finally he bent his head in acknowledgment and walked out. She heard the throaty engine of his pickup, loud at first and then fading.

Tears hot in her eyes, she locked the front door, leaving the porch light on, and tucked Molly under the covers in her bed. "I'll be right back," she whispered and hurried to the kitchen for her makeshift weapons, setting them within reach in the bedroom. Then, cold all the way to the bone, she slipped under the covers with the little girl who scrambled to cuddle right up to her, knees digging into Savannah's belly.

If only she already had that gun.

She'd have to get a safe, too, of course. She wondered how long it took to unlock one and yank out the gun. Would she be quick enough?

Fear didn't keep her awake; no, the sense of betrayal did that all on its own.

ANGRY AND FEELING SICK, Logan drove away too fast. He'd let past convictions build doubt in his mind before he so much as heard a word she said, but when she'd stared at him with bottomless pain in her eyes, he'd known what he'd done. Woman and girl needed him, but Savannah wouldn't call him again no matter what happened.

Sure, he'd been concerned, after that phone call Savannah had taken from Jared's so-called boss. But he'd spent a couple of nights now convincing himself that there was nothing to worry about there. Nobody knew where she and Molly were, and she'd talked to the San Francisco cop about the situation. He had a lot on his plate, and he wasn't going to add to it with needless conjecture from a woman with a history of being the center of attention, especially since in all of his father's years of ranching, he'd never had a break-in. Obviously, the Circle

B hadn't, either. In fact, that kind of crime was rare to nonexistent in these parts.

It didn't help that Logan had detested Gene Baird for years. His phone call had been all but frantic, because his precious daughter had been threatened. If Jared had been, he'd have probably growled, "Deal with it," and rolled over to go back to sleep.

Driving over here, Savannah on his mind, Logan remembered the rodeo princess, the homecoming queen. The center of attention, except now her pretty niece had taken that place.

The icing on the cake was that he couldn't help remembering what he'd said while they drove back from town a few evenings ago—and how she'd responded.

He'd suggested that her brother had expected a lot from her. She agreed it had been a shocker.

Especially when we didn't hear from him, and it sank in that I was all she had. I had to quit my job. Molly was too traumatized to settle into the only day care available, and she had so many nightmares, I started feeling like a zombie. There were moments—

He thought that was what she'd said, almost word for word. She'd backed off fast after that.

Moments that what? The only interpretation he could come to was that she had times when she quaked at the burden she'd taken on. Thought it was more than she could bear.

Even if that was true, did he really believe she'd do something so despicable as terrify an already traumatized child with a spotlight-grabbing stunt?

He'd *seen* her with Molly. No. He wouldn't believe it. Was he stuck in the past, assuming she was the pampered girl he used to know? Or had he really known her at all?

Throat so tight he couldn't have swallowed, he steered onto the shoulder of the road just short of his own driveway and put the truck into Park.

Would she accept an apology?

Logan couldn't imagine.

SINCE SAVANNAH HAD plans for the morning that didn't include working, and she and Molly were up plenty early, she made pancakes for breakfast instead of setting out the usual cereal and milk. She even tried to pour the batter to form some recognizable shapes, but without a lot of success. Dad had been skilled at that, she remembered suddenly. His horses looked like horses. He'd done that every so often, to her and Jared's delight.

The memory held a bittersweet sting.

Molly giggled when Savannah delivered a plate to her with two pancakes that were supposed to be, yes, a horse and a crescent moon, but she scarfed them down happily, eating more than she usually did.

Savannah finished her own breakfast—her pancakes looked more like blobs of sagebrush than anything, she decided—and then smiled at her niece. "Honey, I think it's time you tell me what you remember about your mom."

Molly's eyes widened in alarm. "I don't want to live with her," she whispered.

"No." Savannah reached over the table to clasp the small hand snugly in hers. "Never, never, never. You're *my* little girl now. I'll fight anyone who tries to take you away from me. You understand?"

Maybe she'd spoken more fiercely than she should have. Maybe she shouldn't have even hinted that anyone *might* try to take Molly. But those blue eyes stayed fixed, unblinking, on Savannah's face for longer than was comfortable.

Then she nodded.

"Good. I'm glad we've got that straight." She smiled, and Molly relaxed enough to smile back.

It took some more coaxing, but eventually the four-year-old did share confused memories of when she'd lived with her mother. Memories that horrified Savannah.

There had apparently always been other people living with them. Or else Molly and her mother had moved frequently to stay with anyone who'd take them in. Savannah couldn't tell. Molly's mommy had sometimes tried to be the mother she needed to be, but sometimes she slept a lot or just sat staring straight ahead and didn't even hear when Molly spoke to her. It sounded as if Molly had crept around trying not to attract any attention, because she knew the other, rotating members of the household thought she was a nuisance. She'd fed herself, mostly cereal and bread, when no one thought to offer her anything.

Then one day her daddy had swept in and taken her away. She *thought* they'd driven a long ways in his car, but she'd fallen asleep and didn't really know whether it was all night or not.

"I liked being with Daddy," she added, "'cept he worked a lot, and then I had to stay with Julie." Her nose crinkled. "This boy she took care of was mean to me, but Daddy said I couldn't go to work with him, and at least I could play and watch TV and stuff at Julie's 'partment."

"I see." Molly must have felt a déjà vu when her auntie left her during the day with Brenda. "Did you get to say goodbye to your mommy?"

Molly's eyes filled with tears. "Uh-huh. She looked sad, but she said I would be better with Daddy. Only... I was scared, 'cause I didn't know him." She sniffed. "Is Mommy dead, too?"

"I...don't know, but I do think she was right. You were better off with your dad, and now with me."

"I like living with you best," her niece said simply.

"Good." She half stood, scooped Molly up in her arms and sat back down. "*I* like living with you, too."

Nothing Molly had told her came as a surprise. The mother had very likely been a drug addict, too. How and why Jared came to learn about his daughter would remain a mystery, but she was glad to know he hadn't hesitated to leap into action, even if single parenthood didn't conform well with his lifestyle. He'd made Molly feel loved, though.

Unfortunately, Molly hadn't said anything that would help Savannah find the mother. Maybe that was just as well. She wouldn't be turning to Logan for help, that was for sure.

Savannah sent Molly to get dressed and stood up to load the dishwasher.

Her phone rang. She saw exactly what she'd expected: instead of a displayed number, her screen showed that the number was blocked.

Oh, God. Not answering didn't seem to be an option. *Please let Molly dawdle over picking out clothes.*

She answered the call and triggered the recording app, hoping she'd done it right and it would actually work. "Hello?"

"Ms. Baird." The voice was familiar from that last call. "I hope we didn't alarm you too much last night."

"You're kidding, right?"

"We need you to know that we're serious. That you can't hide from us."

This was hopeless, but— "You're barking up the wrong tree," she said. "I told you the truth last time. If Jared had something he shouldn't have had, I'm the last person he'd have passed it on to. I'd always been careful during our rare conversations not to ask what he did for a living. If he wanted something done, he wouldn't have depended on me. We were virtual strangers."

"But, you see, I don't believe you," the man said, almost gently. "*You* were the last person he called. He entrusted you with his child. He knew you'd raise her the way he wanted you to. You can't deny that."

"I can't, but a little girl is different than...than whatever you're talking about. Of course I'd take my niece, no matter how I felt about Jared! Why can't you see that?"

"We have considered all other possibilities," the man assured her. He sounded so businesslike, it was surreal. "We're left with only one. You."

"My brother didn't give me anything. He left no instructions, only paperwork giving me legal custody over his daughter. You're wasting your time."

"It's ours to waste, but we are getting somewhat impatient." That voice took on an edge. "Last night was a gentle warning. Please take another hard look at every message your brother left you, every single thing he passed on to you along with his *precious* daughter."

The emphasis on *precious* scared the daylights out of Savannah.

"We'll call again," he said. "If you don't have an answer, we may have to apply some real pressure."

Her mouth opened, even though she had no idea what to say, but she knew immediately that the caller was gone. The connection was dead.

Bad choice of words.

Disturbed, she sank down in a chair, dropped the phone onto the table in front of her and stared at it as if it was a coiled snake rattling its tail.

Chapter Eight

Hearing the sound of the toilet flushing from down the hall, Savannah didn't move. Her mind whirled. Now what?

Search everything Jared had left again, yes, but she'd already done that. The obvious item of interest was his phone, and she'd gone through it several times already, finding nothing. Who knew why he'd discarded it? Anyway, if she found something, what would she do with it? Hand it over to the creeps who were threatening her? She didn't think so.

Otherwise…she would definitely let Detective Trenowski know about the call, for what little good he could do her. Logan? She supposed she almost had to. At least he'd have to believe her, since he could listen to the wretched conversation himself—unless she had done something wrong and failed to record it. But what would he do, sheriff with authority over an inadequate number of officers already stretched too thin? Savannah had no doubt tracing the phone the call had been made from, assuming he could do that, would be useless. She'd recently become well aware of the cheap phones anyone who was criminal-minded or just didn't want to be found could use, toss and replace.

So. Pack up, the way she'd intended, and run with Molly for their very lives? Try to find someplace they could live off the grid, preferably with some protection? But she didn't know how her brother's "employers" had pinned down where she and Molly were so quickly. How could the two of them make a getaway sure they were unseen?

Especially since she'd sold her own car to another ranch hand back in New Mexico and was currently borrowing an old pickup used around her father's ranch. If she disappeared with it, of course, she felt sure Dad wouldn't call the cops to report grand theft auto, but she'd undoubtedly have to dump it somewhere so she and Molly could hop buses and zigzag across the West undetected until they found what appeared to be a safe roost.

And she couldn't let herself forget how happy Molly was here, with grandparents as well as her aunt. Savannah tried to picture leaving Molly, if only temporarily, with those grandparents, but aside from understanding that Molly would feel abandoned for the third time in her life, she couldn't forget the way that man had described Molly as Jared's *precious* daughter. If that wasn't a threat, she'd never heard one.

Staying here, Molly would still be vulnerable, and what more powerful lever could evil men find than the child whom Savannah loved?

Not a single option seemed to offer any hope at all.

MOLLY BEGGED FOR her fine blond hair to be French-braided, and then insisted on wearing those pink cowboy boots even though she probably wouldn't go near a horse this morning, but finally Savannah walked her to the big house. She found only Mom in the kitchen. Molly ran to her for a hug.

Mom looked worried. "Your father said it sounded like someone was breaking into the cabin last night?"

Molly visibly shrank.

Glancing meaningfully at her, Savannah said only, "Or... taunting me. It was scary, but we were okay, weren't we, pumpkin?"

The child's blonde head bobbed, but her body language showed tension.

"I need to go into town to do some errands," she said. "You don't mind Molly staying with you, do you?"

"Of course not!" Her mother beamed at her granddaughter, although she still looked anxious. "We can read some more, and bake pies, and—"

Molly had perked up, and they were still talking about how they could fill the day when Savannah left.

A gun store was her first stop. She tried out half a dozen handguns the owner recommended for women. She hadn't fired one since she was a kid and her father gave her and Jared lessons aiming at the classic bottles on fence posts. Target shooting had never appealed to her, and didn't now, but she was glad to find that she was still reasonably accurate. She also agreed to come in and spend some time in the range. For Molly's sake, she had to become comfortable with the gun in her hands.

The background check was quick in the state of Oregon, as was approval for a concealed carry permit, and she was able to leave with her new Sig Sauer P365 tucked in a holster and bagged along with a small gun safe that would sit cozily on her bedside table next to her clock and lamp. Just what she'd always wanted.

Had Jared carried a weapon on a day-to-day basis? she wondered. If so, it had been stripped from him.

For a dose of normalcy, she loaded up with groceries, stopped by the pharmacy and chose a couple of new games and toys for Molly, including a particularly cute stuffed sea turtle, then turned in their library books and picked out a dozen new ones to read to Molly, plus a couple for herself. Somehow, the mysteries didn't appeal to her right now. She chose fantasies.

She thought seriously about making calls to horse owners in her contacts list, asking them to spread the word that she was looking for a job, but decided to leave that for another day. Part of her, the Savannah who was angry at Logan, not to mention feeling sick with roiling panic, still wanted to pack and go right this minute. But how? Even if she persuaded Dad or even one of the ranch hands to drive her and Molly someplace less obvious than town to catch a Greyhound bus, they could be followed.

Anyway, she kept thinking about the way Molly had run to her grandmother this morning, how much she loved her new bedroom and how she'd lit up when Savannah promised her a pony of her own. Then there were the horses Savannah had started to work with. Would those owners be willing to transport them to another ranch, even assuming she could find a place where she'd be able to take on outside horses? And how could *that* happen without any pursuers being led right to her?

Little as she wanted to move back into her parents' house, she'd do it if she believed she and Molly would be safer there. But would they really be?

And…if her worst fears were true, did she want to risk her parents, too?

Didn't it figure that, when she came out of the library, a sheriff's department SUV approached down the street. Not even giving herself a chance to identify the driver, she hustled for her pickup and leaped into the driver's seat. Maybe he wouldn't recognize the borrowed truck. She wasn't ready to talk to Logan…but it was too late. By the time she'd fired up the engine, the marked SUV swung abruptly into the library parking lot and braked in front of her, blocking her in.

LOGAN HAD DETOURED by the Circle B before going into work, but didn't stop to knock on doors or talk to anyone once he'd seen that Savannah's pickup was missing. After that, he'd been delayed with business at headquarters, but once he set out on the road again, he drove slowly through town looking for her. He'd begun to think he'd missed her.

His relief when he spotted her was powerful enough to awaken uneasiness again, but he blocked out that part. She hadn't packed up Molly and taken off this morning for points unknown. For the moment, that was enough.

He hopped out, walked to the driver side of her vehicle and twirled his finger to ask her to roll down her window.

Fingers gripped tight on the steering wheel, she just stared at him for a minute, and he wondered if she'd ignore his request. She'd probably consider it a demand.

Finally, she closed her eyes for a moment, then complied with obvious reluctance. "Sheriff."

"Where's Molly?" he asked.

"With Mom. Where else?"

"I called your dad, but he said he hadn't had a chance to talk to you this morning," he said.

Her mouth tightened. "No. Little as I like the idea, I did intend to call you."

"You did?" God. Something else had to have happened.

"First, why don't you spit out whatever it is you're determined to say?"

"You've never made a mistake?"

Her vividly colored eyes held his. "Plenty of them, but you didn't make a mistake. You've disliked me for most of your life, and you made that obvious again. At a bad time, too."

In one way, she was right, and he hated knowing that. What she'd forgotten or never guessed was the flip side, his fondness for the scrappy little girl who'd idolized him and her brother, the attraction that had plagued him the last couple of years of high school—and since she'd returned to town.

"I...had a moment of doubt." He didn't much like humbling himself, but if she wouldn't forgive him— He couldn't let himself think about that and went on. "I let myself...wonder."

Her short laugh held an edge sharp enough to slice vulnerable skin. "Uh-huh. Well, I'm sorry to say I didn't dream the whole thing. I got another call first thing this morning."

"Did you record it?"

"I did." She reached in her bag and then handed him the phone.

Since he'd installed the app, he pulled up the call quickly. The man's voice came from the phone, crystal clear. Logan's gaze never left hers as he listened, his body rigid.

"Ms. Baird. I hope we didn't alarm you too much last night."

Her protest went ignored. "We need you to know that we're serious. That you can't hide from us."

The thrust of the call got worse and worse.

"Last night was a gentle warning. Please take another hard look at every message your brother left you, every single thing he passed on to you along with his *precious* daughter."

The implicit threat enraged Logan.

"We'll call again," the SOB said. "If you don't have an answer, we may have to apply some real pressure."

Either she hadn't had a chance to say anything more, or she'd been cut off. Logan cursed, but his outburst didn't help vent any of his tension. He handed the phone back to her.

"If you come into the station, I'd like to make a copy of that and put a trace on the original call."

"Like that'll do any good," she scoffed.

Unfortunately, she was right. Who in their right mind would issue a threat from a phone number linked to an identifiable business or individual?

"I plan to share this with the detective in San Francisco," she said. "I wanted to get my errands done first."

His gaze fell to the passenger seat and the floor in front of it, crowded with bags. He recognized one of them, printed like desert camouflage.

"You bought a gun."

"Yes, I did."

"You're lucky someone didn't break in if you left that in sight while you were in the library."

"You mean, there is crime in the county?" she exclaimed in mock astonishment, before dropping it and reverting to a flat "I made sure it couldn't be seen."

"You going to be able to lock it up?"

"Yes, Sheriff, I bought a gun safe, too. Now, if we're done?"

He gripped the bottom of her window frame, even though he knew full well he couldn't stop her from rolling up the window.

"Damn it, Savannah! I'm here for you. I came last night without hesitation. And, yeah, I screwed up, but, like your father, I'll come running anytime you need me. I swear it."

Her remote expression chilled him. "I'll keep that in mind, but I don't plan to need you." She looked pointedly at his hands. "I have to get home."

Home. Did that mean she didn't intend to leave? He thought he'd pushed it enough for the moment. Asking her future intentions probably wouldn't be smart.

After a moment, he let his hands drop to his sides and backed up. "Don't let hurt feelings put you or Molly at risk."

Now her stare blistered him, but she didn't say anything. He could only nod and walk back to his SUV, get in and drive away. Logan hoped like hell she didn't try to disappear the way she'd said she would.

Being brutally honest with himself, he wasn't sure how much of that hope had to do with keeping woman and child safe… and how much with this morass of emotions that kept surfacing where she was concerned.

APPARENTLY DETERMINED TO do his best to know where she was and what she was doing, Logan stopped by the ranch at least once a day during the following week. The only news she shared was that she'd received Jared's ashes, which she was currently storing in her closet so as not to disturb Molly. Most often, she was able to ignore Logan, although his very presence leaning on the fence surrounding the outdoor corral or sitting on the bleacher-style benches in the indoor arena challenged her ability to maintain concentration as she worked with horses she had in training. She could *feel* his eyes on her, even with her back turned. When she let her own gaze slide indifferently over him, he was always looking back. Watching.

Well, to hell with him. She couldn't ban him from the property, since she didn't own it—in fact, a couple of times her father joined him and they talked for a few minutes. And, no, she wouldn't cut off her nose to spite her face—one of Mom's pithy sayings—and reject the help she would likely need from local law enforcement, but that still didn't mean she had to talk to him. What annoyed her most was when she spotted him walking up to the house a couple of times and disappearing inside long enough to have a cup of coffee and probably charm Molly.

And, yes, she was petty enough to want him to stay away from Molly, too, but she knew talking to Sheriff Quade wouldn't hurt any child. He'd been astonishingly natural with Molly, surprisingly so considering he apparently didn't have any kids of his own. Maybe seeing him around and learning to trust him would even build Molly's sense of security. Savannah wished that was working for her. Instead…just the sight of him stirred up her tangled feelings for the boy he'd been and the man he was now. Examining them didn't seem to do any good. Afraid for herself and Molly and wishing she could trust Logan, she never had a peaceful moment.

Truthfully, her concentration when she was on horseback was poor even when Logan wasn't here, watching.

Once Molly had fallen asleep each evening, Savannah searched everything that Jared had sent with her. She got desperate enough to cut open the tube of toothpaste, hoping Molly wouldn't wonder too much why her auntie Vannah had replaced it. The doll, with its hard body, didn't seem to offer any possibilities, nor did the doll's wardrobe, although Savannah studied every garment carefully. Feeling even worse, she sliced seams on the stuffed animals that had come with Molly, running her fingers through the foam pellets in one case, the white polyester filling in the others. She felt nothing hard, like a thumb drive, or crackly, like paper. Having planned in advance, she'd sneaked into Mom's sewing room to borrow a needle and thread so she could stitch the poor stuffed animals back together again. She examined the duffel bag in case Jared had added a pocket that wasn't obviously visible. No to that, too. Molly's clothes, her coat, her shoes, got scrutinized. Oh, and the board games—a good place to disguise a code or password, maybe.

She didn't find a thing.

The week was so quiet, it was as if she'd imagined that last phone call. She wasn't at all reassured. *Disturbed* was a better description. The only times her phone rang, the callers were friends or trainers she knew. Meantime, whatever Dad had said to her, he'd instructed hands to keep an eye out for anyone who might be trying to slip onto the ranch unnoticed. Logan's regular stops probably had a similar intent, as did the occasional sheriff's deputy vehicle she saw out on the road and even, a couple of times, coming up to the house before circling and going back out.

The efforts to keep her safe continued to undermine her original determination to pack up and leave. People were watching out for her here. Molly loved the time she spent with Grandma, who was totally devoted to her, and she loved equally the short horseback rides Savannah took her on. So far, they had stayed in the open, close to ranch buildings. Trails that wound among junipers, along a stream lined with cottonwood, or over a crumbling basalt rimrock that was one of the more distinctive features here on the ranch, all were off-limits.

She'd put off buying Molly a pony in case they had to move on, but she couldn't explain why without scaring Molly even more than she already was. She kept repeating, "I haven't found the right pony yet."

Savannah drove to the gun range to practice several times, but felt uneasy the whole time she was gone. Mom had agreed to lock the doors when Molly was with her, but how hard would it really be for someone to break in? Dad was sometimes nearby in the barn or corrals, but more often, given the time of year, he joined his foreman and the hired hands checking fences and hauling feed out to far pastures with the tractor.

The next time she planned to go to the library, Molly begged to come. She'd attended the story time put on by the children's librarian and wanted to go again.

"I can pick out my own books," she declared, too.

Savannah laughed and capitulated.

During the story time, Molly sat cross-legged on the carpeted floor beside another girl who looked about her age. That girl was a lot bolder than Molly, whispering in her ear and giggling, Molly shyly pleased. After the story time was over, the girl tugged her mother over and said, "Can Molly come over and play someday?"

The woman chuckled. "I'm Sheila Kavanagh, and this is my not-so-shy daughter, Poppy."

Savannah introduced the two of them, and they determined that both girls would be starting kindergarten the next fall. They exchanged phone numbers and addresses, and made a date for Molly to go to Poppy's house first. Poppy had a Barbie house *and* car, while Molly could bring the Barbie horse and dolls her grandma had recently bought for her.

Not until they parted in the library parking lot did Savannah realize she'd just committed to something almost a week away. And yet...wasn't this what she wanted for Molly—the start of a friendship, a chance to be part of a small community in complete contrast to the scary places she'd lived in the past?

Maybe it would be better if she and Molly moved into the house for now.

Except...nothing else had happened. There'd been no followup at all, neither calls nor, as far as she could tell, any sign of a tail when she left the ranch. She hated as much as ever the possibility of either of her parents trying to stop a cold-blooded man—or men—determined to grab her *or* Molly. In the cabin, she could fire her new handgun at will. Which circled her back to staying in the cabin by herself, Molly tucked in an upstairs bedroom at the house.

Only listening to Molly's chatter with half an ear, she guiltily checked her rearview and side mirrors for anyone seemingly trailing them. This being midday, of course there were other cars on the road, so how was she supposed to tell?

But gradually, the other vehicles turned off. As she neared her own turnoff, an SUV closed in on her from behind, exceeding the speed limit. Tensing, Savannah watched it approach and debated pulling out the handgun she'd taken to carrying in a holster, but as far as she could tell, there was no one else in the vehicle but the driver. She stuck exactly to the speed limit, put on her turn signal…and the SUV swerved into the other lane and sped past her. As far as she could tell, the male driver didn't even turn his head.

He just wanted to drive faster than she'd been going.

Idiot. Most country roads in the county had yellow stripes down the middle and next-to-no shoulders. You'd find yourself in a ditch if you were even a little careless. Or tangled in a sagebrush-choked barbed wire fence, even more fun.

Speeders weren't uncommon, but she found her heartbeat had accelerated, and she felt shaky as she rattled over the cattle guard and drove slowly up the packed-earth ranch lane. Her gaze kept going to the rearview mirror. Maybe she shouldn't have turned where a passing driver could see her. Except… somebody had already found her, so it was a little late to pretend she and Molly didn't live here.

Another night came in which she slept only restlessly, prepared to turn the dial on the small safe to the last number in an instant. She'd rehearsed the act—opening the safe, snatching out the gun, flicking off the safety—dozens of times.

But morning came with no scares, no phone calls, only the routine of feeding herself and Molly, getting dressed, planning which horses she'd work with today. As she and Molly walked the distance to the house, she saw the green tractor pulling a trailer piled high with hay bales rumbling through a gate, then on through the pasture.

Mom was waiting for Molly, who said, "Auntie Vannah says we can ride later! After lunch."

Mom laughed as she tugged off the little girl's mittens and then hat, and started unzipping her parka. "That sounds fun, but I'll bet we can have fun right here, too. What do you think?"

Molly nodded vigorously. "I liked painting. Can we paint again?"

"Of course we can."

Savannah doubted her niece even noticed when she left. She paused on the porch, however, until she heard the dead bolt snap shut on the back door. Glad Mom was taking the threat seriously, whether she believed in it or not, Savannah headed for the barn. She actually liked mornings like this, when she would likely have it to herself. Despite her sheepskin-lined jacket and gloves, she was very conscious of the cold and light layer of frost. It wouldn't be a problem in the arena, though.

She'd left the metal barrels out yesterday in the corral, so she'd start with a mare she was training for a teenage daughter of a longtime customer. The prosaically named Brownie, whose coat was indeed an unrelieved brown, had real promise.

Savannah patted noses, distributed sugar cubes she'd pocketed earlier and worked her way down the aisle to Brownie, who hung her head eagerly over the stall door. As always, she'd start by cross-tying her and doing a light grooming.

Trying to dodge Brownie's head butts, she reached for the latch on the stall door. A soft sound came from behind her. A barn cat, maybe, or had one of the hands stayed behind? She had started to turn when a blow slammed her against the stall door.

Chapter Nine

Savannah saw the next blow coming. She managed to twist as she slid down the rough wood of the stall to the hard-packed floor in the aisle, cushioned with a couple of inches of shavings. She didn't know what the man looming above her was wielding, but it looked like a flashlight, only longer—

As he swung it, she kept twisting. She heard the weapon whistle through the air, but it connected only with her shoulder. It hurt terribly. He'd kill her if he struck her head—

Screaming now, she flung herself facedown and rolled toward the man's booted feet with some vague idea of knocking him off-balance. It didn't work. He dodged her even as he readied for another blow. She tried to grope for the gun she wore in a shoulder holster, but she'd zipped the coat. Lousy planning.

Smash. Her upper arm again. Oh, God, was it broken?

On a distant plane, she thought, *That might be a flashlight, but why does it have a ball on the end like a baseball bat to ensure a secure grip?*

She gave up on screaming. All she could do was keep moving, watching for his backswing and responding desperately, trying to evade the blows. She got up as far as her knees once, but he kicked her backward. All she managed was to protect her head. The pointed toe of his cowboy boot lashed out again, this time connecting with her belly. She retched, tasting bile as she curled protectively around an agony in her midsection that had to be a broken or cracked rib.

The attack went on and on. She wound down. No one had heard her screams. Would he kill her?

When finally she had rolled into a ball and tried to protect as much of her body as she could, knowing tears and snot wet her face, the man nudged her hard with his toe.

She peered at him through a slitted eye. Her right cheekbone was on fire, so one of the many blows had struck her face after all.

He was dressed like any man around here: faded jeans, cowboy boots, heavy jacket—and a ski mask that covered his whole head. Only his eyes glittered. Brown. As if it mattered.

He crouched. "Appears you didn't pay attention to our first message. This is your last chance to give us what we need. Next time, we won't hold back." He was smiling, she was sure of it. "Be smart. We can get you anytime, anywhere. Expect a call."

He walked away.

Savannah would have shot him…if she could have made her battered body obey any commands at all. If the pain wasn't swelling until darkness crept over her remaining vision.

TEN O'CLOCK OR SO, Logan's phone rang. Driving hands-free since he was patrolling in place of an officer who'd called in sick, he answered immediately.

"Logan?" The low voice sounded…thick. "It's 'Vannah."

She might have said her full name. He couldn't tell.

With a bare glance in his rearview mirror, Logan braked hard enough to burn rubber and then spun the steering wheel to accomplish a high-speed U-turn midhighway. "Savannah? Are you hurt?"

"Yah. Barn."

Slammed by fear, he stepped hard on the accelerator and activated lights and siren. "I'm on my way. Ten minutes. Are you alone?"

"Yah," she said again. "Don't want… Mom…come out."

"I'm calling for an aide car, too. I should get there first."

Whatever she said, he didn't make out. "Savannah? Stay on the line."

But she'd quit speaking. No, disconnected.

He drove a hell of a lot faster than was safe.

The few drivers he'd passed going the other way rubbernecked. Exactly seven minutes later, he passed his father's ranch. He slowed but still skidded on the packed earth to turn into the Circle B. He accelerated even before he'd gone over the cattle guard. Hell on tires, but he didn't care.

No flashing lights showed ahead, and he thought to turn off his siren so he didn't frighten Savannah's mother up at the house. Although…where the hell was everyone else who worked on the ranch? His SUV slid to a stop right in front of the wide-open doors leading into the huge barn. Logan leaped out, unholstered his sidearm and ran inside.

He saw a small ball of human being right away. She lay terrifyingly still. Anguish squeezed his chest in a vise. Savannah wasn't dead. She couldn't be. She'd called him. Horses thrust their heads over the stall doors, and he heard more clomping, hard kicks on wood partitions and shrill neighs. The attack had stirred up the inhabitants of the barn.

Where were the damn dogs? But he knew: with the ranch workers, wherever *they* were.

What little he could see of her face was battered. Lying on her side, knees drawn up toward her chest, she had to be trying to hug herself with her arms. No, arm. One lay awkwardly.

Swearing, he reached her, holstered his weapon and fell to his own knees. She moved, just a little, and moaned.

Thank God.

"Savannah." He couldn't *not* touch her, smoothing hair from her forehead with his fingertips. "Who did this?"

Squinting up at him, she mumbled, "Man. Mask."

"Did you hear a vehicle?"

"Nah. Just…" She struggled to swallow. "Here. Gone."

Her lips were swollen and split. Damn it, damn it, damn it.

"The lights may bring your mother out," Logan warned.

"Don't want Molly—"

"To see you? No. I'll head them off, but first, let me take a look at you."

He thought her shoulder might be dislocated rather than her arm being broken. He hoped so. Her pupils were equal and re-active—what he could see of them with the one eye swollen.

"Think...ribs," she managed to say.

Yeah, given the way she had apparently unconsciously tried to protect them, he agreed that was a likelihood. His gentle, exploring hand determined that she'd been beaten to the point where he wondered if she might have lost consciousness. She didn't seem to know—but her assailant had stopped well short of killing her. Or landing her in the hospital for a lengthy stay. Logan's guess was that she'd mostly suffered bruises, the dis-location or broken arm, and cracked or possibly broken ribs. These bastards needed her to be able to comply with their de-mands.

He wanted to kill somebody.

Tipping his head, he said, "Here comes the ambulance. I'm not going far, but I'll stop your mother and Molly from com-ing in."

She gave an infinitesimal nod, those haunting eyes fixed on his face. It was all he could do to make himself leave her side.

SAVANNAH VAGUELY RECOGNIZED one of the two EMTs. They'd gone to school together, she thought. Both seemed efficient. They placed something around her neck to stabilize it and shifted her carefully onto a backboard before "packaging her." Or so she heard the man say.

Logan walked beside her out to the ambulance, his gaze never leaving her face, his hand resting close enough to her side to brush her own hand.

"I'll follow you to the hospital as soon as I can," he mur-mured.

Strapped down as she was, Savannah couldn't even nod.

Naturally, she lost sight of him as soon as they slid her into the back of the ambulance, but when she closed her eyes, she kept seeing his face. It was as if he'd aged a decade or more, creases in his cheeks and forehead looking as if they'd never smooth out again.

Worry, simmering anger, tenderness and more were all betrayed by the darkness in his gray eyes and those careworn lines. Drifting, she reminded herself that it didn't matter how sexy, even handsome he was. *Can't trust him*, she thought fuzzily. Except…he was right. He'd come running every time she needed him.

A phone rang, and she realized it was hers, but the EMT— what was her name? Something starting with an *N*—shook her head sternly at Savannah and deftly plucked the phone out of her pocket, setting it somewhere out of reach.

"How do you feel?" Nellie—no, Naomi, that was it—asked.

"Bet…" Savannah licked her lips. "…you can…guess."

Naomi smiled. "Just hold on. Once we get X-rays and maybe a CAT scan out of the way, we'll be able to give you pain relief."

How long would *that* take? Savannah wanted to whimper, but held on. She hurt, but no worse than she had the time she'd ridden a bucking bronco in a futile attempt to impress Jared and, even more, Logan. If she'd survived that, she'd survive this. Mom and Dad had been so mad. She thought she'd been twelve, smugly certain she could ride any horse, however it twisted and spun and bucked.

Her brother had knelt at her side while Logan ran for help. "Didn't make it eight seconds," Jared had informed her. "Where were your brains?"

Good question. What she remembered was that as she'd lain there on the ground waiting for her father to come, or for him to get an ambulance out there, whichever came first, she hadn't been looking at Jared's face. Oh, no. Just like today, she'd watched Logan for as long as she could see him.

In those days, she hadn't analyzed why he drew her when no other boy in their town did, but now she thought someone must have cast a spell on her. One that hadn't dissipated despite the intervening years.

The sad thing was, *he'd* never gotten over disliking her. And yet his touch a few minutes ago had been so gentle, his rage on her behalf strangely comforting.

As she was wheeled into the hospital, she had to close her eyes against the bright lights. She was dizzy, everything swaying around her.

Her mother showed up first, just after Savannah had been brought back to her cubicle from getting X-rays—shoulder, rib cage, back and right hip, which had begun to throb. Maybe everywhere. Her head. She seemed to remember that. Which made sense when the throbbing seemed to get worse rather than better.

Her feet felt fine, she thought.

"Savannah!" Mom cried, snatching her daughter's hand. "I've been petrified since I saw the flashing lights and then Logan told us what happened. Your dad—"

"Where… Molly?"

"I left her with Logan's dad and his housekeeper. It was going to take your dad too long to get back to the house. Molly wanted to come with me, but I wasn't sure that would be a good idea."

"No," Savannah said definitely.

"Has the doctor told you yet what—"

The curtain rattled and the doctor, who didn't appear any older than Savannah, walked in. His eyebrows rose. "Mrs. Baird?"

"Yes."

"Well, the news from the X-rays is mostly encouraging." He focused on Savannah. "We think you have a cracked rib or two, and you'll want to keep your rib cage wrapped tightly for comfort, but there are no obvious breaks. Your shoulder is dislocated, as Sheriff Quade suspected. We'll be dealing with that immediately, and you should feel a lot better when we've popped the ball of your humerus—" he lightly touched her upper arm "—back into the joint where it belongs. The relief will be almost immediate."

That was where the blazing coal of pain centered. She had to grit her teeth to swallow the scream at the contact.

"When—"

"I have someone on the way to help me," he assured her. "To finish the catalog, your hip is bruised, your cheekbone cracked, but there's not a lot we can do for that, and you'll find the swelling goes down reasonably quickly. Ice will help with that. Lots of ice. Ah, you have one broken finger—I'm guessing you know which one."

With everything hurting, she hadn't thought, oh, my finger is broken, but now that he'd mentioned it, he was right. She could feel it. It was the small finger on her right side.

"As you may know, we'll bind it to the next finger, which will serve as a sort of splint. It's annoying, but shouldn't keep you from using your hands in most ways."

Reining a horse? She thought she could adapt, although at this exact moment, the idea of heaving herself onto a horse's back seemed as unlikely as her setting out to climb any of the Cascade volcanoes for a fun outing.

Start with Mount Hood, she told herself frivolously.

Another man slipped into the cubicle, they politely asked Savannah's mother to wait outside, and they deftly popped the joint back into place. The doctor hadn't mentioned how much *that* would hurt, despite the pain relief they were already giving her through her IV—but he was right that the stab of agony in her shoulder subsided so quickly afterward, she sighed and sank back into her pillows.

Okay. I'll survive.

As fuzzy as her head was, though, she couldn't forget what the man had said: *This is your last chance to give us what we need. Next time, we won't hold back. Be smart. We can get you anytime, anywhere.*

Part of the memory was the way his mouth had curved. He'd

savored both the process of brutally intimidating her *and* issuing the verbal threat.

Her eyes stung, and she was afraid she was crying, something she *hated* doing.

Jared, how could you do this to us? she begged.

THERE WERE SO many reasons to be furious, Logan had trouble focusing on just one.

No, not true: the shadows cast by the past and the mixed feelings that had kept him from 100 percent supporting and believing in Savannah came out on top.

When he was finally able to sit at her bedside and watch her sleep, he acknowledged another reason for his rage: the fact that she'd been beaten by an expert who knew how to precisely calibrate the strength of his blows and kicks. Enough to make his point, to ensure she suffered, but not enough to cripple her. Oh, no, by tomorrow she'd be able to jump right on their demands, whatever they were. The *care* taken almost made the vicious assault worse. The guy was doing his job, that's all.

Logan had no intention of leaving her side from here on out, no matter what she had to say about that. He'd hire a husky ranch hand to help his father from here on out, and he'd do as much of his work for the sheriff's department as he possibly could remotely. The county council wouldn't like that, but to hell with them.

He'd sent her mother home, gently suggesting that Molly needed her, and taken what calls he needed to by stepping out into the hall. The one call *he* made was to Detective Trenowski in San Francisco, who sounded as appalled as Logan felt.

Trenowski was also openly frustrated. "I'm not getting anywhere with figuring out who Jared might have been working with in law enforcement, if anyone. The DEA is giving me the runaround, and the local FBI office claims they've never heard of him, although the agent I spoke with sounded bored answering my questions. I couldn't tell if he even looked up the name."

Logan growled.

The detective gave a short laugh that held zero humor. "Got to tell you, the Feds always rub me the wrong way. They seem to go out of their way *not* to be cooperative."

"I know what you're talking about. I've met a couple of exceptions," Logan said, "but that's what they are."

During their first conversation, he'd shared his history with Trenowski, which had erased the initial wary barricade. Big-city cops didn't fully respect sheriffs and officers in rural counties. Logan understood that. His deputies didn't have the same level of training, equipment and competence as their urban counterparts. Some of his focus since he'd arrived had, in fact, been training, building morale—and firing the one deputy who'd been on the job for ten years and resented the implication that he was better at swaggering than he was at actually protecting local citizens.

Trenowski asked, "You think about packing her and the girl off to someplace they might be safer?"

"And where would that be? Do you have a safe house to offer? Manpower to guard it?"

Silence.

"They traced her here with remarkable speed. And, yes, it was her brother's hometown, so that made sense up to a point. But in these parts, people keep an eye out for each other. They notice strangers. We're off the beaten path enough not to get tourists. There's not so much as a dude ranch in the county. So how did these men—or maybe it's only one man—watch the ranch *completely undetected* for what has to have been a week or more now?" He hoped the detective didn't hear him grinding his teeth. "I've stopped in at all the neighbors to ask whether they've seen an unfamiliar vehicle tucked into a turn-out somewhere nearby. Do they have an unused outbuilding where someone could have been hiding? The answers are no. This guy has to have been sneaking around on foot, or conceivably on horseback—"

"Muscle for a drug trafficking outfit?" the detective said incredulously. "On a *horse*?" Trenowski sounded as if he'd never seen the animal in real life before.

"Hard to picture, but he's been invisible so far unless he wants to be seen. Savannah says he wore faded jeans, cowboy boots and a sheepskin-lined coat that would allow him to blend in around here. People might see him and assume he's a new hire at one of the couple dozen ranches, large and small, in this county. Pay isn't great for ranch hands, they're frequently let go over the winter, so they do come and go."

"That makes sense," Trenowski said thoughtfully. "Any chance he has taken a job close by? That would give him access to a mount."

"I've asked about that, too. No one nearby has taken on anybody new in the recent past. If they had, they'd have noticed his strange disappearances. Otherwise, how's he getting out here? Where is he staying? The hands at the Circle B would have said if they'd seen anyone unfamiliar hanging around."

"Could they have found a local willing to do their dirty work?"

"How? Not the kind of thing you can advertise for in the *County Reporter*. Besides, this beating was done by a professional who knew exactly how far to go. I'd swear to it."

There was a pause. "You have time to ride around in case he's camping out nearby?"

"I'll do my best to get other people to do that. Me, I'm going to stick with her and the girl as close to around-the-clock as I can. I can do a lot on the phone. I'm calling every dump of a motel, resort and bed-and-breakfast within a couple of counties, for example. My bigger worry is that he's squatting in a falling-down barn or at one of the ranch properties that's been long-vacant and for sale. Even if he's found a house, there'd be no utilities. If he started a fire in a fireplace, someone might see the smoke. It's getting cold here, so if he is roughing it, he's got to be miserable."

"We can hope."

Logan grunted his agreement, although he wanted far worse

for the man who'd slammed some kind of truncheon into Savannah and kicked her hard enough to crack ribs. If he came face-to-face with this bastard, he'd have a hard time holding on to the dispassion required to make a clean arrest.

The two men let it go at that. Logan returned to Savannah's room to find her awake if glassy-eyed, and looking nervously around. Her gaze latched right on to him when he appeared around the curtain.

"Hey, sunshine," he said, finding a smile somewhere as he also took his seat and reached automatically for her hand. "I was just making a call right outside your room."

"Molly's…favorite…song." Her face made some gyrations he thought were intended to be a scowl. "Don't…have to…stay."

"I do." Seeing her trying to work up a protest, he added, "Live with it."

"Bossy."

"Yeah." He outright grinned, even though he didn't feel much amusement. "So I've been told."

"Sister."

"Yep."

"Can't I go home?"

Logan was getting good at understanding her slurry words. "Doctor is keeping you overnight. They want to watch you because you suffered a concussion. They don't like giving you pain meds on top of that, but it's kind of unavoidable."

Savannah made a face he thought was cute, despite the distortion of her features. "That's why…head hurts."

"Yep." He showed her how to use the button to boost her load of those pain meds, even though he was sure the nurse had done the same. Then he said, "Sleep as much as you can, sweetheart. I'd promise you'll feel better tomorrow, except—"

Sweetheart? Had he really let that slip out?

Yeah. Might be good if she hadn't noticed.

But her eyes were suddenly unexpectedly clear, and that might be color in her cheeks. She didn't comment, though, only said, "I'd know you were lying."

Lying? Oh, about tomorrow.

"Given what you do for a living, I suppose you've been hurt a few times."

She gave the tiniest nod. "Bucking bronco."

"I'd almost forgotten. You scared the living daylights out of me. Jared, too." He grimaced. "Your dad blamed us even though you didn't tell us what you intended to do."

"Jared," she mumbled. "He got in trouble. Not me. Dad... wouldn't believe me."

Logan didn't feel a trace of doubt. She'd defended her brother, and her father had smacked Jared anyway. Jared had only shrugged the next day and said, "You know Dad. Savannah tried."

How often had Jared said something similar? Logan wondered. Why had he been so sure Jared had lied, that pretty, perfect Savannah had been smirking in the background while her brother was unfairly accused and punished?

Had he been scared to feel so much for a girl?

Logan wished he knew.

Chapter Ten

Savannah cast an uneasy glance at the spot in the barn aisle where she'd been pummeled. Somebody must have shoveled up any bloody shavings. Inhaling the sharp scent of the fresh wood chips that had been raked smooth, she should be happy stroking Brownie's neck after giving her a couple of lumps of sugar.

Logan, who'd just tossed her saddle effortlessly atop Akil, the Arabian gelding, glanced over his shoulder at her. Amusement glinted in his eyes. "You planning to take a swing at me?"

"No! But I hate this!" Mad at herself the minute the words burst out, Savannah made a face and then immediately regretted doing so because it *hurt*. "I'm sorry! I don't like feeling helpless, but… I like even less being a whiner."

"You're entitled," he said with a shrug. "You must ache from head to toe." He slapped Akil's belly before yanking tight the girth strap. "I still think this is too soon for you to ride."

"My toes are fine, thank you. And you know I'll be better off if I get moving." Her doctor had discouraged her from raising her arm high enough to saddle a horse, however, even assuming she'd thought she could handle the weight combined with the upward swing. She couldn't even slip Akil's bridle on in case he tossed his head at the wrong moment and her arm was pulled too high.

Since she'd acquired a 24/7—or pretty close to it—bodyguard, though, it was just as well she could put him to work. Even better that he knew his way around horses.

She *hadn't* told him that part of her insistence on this outing had to do with being stuck with him in the cabin, which seemed to have shrunk now that he'd moved in with her and Molly. It wasn't just because he was a big man who took up more space than he should. No, her problem was that an accidental brush of shoulders passing in the hall, hands touching as they both reached for something, even the *sight* of him, made her body hum, whether she liked it or not. Rather than spend most of the day trapped alone with him in the cabin while Molly was entertained by her grandma, Savannah had grasped for any excuse to escape.

He'd given her a thoughtful look, his objections mild. Maybe he wanted a change in scenery, too, or just crisp, cold air to clear his head.

She waited while Logan saddled a second mount, a quarter horse gelding belonging to her father, and a few minutes later they rode out of the barn. After he leaned to the side to open a gate and then close it behind them both, they trotted into the empty pasture. Almost a mile out, she could see small clumps of cattle grazing the winter-brown wild bunchgrasses in the next pasture. Most of Dad's herd had been turned loose on federal land in the late summer and fall, giving the grass closer in a chance to rebound. By February, the pasture closest to the barn where she and Logan now rode would be full of pregnant cows to ensure none gave birth out in distant reaches of the ranch.

The land rose gradually, clusters of juniper growing where enough elevation was gained. If she squinted, she could make out a basalt rimrock, betraying how recently volcanic activity had formed this landscape even as it looked like the remnant of a medieval castle wall. No, she and Logan wouldn't be going anywhere near it today. Trail rides were out; Logan claimed not to worry about a sniper, but still made decisions based on keeping her a good distance from any possible cover.

Savannah had pointed out that her caller didn't want her dead, he wanted her treasure hunting for his benefit, but Logan remained adamant once he made a decision.

She had to remind herself every couple of hours, silently, of course, that he was apparently willing to lay his life on the line. For her.

The horses' hooves crunched on the morning frost that still lingered. Just being out under the cold blue sky, sharp air in her lungs, was exhilarating. It smelled different here than it had in the red rock country in New Mexico where she'd last worked, or the couple of ranches in western Oregon, for that matter. It had to have something to do with the volcanic soil, along with the ubiquitous sagebrush, so aromatic when the needles were crushed. Junipers, too, and even the more noxious-smelling rabbitbrush that was hard to eradicate.

The relaxation that allowed her to move as one with the horse was definitely compromised, she realized with annoyance. Her hip wasn't happy, and instinct had her holding herself stiffly because of the ever-present pain from her rib cage. Otherwise... she wasn't any worse off than she would have been lounging on her new sofa in front of the TV.

Logan reined in his mount, tipped back his Stetson as his eyes met hers and asked, "How do you feel?"

"Not too bad," she decided. "I'm not quite up to working any of the horses, thanks to the cracked ribs, but I usually heal fast."

His dark eyebrow expressed his skepticism, and she grinned back.

"I stink at sitting around."

"I've noticed." His voice grew rougher. "Any new ideas?"

She didn't have to ask what he was talking about. Two nights ago, her first after being released from the hospital, he had joined her in reexamining everything that Jared had sent with his daughter. They could dismiss some of the toys quickly: all they'd done with the hard plastic doll was give it a good shake to be sure Jared hadn't pulled off a leg or the head or something to insert a thumb drive into the body, for example. They'd gone so far as to steal Molly's beloved and battered stuffed bunny out from under her arm after she was sound asleep so they could more thoroughly disembowel it than Savannah had the first time around. It had taken her quite a while to stuff the poor thing again and stitch up the seams, especially given her so-so sewing skills.

Yesterday, Logan had run numbers from the outgoing and incoming lists of callers on Jared's phone. They all traced to San Francisco businesses. He'd been particularly fond of one pizza parlor. Other than that, Logan had turned up nothing of value there, and he thought Jared might have just thrown his phone in with his other things, knowing he had a burner on him.

No surprise, Molly had been terrified from the minute she saw Savannah's swollen, bruised face. Really, she must have been from the moment she heard that Savannah had been injured and taken to the hospital. She understood that Logan hadn't moved in with them and slept on their couch as a fun sleepover, but rather to keep her auntie Vannah safe from a bad man. Naturally, her nightmares came more frequently again. She still didn't remember details or couldn't adequately articulate what she saw. Each time Savannah had gotten up to go to her, she'd been aware of Logan standing in the hall watching.

Guarding them. Worrying about them.

The two nights since she'd come home had left all three of them tired, and Savannah's tension stretched like a rubber band being pulled until it must be close to snapping.

Now she admitted, "A new idea? Not a one. You?"

"You're *sure* you haven't forgotten something that came with her?" His frustration was understandable.

"I haven't thrown a single thing away, even though some of her clothes are ready for the ragbag. Well, and her shoes, too." The sneakers Molly was rarely willing to put on these days instead of her prized cowboy boots.

"Jared was too smart for his own good," she said, before closing her eyes. More quietly, she added, "Or for *our* good."

Logan watched her with keener perception than felt comfortable. "It's got to be the damn phone," he growled after a moment. "I wish I was better with technology. I think the time has come to bring someone else in on this."

She couldn't help teasing, "What, you never solved investigations by unburying a cleverly hidden clue on someone's laptop or phone?"

Logan gave her a dark look, although his mouth twitched. "Gangs in Portland weren't that sophisticated, and women in domestic disputes rarely pause to type a confession and hide it in the cloud before shooting their husbands."

"Or vice versa?"

"Yeah," he agreed. "Goes both ways. Same-sex relationships aren't immune from violence, either. And armed robbers? Not given to hiding their bank account numbers on the cloud. Or, let's see, my last investigation—" He slammed to a stop.

"Your last case?"

He said reluctantly, "An attack on a homeless man."

She had a bad feeling that it hadn't just been an attack, it had been a homicide, but she wouldn't push.

"That…sounds like a stressful job." She now knew that Logan had mainly worked homicides in Portland. No wonder he'd perfected an appearance of calm and control she couldn't match.

Whatever turmoil existed under the surface, Logan's body moved in the saddle with the ease she'd always taken for granted. His hand stayed light on the reins as he controlled his horse with his legs. He looked as if he belonged on horseback, instead of having spent close to half his life in college and then a big city.

At the moment, he'd turned his head away, either to avoid her gaze or because he felt the need to search for any visible danger. Either way, she assumed he was closing the subject.

Yet finally he said, "The job can be tough. With practice, you get so you just tuck the things you see away so they don't haunt you."

"But they'll keep piling up over time."

He flickered a glance at her. "Then you burn out and find another job."

What could she do but nod? They weren't best friends, they

especially weren't…whatever she'd been thinking. Logan was doing his current job, and probably on top of that felt an obligation to defend Jared's sister and child. Why she wanted to pry open his psyche, Savannah didn't know.

Lie, lie, lie.

She eased Akil into a lope. Only a stride later, Logan's mount pulled up right beside the Arabian. Making a gradual semicircle would lead them back to the ranch buildings.

They had ridden in silence for a good ten minutes before her phone rang.

SAVANNAH BROUGHT THE gelding to a stop abrupt enough to jolt her painful torso. As she groped in her pocket for her phone, Logan pulled his mount in almost as fast, eyes sharp on her face.

Her thoughts were jumbled, her fingers cold enough to be clumsy. She should have worn gloves.

Pulling out the phone, she thought, *Please don't let it be* them. *Not yet. It could just be Mom. It could…*

The number was unfamiliar, awakening dread. She held it out so Logan could see the screen, then took a deep breath and answered.

"Ms. Baird?" a man said. Not the *same* man, but she wasn't reassured.

Gaze latching on to Logan's, she put the call on speaker. "Yes."

"Why the hell haven't you been in touch with me?" he demanded, before falling abruptly silent. "You have my call on speaker. Who else is listening?" he asked, sounding suspicious.

She jumped on his rudeness before she thought better of it. "What business is that of yours? You haven't even done me the courtesy of identifying yourself."

Logan winced.

Oh, God…even if this wasn't *him*, it might be one of his confederates. She had to be conciliatory for now, try to buy time.

"Your brother swore you were reliable," her caller snapped. "That I could depend on you to get in touch if anything went wrong."

Savannah couldn't remember the last time she'd blinked. All she saw was Logan, who effortlessly controlled his horse. *He* didn't look away from her, either.

"You still haven't told me who you are." Her voice was a husk of its usual self.

Still sounding annoyed, the caller said, "Cormac Donaldson. I'm an agent with the Drug Enforcement Administration."

The initial rush of relief didn't last. What if he was lying?

"Did you speak to a San Francisco PD detective?" she asked.

"No. I've been waiting to hear from Jared, and when he didn't surface, I did the research to find out he was dead."

"That's…kind of an awful thing to say, you know."

"Awful? What do you mean?"

"*Surfaced?* After his body was found in the bay?"

There was a pause before he said stiffly, "That was tactless. My apologies." He waited, but when she didn't say anything, he continued. "I did note the detective of record." Paper rustled. "An Alan Trenowski."

That might have been reassuring if she hadn't been certain the killers knew who was investigating the death, too.

Logan mouthed something. She caught only the gist, but nodded.

"I'm not going to answer your questions until I verify your identity."

He muttered something she suspected was uncomplimentary, but still sounding stiff, he said, "That's fair enough."

"Have you…dealt with Jared before?"

"He didn't tell you?"

"No. I had an impression…but I was never sure."

"Your brother was a confidential informant. A really valuable one. We hoped the newest information would allow us to bring down the entire organization, or as close as we ever come."

She heard weariness in the last thing he'd said. She'd read

enough to know that some drug trafficking organizations operated internationally and certainly in many states. They had as many limbs as an octopus. Jared's supposed information had to be limited, didn't it?

Logan leaned forward and said, "Agent Donaldson, this is Sheriff Logan Quade. I'm sticking close to Ms. Baird for now because of threats."

"They've found her?" The alarm seemed genuine.

"Yes. Can you give us a few hours and then call back?"

"As long as you understand that they may be clearing out warehouses and changing shipping dates even now. Sooner is better than later."

"Our trust is a little shaky right now."

"I can understand that. I'll call again from this number."

No goodbye, which didn't surprise Savannah at all.

She shoved her phone in her pocket and announced, "I didn't like him."

Logan gave a choked laugh.

ONCE THEY WERE back at the cabin, Logan sat down at the kitchen table, opened his laptop in front of him and started making phone calls in between pursuing new information online. Savannah poured two cups of coffee and then plunked down across the table from him presumably to remain within earshot, although she got bored enough to play a game on her phone—or pretend she was.

It took a while before Logan reached an agent in the Seattle division of the DEA he'd known from a task force they had both served on. At the time, his impression had been mostly positive. Ray Sheppard wasn't all ego, the way Trenowski had described too many Feds. Logan thought it was a long shot that the guy would remember him, but kept his fingers crossed.

When the agent finally came on the line, he said immediately, "Logan Quade? Portland Police Bureau?"

"That's me," Logan agreed. He described his changed circumstances before segueing into the mess Jared had dumped on his sister, saying, "She's received several threats and there have been two incidents, including a vicious beating. Apparently Jared hid information they are determined to keep her from passing on to investigators. The reason I'm calling now is that we just heard from a man who identified himself as a DEA agent named Cormac Donaldson. He seemed to think Ms. Baird would know who he was, but her brother never mentioned the name. I presume the guy is with the San Francisco division, since Jared lived in the California Bay Area and was murdered there, but I can't be sure. We need to verify his identity before we dare talk openly to him."

"Back a few years, I knew a Donaldson when we were both assigned to the DC office. Huh. Let me check." The silence had to have lasted five minutes before he came back on the line. "Yeah, Cormac is based in San Francisco now. Why don't I call him, make sure it's really him you talked to, then call you back?"

"I'd be grateful," Logan said. When he set down his phone, he cocked an eyebrow at Savannah. "Did you hear that?"

"Most of it." Anxiety darkened her eyes. "If only Jared *had* told me about this agent."

And about the load of trouble that would be dumped on her head, Logan couldn't help thinking. It was great Jared had turned his life around and was trying to atone—Logan thought that was the word Savannah had used. He'd obviously been scared enough to try to ensure his daughter's safety, too. All good, except he'd messed up, big-time, by being so close-mouthed. If Logan had been able to come face-to-face with his old friend right now, he might have planted a fist in his face.

"Something I've been wanting to talk to you about," Logan said slowly. Maybe this was lousy timing, but he thought distraction would benefit Savannah. And…he needed to know where he was going with her. Whether any kind of do-over was possible. Staying in close quarters with her had ratcheted up his hunger for her, and more. She was amazing with Molly.

He felt especially bad that he'd doubted how committed she was to the little girl.

"What's that?" Savannah asked in obvious puzzlement.

With an effort, he kept his hand on the table relaxed. His other hand, resting on his thigh and hidden beneath the table, balled into a fist. "You and me," he said. "I'd really like to know if you'll ever trust me."

Her expression altered by slow degrees. The distraction had worked that well. Tiny creases formed between the arch of her eyebrows, and her eyes sharpened on his face.

"I'm...grateful for what you're doing now. I trust you to do whatever you can to protect me. Molly, too. Of course I do. Are you afraid I'll go raring off in some direction without consulting you?"

"No. You're too smart to do that." He hesitated. "My question was...more personal. We have a history."

He wasn't surprised when her eyes narrowed.

"You could say that."

Logan made himself go on. "I had something of an epiphany while I was trying to sleep the other night." He'd had long wakeful periods, in part because her sofa was too short for a man his height. He wasn't about to tell her that, though.

"An epiphany?" She looked wary, as if she wasn't sure she wanted to hear what he had to say.

"I really liked you when you were a kid." He smiled crookedly. "Trailing after Jared and me, annoyingly persistent but also gutsy and funny."

Surprise showed on Savannah's face, as if, after everything that came after, she'd forgotten the way her brother and Logan teased her, boosted her up to a tree fort she couldn't have reached on her own, taught her how to throw a ball like a boy instead of a girl. If he hadn't been so nervous, he would have smiled at how furious she'd been at that description. She'd declared that girls could do anything boys could, and did her best to prove it, over and over again.

Years' worth of those kind of memories shaped how he knew

the woman sitting across from him. Given that, how had he ever come to doubt her? Yeah, that question had been part of his epiphany.

"As your father started to come down on Jared harder and harder," Logan went on, "and I could see how much it hurt him, I started to blame you. I guess you know that."

"You think?"

Looking into the past, he said, "Jared did complain sometimes. He couldn't do anything right, you couldn't do anything wrong. I started to get this picture in my head at the same time you were…maturing physically. I could see you were going to be beautiful." Pause. "Already were."

"Beautiful?" She barely breathed the word. "When I was twelve? Thirteen?"

He cleared his throat. "Both. And fourteen and fifteen. Especially those last couple of years before I graduated."

She gaped. "You thought…"

"I did. The trouble is, I had to stay loyal to Jared. I convinced myself that, sure, I noticed the way you walked, your smile, your grace, your voice. Hearing you talk is like listening to music, you know."

She still looked stunned.

He cleared his throat. "None of that meant I was really attracted to you, though. That if you hadn't been Jared's sister—"

She pushed her chair back, the legs scraping on the wood floor. "You hated me!"

Holding himself rigidly, he didn't move. "It was…self-defense. I thought Jared was dead, you know. I even wondered sometimes if he and your father really got into it, and Jared was buried somewhere here on ranch land."

A quiver ran over her. Had she wondered the same?

"Him just disappearing…haunted me. Part of me had come to believe that if you didn't exist, your father would have loved Jared. You were…a mirror that distorted your dad's view. It had to be your fault. You know the deep spiral he went into. Watching him was so hard. I thought I was helping him when I set limits, but I think all I did was hurt him. I should have been there for him. Solid. I felt guilty enough about that."

How long since she'd blinked? "Jared must have thought that way about me," she said, so softly he just heard her. "How could he not hate me?"

"I thought he did." This was a hard admission. A hurtful one. "But now when I remember the way he'd talk about you, I know that wasn't ever true. Your dad had seriously eroded his self-esteem, you know. Even so, he talked as much about the way you tried to stand between him and your dad as he did about how you were just so perfect, he couldn't measure up."

Savannah's lips trembled, and she looked down at the table. After a moment, she swallowed hard enough, Logan wondered if she wasn't fighting tears.

He hated feeling vulnerable, but he owed her. He pushed himself to get this said. "I couldn't let myself betray my best friend in the world, so I refused to admit even to myself that I'd have been hot for you otherwise." That maybe he'd even been in love with her, as much as a boy that age could be.

Her head came up, and they stared at each other.

"Jared wasn't the only one you hurt," she said at last, in a voice that shook. "You hurt *me*. I had a crush on you from when I was, I don't know, a girl. Not very old at all. You were the first boy I thought I loved. When I reached an age where that really meant something, you'd become cruel to me."

He hated the expression on her fine-boned face, the darkness in her beautiful eyes. Beneath the table, his fingernails drove into the palm of his hand. He might even have drawn blood.

"Then Jared was gone, and you pretended I didn't exist." Her voice was rising, sharpening like a blade she'd been honing. "If you couldn't get away with pretending not to see me at all, you sneered like I was a pile of steaming, stinking manure you'd just stepped in and had to wipe off your boot. I had tried so hard to protect Jared from Dad, and you—" She shook her head. "I don't even know what you're asking, but—"

Logan cut her off before she could say, *Hell, no. Never.* "I messed up because I never understood how your father could treat Jared the way he did. My view of what went on in your house was skewed. I'm trying to tell you how sorry I am, and that I was so determined to be loyal to Jared, I couldn't let anyone see how I really felt about you."

Now her eyes searched his as if she was rewinding a tape, puzzling over scenes that she'd been sure were deleted from whatever film she saw. "You *had* to have known," she whispered.

His lips twisted. "Amazing what you can bury under a shovelful of guilt."

They sat in silence for an uncomfortable length of time. Logan tried not to twitch.

She sighed at last. "I don't know what to say. No matter what, there's so much going on. I have to focus on keeping Molly safe. That you're standing up for us means a lot to me, but—I can't think about anything else."

He made himself nod. "Fair enough. There'll be plenty of time down the line—"

His phone rang.

Chapter Eleven

The call was from the front desk clerk at the sheriff's department wanting to pass on phone messages. Even as he jotted them down, Logan was aware that Savannah had jumped up and appeared to be reorganizing the canned goods cupboard. Her mother had grocery shopped for them yesterday, and either didn't know Savannah's system, or else she was shifting cans from shelf to shelf just to occupy herself. She'd certainly seized the moment to end their conversation, and he had to accept that.

When she rose on tiptoe to put some of those cans on high shelves, he had to work to keep his mouth shut. She didn't raise her left arm, and she'd probably blow up if he tried to make her sit down until he could help her.

His phone rang twice more in the next hour, each time from someone at the sheriff's department needing direction. Even if he'd felt inclined, he couldn't *not* answer those calls. The last question from a young deputy had him shaking his head in something close to disbelief. Damn. He had to hope no serious situation erupted while he was working from the Circle B ranch. Not even the couple of more experienced deputies seemed capable of making real decisions in his absence. With permission from the county council, Logan had already posted the position of assistant sheriff, but hadn't had a chance to study any applications. Maybe he should make that a priority tonight when he couldn't sleep, which was inevitable. Of course, there was a chance nobody had applied. This small county in the high desert wasn't most people's idea of paradise.

The other deputy patrolling today called to let him know that he'd driven into several abandoned ranches and seen no sign of recent occupation.

Savannah had decided to heat them some soup, and was opening cans when the next call came in. It was about damn time—two hours and three minutes. His eyes met Savannah's, and she abandoned the lunch makings and returned to the table.

He accepted the call. "Ray?"

"Sorry it took a while to track down Donaldson. I did reach him, though, and he's the guy who called you. Sounds like losing this Jared seriously upset the applecart for the agents who thought they had a wedge into a nasty organization."

Logan rubbed his forehead. "All right. I hope he can help us find this information everyone seems so damn sure Jared had. Would have been nice if he'd spread some bread crumbs for his sister to follow."

Ray grunted. "If he had, his bosses might have followed them before she had the chance."

"Yeah, but at the moment we're clueless."

"Give Donaldson a chance. He sounded a little embarrassed. He's not usually abrasive."

Savannah definitely heard that, because she rolled her eyes upward.

"We all have our moments," Logan said diplomatically, then thanked Ray for his help before cutting the connection.

"He's supposed to call us," she said. "I suppose we just have to twiddle our thumbs until then."

Logan's phone rang, and he half smiled when he saw the DEA agent's number. "Neither of you seem to be the patient type."

This time, they were all on their best behavior. Logan described their search of everything that Jared had left along with his daughter in that doorway. The agent said that he'd met with

Jared a few times in the past three or so years, but that usually Jared shared what he'd learned by electronic transfer.

"I had the feeling he was using someone else's computer. Maybe even one at the library. In this case, the fact that he left a phone with you is meaningful."

"This model is only a year or two old," Savannah said, "but the number is the same one he's had since he was a teenager. Um...there was a phone left on his body, too, but Detective Trenowski implied it was something he'd picked up recently, and had almost no information in it."

Logan leaned forward to be sure he was heard. "The only name in the contacts on that phone was 'sister.' He wanted his body identified quickly, and his killer cooperated in making that happen."

Donaldson swore. "Why didn't he contact me? We could have moved fast, pulled him out. We'd talked about how to do that."

Pain made Savannah's face almost gaunt, but seeing his eyes on her, she donned a mask. "He... When I talked to him that morning, he said 'they' were suspicious. I think they must have been following him. His entire focus seemed to be on getting his daughter, Molly, to me. Molly is only four years old. I know he must have *hated* leaving her alone the way he did. He may have thought he'd shaken them very briefly, then decided to draw them away."

"Was his body found the next day?"

"No, it was almost three weeks later."

"I'm assuming you called him."

"Only once. Then I found his phone in the duffel bag and realized it had been ringing in the trunk of my rental car. I never had an address for him, or so much as the name of a friend. There was no way for me to reach him, short of hiring a PI, and I had a feeling that might just put him in more danger."

"Hell," the DEA agent said, sounding more human than he had. "Ah...what kind of phone is it?"

When she told him, he groaned theatrically.

"What?"

"You haven't read about the battles various law enforcement agencies have waged with the company?"

Logan could all but hear the guy's teeth grinding and understood.

"I remember something about that," she said, sounding puzzled, "but…this phone isn't password-protected. We don't *have* to break into it."

"Do you by rights own it now?"

"Well…he put it in the duffel bag for me to find. He must have stripped any protections to allow me to open it."

He was quiet for a minute, then asked Savannah to get her brother's phone. After discussion about Logan's identification of the numbers called from the call log, Donaldson tried to start walking her through recovering any apps or files. After a minute, she pushed it across the table to Logan.

"I use only the most common apps," she admitted, low-voiced. "I train horses. I talk, text and email. That's all."

For all he'd told her, Logan was more aware of all the capabilities of a modern smartphone than she was. He followed instructions with it, not at all surprised to find Jared had set up a single file called "Info." The attempt to open it produced a not-unexpected demand for a password.

That was where they hit a dead end. They wasted a good half hour trying variations on the passwords Savannah knew her brother had used before, ones that included Molly's name, the name of Molly's stuffed rabbit—Walter—and everything else that came to mind for either Savannah and Logan, unlikely as it was for Jared to think Logan would somehow be involved. Still, they tried the year he and Jared had played on a state championship baseball team. Jokes about the nerds in the high school computer club. Favorite horses, profanities, local landscape features.

Nothing worked.

Logan had a full-blown headache by now, and Savannah

looked like she might, too. It was Donaldson who called a stop to their efforts.

"We're spinning our wheels. This password *has* to be something he thought would be meaningful to you, Savannah."

"Aren't there computer programs that can figure out passwords?"

"They're not foolproof. We can try that, except..." Donaldson hesitated. "Did Jared will all his possessions to you?"

"No. I'm named in his will only as guardian to his daughter. What money he had is for her."

"How was it worded?"

She went to get the will so she could be sure.

"In other words, he did *not* will his phone to either you or the child. There's none of the usual general language about all his possessions."

"No," she said. "I assumed that's because he didn't have anything else to leave."

"Except his phone."

"But...he clearly wanted me to have it."

"That's clear to you and to me." Tension infused the agent's voice. "The problem is, if we start messing with the phone and do break into the file, will our possession of it be deemed legal? I'll need to talk to the lawyers to find out where we stand."

"What?" she said again.

Logan spoke up. "I'll explain your issues. If worse comes to worst, we may need to take a chance. But for now, I agree with you. Jared wanted Savannah to be able to open this thing."

"Your brother would have seeded a strong hint," Donaldson agreed. "I'm betting it will come to you."

"I...have a feeling my deadline might be tight," she said, more strain in her voice than she'd like them knowing.

Logan liked the agent a little better when his response was almost gentle. "I'm guessing we'll have a few days yet. Try not to obsess about it. Odds are, the answer will float into your head when you least expect it."

Her eyes held desperation when they met Logan's, but she

said, "Okay," and they agreed to talk again tomorrow, once they'd all had the chance to think some more.

With the call over, Logan shoved his chair back and held out an inviting hand. "I know you're mad at me, but will you let me hold you for a minute anyway?"

SAVANNAH STARED AT HIM, torn between outrage and yearning. Despite everything, she wanted to feel his arms around her, be able to lean on his strong body just for a few minutes. And… whatever their past, he was here now.

Somehow, she'd come to be on her feet and circling the table. "I am still mad. Just so you know."

And yet, when she reached him, he lifted her high enough to deposit her on the powerful thighs she'd ogled while they rode today, and then wrapped her in the most comforting embrace that she could remember. There must have been times when she was a child, but later, she'd never felt absolute trust in either of her parents.

I don't feel it for Logan, either. No, she didn't, but right now, she trusted him more than she did anyone else in the world, at least in his determination to protect her.

She laid her head against his wide shoulder and looped one arm around his torso. Savannah tried to empty her mind, instead soaking in the moment. His chest rose and fell in a regular, soothing rhythm. She studied the strong, tanned column of his neck and that vulnerable hollow at the base of his throat. Dark tufts of chest hair showed, too, tempting her to touch. Were they silky, or coarser than the hair on his head?

She almost smiled, remembering times they'd gone swimming at the river, Jared and Logan both tall but skinny, too, their chests more bony than brawny and completely hairless. Later, she'd seen hair first appearing on their chests and underarms, along with the unpredictable deepening of their voices that embarrassed them so.

Of course, she'd been embarrassed when her body started maturing, too, starting to wear sacky sweatshirts and leaving a T-shirt on over her bathing suit when they splashed in the cold river water. The first time she'd done that and looked down to see that the shirt was now transparent and clinging to her, she'd jumped out of the water and run to wrap herself in a towel. Jared had teased her sometimes about her not-so-womanly figure, but of course Logan had never given any indication he'd even noticed. By then, he'd cooled off toward her.

She'd been wrong, though. He *had* noticed. And thought she was beautiful? What could be more staggering than having him say that?

Her wary self roused. He could turn on her the next time his deep-seated suspicion told him that really she was self-centered and shallow, might be capable of anything.

She'd started to stiffen when his arms tightened and he rubbed his cheek against her head. Their relationship was so complicated. How was she supposed to pick out the truth?

He spoke up. "Is it a relief to find out that Jared really was trying to do the right thing?"

She felt the vibration of his voice as much as heard it, but didn't let herself enjoy the sensation too much—or imagine how much better it would sound if she were lying with her head on his *bare* chest.

Unfortunately, his question pulled her back to the terrible tangle of events that had led them to this moment. She had to think for a minute.

"In a way," she murmured finally, "but in a way I'm also furious with him for risking his life instead of extricating himself and actually looking for happiness. You know? And Molly makes it worse. Couldn't he see how much she needed him? He said she was everything to him, but that wasn't true, or he would have made different decisions."

The warm, muscular chest lifted and fell in a long sigh. "Yeah. I've…had the same thought. If he could walk into the kitchen right this minute, I'd be incredibly relieved, but I also might punch his lights out for what he's done to you and Molly."

She choked out a laugh. "Yes. I'd have a lot to say, but I want him to be alive."

One of his hands made circles on her back, pausing to gently knead here and there. He had to know where she hurt and where she didn't, because he was so careful. She shouldn't be doing this, letting him take care of her, but it felt so good.

"It breaks my heart, hearing that Agent Donaldson met him in person." That just popped out. "Why, *why*, didn't he ever visit? If I could have seen him just once!"

In a way, it occurred to her, Logan had even more reason to have this awful hollow feeling. He and Jared had been best friends, and yet Jared had never so much as called and said, *I'm alive. I think about you sometimes.*

Yet when Logan resumed speaking, it was his frustration that had reemerged. "If this morning I'd known we'd be contacted by the DEA agent Jared worked with, and had likely located the file everyone wants so damn badly, I would have thought we'd be able to see a way out of this mess. Instead..."

She finished the sentence for him. "We're no closer than ever to being able to fend off these monsters."

No, they weren't, but one thing had changed, she realized. She had used the word *we* and believed in it. It was no longer only she who would do anything to protect a child who'd already been neglected, abandoned and traumatized more than enough for a lifetime.

She *did* trust Logan, at least to that extent. She couldn't really believe he'd ever turn on her again, especially now when she needed him so much. That certainty let her straighten on his lap so she could see his face when she told him what scared her the most.

"Agent Donaldson talked about 'bringing the organization down,' as if they'd be able to arrest everyone from the top down to the muscle they sent to threaten me, but that isn't possible, is it? Even if I do figure out that password, and the contents of the file really are what the DEA thinks they are, what's to say they'll forget about me?" She pressed her lips together, then finished. "Will Molly and I have any future if we don't just vanish and take new identities?"

She saw Logan's shock…and the unwelcome answers to some of her questions.

No, he didn't think any more than she did that handing over Jared's information stash to the DEA would mean she'd be forgotten by the men who were determined to keep her in fear for her life. In fact, they'd be enraged.

And yet the only way forward was to figure out that damn password.

LOGAN HAD MIXED feelings about continuing to let Molly spend a good part of her days up at the house with her grandmother. That had started as a necessity; he understood that. Savannah had to work. Right now, she wouldn't be doing that, though, and Logan felt certain the bastards pressuring Savannah hadn't forgotten Jared's small, vulnerable daughter. Kick in the kitchen door at the house, grab the kid and they'd have Savannah crawling across hot coals to please them.

Considering that he and Savannah had trouble setting aside their awareness that they were walking a tightrope over an abyss, though, he also knew that in some ways, it was healthy for Molly to have a break from the forced good humor the two of them assumed for her benefit.

He was on the phone with a deputy prosecutor discussing whether or not they'd go to trial after an arrest that had happened not long after he stepped in as sheriff when Logan heard a sharp rap on the back door. He shot to his feet and got far enough to see into the kitchen, where Savannah was letting her father in. He hadn't heard her call, "Who's there?" but had confidence she'd peeked out the window over the sink.

Gene didn't give any indication he noticed Logan lurking in the hall outside the kitchen. He hung his hat on a hook just inside the door, poured himself a cup of coffee without asking, then sat heavily on one of the chairs at the table.

After locking the door behind him, Savannah sat again,

too, in front of her open laptop. She stared straight ahead, occasionally mumbling to herself, after which her fingers would fly briefly on the keyboard. He made out a word here or there. Aurora was the name of the horse she'd loved dearly as a girl and mourned as if she'd been a sister.

Good thought. Jared knew how much she'd loved that horse. Muffin had been her cat, Bramble the dog as devoted to her as she'd been to him.

Apparently none of those panned out, although he knew she was listing them anyway. Problem was, the password would undoubtedly include numbers and/or symbols, too. Putting it all together would take a miracle, he was starting to think.

Maybe she thought if she gazed into the brightly lit screen long enough, it would become a crystal globe displaying a string of letters and numbers.

God. What if the mysterious password wasn't anything familiar at all? What if Jared had used a nonsensical jumble of letters, symbols and numbers, sure he'd get a chance to pass them on to Savannah?

Logan frowned. Well, then, why hadn't he? Or could they have been jotted on a tiny slip of paper that fell, unseen, out of Molly's suitcase or the duffel, say in the hotel room that first night?

No. Just...*no.*

While he'd brooded, Gene Baird had leveled a scowl at his daughter, who waited him out.

At last, the man said, "Guess I'm lucky Logan sees fit to keep me up to date with what's going on."

She raised her eyebrows in innocent surprise. "Does it matter which one of us keeps you informed?"

"You are my daughter," he snapped.

"I'm scared," Savannah said softly. "Trying to see a way out of this trouble. I appreciate you and Mom taking us in, but the ranch didn't turn out to be the refuge I thought it would be. I've never sulked in my life. If I were mad, you'd know it."

"If I could get my hands on that son of mine— Putting you and his own child in danger."

She stared at him for a long time before giving a laugh that lacked a grain of humor. "Did you ever love Jared?"

He reared back. "What are you talking about? Of course I did. If that kid hadn't been so determined to butt heads with me—" He stopped, shrugged, apparently thinking that was all there was to say.

And maybe he was right, Logan couldn't help thinking. What good would it do now to force him to understand how he'd wronged his son? If Gene ever saw his treatment of Jared the way everyone else had, what would it do to him, a man who had to believe he loved his family?

Logan didn't have to see Savannah's face to know what she was thinking. She'd have tried before. Even Jared admitted that his mother had tried to reason with his father. If Savannah gave him a hard shake right now and tried again, Gene still wouldn't get it. He'd probably just look at her as if she was crazy.

"Um...why are you here?" she asked.

"I still say Molly would be safer sleeping upstairs at the house instead of here. But I suppose you don't agree." Still scowling, Gene shoved back his chair, rose to his feet and stomped to the sink, where he dumped out his coffee.

"Logan is here, on guard and armed."

"I am, too."

"I...need to have her close." Savannah spoke so quietly, Logan just made out what she'd said.

Her father grumbled and growled some more, but did pause to lay a hand on her shoulder before he let himself out the back. Logan couldn't help noticing how gnarled that hand had become.

Her father out the door, Savannah pushed her laptop away and bent forward to clunk her forehead on the tabletop. "You can come out of hiding."

Logan stepped forward into the kitchen. "I wasn't hiding.

He should have seen me." He cocked his head. "How'd you know I was there?"

She twisted in her seat to make a face at him. "Heard the floorboard squeak."

She was more observant than he'd known. He had made a point of memorizing every place in the cabin where the plank floor complained at even a light footstep.

Pulling out the chair kitty-corner from her, he sat down. "He'd say you're the bullheaded one."

Her startled laugh made Logan smile.

"That's Dad. I truly believe he loves me, but sometimes it's hard to convince myself. He's not exactly generous with words."

Logan remembered things differently. "He used to praise you all the time."

Quiet for a minute, she met his eyes. "I'm not so sure that's what he was doing. Especially what you heard. If you were there, so was Jared. I think Dad was more aiming barbs at Jared than he was patting me on the back."

Having something so basic flipped on end took Logan aback, even though it shouldn't. How much that he'd been so sure he knew hadn't been anything approaching the way he'd seen it? Increasingly, he felt as if he'd been spun in a dryer until he didn't know up from down.

"I…can see that," he said slowly. "Is he softer with your mother?"

"In all those tender moments? No. His idea of a compliment is an occasional grunted 'Good dinner' before he heads for the living room and his remote control. Was your father any better with your mother?"

"Yeah. He'd be embarrassed, but every so often Mary or I'd catch them cuddling. Or worse. He'd turn red and glare at us."

A smile trembled on Savannah's lips. "That's sweet."

Logan abruptly stood and tugged her to her feet. "Went like this," he said in a rough voice and bent his head. His lips inches from hers, he made himself go still and wait to see if she'd refuse him.

Chapter Twelve

Dream come true, Savannah thought dizzily. That he was waiting so patiently for her response broke her determination to keep hugging her hurt feelings to herself. Really, she'd spent half her life imagining that someday this would happen. Logan Quade would actually want to kiss her.

Unable to resist, she lifted her hand to his shoulder, pushed herself up on tiptoe and pressed her lips to his. With one arm dangling uselessly, this felt clumsy, except he took charge so fast, she had no chance to feel embarrassed.

They went from the first gentle brush of lips to an open-mouthed, passionate kiss in what seemed like seconds. He tasted like coffee and man, or maybe it was just him. He stroked her tongue with his, and she returned the favor. What had been some distance between them evaporated, with her having come to be plastered against that hard, strong body. One of his big hands kneaded her butt, lifting, while the fingers of his other hand slid into her hair and cradled the back of her head so he could angle it to please him.

The stubble on his cheeks and jaw scraped her softer skin, but she didn't care. Savannah's knees wanted to buckle, but more than anything she needed to be as close to him as she could humanly get. His hips rocked, and she rubbed against him. Nothing had ever felt so good. She moaned when his mouth left hers to skim down her throat. Her head fell back, and she reached with her injured arm to anchor herself even more tightly against him.

The stab of pain broke her out of the moment, and she went still. Stiffened. Her ribs hurt, too, but that hadn't softened her from wrapping one of her legs around his. An alarm blared. What was she *doing*? This was as far from a wish-fulfillment kiss as it could get. Would she even have remembered if Molly had been home?

He nipped her, just hard enough to sting, but he had also gone completely still. Then he carefully set her back on her feet, smoothed hair from her forehead with a hand that had a tremor and finally kissed her lips again lightly.

"That…went a little further than I intended," he said, low and scratchy.

"No. It's…okay." Startled by the heat in eyes that were often icy, she took a step back. "I'm pretty sure *I* kissed *you*." Already blushing, she made the mistake of lowering her gaze to find herself staring at the thick ridge beneath his jeans.

Heat flooding her face, she jerked her gaze back up.

One side of Logan's mouth lifted. "I think you did, too. Thank you for that."

"I didn't expect—" She hesitated. Oh, why couldn't she simply have said, *Not ready for anything that intense, guy*, and at least pretended to be more experienced than she was?

He arched an eyebrow in that way he had. "What did you expect?"

She just about had to answer. "I suppose…whatever I imagined kissing you would be like when I was a teenager." She managed a shrug. "Since at that point I'd never been kissed, my imagination was pretty tame."

"I had the impression once you were in high school that guys were hot for you."

"As a freshman?" She wrinkled her nose. "Mom and Dad would have had a fit. I didn't really date until after you were gone."

Not that she'd ever raised the subject with her parents, not when the only boy she wanted was Logan Quade, who at his kindest pretended she didn't exist.

This pain was sharper than the one in her shoulder, even if he had apologized and claimed a lot more had gone on in his head than she could have dreamed. He'd still wounded her. He couldn't take that back.

No, her body had begun a meltdown, but her trust only went so far, especially after he'd doubted the danger to her and Molly.

"Do I even want to know what you're thinking?" he asked.

"Nothing that would surprise you. I keep tripping over the past. It's hard not to."

He lifted a hand to squeeze the back of his neck. "Yeah," he admitted gruffly. "We've both come home, and it's changed at the same time as it hasn't."

"I haven't said so, but I feel bad about your father." A detour in topic seemed safer. "I mean, you're here in Sage Creek because he needs you, and instead you're hanging around here."

He grimaced. "Mind if I pour myself a cup of coffee?"

"Oh. No. Of course not. I wouldn't mind—"

He poured two cups full and brought them to the table, where they both sat down and looked at each other. He'd deliberately, she assumed, chosen the chair her father had sat in earlier rather than the one closer to her.

Logan sighed. "Dad insists he doesn't need me, you know. We were butting heads two or three times a day. He's probably thrilled to be able to order around the extra ranch hand I hired instead of sucking it up and admitting he did need me to handle things he can't anymore."

"I'm sorry." She reached out tentatively, then started to pull her hand back. Moving with startling speed, he captured it with his. She'd been determined to open distance, and now they were holding hands, their fingers twined together. It felt so good. Too good.

She was in such trouble, now on a new front.

"Something I need to say," he told her gruffly. "I'm really glad I came home when I did. If I hadn't, I wouldn't have been here when *you* needed me. If I'd found out later—" He swallowed hard, but didn't finish.

As if he'd been pining for her? She didn't think so. Why on earth was she holding hands with him? When she tugged, he let her go without resistance.

Chin up, she said, "You're glad to be here for Jared's daughter. I'll bet you hadn't given *me* a thought in years."

"You'd be wrong." The expression on his face was odd. "No, I guess I didn't often, but I knew you the minute I saw you in the pharmacy that day, and I was mostly looking at your back."

"But you saw Molly."

"It was you who stopped me in my tracks. I knew you—and then I saw Molly and thought…"

"That she was mine."

"Yeah," he agreed, an indefinable note in his voice.

"Well." It would be childish to keep arguing. *You didn't know me. Yes, I did. No, you didn't.* "It doesn't really matter, does it?"

This time, he kept his mouth shut, forcing her to realize she *wanted* to keep arguing. It was a way of releasing this otherwise unrelenting tension.

Her gaze dropped to his hand, still lying on the table, and the powerful, tanned forearm exposed below his rolled-up shirt-sleeve. Even given the sprinkling of dark hair, veins and tendons stood out. A few hairs curled on the backs of his fingers. Her hand tingled at the sensory memory of his calluses. She remembered how he'd gripped her while she all but tried to climb him.

How long since she'd blinked? Could he guess what she was thinking? Sex would be one way to release a whole lot of tension—

She jumped up. "I'm going up to the house to spend time with Molly." If she could just get a break from him for a few minutes…

"I'll walk you."

Of course he would. Savannah closed her eyes, breathed in, breathed out and managed a nod.

THE NEXT MORNING, they took Molly along for their ride and succeeded in making two loops of the large pasture. In the barn, Logan suggested Molly ride in front of Savannah.

"Can I?" the little girl begged.

She obviously hadn't known the "suggestion" was a thinly disguised order. Not that Savannah intended to argue. If something happened, Logan could deal with it better than she could. The one thing she did really well was ride. She could get herself and Molly back to the barn with incredible speed. That was what quarter horses were known for—lightning-fast acceleration and unmatched speed over the first quarter mile. Today she rode one of her father's, a mare who showed promise for barrel racing.

They started at an amble, and Savannah was pleased to discover her body moved more naturally than it had yesterday. Logan chatted with Molly, which she thought was really nice of him until she tuned in to one of his questions.

"What did your daddy tell you about your aunt?"

Wait. What?

Molly screwed up her face in thought. "He said she was pretty. And he could have listened for *hours* when she sang."

"You're lucky because she sings to *you*."

Molly offered him a glowing smile. "Uh-huh!"

"What else?"

This wasn't conversation—it was an interrogation. But she didn't intervene because he was right to get Molly to open up. What if Jared had counted on his daughter passing on some tidbit that would make the password appear in Savannah's mind, lit in neon?

Molly thought about Logan's question. "Daddy said she could ride horses better than *him*, even." Her expression betrayed doubt, even if she'd never seen Jared on a horse.

"That's probably true," Logan said, looking amused, "but your dad was a good rider, too. Did he talk about the rodeos we competed in?"

Sounding uncertain, she said, "He talked about roping calves."

As if she had no clue what her dad had been talking about.

"This summer we'll go to some rodeos," Savannah suggested. "They're fun to watch. There's calf roping, bucking broncos and bulls, and barrel racing."

"Like you do with Akil." Molly appeared delighted.

"Right."

"That's what I want to do when I get bigger," she declared.

Logan and Savannah exchanged a smile, not complicated as so much of their relationship was, and they moved straight into a lope instead of trotting. Every so often they slowed to a walk, and he encouraged Molly to chat some more. She clearly *liked* Logan—and why wouldn't she? Savannah smiled encouragement as if she wasn't irrationally irritated.

Unfortunately, Molly didn't say a word that rang any bells for Auntie Vannah. She veered into talking about how Grandma let her paint. Did Logan know she had her own easel in Grandma and Granddad's kitchen? And she'd rolled out piecrusts yesterday, and today Grandma said they'd make cinnamon rolls.

She *loved* cinnamon rolls.

Logan grinned at her. "Who doesn't? Do we get any of them?"

Molly giggled, knowing full well that Logan had scarfed down plenty of yesterday's oatmeal-raisin cookies.

After the ride, Savannah and Logan ate lunch with Molly and Grandma—Granddad was off doing unspecified chores—before leaving them to their afternoon activities.

"Neither of our phones have rung this morning," Savannah said into the silence as they walked the distance to the cabin.

Logan raised his eyebrows in that expressive way he had. "You complaining?"

"No! Just—" She choked off the rest.

He took her hand and gently squeezed. He didn't have to say, *I get it.*

His phone did ring that afternoon. He'd been trying to work on scheduling on his laptop, but spent most of the afternoon talking instead. Savannah watched in fascination as the expressions of exasperation, impatience and incredulity appeared on his face even as his voice remained professional, even soothing.

Her frustration climbed. She was running out of ideas. What had meant enough to her and Jared—or just to her—that he would assume she'd be able to guess his password? The inside of her head was starting to feel like an old-fashioned pinball machine, the ball bouncing around unpredictably. *Whack!* There it went, until it connected with another wall or paddle and sped in another direction.

It would help if she could turn her thoughts to something else, the way Logan was doing, but what? Yes, she had a schedule on her laptop of when she'd work with which horse, and notes about progress, behavioral issues, minor injuries should they arise. Those notes made it easy to keep her outside clients up to date. Unfortunately, right now she had nothing to add to either her schedule or notes. How could she, being unsure of when she could resume riding beyond plodding around the pasture?

Tomorrow. She let out a sigh, soundless so that she didn't catch Logan's attention. Maybe the day after. She could start with getting the cutting horses back in the ring. She hardly had to do a thing except send signals to them that took little but a twitch of her finger or slight pressure with one knee or the other. Thank goodness that thug had beat on her left arm and shoulder instead of the right!

A silver lining.

"What are you thinking?"

Startled by Logan's question, she gave the one-shoulder shrug that was coming more naturally. "Training. Which horses I should work with first."

"That's not it."

She frowned at him. "If you must know, I was thinking what a blessing it is that my left shoulder was injured, not my right. And that brought a fleeting memory of how it happened."

He growled, "I can't believe we haven't been able to put

our hands on that creep." Except he used a much worse word. "Where the hell is he?"

She would have given a great deal to know. Jared's "employer" knew too well where she was and what she was doing. It had gotten so that even guarded by Logan, she had the crawling sensation of being watched whenever they stepped out the door. He hadn't argued at her keeping blinds and curtains drawn when they were inside. Mom didn't, and the bright interior of the kitchen and dining room made her want to hide under the table. She wasn't alone, either—she'd noticed Logan's gaze flickering from one window to the next, barely pausing on the face of whoever was talking.

He couldn't be sleeping any better than she was. Savannah never got up with Molly that she didn't see that shadow in the hall and know he'd probably opened his eyes at the first whimper, if he'd managed to close them in the first place.

The last thing he did every night was walk the perimeter. He invariably waited until Molly was asleep, at which point he quit hiding the handgun he carried all the time these days. Some nights when Savannah was sitting on Molly's bed reading stories or singing softly to her, Logan hovered in the hall. Other times, he stepped in and sat at the foot of the bed, listening.

Last night had been a first. After story time, Savannah had hugged Molly, kissed the top of her head and tucked the covers around her. She'd barely risen when the little girl said, "Can Logan hug me, too?"

Savannah didn't think she'd ever forget the expression she saw on his hard face. He hid it quickly, as he did most vulnerability, and stepped to the side of the bed.

"Of course I can. Now, whether I *will*..."

In complete faith that she was being teased, not doubting him for a second, she giggled and pulled her arms from beneath the covers to hold them up. Logan gave her a squeeze, kissed her forehead and then gently tucked her in again.

Heart aching, Savannah backed into the hall. A moment later, Logan followed her, turning out the overhead light and pulling the door toward him, leaving it cracked the requisite six inches. Of course, he'd noticed how she left it every night.

Both quietly retreated to the kitchen. Savannah couldn't remember the last time she'd so much as sat down in the living room. The only time she turned on the TV was for Molly.

Again, she stayed opposite Logan. "Thank you," she said.

He looked surprised. "For what?"

"Well... Molly."

His mouth thinned. "She's a sweetheart. Even if it weren't for her connection to you and Jared, she'd have made her way into my heart." He said the last word belligerently. "Okay?"

Savannah pressed her lips together and nodded. Looking down at the tabletop, she said, "I'm just so scared for her. For me, too, but if she loses me—"

"I won't let that happen."

His absolute confidence allowed her to lift her eyes to meet his. What she saw there...scared her in a different way. What would it do to him if she were killed under what he considered his watch? He was only one man.

Nobody wants to kill me, she reminded herself.

Not yet.

She shot to her feet. "I think I'll go to bed."

"That's a good idea," he said huskily. "We're all getting tired. I think I'll stay up a little longer, though."

Her head bobbed, and she fled, even knowing that she wasn't truly escaping the tension between them. Oh, no—it was hardest to ignore at night. That intense awareness of him looking on when she comforted Molly or lay down beside her while she fell back asleep after a nightmare. The times when Savannah needed the bathroom, and couldn't resist one glimpse into the dark living room. The night-light she'd plugged into the hall for Molly's sake was enough to allow her to see the man sprawled on the sofa. Usually, his bare feet were propped on the arm of the couch.

And then there were the times he got up and prowled the house, silent but for an occasional squeak of a floorboard or rattle of a blind when he peered out. Or the way he blocked the faint glow of the night-light when he paused outside Savannah's bedroom and she knew he was looking in.

Waiting. Just as she was doing, however much she denied it to herself.

Chapter Thirteen

The call came the next morning. Logan, Agent Donaldson and Savannah had discussed what she needed to do: buy time.

She and Logan had already walked Molly up to Grandma and Granddad's house, thank God; Logan didn't want that cute kid hearing any threats. She'd been through enough. That she'd seen Savannah's battered face and knew the ranch had become an armed camp enraged Logan as it was.

Savannah's phone rang just as they let themselves into the kitchen of the cabin through the back door. He automatically locked it behind them, then raised his eyebrows at her.

Her breathing was noticeably shallow. She nodded. Yes, it was *him*.

Had he used the same phone number twice?

"Hello?" Her hand shook as she put the device on speaker and set it on the table, although her voice remained stable. Logan lifted his chair so it didn't make any noise scraping on the plank floor, then sat down.

"I've been waiting for you to call *me*," the man said.

"Oh." She managed to sound startled. Her gaze held Logan's. "You didn't say. You haven't used the same phone before. Or at least not the same number."

There was a brief silence. "Do you have what I want?"

"Yes and no—"

"Don't play games with me," he snapped, voice icy.

"I'm not! I found an unidentified file on Jared's phone. I can email you the link. The problem is, it's password-protected. Unless you know what password he would have used—"

"Your brother was stealing from us. Of course I don't know what he'd have used. But *you* do." Three words, and enough menace to raise the hairs on the back of Logan's neck.

He reached over and covered one of Savannah's hands with his. It felt chilly.

"You've scared me adequately, okay?" she said. "I'm trying so hard to figure out what Jared could possibly have assumed I'd know. I told you how many years it's been since I've seen him! We rarely talked. Thinking back to what he'd know had meaning to me isn't easy. Please." Now a tremor sounded in her voice. "I need some more time."

"I think you're playing me."

"No! I swear I'm not."

This time, the silence drew out long enough, Logan's gaze flickered to the phone. Had the connection been cut?

Savannah said more strongly, "The file may be saved on the cloud. I can't tell. If you don't give me the chance to succeed, it'll stay out there. There's always the chance someone else could stumble on it. Maybe hack into it. That's not impossible, you know. Please. Just a few more days…"

Logan wasn't given to imaginative leaps, but he'd swear the fury he felt wasn't his own.

And, indeed, when the caller spoke again, his voice had dropped a register or two and roughened. "We'll see."

Savannah snatched up the phone. "What do you mean? Are you still there? Please…"

The SOB was gone.

Her teeth chattered when she looked at Logan again. "What will they do next?"

None of the possibilities that came to mind were good.

SAVANNAH WENT INTO his arms again, dangerous as that was. She needed the closeness, the awareness of his strength, both physical and emotional. She didn't stay as long as she'd have liked, though. Her body felt like barbed wire strung too tight. If it broke, it would snap back and wrap her in vicious prongs that tore her skin. As terrified as she was, it had to be insanity that allowed her to feel anything sexual…but she did. She did. She wanted more than anything to release this tension some-how—and sex was one way.

She felt his body hardening, his heartbeat kicking up. He'd gone very still. Savannah stared at his throat, at the pulse she could see, the bare hint of stubble on his jaw. She ached.

If he turned his head far enough to seek her mouth, she might not have been able to say no. Neither of them moved as she shored up her resolve. When she scrambled off his lap again, his arms opened to let her go.

He was letting her make the decision, and she was glad. She'd hate to let herself get swept away and then have second thoughts. This was better.

Unless I die never having made love with Logan Quade, a voice in her head pointed out tartly.

She sniffed. Really? She'd be dead and not care.

Safely across the table from him again, she let herself meet his eyes. "Now what do I do?"

He let out a long exhalation, then rolled his head as if his neck had become unbearably stiff. "The same thing you're al-ready doing. If you keep at it—"

"I may never figure this out!" she cried. "And if I do? What? I hand it over? I'll bet Agent Donaldson would love that!"

"I'd like to think he has a plan," Logan said slowly. "It's time he shares that with us."

Agent Donaldson did answer his phone. He listened to the call Savannah had recorded, then asked, "Ms. Baird, have you made any progress at coming up with the password?"

She leaned over so her mouth was closer to Logan's phone. "Are you asking if I lied to him? I didn't. Nothing I've thought of so far has panned out."

"I'm still of a mind to hold off taking the phone from you.

Our right to dig inside it could result in convictions that get thrown out."

That was the last thing she wanted, too.

"I don't know if you're aware that your brother was something of a computer wiz," he continued. "I gather he was the IT expert for this organization. But he knew you well enough, he wouldn't have made this password very complicated given that he expected you to figure it out."

"Thank you," she said dryly.

Donaldson was still an ass.

"Thank you?" His initial confusion shifted into annoyance. "That wasn't meant as an insult."

Sure.

"Let's cut to the chase," Logan interjected. "I took his closing remark to be a threat, not an agreement to give her more time. We need a plan from *you*."

"You were right, though, Ms. Baird, and he has to see it. What good are you to him if you're dead?"

"If they get to her, *your* ass will fry," Logan declared, every bit as menacing as the drug trafficker had been.

"I don't appreciate threats, Sheriff. What is it you suggest I do?"

"Put her into a safe house."

"For how long? At what expense? What if she never figures out this damn password?"

"Then she gets relocated with a new identity."

Shocked, Savannah stared at him. So much for her reawakened emotions for Logan. She appreciated him wanting to keep her alive, but apparently he was willing to wave bye-bye without a second thought.

"It's not that easy," Donaldson said stiffly.

"How long have you been working on bringing down this organization?" Logan asked. His light silver eyes held hers, but she couldn't seem to read anything he felt.

"Ah…close to two years. You must be aware how complex these kinds of investigations are."

Logan snorted. "You don't have any approved warrants?"

"Mr. Baird was going to deliver all the details I needed for that," he said. "Without, I don't have enough."

Logan swore at length, creatively.

Donaldson didn't say a word.

Feeling a burn under her skin, Savannah said, "I'm beginning to wonder why Jared risked so much when you couldn't do anything for him or his family in return."

"He wasn't doing it for the DEA," the agent said quietly. "He was cooperating with us in hopes of saving young people from becoming addicts."

Shamed, Savannah bent her head. "You're right."

"I'll try to get permission to send an agent to reinforce you, Sheriff Quade," Donaldson added. "I can do that much. If you'd prefer for Ms. Baird to come to San Francisco, I might be able to arrange for a safe house."

She gave a panicky shake of her head. Logan took in her expression and said calmly, "We'll get back to you on that." He ended the call and reached for her hands. "That's a no, I take it."

She tucked them onto her lap and knotted her fingers together. "I'm supposed to pack up, tell Molly that, gee, we're going to hide out in an apartment or house in a strange place, surrounded by strange men, but everything will be fine?" Her voice rose as she went, and she didn't care. "I'd rather take her and do my best to disappear on our own. If that's what you want me to do—"

"Let's get one thing straight. Whatever you do, I'll be going with you." His voice was guttural. "I'm not leaving your side."

What a humiliating moment to burst into tears.

LOGAN CIRCLED THE table and had her on her feet and into his arms so fast, she probably didn't see him coming. How could she think he was tired of being her protector? Where had she gotten that idea?

Cheek pressed to her head, he held her, rocked on his feet and murmured whatever came to mind—probably useless platitudes. Still she cried. Instead of wrapping her arms around him, she gripped wads of his shirt in her hands. He expected to hear the fabric tear.

At last he said, "Enough! You'll make yourself sick."

She went still.

Feeling a wrench of...not pity, he didn't think, but he wasn't sure he wanted to identify the emotion, Logan pried her hands from his shirt, then bent and swept her up in his arms. He carried her to her bedroom, laid her down as gently as he could on the bed and stretched out beside her so that he spooned her. He slipped his arm beneath her neck to allow her to use him as a pillow.

"Relax," he murmured. "I know you're scared, and you have to get this out."

She sniffed a few times.

His smile wouldn't form given the storm whipping inside him, but he groped in a pocket and produced a red bandanna, which he handed to her.

Lying behind her, he couldn't be sure, but thought she was wiping up her tears. The sound when she blew her nose was unmistakable.

"Thank you," she mumbled.

"S'okay." Instead of her usual braid, her hair had been captured in a ponytail but was now slithering out, tickling his face. He loved her hair, thick, silky and fragrant. He'd swear that was vanilla he smelled.

Her body moved slightly with each breath. He was acutely conscious of that body, sharp shoulder blades, delicate nape, long, slender torso that curved into womanly hips.

He didn't hear anything to make him think she was still crying. With the blinds closed tightly, the light was dim despite this being midafternoon. Maybe he should pull a blanket over her...but he was reluctant to move. Some of the reasons for that weren't praiseworthy. In fact, he'd had to inch his hips back from her firm, shapely ass. She'd be rightly offended if she felt his arousal. She'd said no, and he had to accept that.

What counted was keeping her and Molly safe. Later…no, not even later. After the way he'd blown it, she had to make the move, or it wouldn't happen.

Who'd have thought that his teenage, hormone-ridden confusion going head-to-head with his determined, misguided loyalty to his best friend would have altered the course of his life so profoundly? The girl he'd wanted so much in high school was now snuggled up to him, but because she had no one else to stand beside her against the threats to her life, not because she felt anything like he did. The basic attraction was there, but the deep-down trust wasn't.

My fault.

They'd been quiet for a long time. Ten minutes? Twenty? Logan had no idea. He wasn't sleepy, too busy working out how to combat the danger to her even as, weirdly, he felt a sense of rightness and contentment just because she was here in his arms.

When she stirred, he tensed but lifted the arm he'd tucked around her waist. If she was ready to get up—

Instead, she pulled away only enough so she could roll to face him. An observant but distant part of him noted that her eyelids were still a little puffy and the bruises and swelling diminished but far from gone. Tiny hairs that had broken off curled on her temples and forehead. A desperate expression in her hazel eyes riveted him.

She searched his face, looking for something he'd give anything to provide, then whispered, "Will you make love with me?"

SAVANNAH HADN'T EVEN known she was going to do this. It had to be a way of fighting her sense of helplessness, frustration, fear. Take control of *something*.

It was also the kind of thing she'd regret later. Baring herself to a man whose emotions were still opaque to her? Essentially, begging him to have sex with her?

The seconds drew out and he stared, unmoving. Oh, God—

what was he thinking? About how he could politely refuse? That wouldn't be hard, at least; he could just pat her and say, "You're too battered for anything like that." And maybe he'd even be right, but—

"You mean that?" His voice was deep, strained.

She bobbed her head. Almost said *Please*, but thought better of it. No more begging.

"There's...not much I want more." He lifted his free hand and cupped her face, smoothing hair back, thumb pressing her lips.

She couldn't help herself: she flicked her tongue over his thumb, savoring the saltiness and how he jerked.

Moving faster than she'd known he could, he whisked her onto her back and leaned over her. As bossy as he could be, she'd have expected him to descend on her like a conqueror, plundering her mouth, claiming her. Instead, he cradled her face in both hands, the touch extraordinarily gentle in deference to her injuries. He kissed her tenderly, his mouth brushing over hers until he sucked her lower lip and grazed it with his teeth. She felt as if she were floating on air, all her aches and pains gone.

For a minute, she looked up into eyes that were as far from icy as it was possible to be. She took in the angles of his face, his thick lashes, the dark stubble on his cheeks and jaw, the faint crinkle of lines fanning out from his eyes, even the shape of his ears. She had been fascinated by Logan's face from the time she was a girl. Now she lifted a hand to stroke and really let herself feel the textures.

His lips were unexpectedly soft, and she shivered.

Something about that brought her to life. She gripped the back of his neck and pulled herself up enough to kiss *him*. And, oh, maybe it was clumsy and too hard, but she *needed* him. He took over the kiss, deepening it, their tongues tangling, she more conscious than she'd ever been in her life of the sheer size and power of the man whose weight she wanted to feel fully on her body.

He explored her throat with his mouth, tasting and nipping, even as he deftly unsnapped her shirt and spread it open. She was hardly aware of the moment he opened her front-closing bra and brushed it away from her breasts, too. But the way he stared, dark color slashing across his cheekbones—that, she noticed. He must want her, he must, or he couldn't possibly look at her like this.

He muttered, "If you had any idea how often I dreamed of seeing you like this."

At least, that was what she thought he'd said. She tore open his Western-style shirt, the snaps giving way to her determined tugs. Savannah felt a tiny moment of amusement at her recollection of the skinny, lanky boy she'd seen shirtless so many years before, but it didn't last when she could stroke and knead a muscular, tanned chest. Dark hair formed a mat that had a softer texture than she'd expected.

Somewhere in there, their mutual explorations blended together, became something more, something so powerful she was swept away as she'd never been before. They undressed each other, her one moment of clarity coming when she saw how carefully he set his gun within reach. He hadn't forgotten the threat to her, but after that, he was free to cup her breasts, to kiss them, suck them, make his teeth be felt on her nipples before returning to her mouth for more drugging kisses.

She pressed herself against him, hungry for something she'd never felt. A wish to get under his skin, to be part of him. She was intensely grateful when he rolled away for a moment and she heard him tearing a packet. For once in her life, she wouldn't have thought of that.

Then he finally moved between her thighs and she could grip him fiercely with her knees and her arms, trying to hurry him as he growled words she didn't catch but did push against her opening.

He filled her, moving slower than she wanted, but also momentarily snapping her back to herself. This was almost too much...except that wasn't true. He retreated, drove deep, and she struggled to move with him, to meet him.

Just once, she thought, *This is Logan Quade. At last.* Only her mind couldn't hold on to anything so coherent. It was all sensation, the power of his body dominating hers, claiming her.

And then she simply imploded, and felt him shudder and heard a guttural sound escape his throat only moments later.

Tears burned her eyes. Just a few, and maybe it was inevitable. She'd had so many dreams. No wonder she'd felt so much.

"Savannah," he murmured, a wealth of meaning expressed with just her name.

If only she could believe in it.

Chapter Fourteen

Logan felt Savannah's almost-immediate subtle tension that seemed as if she was trying to pull back from him without actually moving. Still holding her, he wished he could think of the right thing to say. She didn't utter a word, but began to retreat in body as well as in spirit. He had to release her.

"In a hurry, are you?" He could have kicked himself for a tone that teetered on the edge of being antagonistic, but damn it, he was both hurt and offended.

"No, I... I need to fetch Molly."

What could he do but retreat behind the mask he'd had to create as a cop? Unfortunately, the silence between them stole his euphoria and the pleasurable state of relaxation.

"Fine," he said curtly.

"Logan..."

"Get dressed."

Once she got up off the bed, she turned her back on him as if ashamed of her nudity. She pulled on her clothes with impressive speed.

He emulated her, stamping his feet into boots at the same time she did.

"She worries if I'm late."

That might even be true, and he was being a jackass. *He* could have told her how amazing their lovemaking was, but hadn't. He didn't like wondering if she felt a sting from his withdrawal, too.

"I'm glad you put dinner on," he offered. She'd started a stew in the slow cooker that morning. "I'd rather we didn't walk back after dark."

He thought she shivered.

"No. I'm getting so I don't like the dark at all, which makes no sense given that I was attacked on a sunny morning."

"I prefer to see what's coming."

On that note, they hustled to the house, where inevitably her mother cried, "Oh, you're not staying for dinner? You know you're always welcome. Molly is turning out to be such a good cook's helper."

Logan just bet.

Savannah bent to kiss her niece. "She can help me make biscuits to go with our stew. She cuts them out and puts them on the cookie sheet for me."

"I'm real careful," the little girl assured her grandma, whose resistance melted into a smile.

"Of course you are! Oh." She focused on Savannah again. "Your dad and I are making a Costco run tomorrow. You could stock up, too, and with us all going, it will be fine—" The whites of her eyes briefly showed as she obviously didn't want to talk about risk in Molly's presence.

"I don't know." Savannah turned to him. "What do you think?"

Logan mulled over the idea. He absolutely had to put some time in at headquarters in the near future; there were conversations he needed to have face-to-face. Even if Gene and Savannah carried guns, he wasn't easy with the idea, though.

"That would give me a chance to go into work," he agreed slowly, "but I still want you to have backup. I can send a deputy out to tail you to Bend and back. If he walks you to the entrance and you call him when you're ready to come out, the trip should be safe enough."

"A deputy?" Savannah looked astonished. "Really? Can the department afford to have a deputy trailing us on a shopping expedition instead of patrolling?"

"Nonnegotiable," he said firmly.

She didn't protest any further, which made him wonder if she wasn't at least a little relieved. For all that she'd proved her marksmanship to him, accuracy at a range wasn't the same as shooting a man, and especially in the middle of an attack. He suspected her father was a better shot with a .22 rifle, probably what he carried to protect his calves from aggressive wildlife. Gene hadn't served in the military, however, and was therefore unlikely ever to have shot at a human being, either.

That said...the young deputies Logan was trying to whip into shape hadn't, either. It wasn't just their inexperience; most cops retired after long careers without ever having to pull a weapon on the job. *Not* having to pull that weapon was their goal, unless they served on SWAT or the like.

He took Gene aside while Molly put on her boots and her grandmother fetched her coat and mittens.

"Keep a sharp eye on the mirrors tomorrow, not just the road ahead of you," Logan said. "If you can help it, don't let a vehicle sneak in between you and the deputy."

"I take Savannah and Molly's safety seriously," the older man said, his expression grim.

Good.

Back at the cabin, Logan was glad it was just him, Savannah and Molly. Dinner was excellent, the biscuits Molly helped make mouthwateringly delicious, and thanks to the chatty child, conversation even flowed comfortably.

"I wanted to ride tomorrow," she said, in a rare moment of sulkiness. "Why do we have to go shopping? Shopping is no fun."

Savannah's amused gaze fleetingly met Logan's. "Chances are good we'll do some shopping for *you.*"

Molly bounced in her chair. "Are we going to look at a *pony*? Is that what we're doing?"

Savannah laughed. "No, sorry. You don't shop for a pony the way you do for...for a new doll. I've let people know I'm looking. When I hear about one that sounds like a good choice, we'll go meet it and—*maybe*—you can ride it so we can be sure it really is the right pony."

Molly's eyes narrowed. "What do you mean, *maybe*?"

Buttering a second biscuit for herself, Savannah only smiled. "I might decide to surprise you."

"Oh." Clearly, the girl wasn't sure whether she liked that idea or not.

Logan chuckled. "Your aunt has good judgment where horses are concerned, you know."

She wrinkled her nose. "So what *are* we shopping for?"

"Paper towels, toilet paper, canned goods like beans. Everything we need to bake and cook." Seeing a storm brewing, she held up a finger. "Costco does carry clothes your size, children's books and toys. We might take a look if you're patient while we load up on the everyday stuff. Deal?"

Molly slumped. "I guess."

Grinning by this time, Logan wished he could go with them. But the drive was an hour or more each way to Bend, eastern Oregon's largest city and home to the only Costco on this side of the mountains. Add in the shopping, possibly lunch there in the store and the round trip, and he should have a good four to five hours to be sheriff instead of bodyguard. If he could get out of the station soon enough, he wouldn't mind taking time to check out more of the many abandoned ranch buildings in the area. He hadn't asked his deputies to exit their vehicles, only to drive in, look for any sign of a recent visitor, then report to him. Despite his greater experience, he'd probably do the same. He'd rather plan a raid than do anything foolish.

Even as he made his own plans, he brooded about the miles of often empty highways the Bairds would have to travel. So far, though, Savannah's assailant had passed unseen. Taking on two armed adults and a law enforcement escort seemed unlikely in the extreme. There were easier ways to scare her.

The closer bedtime came, the more distant Savannah was. With a pleasant "Good night," she disappeared into her own room shortly after tucking in Molly, and definitely before he could suggest they talk or at least sneak in a kiss.

Disgruntled, uneasy, uncomfortable on the damn sofa and still less than happy about Savannah and Molly's outing tomorrow, Logan was lucky for snatches of sleep.

THE FORMALITY AND cut of Logan's dark green uniform reminded Savannah how imposing he was physically. His inscrutable expression, along with the badge pinned to his chest, made him look stern this morning. It was a little unsettling. Enough days had passed since she'd seen him in uniform that Savannah had become used to the more relaxed man in jeans and a flannel shirt indoors, fleece-lined coat outdoors.

"Walk me out," he commanded when it came time for him to go. He did sweep Molly up, swing her in a circle as she shrieked and laughed, hug her and set her down gently before raising his dark brows at Savannah.

She should be bristling at the spoken and unspoken command, but didn't because…she wished he wasn't going, even if she'd see him again in a few hours.

"Finish getting dressed," she told Molly. "We need to be ready when Grandma and Granddad get here." She grabbed a jacket hanging by the door before she went outside with Logan.

"Ah," he said. "Deputy Krupski is here. Good."

She followed his gaze to see the white SUV marked by a green stripe and the insignia of the sheriff's department and topped with a rack of lights. It was just turning onto the ranch road.

She walked with Logan the short distance to his personal SUV. It beeped and he opened the door.

"Stay sharp," he said. "I don't know how observant your father is."

"This is supposed to be a safe outing. You gave your permission for it." So easily, her pulse took a jump.

He rolled his shoulders in a tell she'd begun to recognize.

"I'm sure it'll be fine." His voice became gruffer. "I'll be glad when you're home again, that's all."

"I will be, too," she admitted. "I want all of this to be over."

"Yeah." He gazed down at her for a minute, bent his head and kissed her lightly. "Call me when you get back."

Lips tingling, she bobbed her head. "Yes, sir. Immediately, sir."

He grinned, sending her pulse stampeding for an entirely different reason, then swung up behind the wheel. She stepped back; he closed the door and drove away.

She watched long enough to see him brake and roll down a window to exchange a few words with the deputy before continuing toward the main road.

Savannah stayed to greet Deputy Krupski, round-faced and absurdly young-looking, tell him when they planned to leave and offer to refill his insulated coffee mug before going back inside herself to finish getting ready.

A few minutes later, Dad gave a tap on the horn when he stopped outside the cabin. She and Molly came out to be swarmed by four dogs who'd come running at the sound of the horn and threatened to knock Molly over as they twirled around her and Savannah, tails whipping.

Molly was giggling when they climbed in the back of her grandfather's extended-cab pickup. Thank goodness the heater was already doing its magic.

Savannah's mom beamed at them, twisting to watch as Savannah put the booster seat in place, waited for Molly to scramble into it and for Savannah to buckle her in before doing the same for herself.

Starting down the driveway, her father checked out the rearview mirror, where he could see their escort vehicle. "This is overkill," he muttered. "Don't know what Joplin will have to say about this once he hears."

Roger Joplin chaired the county council, which made him Logan's boss. She'd heard Logan talking to him several times.

"Mr. Joplin thinks a lot of you, Dad," she said mildly.

"You know he'll want to support you and your family any way he can."

Her father made a few grumbly sounds, then subsided. Savannah suspected that Dad's pride had been hurt because Logan didn't think he alone could protect his family.

Mom threw out a couple of remarks, but it was hard to hear from the back seat and they soon gave up. Savannah hadn't slept very well last night—not hard to figure out why—and found her eyelids growing heavy. She shook herself, remembering what Logan had said.

Stay sharp.

That was easier said than done from the back seat. None of the mirrors offered her the kind of view she needed to see traffic ahead or behind, and it was awkward turning her whole upper body to allow her to see out the back window, partially blocked by an empty gun rack.

Mom cast a smile over her shoulder at the sight of Molly, whose gradual sideways slump had ended with her sound asleep, her cheek planted on the door. Savannah smiled, too, but reminded herself, *Stay sharp.*

She touched the butt of her sidearm, tucked beneath her armpit, in a kind of reassurance. The seat belt crossed over it, which would make drawing slow unless she released her belt first. *Okay,* she thought, *then that's what I'll do.*

She knew when her father turned from the country road onto one of the many minor highways that connected Oregonians in these remote parts to each other. As he accelerated, the tires hummed on the road surface. She really wanted to nod off but wouldn't let herself. Probably half an hour later, she was hanging in there enough to notice a sign that said Entering Crook County. They were at last halfway, then. This was empty countryside, the only indication of human habitation a few minor roads turning off, one gravel and a handful of what were obviously private drives to ranches or farms.

After stopping at a blinking red light, Dad took a shortcut, yet another two-lane road posted fifty miles per hour that Savannah knew would shortly meet up with Highway 26. Strange that she hadn't seen any traffic yet, Savannah mused. Or maybe not. Once they got on 26, there would be plenty of other travelers. And they *had* gotten an early start.

Needing reassurance, she craned her neck again to look back—to see only empty highway. Alarm flared. Maybe the deputy had just dropped back a little, but... Had he not made the last turn with them? Wasn't Dad paying any attention?

She leaned forward. "Dad! We've lost Deputy Krupski."

"What?" He looked into the rearview mirror. "Where the hell did he go?" His foot must have lifted from the gas pedal, because they began to slow.

Heart thundering, fumbling for her phone, she said, "I don't know, but I think we should turn around. We shouldn't go on without him."

"No. Okay." Astonishing that he'd taken Logan so seriously. The pickup drifted toward the shoulder. Only... A black SUV was coming fast toward them from the opposite direction. Too fast.

"Dad, hurry!" she cried.

"I don't want to put us in a ditch!"

Panic changed Mom's face to someone Savannah hardly recognized. Her father swore, and she looked over her shoulder to see that a second vehicle was closing in on them.

Please let it be chance. She didn't believe it. This was a classic pincer movement.

Molly woke up with a start. "Auntie Vannah?"

Savannah pushed aside the seat belt so she could pull her handgun and flick off the safety. Her hands shook, she saw as if from a distance. That wasn't good.

They'd reached a near stop and her father cranked the wheel to make a U-turn, but by that time the black SUV had swung sharply across both lanes and slammed to a halt blocking the highway going forward. The sedan that had approached from the rear did the same behind them.

"What do I do?" her father yelled.

"Keep going! You're bigger than that car. Slam into it and push it out of the way if you have to!"

She was thrown back against the seat as he stepped hard on the gas again, but two gunshots sounded and the pickup jerked. To her shock, a hole appeared in the side window.

"Dad!" she screamed.

He was yelling, "Get down, get down," and still trying to drive, but more gunshots had to be taking out tires—they rocked now, and she could tell they were riding on rims—and she couldn't see well enough to take a shot of her own until they came to an abrupt halt.

A masked man appeared by Savannah's window. She tried to fire, but her arm wouldn't lift. She'd lost sensation, which meant she had to have been shot. He blasted a hole in the glass, then used the butt of his gun to smash it until he could reach in to open the door. Her gun...it must have fallen from her hand.

Mom was struggling with her seat belt and both screaming and crying. Dad—he'd slumped forward. Another masked man finished smashing the glass and swung the butt of his gun at Dad's head. Savannah realized Molly was screaming and so was she, but they were dragging her out, throwing her on the pavement.

"Molly!"

A hard kick felt as if it was caving in Savannah's already painful rib cage. She curled into a ball, even as another man hauled Molly out right over Savannah.

Molly kicked and flailed and sounded like a steam engine, but she was too small to be effective. A backhanded blow rocked Savannah's head. That was her last sight of Molly. Somehow, Savannah pushed herself to her feet, where she stood unsteadily. Which direction had they carried Molly? Only one man was throwing himself into the sedan, so probably the SUV.

But...what if he'd closed Molly in the trunk first? Desperate, she scrambled back to the open door and spotted her gun lying on the floorboard. She flung herself back out and propped up her good hand with her injured one to lift the weapon and pull the trigger.

Glass in the back window of the sedan crumbled. She didn't dare hit the trunk, in case. Tires.

Crack, crack, crack.

The car lurched, then spun out and hurtled off the road. Savannah didn't care if she'd killed the driver. Whirling the other direction, she almost tripped over her father, stumbled and kept her gun level.

The SUV was receding. She ran after it, shooting, shooting, until she had no more bullets. She kept running down the middle of the highway, breath burning in her lungs and throat, face wet, until she couldn't see the SUV anymore. She slowed, swayed on her feet…and collapsed onto her knees on the pavement.

GIVEN THE SPEED he was traveling, Logan hoped like hell he didn't encounter any other traffic and that no whitetail deer or pronghorn decided to bound across the highway in front of him. He'd thought he was scared the last time Savannah was attacked, but that had been nothing.

All he knew was that she'd been hurt, Molly was missing and someone else was injured, presumably on top of Deputy Krupski's life-threatening injury.

Apparently, Krupski had been shot and gone off the road. The first call had come in when a passing motorist saw his vehicle half-buried in a mess of sagebrush and stopped to investigate. Logan had passed that mess a minute ago; flashing lights everywhere, including those on an ambulance. Presumably the other car stopped on the shoulder belonged to the Good Samaritan. Under any other circumstances, he'd have braked long enough to check on his deputy. The thought hadn't even crossed his mind. Thank God the Crook County sheriff's department had called Logan's department immediately. Unfortunately, Krupski had suffered a head shot. Unconscious, he hadn't been able to tell anyone what had happened.

But Logan had known instantly. The deputy had been ambushed before making the turn onto the highway that Logan saw right ahead. Perfect timing; it would have taken Gene and Savannah a few minutes to notice his absence.

Had these bastards *known* where the Baird family was going this morning? Could they somehow have gotten into the cabin or the main house and hidden an electronic ear? Or had they just been waiting, assuming Savannah and Molly would go out eventually? It wouldn't have taken long to guess where they were headed. There wasn't a lot between Sage Creek and Bend, central Oregon's largest city. If you'd spread out your troops, it wouldn't be hard to set up a two-pronged ambush.

Logan berated himself for not guessing that they would have increased the manpower locally.

Ignoring the flashing red light, he burned rubber making the turn and zeroed in on the multiple emergency lights ahead. He didn't slow until he was nearly upon them. To his right, an unfamiliar car had gone off the road, bullet holes in the rear window and the windshield. A backboard was being maneuvered up the incline to the ambulance waiting on the road verge. Neck collar.

They'd better not be transporting this scum before Savannah and her family had been taken care of.

Another hundred yards, and he ran right over some flares before slamming to a stop as close to Gene Baird's pickup truck as he could get. Yet another ambulance was screaming away.

What if Savannah was in that ambulance, out of his reach? If that was so, Logan didn't know if he could stay at the scene and figure out what, where and who with even a grain of dispassion. All he'd want was to go after her.

He jumped out and ran toward the pickup, which sat on three flat tires. Metal dented, glass glinting on the pavement, bullet holes in the windshield, side windows smashed out.

There was one still figure in the midst of the activity. Savannah, sitting on her butt on the pavement, seemingly oblivious to the medic crouched beside her, wrapping her arm in white gauze.

And yet somehow his footsteps penetrated her shock. Her head turned, and she didn't so much as blink as he walked straight to her.

Chapter Fifteen

She hadn't even realized how desperately she hoped that Logan would come. But once she saw him, she knew she'd held no doubt. She'd been waiting, that's all.

His savage expression was what she needed to see. He flickered a look at the bulky bandage on her arm, then transferred it to the medic.

"Her injury?"

"Gunshot wound," the woman said. "A severe blow to her rib cage. She needs to go to the hospital, but she is declining to do so."

His pale eyes met hers again. "Savannah?"

"It can wait. I couldn't leave until…until…" Her voice hitched and kept hitching, and she didn't care that the salty tears now running down her scraped cheeks burned. She didn't so much as bother to lift a hand to wipe them away.

Logan looked even angrier. His hands tightened into fists at his sides. He would hate feeling helpless, and she knew his first instinct would be to blame himself for letting them go without him. Savannah was glad he didn't take her in his arms, as she suspected he wanted to do. She'd fall apart, and she couldn't afford that yet. She had to tell him what had happened, make sure he mounted a hunt for the little girl Savannah loved so much.

"They took Molly." That was the hardest thing to say, even if he must already know. She couldn't look away from him. As far as she was concerned, no one else was here. "I couldn't stop them. I couldn't do anything. I thought I was prepared, but I was useless! Please, please. Find her, Logan."

"I'll do my damnedest. Trust me."

"I do," she whispered. "I'm so scared."

The medic shrugged, packed away her supplies and walked away.

"You must hurt," Logan said. "You should go to the hospital."

"No." She shook her head. "No. It doesn't matter. Molly matters."

"Okay." He coaxed her to stand so that he could lift her onto the tailgate of her dad's pickup. Then he leaned a hip beside her. Crook County deputies were watching him, but must know who he was and were deferring to him for the moment.

"Tell me what happened," he said. "Looks like you got about halfway to Bend."

"Did we?" She turned her head and scanned their surroundings, high mountain desert that could have been almost anywhere in this part of the state. Then her gaze latched back on to his. "We hadn't seen any other traffic in a while. I kept turning to look out the back, and I suddenly realized the deputy wasn't there." Oh, dear Lord—she'd forgotten about Deputy Krupski. "Do you know where he is? *How* he is?" If he'd had something like a flat tire, he'd have called her.

Logan said grimly, "He was shot and went off the road. Somebody saw his vehicle and called in what was assumed to be an accident. That's what started this response."

"He's dead?" She wished she could feel numb.

"No. He's on his way to the hospital. Unconscious, but I don't know any details yet."

Her teeth chattered, although talking seemed to help. She related events as she'd experienced them. It must sound jerky. From Logan's expression, nothing she said surprised him. Big SUV blocked the narrow highway, car raced up to prevent her father from completing a U-turn, and bullets started to fly.

His jaw muscles knotted. "Sounds smoothly enough executed, I'd say it isn't the first time these men have done it. You couldn't be expected to react fast enough to stop them." He shook his head. "I didn't foresee anything this sophisticated. They have to be getting desperate. Whatever Jared had on them must be dynamite."

"But…they didn't even call again."

"They wanted something to hold over you."

Something. An already traumatized child. Savannah hated at that moment as she'd never imagined she could. But she dragged herself back to her narration.

"Dad…" Beginning to stumble over words, she was winding down. "They threw him down. Slammed the butt of a pistol against his head. He's…unconscious, too."

"Your mother?" Logan asked gently.

"I think…she's mostly all right. Terrified. She went in the ambulance with Dad."

"That's best for both of them."

She couldn't decide if he wished she'd gone as well, but was sure he understood why she'd refused.

"One of them stepped right over the top of me and yanked Molly out of the truck. I couldn't see which direction they went." She sounded piteous to her own ears. "I… I thought they might have shut her in the trunk of the car."

Thought wrong. She wouldn't forgive herself for that.

"Ah. Then it was you who shot out the tires and sent him flying off the road."

"Did…did he get away?"

"No. He didn't take the time to fasten his seat belt. Flew through the windshield, which already had some bullet holes. I'd give a lot for a few minutes with him, but he's not looking good. I doubt I'll have the chance."

"You mean… I may have killed him." Shouldn't she feel more shocked?

"Are you sorry?" he asked.

After a moment, she shook her head. She wasn't feeling so

good. In fact… She barely made it to the ditch and dropped to her hands and knees before she started to heave.

Logan crouched beside her and rubbed her back, giving her the gift of silence. He produced some crumpled tissues from his pocket when she finally pushed herself up. Still quiet, he waited as she wiped her mouth.

Then he said, "You need to go to the hospital. Nausea suggests you have a concussion again. That's bad so close after the last one." When she opened her mouth, he shook his head. "No. If you can answer a couple more questions, I need you to go get checked out."

As it turned out, she couldn't provide any useful information. Oh, how she hated to admit that she hadn't been observant enough. No, she hadn't seen a license plate on the SUV; her best view of it was from the side after it had swung around to block the highway. No, she wasn't sure of a model, except that it was big. Something in the size range of a Tahoe was the best she could do, even knowing how many models there were now.

She couldn't come up with any identifying characteristics on the two men she'd seen best, either. Both had worn black knit ski masks. The one who shot out her window had brown eyes, she thought. Both were Caucasian. She'd tried shooting after the SUV when it took off, but didn't believe she'd hit it. She thought there'd been two men in it, but there could have been a third.

"If I'd shot out those tires first—"

Logan kept his gaze steady on her. "The guy in the sedan would have taken you out, or the others would have come back. You were outgunned from the beginning." Undoubtedly seeing her misery, he told her, "Crook County got out a BOLO pretty quickly. To neighboring counties, too. We can hope a black SUV catches someone's eye." He paused. "It looks like your father got off a couple of shots. If we're lucky, that SUV has a suspicious dent or two, or a nice round hole through one of the windows."

"I…didn't know he had a chance."

"Too much going on." He hugged her, and she realized he must have caught the eye of the medic, because there she was. "I'll get to the hospital as soon as I can. You'll be able to check on your parents once you're there."

She managed a small nod. He could do his job better once she was out of the way.

"You have your phone?"

"Yes."

"Find her," she begged, even knowing how hopeless this was. "Please."

"Nothing is more important than bringing Molly home," he murmured and kissed her forehead.

She let herself be steered away.

THE DEVIL OF it was, there was damn little Logan could do. He was out of his jurisdiction. He'd have called in extra deputies to join the hunt for the SUV, except when last seen it had been speeding west, toward the Deschutes County line. Deputies there were watching for it, but he thought these men were too experienced to do anything so predictable. No, they'd turn off on minor roads, circle back toward Sage Creek or head north or south. God knew.

Savannah must know as well as he did what would happen next. Her phone would ring. Her caller had upped the stakes—and she still couldn't trade what they would want for Molly Baird. Logan suspected they wouldn't return the little girl anyway; she might have seen faces, heard things she shouldn't, and her continuing captivity could be used to control Savannah indefinitely.

Unless they had her cabin bugged, in which case they already knew she was cooperating with the DEA.

Speaking of…

He called first Cormac Donaldson, then Trenowski. Both sounded as angry as he felt, even given that neither had ever met Savannah or Molly.

The DEA agent used some creative obscenities to express how much he wanted to bring the organization down.

Logan only said, in a voice he hardly recognized, "Yes."

He checked in with his own department, made sure anyone and everyone knew he could be reached at St. Charles Hospital in Prineville, and activated lights and siren to speed his way.

Neither Savannah nor either of her parents were in the ER waiting room. When he asked, he was allowed back to a cubicle where he found Savannah lying on a narrow bed, looking wan.

He hated to see the momentary hope on her face. He had to shake his head. "I don't know anything. I'd like to be able to talk to your dad."

"I haven't heard a word about him yet. Can you find out what's happening?"

He could and did, returning to report that her father had regained consciousness shortly after arrival at the hospital, and was currently undergoing an MRI that would tell the doctors more.

"Your mom should be here in a minute," he added. "Tell me what the doctor says about you."

Surprisingly, they didn't believe she had suffered a concussion. "I guess stress was enough to make me puke," she said wryly. "Imagine that." The wound on her upper arm had been thoroughly cleaned and bandaged anew, with the recommendation that she consider seeing a plastic surgeon in the near future. "Because I could hardly use my arm right after I was shot, there may be damage to nerves and muscles."

X-rays didn't conclusively show any broken ribs, either. The doctor thought that the fact she'd already had her rib cage wrapped had protected her from further damage, just not from pain.

They held hands, fingers entwined, while they waited for her mother. Savannah kept watching him, her emotions naked. Whatever wall she'd temporarily built after their lovemaking had fallen. Logan had the uneasy feeling she could see everything he felt, too, which was uncomfortable.

Maybe baring himself emotionally was necessary, though. Slammed by so much these past weeks, he had to realize he'd never really opened up to a woman before, never wanted to. All that had been hurt was his pride when Laura declined to consider moving across the state with him. Already, he could hardly picture her face, so shallow had been his feelings for her. Maybe she'd known that.

Savannah's mother finally slipped into the cubicle, only shaking her head when asked about Gene. Logan had to step back from Savannah to let her and her mother fall into a long embrace. Savannah closed her eyes, a few tears leaking as her mother sobbed her fear and anguish.

"Molly must be so scared," she cried. "We have to find her. We have to!"

"We will." Savannah opened her eyes, and it was as if she'd reestablished a direct connection with him. "Logan will," she said, before her face contorted.

He put his arms around both women.

Finally, her mother mopped up and decided Gene would be back from the MRI. Her face was red, her eyes swollen, and she moved as if she'd aged a couple of decades today. Maybe she had, in every meaningful way.

He wet a couple of paper towels with cold water and gave them to Savannah to lay over her face. Then he took her hand again.

His phone rang once, and he stepped out to take the call from his own department. A passing nurse looked disapproving, but didn't say anything. He was able a minute later to return and tell Savannah that doctors had hope for Krupski.

"The bullet ricocheted off his cranium. They've drilled a hole to release some of the internal pressure. They're calling it a coma now and he's still in critical condition. Most people in his state do recover, though." He swore softly. "He's a kid."

Savannah's hand tightened on his. "Would it be any worse if it was an older deputy?"

He rubbed his free hand over his face. "No. I don't know.

It's so damn unlikely for anyone in law enforcement in a small town or rural county to ever get shot. His parents—" He broke off. They'd been so proud. Now they'd be sitting outside Intensive Care at the hospital in Bend, where their son had been transported because of the severity of his condition.

He should call them...but anguish he'd never imagined feeling for a child who wasn't his kept pulling him back to Molly. He saw the joy and trust on her face as he'd swung her in a circle before he left that morning. It shouldn't have been able to happen so quickly, but he loved that little girl as much as he knew Savannah did. Molly was entirely lovable. He kept being hit by the fact that she was Jared's daughter, too, as well as Savannah's niece.

A phone rang, and he realized right away it wasn't his. Savannah pulled out hers, looked at the displayed number, then at him.

"Ms. BAIRD. I think we have something of yours."

Pushing aside the grief to allow room for rage, she said, "Not *something*. A little girl who has already had too many bad things happen to her in her life."

"I should have said, something valuable." The cold voice hardened. "I've run out of patience, Ms. Baird. You've had plenty of chances to do what I asked. I hope you're a little more motivated now."

"You do know that your men badly injured my father and may have killed a cop. Considering we have capital punishment in this state, that seems really stupid."

"Ah, but who will catch my men? Your local law enforcement hasn't been a great deal of help so far, have they?"

"I'm in the hospital, too. Did your hired guns tell you that? One of them shot me. A few inches different, I wouldn't have been around to help you with your problem."

"Perhaps without *you* in the picture, it wouldn't have been a problem anymore. Now, when are you going to give me what I need?"

"We can… We'll have to set up a meeting."

"You've figured out your brother's password."

Savannah met Logan's eyes and lied with remarkable steadiness. "Yes."

"Tell me."

"No. I'll give you the phone with the password when I have Molly back, unharmed."

Logan nodded his approval.

At least she'd provoked a moment of silence.

"When will you be released from the hospital?" he asked.

"I…don't know yet. Probably by tomorrow morning. And in case you had visions of stopping by my room, I don't know the password by heart. I wrote it down and hid it. All I had with me today was a shopping list."

"You really shouldn't antagonize me, you know. That cute little girl's life is in my hands. And let me say, if I get even a hint that you've shared information from that file with authorities, she's dead. Do you understand me?"

"Yes!"

"Don't let your lover spend the night. We'll be watching."

Her mouth opened and closed.

Then came a curt "I'll call you at noon tomorrow with a meeting place. If you're not alone, you know what will happen."

"Wait!" she cried, but he'd cut her off.

Logan muffled her scream against his chest, his arms locked around her.

Chapter Sixteen

It never took long for a woman as gutsy as Savannah to collect herself. Once she had, she said, "What are we going to do?"

"Set up a trap," he answered grimly.

"But…you heard what he said!"

"I did. We'll have to give the appearance that you're alone. That will take some planning. No matter what, we'll need to have enough manpower in Sage Creek, ready to go in an instant. And by God, it's time Donaldson comes up with more than talk."

Donaldson did. He had a team ready and eager to go. When Logan told him about the specific threat to Molly if the traffickers caught even a whiff of rumors that a move was being made on them, the agent was able to reassure him. He'd set up a fake investigation to explain why agents were being sent to Oregon. They'd fly to Portland immediately, then drive through the night if necessary to be available in the morning. They discussed where they could wait so as not to draw any attention at all, assuming Savannah's watcher was still loitering.

Not liking to rely entirely on anyone else, Logan called a couple of his most capable deputies to be ready as well.

He'd no sooner gotten off the phone than a nurse let him know that he could see Savannah's father.

Not surprisingly, Gene couldn't produce a breakthrough piece of information. He had no idea of a license plate. The man who'd grabbed him was dark-haired; he'd seen the hair on his forearms.

"A big bruiser," he mumbled past swollen lips. He'd lost a couple of teeth, which didn't help his speech, either. "Near my height, but broader than me. I grabbed for his mask, but he had me on the ground too fast."

"What did he wear?"

"Shiny black cowboy boots. Saw those."

Logan winced. Baird and Savannah had both been kicked. That seemed to be a favorite punishment handed out by the trafficker's enforcers, especially effective with pointed-toe cowboy boots.

"Luck they didn't hurt Susan." The shame in Gene's eyes echoed Logan's knowledge that he'd failed Savannah and Molly. "I should have reacted quicker."

Despite Logan's old anger at this man, he laid a hand on his shoulder. "You're not a special ops soldier. It takes intensive training to be ready for something this out of the ordinary. If anyone is to blame, it's me for okaying this expedition."

Gene grimaced. "Craziness."

"It was."

Logan was incredibly glad to be able to take Savannah back to the ranch. Doctors wanted to monitor her father for the night because of his head injury, and despite his gruff insistence Savannah's mother go home, she dug in her heels and stayed with him.

Logan couldn't take her to his dad's place. He didn't want to endanger his father, and anyway, Savannah was in no state to have an obligatory conversation with his father and Mrs. Sanders. Logan hoped the Circle B ranch wasn't being watched at this point; he'd rather these scumbags not know that, contrary to what she'd suggested, she wasn't actually being held another night at the hospital. He frowned. What if they went to a motel?

Once he'd lifted her into his truck and gotten behind the wheel himself, he asked what she would prefer.

He had the feeling her thoughts were turning slowly, but finally she said, "Home. I mean, the cabin. If you don't mind."

"Of course I don't."

He worried during the hour-long drive, stealing frequent glances at her. She'd crawled deep inside herself. The couple of times he tried to initiate conversation, she would turn her head, look vaguely surprised to see him and say, "What?"

These scum suckers had already made their point in a powerful way. Despite knowing how unlikely it was that he and she would be attacked, Logan stayed hyperalert watching for other vehicles, paying special attention as they got closer to home.

He parked as close to the back door of the cabin as he could get, helped Savannah out and hustled her in. He sat her down at the kitchen table and then cleared the remaining rooms. Finally, he mounted a search of any obscure place a bug could have been concealed but found nothing. As far as he could tell, Savannah didn't even notice what he was doing. She sat where he'd left her, staring straight ahead, eyes unfocused.

"Are you hungry?" he asked.

Her gaze wandered slowly his way. Her forehead crinkled slightly; predictably, she shook her head.

To hell with it. He was starved, and needed fuel to do his best thinking and prepare for action.

He was glad to find a lasagna he knew she'd made in the freezer, since cooking wasn't one of his best skills. He stuck it in the microwave to defrost and then heat, cut up broccoli and put it on to cook, and even found some French bread, which he buttered. No garlic salt to be found in her spice cupboard, but he did come across garlic cloves and crushed one so he could spread it over the bread.

His phone rang several times with updates, none important enough at the moment to intrude on her fear and grief. Deputy Krupski seemed to be getting more responsive, thank God; eyelids moving, fingers twitching, that kind of thing. He called Savannah's mother, who said Gene hurt and was mad. She didn't have to say that he was scared, too. His truck had been towed to an auto body shop in Sage Creek. It would need some significant work. The same shop did the work on sheriff's department vehicles, so they had that car, too, by this time.

A sergeant with the Crook County sheriff's department reported that the driver of the crashed sedan had died. The car was a rental. They'd pulled some fingerprints that matched those of the dead man and had a name for him.

Jimmy Barraza had used a fake driver's license to rent the car. However, his fingerprints were in the system. He was a San Francisco resident who'd served several stretches in state penitentiaries for violent crimes. Calls to the San Francisco PD suggested that while rumor linked him to a drug trafficking organization with ties to a Mexican cartel, proof was scant. He hadn't been arrested or charged with any crime in the past eighteen months.

"We think a couple of bullets we removed from the interior of Mr. Baird's pickup will match up with the Colt Barraza carried," the sergeant added. "Nice if we could have charged him, but—"

Burying him was easier all around, Logan thought.

THE AFTERNOON AND evening felt interminable. Logan suggested Savannah lie down, but how could she sleep? Waking nightmares flickered through her head like poor-quality film.

She relived the minutes from when she'd noticed they'd lost their escort until she'd collapsed screaming on the roadway. Over and over, her last glimpse of Molly being pulled out of the pickup, right over her, played. The terror, the instant their eyes met, Molly not understanding why her auntie Vannah didn't *stop* that man. Daddy said she could *trust* her aunt.

The very young brother she'd loved kept coming to her, and sometimes she felt only grief, other times rage because this was *his* fault—except it wasn't all, she knew that—and ending in guilt, because he had trusted her to protect his "everything." Worse, because she loved Molly for her own sake, loved her as if she was her own.

Savannah was dimly aware of Logan on the phone, restlessly pacing the kitchen, slitting the blinds to peer out—and watching her. She did let him persuade her to eat some dinner. She wasn't hungry, but he was right; she needed to be ready tomorrow for whatever came. Aware, *smart*, not the zombie she felt right now.

A couple of times, she shut herself in the bathroom when she absolutely had to cry. Not that she was fooling him. It was hard to hide puffy, bloodshot eyes. She didn't even know why she had tried, except she didn't want him to feel worse than he already did.

She worked up some resentment because, while he felt he'd failed her and Molly, he was still able to plot, to weave the strands surrounding him into something meaningful. He talked with fellow cops from several jurisdictions, hospital personnel, the DEA agent who was zealous enough to be on his way to Sage Creek, Oregon, along with his fellow agents.

Logan pulled up USGS maps of the county on his laptop, comparing them with paper maps he brought in from his department SUV. Savannah did rouse herself enough to ask how he could possibly think he'd be able to predict where these monsters would choose to set up an exchange.

Face heavily lined, he said, "I can't, of course, but I'm eliminating possibilities and trying to see through their eyes. How much have they actually driven around the area? Is their hideout also a logical place to meet you? They have to know you'll do your best not to be alone, despite their demand. Fortunately, I doubt they'll expect federal agents, but they know I'm the sheriff and will try to corner them if I can."

That alarmed her. "Will you? If they have Molly?"

He shook his head. "Not until the trade is made." He hesitated. "If it's made. I expect they'll bring her, but what if they want to keep a hold on you?"

"Why?" she cried. After a moment, her shoulders sagged. "Because they think I might keep a copy of the file so I can pass it on to somebody like the DEA." She had to say this aloud, however horrible it was. "They don't really plan to give her back to me at all, do they?"

Expression compassionate, he was still honest. "No. I don't think they do." Then he shook his head wearily. "They're going to assume we'll try to set them up. That…introduces danger."

"Maybe…maybe we shouldn't. What if I really did go without anyone—"

He took one of her hands in a warm clasp. "They have zero ethics, Savannah. No sense of morality. They don't care that Molly is a scared kid, or that you're her terrified mom." When she opened her mouth, he said, "Aren't you?"

Her eyes got watery again. He apologized, and she jumped up to retreat to the bathroom again. Except this time she felt compelled to bypass it and go to Molly's bedroom. Pink and purple, unicorns and night-light, a lamp with a base of a rearing china horse that Savannah had forgotten all about but that Mom had retrieved from the house.

Hugging herself, she turned slowly in place. They'd probably gotten carried away with the toys and games. Stuffed animals especially; Molly loved them, although it was the rabbit with worn fur and a tattered ear she'd loved most. Savannah wished suddenly that Molly had taken it with her this morning. Maybe she could have held on to it. Maybe *they* would have let the kid keep it, if it would keep her quiet.

Or…maybe it would have been lost forever.

Just so Molly wasn't.

Savannah sat down on the edge of the bed, picked up Rabbit, studying him and finally pressing her cheek to his furry stomach. He smelled a little peculiar, but she imagined some of that was Molly.

She heard the high, sweet voice.

Will you sing "Sunshine" to me?

Her voice wanted to crack, but she began to sing, "You are my sunshine, my only sunshine." By the time she reached the part where she was begging for her sunshine not to be taken away, her nose was so clogged that she could hardly breathe.

How terribly fitting the lyrics had turned out to be! If she never saw Molly again, Savannah knew she'd never listen to this song again, much less sing it.

How strange that Jared had remembered it as her favorite.

As if she'd been hit by a Taser, she quit singing midphrase. Wait. Why hadn't it occurred to her that *this* was the one oddity Molly had shared? The only thing that resembled a message for her? A song she had had to learn off the internet? He'd been there when she was growing up. He'd have *known* their mother either didn't know it or didn't like it for some reason.

He'd all but *made* Savannah learn the lyrics.

Stunned, she felt her chest swelling with hope. This had to be it. It *had* to be.

She set Rabbit on the pillow, jumped to her feet and called, "Logan! Logan!"

SHE'D ABOUT STOPPED Logan's heart. The way the day had gone, he expected a cherry bomb had exploded through the window, at the very least.

Her face was wet with tears, but her entire expression had changed. Standing by Molly's bed, the worn stuffed rabbit lying askew on the pillow, Savannah fairly vibrated with new energy.

She rushed to explain and said, "I think 'You Are My Sunshine' *has* to be at the heart of that password. It's the first thing that makes sense."

She was right. He was careful not to say, *Being able to access the file may not help us bring Molly home.* Savannah had to know that.

They went back to the kitchen to try to figure this out. Savannah detoured on the way to grab a printout of the lyrics for a song that had originally been embraced as country music. Once they'd sat down at the table, he skimmed over the lyrics and was horrified. The damn song was heartbreaking. It wasn't a reassuring love song; it was about heartbreak. Hadn't

Jared *noticed*? Or was his choice influenced by his own sense of impending tragedy?

Logan looked up. "You don't sing the whole thing to Molly, do you?"

"Heavens no! It's beautiful, but awfully sad."

They finally got out a notebook and wrote numerous alternatives. *YouAreMy. MySunshine.* On and on. Logan eyed the line about how the lost love would someday regret leaving the singer. At the moment, that sounded like a threat.

They moved on to possible numbers. Molly's birthday seemed most logical, so they played with that. Symbols? How were they supposed to know?

Except Savannah said suddenly, "An exclamation point. I was way too fond of them when I was a kid. Even my teachers had to constantly replace them with periods and write me notes in the margin about how overuse weakened the punch. Jared gave me a hard time about being so sunny—" she faltered there "—that everything had to be *great*!" She was obviously mimicking her brother with the last part, each word bouncing high.

"I remember that." He stretched with both arms over his head while he thought about it. "I don't think this is about Molly at all. It's about *you*. He may have been using this password before Molly even came to live with him. Clearly, he's always had you in mind as his backup."

Savannah stared at him, seeming stunned. "Me?"

"He constantly used the word *sunny* when he talked about you. I'd...forgotten." Even his memories had been filtered through his biases. He wanted to give himself a kick in the rear. "Jared knew sometimes you were pretending, but he said you did it well. So let's try parts of *your* birthday." Logan paused. "He loved you."

Savannah swallowed and nodded.

Back to symbols. She pulled up texting on her phone to stare at the options. "What about 'at'?"

He jotted down his version of @.

"The symbol for *number*. He and I constantly played tic-tac-toe, especially on trips when we were crazy bored in the back seat. Naturally, I never had a chance after he figured out how to inevitably win, and it took me ages to realize that if he'd ever let me go first, *I* could have won. We'd end up squabbling, and Dad would yell at us, but—"

went down on their list.

Thank God Jared hadn't set the log-in—or, even worse, the file itself—to self-destruct when someone made too many attempts at passwords. Logan lost track of the number of alternatives they tried, and that was just today's effort. Then she typed in just the day and month of her birthday, followed by #, MySunshine and an exclamation mark.

And they found themselves looking at a letter.

Vannah,
I hope the worst hasn't happened and you're reading this. If it has—God, I'm so sorry. I guess you've figured out that I'm doing everything I can to bring down the entire drug trafficking organization that got their talons into me when I was at my weakest. Give this file to DEA Agent Cormac Donaldson.

Jared used the #, followed by a phone number Logan already knew.

I know how hard you tried to protect me from Dad. I wish I'd been mature enough to let his abuse roll off my back. I could have had a different life. But I didn't, and I can't regret Molly.
My love to you both. Always.
Jared

Logan's first thought was that Jared had provided the permission the DEA needed to use this document.

Savannah leaked a few more tears, they flipped through

some of the multiple pages that followed, and she said finally, "Should we call Donaldson?"

Logan didn't hesitate long. "No. He can wait. I don't one hundred percent trust that he wouldn't get excited and push for a warrant, assuming it could be kept quiet. His priority and ours aren't the same."

They copied the file to Logan's laptop and to Savannah's, too, then closed it on the phone.

"You're a genius," he told her, and she gave a watery laugh.

"Hardly, but no matter what, I'm glad we did figure this out. Except for getting Molly back and loving her, this is the last thing I can do for Jared."

"Yeah," Logan agreed gruffly. "Now we'd better try to get some rest. Do you think you can sleep?"

Exhaustion and strain making her look fragile, Savannah said, "No, but I'll try. Only...will you lie down with me? I mean, not to—"

"I know what you mean." He managed a crooked smile.

"I shouldn't ask, since you can't stay."

That was part of the plan. She had to appear to be compliant. She also knew that two deputies, six DEA agents and Logan would by morning be spread out across the county so that at least a couple of them should ideally be close once she was told where to go.

That, of course, was assuming Logan was able to overhear the instructions the way they'd planned.

"You don't know how much I'm going to hate leaving. Right now... I need to hold you."

As usual, he made a perimeter walk outside before checking all the locks and turning out lights. Then he went to Savannah's room. She'd removed her boots and jeans, but hadn't bothered taking off her T-shirt and, he presumed, her bra and panties. Logan followed her example, leaving his boots beside the bed where he could put them on quickly and tossing his jeans over a chair. Then he climbed under the covers, stretched out and gathered the woman he loved into his arms.

He felt her letting go of some of her tension. Tonight, that was enough.

SHE SET OUT in the aging pickup truck at 12:05 on the nose. Ranch hands may have known what was happening. She didn't know, only that they watched her as she started down the driveway, their expressions grim. They probably assumed she was on her way to see her dad in the hospital.

Savannah would have been scared spitless, except she clung to her hatred for these monsters as if it was a supercharged heating pad that kept her from the creeping cold she'd battled since Logan had slipped out of bed in the middle of the night and left.

She'd dozed off and on until then, but the moment she'd felt him lift his head to look at his phone or the clock, she'd lost any ability to sleep.

He brushed her nape with his lips—she couldn't think what else that sensation could be—and then murmured, "If I had any choice, I'd have stayed with you as long as you needed me. I hope you know that."

She'd heard her own croaked "I... I do."

"Good. Remember, I won't be far."

She thought she'd nodded. Then he slipped out of bed. A few rustles and a faint squeak of the floorboard told her he was getting dressed, and not a minute later the back door closed.

Now, following the directions the cold voice had given her, she held on to Logan's promise.

I won't be far.

How he'd accomplish that, she had no idea, except that, using Jared's phone, she had the line to him open and her own phone on speaker. She could only hope he heard enough snatches of the directions she'd been given through her phone.

Unfortunately, the man hadn't been stupid enough to give her a final destination. She could only drive, trust in Logan and make the silent vow to do anything to save Molly.

Chapter Seventeen

The two phones might have started lying next to each other on the passenger seat in Savannah's ancient pickup, but once she started driving, Logan suspected they'd slid apart. The creep giving the directions was both angry and incredulous when she told him she didn't have Bluetooth. Ticked that the phone was on speaker, he remained suspicious but evidently resigned himself when she snapped, "I can't clutch a phone in my hand and drive safely, especially when I'm already rattled!"

Logan had no trouble hearing that. The rejoinder was a little muffled.

"If you have someone else in the vehicle with you, this meeting is canceled."

"I don't! I'm telling you the truth."

Clearly, they weren't able to use GPS to locate Jared's phone. He'd probably had multiples, and they'd never known this one existed.

Logan was doing some serious sweating. He'd had to make choices, knowing how flawed they could be. But he didn't have an army to disperse on this battlefield. What he did have was fewer than ten men—and superior knowledge of this county. Some of that was courtesy of his childhood, but once he'd accepted the job of sheriff, he'd driven as close to every inch of his new territory as he could come. He knew which ranches were for sale, some still under operation, others long deserted. He knew the dead-end roads where teenagers parked, the falling-down barns where those same teenagers held keggers. He'd also had an epiphany yesterday as he studied the maps.

On a road map, the county was laid out like a spider's web, with the town of Sage Creek being the spider at the center of it. The main highway—if you could call it that—crossing the county went right through town, the speed limit dropping to twenty-five miles per hour. Otherwise, most roads of any significance radiated outward. His conclusion was a gamble, but he also thought it would prove to be right: the guys who'd terrorized Savannah, who'd been able to appear like wraiths in the night on her father's ranch, hadn't been driving from some distant part of the county. As strangers in a place where everyone knew everyone else, they wouldn't have wanted to be seen passing back and forth through town every time they went out to the Circle B to keep watch—or beat the hell out of a woman.

Logan concluded their hideout had to be in the same quadrant of the county as his own dad's ranch *and* the Circle B. Theoretically, his few patrolling deputies had been looking for likely places for out-of-towners to squat temporarily, but there were a lot of them. Ranching as a family-run business was failing, and not only locally. Corporate-owned ranches were taking over, but not a one of them was situated in this notoriously dry part of eastern Oregon. His dad and the Bairds had hung on, along with half a dozen other ranches in the county, but most had gone under or were now only a hobby or a sideline to people who held other jobs.

On the map, he'd long since pinpointed half a dozen possible hideouts within four or five miles of the Baird ranch and had them checked out by deputies, although now he wished he'd done it himself. He added half a dozen other locations where passing traffic wouldn't be able to see today's meeting. He'd spread a couple of his too-few troops farther away...but damn, he hoped he was right.

He was waiting at a spot that seemed a good possibility—one of the closest to the Baird ranch—but he was also ready to hustle and move if he proved to be wrong.

Right now, he sat tensely, knowing she must be approaching the stop sign where one of the big decisions would be made.

Her voice came through the speaker. "Which way do I turn?"

"Left."

Logan breathed a prayerful thanks. Right would have taken her toward town, straight ahead into some mighty bleak country without a lot of habitation. Left had plenty of turnoffs that would put a man within riding or hiking distance of the ranch.

Silencing his own phone very momentarily, he used his radio to inform everyone else waiting. A couple of them—a deputy and a Fed—would be leaping into their vehicles to speed this way.

He had a good idea when she drove past his preferred location where he waited. A moment later, the voice said, "Left on the next dirt road."

"The one with a falling-down sign that says Horseback Riding?" she asked, voice clear.

The scum whose voice Logan had grown to hate answered with a clipped "Yes."

Logan murmured into his radio, then grabbed his phone. Wearing his flexible tactical boots rather than the cowboy boots that let him fit in locally, he set out cross-country at a hard run. Fumbling as he went, he poked in an earbud so he could hear any additional directions to Savannah, then unholstered his weapon and raised it into firing position in case he encountered a surprise.

SAVANNAH HAD PAID more attention yesterday than she'd realized to Logan's calculations with the maps. He'd left one of the maps he'd marked up for her to take today, with Xs telling her where surveillance would be set up.

This was one of those places. The moment she made the turn, she crumpled the map in her hand and, bending, stuffed it under the seat.

A family had lived here until Savannah was ten or so; a couple of kids had ridden her school bus. But they moved away, and Dad had said there'd never been an offer on the ranch, not even a lowball one. She drove as slowly as she could without occasioning suspicion, her heart drumming harder and harder as she watched for any sign of life. The ground wasn't frozen today, and dust rose behind her, announcing her arrival. Had whoever was watching her been staying here? A deputy must have driven in here sometime, but had he gotten out of his vehicle to walk around the derelict ranch buildings? Would he have been gunned down if he had?

Had they watched him come and go, and now felt safe here because they'd been undetected?

This land was slightly higher than her father's ranch, and lacking a stream, if she remembered right. With no cattle grazing, what had once been pasture was growing up in the junipers that ranchers, and even the state, often tried to eradicate. Scruffy trees, they made it hard to see ahead.

"There's a gate on your right," the man said abruptly. "Turn into it."

She wouldn't be going as far as the house or barn, then. Bile rose until she could taste it. If there was a cop here somewhere, he or she would be somewhere near the ranch proper, but she had no choice but to follow directions.

Gate was a generous word for a rusting barbed wire section that had been strung to a post not set in the ground so that it could be pulled aside. She bumped slowly over hard, uneven ground. The shock absorbers in this pickup had needed replacement at least a decade ago, and now each jolt felt like it was giving her whiplash. Oh, God—what if this led back out to the paved road, after which she'd be directed somewhere else altogether?

But then she saw a glint of metal ahead. She shifted her foot to the brake. An all-too-familiar large black SUV backed up to a tumbledown shed with a juniper growing right up through the roof. There was a second vehicle here, too, parked facing her. A nice shiny pickup truck. Another rental?

A part of her was astonished that she could still think at all.

"Stop," said the hard voice. "Get out of your truck."

Please don't let me be alone here, she begged, before turning off the engine and touching her side to be sure she had her own gun. Would she dare fire if they'd really brought Molly? She took a couple of measured breaths. Then, leaving her own phone on the seat, she picked up Jared's, opened her door and stepped out. She didn't move beyond that, though, using the open door as a shield the way cops on TV shows always seemed to do.

A man walked toward her, halting about halfway between the SUV and her pickup truck. Medium height, not lean, he clearly wasn't the muscle here. He had long dark hair smoothly pulled back from a terribly ordinary-looking face. She was still studying it when he lifted a gun she hadn't noticed and fired twice. Instinctively, she crouched as her pickup jerked. Tires. He'd shot out her front tires. Savannah had to force herself to rise to her feet again.

"Just in case you had any ideas," the man said coolly.

It was *him*. She knew that voice from his first call. Hate came to her rescue, steadying her hands.

"Do you have the phone?" *he* asked.

LOGAN WAS CAREFUL not to accidentally brush against the bristly branches of any of the junipers and therefore betray his approach. His lungs burned and, winter or not, sweat stung his eyes by the time he was able to hear a voice.

"Stop. Get out of your truck."

His blood ran cold. He didn't slow down, but stayed low as he wove between trees, sagebrush, rabbitbrush and a few outcrops of volcanic rock.

Savannah apparently turned off her engine. Her door had a distinctive squeal as it opened.

Close now, Logan scanned for movement. Yeah, there was someone beside the SUV, the first vehicle he could see clearly. Two men—no, three, one standing beside a pickup that from his vantage had hidden behind the SUV. This guy held a rifle loosely in his arms.

Crack. Crack.

Terror ran through Logan like an electric shock. If that bastard had just shot Savannah, he was dead.

He ordered himself not to let panic drive him into acting prematurely. Taking each step with care now, Logan eased himself behind cover where he could finally see her rusting truck and crouched low. She stood behind the open driver-side door. So who'd shot, and why— Flat tire. They'd shot out at least one of her tires.

A federal agent had been positioned at the barn. Logan hoped he'd ever set foot outside a city and knew how to approach without crashing through the high-desert vegetation. If he'd been listening to his radio, he should already be here, set up in a position that would allow him to intervene. Cormac Donaldson himself should be approaching from the next abandoned ranch to the north. He'd have had a longer run than Logan's. Logan hoped neither man was trigger-happy.

"Do you have the phone?" the man standing in the open demanded.

"Yes." Savannah lifted it so he could see it.

"Bring it here. Let me see the file."

She didn't give away any of the fear she must feel. She typed what he presumed was the password into it, then walked forward but stopped a few feet short of the bastard. "Where's Molly?"

He jerked his head toward the SUV.

"I can't see her."

He raised his voice. "Let her see the kid."

A back door of the SUV opened, and a man lifted a little blond-haired girl high.

"Molly!" Savannah called, but man and child vanished back inside the vehicle. If Molly had cried out or screamed, Logan hadn't heard her. Would they have her mouth taped?

"Show me," the man said.

"Look but don't touch." She held the phone up so he could see what Logan knew was one of the first pages of the document, detailing shipping dates and locations, rather than the letter.

The man grabbed for the phone.

She snatched it away and backed up a few steps.

"I've closed it. You can't see it again without the password."

"Open it and give it to me," he snarled. "You're outgunned here."

She stared her defiance at him. "Bring Molly to me first. Show me you're a man of your word."

She didn't believe that was even a remote possibility any more than Logan did, but she was pretending for all she was worth. Damn, he was proud of her.

"Bring the kid out," the guy called, baring his teeth.

Again, the SUV door opened, and the same man emerged with Molly in his arms. She wasn't struggling; if Logan had to guess, she'd been doped up. He hadn't thought he could get any angrier, but he'd been wrong.

The guy carrying the little girl approached to within a few feet from Savannah and the SOB calling the shots.

"Password."

"I'll give it to you once you hand my niece over."

"You think I'm stupid?"

She thrust out her chin. "Do you think *I* am?"

Logan held his Sig steady, ready for the moment this scum made the slightest threatening movement.

"Take her back," he snapped, half over his shoulder.

Savannah drew her arm back as if to throw the phone, but the bastard was on her, gripping her wrist until Jared's phone fell from her hand and he forced her to his knees.

"Molly!" she screamed.

Bullets started flying.

IT WAS THE kind of battlefield Logan most feared, the kind where the good guys didn't know where one another were, and the bad guys felt free to fire at will.

He didn't waste any time, taking down the SOB whose brutal grip held Savannah in place and who had just pulled a handgun. He dropped hard, taking her down with him. Unwittingly protecting her with his body, Logan thought with fierce satisfaction.

He tried to wedge himself behind an insubstantial juniper as he took aim and fired again. He'd worn his vest, but was excruciatingly conscious of how much of his flesh it didn't cover.

At least two men were shooting at him, but were either unable to see him clearly or lousy at hitting their targets. Bullets buzzed by.

Guns barked everywhere, and he saw the man holding the rifle drop, too. Not his own shot, so either Donaldson or the other agent were here, too. Or both. Death by friendly fire had become a real possibility.

The engine in the SUV roared to life. He had to get to Molly. As he bent low and ran full out, Logan was horrified to see Savannah crawl, then propel herself to her feet to run the same direction he was. Thank God she wore a Kevlar vest, too, since bullets flew from every direction. He saw her fall. Before his heart stopped, she rolled and scrambled to get up again.

She was too far away and directly in the path of the SUV if it leaped forward.

A hand reached to pull closed the back door. Logan refused to let them accelerate out of this clearing with Molly in there. They wouldn't get far...but would she survive?

Out of the corner of his eye, he saw someone scoop up the phone and then race in the same direction he was. Donaldson appeared and rammed the fool, crashing them both down hard onto the ground. Grunts were followed by curses and thrashing.

Logan wrenched open the back door that hadn't quite latched. The SUV started forward and he had to take a couple of running strides before he could leap in. He saw enough to know there was a driver and a second man in the back seat rearing over the little girl who was curled in an impossibly tight ball. Logan wanted to pull the trigger, but as the SUV lurched over a bump—or a body—he knew he didn't dare. Instead, he flung himself over her.

The pain searing his shoulder came a fraction of a second before the explosive sound of the gun firing rang in his ears. His vision sparked with black, but while he could still move, he made sure he had entirely buried Jared's little girl beneath him.

TERRIFIED BEYOND MEASURE, Savannah dived out of the way of the black SUV, skidding across the ground and ending with a pungent smell of sagebrush as it scratched her face. Whimpering, she backed up...and realized the SUV had shuddered to a stop. Raising her head, she saw that bullet holes peppered the windows.

Two men were advancing on the vehicle, handguns held out in stiff arms. Both had a thickness to their chests that told her they wore Kevlar vests, and the one she could see best had a T-shirt that said POLICE in big letters across the back. Blood ran down the other man's face.

She was undoubtedly crying; why else was her vision so fuzzy and the scratches on her cheeks on fire? The best she could do for a moment was crawl forward, but then somehow she wobbled back to her feet and ran the last few steps toward the half-open back door that first Molly, then Logan, had disappeared through.

"Better let us check first," one of the two unfamiliar men called. He had just kicked a gun away from a prone body.

The second one was crouching to check for a pulse on another.

She ignored them, terrified of what she'd find inside...and rounded the open door. More dead bodies— No, no! The slack face she could see was that of a stranger, but the man sprawled facedown across the seat was Logan. His gun had dropped to the floorboards, and a copious quantity of blood ran down his arm to drip from his fingertips.

"Please. No." That was her. Whispering, or was she screaming? She had no idea. Logan couldn't be dead. He couldn't. And where was Molly? Had one of them gotten away with her? How *could* that have happened?

Logan's body moved oddly.

"Molly?" Savannah whispered.

A small hand worked its way out from beneath him.

"Molly." She stretched forward over Logan.

More squirming. Finally, the smallest voice. "Auntie Van-nah?"

"Molly. Oh, God. You're all right. I love you."

She loved this man, too. One she had feared to trust, but who had been willing to die to protect the child she thought they both loved. Her hand shook as she reached out to touch her fingers to his neck…and felt his pulse.

She screamed for help.

Epilogue

At least this time when Logan woke up, he felt confident he really was alive. The first few times, he hadn't been at all sure. He remembered vaguely thinking, *I should hurt more than I do*.

This time, he did hurt. One hell of a lot. *They must have given me an internal pain reliever during surgery that's worn off*, he decided.

Just to be sure, he squeezed his right hand into a fist. Not easy, but it happened. Alive.

He pried his eyelids open, blinked blearily up at an unfamiliar ceiling, then turned his head on the pillow. Curtains surrounded the bed. Hospital. All that mattered was the woman sitting beside his narrow bed, watching him anxiously.

Savannah. She'd been there one other time, but he'd been sure he had dreamed her.

He croaked her name. Man, she was beautiful.

She smiled. "You sound like you need a drink."

He mouthed the word *Yes*.

She pushed a button that raised the head of the bed, then held a glass of water so that he could get the straw in his mouth and suck down half the contents before turning his face away to indicate he'd had enough. She set the glass down on a tray table to one side.

"You're here," he said, not so intelligently.

"Of course I am. Your dad has been here off and on, too, but it's evening and I sent him home. He looked...shaky."

"Wouldn't have told you that."

She wrinkled her nose. "Of course not."

Savannah had pulled a chair up to the left side of the bed. That arm worked as advertised, and he was able to hold out his hand. To his relief, she placed hers in it. "Chilly," he said.

"It's cold in here."

Was it?

"Tell me what I missed. Molly?"

"Is fine." Her throat worked. "Better than I expected. I think they kept her mostly knocked out. She...doesn't seem to remember a lot, except she's back to being clingy."

"Don't blame her." *He* wanted to cling to Savannah, too.

"No."

"Where is she?"

"Home with Grandma and Granddad. Dad's feeling much better, but not looking forward to getting dental implants. I told him he looks like a kindergartner missing his front teeth, and he glared at me."

Logan's mouth pulled into a smile.

"You're the only one of us who was badly hurt. Donaldson was grazed by a bullet—it left a bloody furrow on his head. The other agent is unscathed."

"Bad guys?"

"Dead or, well, not in jail yet. Actually, two are dead, including the one that went down on top of me. Three are currently still hospitalized, but they'll be locked up as soon as possible."

"They'll fill up our jail."

"Yes. Donaldson didn't sound impressed by your facilities."

He gave a bark of laughter that he instantly regretted. Savannah guided his hand to the button that provided pain relief.

"He's thrilled by the information Jared had gathered, though. It includes physical sites they can search, lots of names, and pages of data on how they laundered their proceeds. He already has a team of lawyers preparing new warrants, and agents serving the warrants they already had almost ready to go."

"Jared did what he set out to do."

"He...he did. Even Dad..." Savannah tried unsuccessfully to smile, but he understood the magnitude of what she felt.

"Your father damn well should," Logan said gruffly.

For a moment there was silence. Savannah broke it, voice thick. "You saved Molly's life."

"I'd have prioritized saving any child," he told her, hoping that wasn't too much honesty. "But Molly...of course I did. She's... Jared's, yours. I love her, too."

Savannah sniffed a few times and snatched a tissue from the box on his table to wipe her eyes and cheeks.

"Thank you."

He shook his head. "Don't need thanks."

She seemed to be looking deep inside him, an unnerving experience. "What do you need?"

This was probably too soon, but... "You," he said simply. "I've fallen hard for you. I know you have plenty of reason not to believe me, but... I hope you'll give me a chance."

"You just risked everything for Molly. How can I ever doubt you again?"

"Not the same thing."

"No." Her smile shook. "I... I love you. I think I always have, or you couldn't have hurt me as much as you did."

He winced. "When I was a teenager, or recently?"

"Both."

His hand tightened on hers. "Never again," he swore, huskily.

She let out a shaky near-sob and stood so she could bend over to kiss him. There and gone, but he probably had lousy breath anyway. He could only imagine how ragged he must look.

"I like my job here," he told her. This would matter to her, and he'd wanted to be sure how he felt about a life spent in his hometown in case he and she ever got to this point. "I'll have to win an election next time around, but—"

"Of course you will. Oh, Logan. You know how I feel working with horses."

"Magic with them. Would never ask you to give it up."

"You're fading on me."

"No." But she was right. "Love you," he managed.

Maybe if he just closed his eyes for a minute…

Savannah loves me. Trusts me. We're all okay. Really believing that all good things could happen, he fell asleep.

* * * * *

THE BODYGUARD'S
DEADLY MISSION

LISA DODSON

To my niece and brilliant forensic scientist, Jillian Lewis.
Thank you for the invaluable insight!

To the Alexa Kings and Brendas in the world.
Embrace your power!

Chapter One

Alexa King dropped the yellow rose she was carrying on the wicker casket. Unfortunately, mourners weren't allowed to stay and watch the casket be lowered into the ground, so the memorial service for her best friend, Tanya Singleton, was officially over.

Walking over to the row of white fold-up chairs near the grave site, Alexa knelt in front of Tanya's mother, Viola Singleton, and took her hand. Tall and athletic in build, Viola was deep in her grief, but it did little to minimize her timeless beauty. Her cream-colored dress with the blouson sleeves was cinched at the waist with a wide tan leather belt. Her curly brown shoulder-length hair was adorned with a single white lily. Viola looked like she was ready to enjoy a picnic in the grassy meadow as opposed to laying her only child to rest. Alexa knew that would be exactly how Tanya would have wanted it.

"You were such a joy to my daughter. She would have loved all you've done to honor her today."

Alexa struggled to get the words out over the lump in her throat. "She was my best friend, and I loved her dearly."

"I know, honey. Thank you for driving all the way here. I know Pittsburgh isn't exactly around the corner from Washington, DC, but this place fits Tanya." Her mother sniffled and dabbed her eyes with her handkerchief. "The environmentally friendly burial was fitting. Thank you for finding it."

Hugging Viola tightly, she said, "You're welcome. And

you're right. She would've loved this place." Alexa kissed her cheek before moving off and letting others pay their respects.

The burial site was on the other side of a meadow. Some people with health issues took advantage of the caretaker's golf cart while most attendees walked.

When she reached the other side of the field, Jake and Margot Stanton King took turns hugging their daughter. Alexa and her parents were all wearing black suits and dark sunglasses. Each had a lapel pin of a gold crown with diamonds. It was a family trademark passed down to each male heir and family for generations.

"How are you, darling?"

Alexa lowered her sunglasses. "My heart is broken, Mom."

Her mother touched her shoulder. "I know, honey. We're so sorry."

"Lex, why don't you come back home with us? Take a few days to rest up and recuperate?"

"I can't, Dad. I have to finish packing up Tanya's apartment."

Her mother frowned. "Alexa, isn't there someone else who can do it?"

"No, Mom. I volunteered. The Singletons have enough on their plate back home with Tanya's brother still in the hospital recovering from surgery."

"I'm sorry he had to miss the funeral."

"We all are, Mom, but there was no way he was well enough to travel."

"Any word from Byron?"

Alexa's hands bunched into fists at her side. "No, and if he knows what's good for him, he'll stay away."

Jake frowned. "It seems strange that he's just disappeared without a trace."

"Well, after the police cleared him of any wrongdoing and the district attorney rejected the case, he decided to make himself scarce."

Margot rested her hand on Alexa's shoulder. "Honey, we know how you feel, but there's no proof."

"I've got plenty of text messages about their arguments and his temper, Mom."

"You know that Tanya never called the police on him, nor did she file a report. He also doesn't have a documented history of violence against his girlfriend. So even if you could produce the text messages, they'd never hold up against cross-examination. The defense will say you could've sent those messages from Tanya's phone."

Alexa blanched. "That's not true."

"It doesn't need to be true, Alexa. All it needs to do is introduce doubt to a jury about their authenticity."

That gave Alexa pause. "He can't get away with this. I don't care what it takes. I'll find a way to ensure Tanya's death wasn't in vain."

"You will be careful," her father warned. "I don't want you getting in over your head, Alexa. Suppose it wasn't an accident? Who knows what Byron could do if he felt cornered. The last thing we need is you to voice your theories on this publicly."

"If there is anything more to find, you let the police handle it," her mother cautioned.

When Alexa didn't readily agree, her father said, "Alexa."

"Okay, I hear you. I won't do anything on my own. I promise."

Her parents relaxed.

"I want you to take some time off work, Alexa."

"Dad, I'm fine."

"You've been working nonstop since she died, Alexa. You need some time to rest and regroup."

"No, I don't. I've got it under control."

Her father looked skeptical but agreed. "Okay, but you take it if you need it."

"I will," she promised.

Alexa's father, a retired intelligence officer for the Defense Intelligence Agency, cofounded J.M. King & Associates with his wife. Her mother headed up the legal side at the risk management firm in Washington, DC. After college graduation,

Alexa went to work there and rose in the ranks to senior cyber threat intelligence analyst. A third-generation corporate lawyer, Margot wanted her daughter to follow in her footsteps and those of her mother and grandmother, but Alexa chose her father's profession.

"I have to go." She kissed both parents. "I promised Tanya's landlord I'd be over in the morning with the movers. Most of her belongings will be donated to local missions and charities."

Jake squeezed her hand. "That's wonderful, sweetheart. Let us know if you need anything."

After their goodbyes, Alexa headed for the parking lot while her parents went to say goodbye to Tanya's family. She had almost reached her convertible Volkswagen Beetle when someone called her name. Recognizing the voice, she kept walking.

"Alexa, wait." The man beckoned. When she ignored him, he ran and jumped in front of her. "Please," Byron Monroe said, holding up his hands. "I just want to talk to you for a minute."

She stepped back. "We have nothing to say to each other. How dare you even be here," she hissed.

"I have every right to be here," he said indignantly. "Tanya was my girlfriend."

"Every right, huh? Is that why you're slinking around and weren't at the grave site?"

He shifted on his feet. His hands shoved into the pockets of his navy blue slacks. "I didn't want to upset the family."

She took in his haphazard suit and unshaven face. "Get out of my way, Byron."

When she went to step around him, Byron blocked her path.

"You must know I would never hurt Tanya—I loved her. We were going to get married. So why would I do her harm?"

"Spare me. That's the garbage you told yourself and my friend, but I'm not buying it." Alexa's expression turned menacing as she jabbed her index finger at his chest.

"I don't know what you're talking about."

"Tanya's death may have been labeled an accident, but we both know differently, don't we?" Alexa pressed, ignoring her parents' warnings. "She finally decides to leave you, and suddenly, she has an accident, trips down a flight of concrete steps, puts herself in a coma and eventually dies from her injuries?" She scoffed. "I don't think so."

Byron wiped his hand across his jaw in agitation. "I won't lie, we were arguing, and she tried to leave. I attempted to grab her arm, but she snatched it away from me, lost her balance and fell backward. It was an accident, Alexa—I swear."

She eyed him with contempt. "I'm not buying that. Save the innocent act for someone who doesn't know your history of losing your temper and taking it out on my best friend. I can't prove it now, but the truth will come out, Byron Monroe. When it does, I'll see that you pay for your crime, and I promise you that I won't stop until you're under the jail."

All pretense at civility was gone. When Byron leaned over, he was so close to Alexa that she smelled his cologne and breath, a cross between stale smoke, cheap liquor and cherry cough drops. She almost gagged.

Knowing that his proximity was an intimidation tactic, Alexa stood her ground.

"Regardless of what you think, I loved Tanya. I didn't kill her, and if I were you, I wouldn't continue digging up imaginary dirt—it's not wise."

"Is that a threat?"

A hint of a smile curled on his lips. Then, standing to his full height, he said, "Merely a warning from a concerned friend."

"We've never been friends. I tolerated you in my life because of Tanya. Nothing more."

"Everything okay over here?" a man called out.

They both turned in his direction.

"Yes, thank you," Alexa said sweetly before turning to Byron.

"If you think I'm going to cower in fear and let this drop, you don't know me."

Alexa shoved past him and strode to her car. Using the remote to unlock the door, she slid inside and started the car.

When she looked up after starting the vehicle, Byron was gone. Taking a moment, she composed herself.

"The nerve of him." Her heart was racing, and her hands shook with suppressed fury and grief. "I will not be intimidated by you, Byron," she vowed.

Her thoughts drifted back to her last conversation with Tanya. It was, of course, about an argument with Byron. She could tell her friend wasn't telling her the whole story. But just as Tanya began to open up, Alexa got called into an important meeting at work.

I'm sorry, Tanya, I'm late for a meeting.
Okay, but you'll call me back?
Yes, I promise.

Alexa had been swamped the rest of the day and into the evening. She'd missed several calls and text messages, two from Tanya. It was almost two o'clock in the morning when Alexa dragged herself through the front door of her condo. Kicking off her shoes, she padded across the room to the couch, where she collapsed in an exhausted heap. She realized almost fifteen minutes later that she'd never called Tanya back.

It's too late to call now. I'll do it first thing in the morning. It's Saturday, and we'll have plenty of time to catch up, she'd promised herself.

Alexa tried to call and text several times the next day but never reached Tanya. When she finally did get a call, it wasn't one she'd ever expected to receive. Instead, it was a police officer calling to inform her that her friend had had an accident and that she should get to the hospital. They had called Alexa because they couldn't reach Tanya's next of kin, and Alexa was listed as her emergency contact.

Hours later, Alexa's world wobbled on its axis at discovering that Tanya was in Intensive Care in a coma with severe head trauma. The prognosis wasn't good, and even worse, the only person with her at the time of the accident was her on-again, off-again boyfriend, Byron.

Flipping through Tanya's phone, police had discovered a

text message that Tanya drafted but never got to send. Chills shot across Alexa's body when she could finally read it herself.

You're right. People don't change, and Byron certainly isn't going to. So I finally broke up with him. But, of course, he insists that he'll win me back. Tanya was in the middle of saying that it would never happen when the text stopped, incomplete.

A horn honk jolted Alexa back to the present. Startled, she saw a car go by with two people waving goodbye.

Resting her head on the steering wheel, Alexa closed her eyes. "I failed you," she whispered into the quiet. "I'm sorry, Tanya."

During the five-hour drive back to Washington, DC, Alexa pondered her conversation with Byron. It made her skin crawl.

Just because I can't prove you're guilty doesn't mean you're innocent.

She disliked Byron with a vengeance and only tolerated his presence because of Tanya. He had never been worthy of her friend's love, and she liked him even less after noticing his mean streak. But Tanya had loved him and defended him regardless. To her peril.

The thought was like a dagger plunged straight into her chest. Fresh tears flowed, causing her vision to blur. Alexa angrily wiped them away with the back of her hand.

The pain closed in around Alexa. It gnawed at her, overtaking her waking hours and invading her sleep. It was the second time in her life that she had lost a friend to a violent encounter—first Shelley Porter, now Tanya. The guilt was so intense it was almost incapacitating.

On the other hand, the fact that Shelley hadn't died was a blessing, but it was bittersweet because her family had covertly blamed Alexa for the encounter in the park. Like she had control over some vagrant man trying to rob them in broad daylight.

Then, as the days turned into weeks and Shelley still hadn't recovered mentally, her mother, Carol Porter, showed up on the Kings' doorstep and accused Alexa of causing the whole incident and not protecting her daughter. Alexa denied any wrongdoing, and her parents had defended her against their neighbor's accusations.

"Mrs. Porter was right. I should forget about having close friends. I'm like a magnet for disaster." She gripped the steering wheel so tight that her fingers went numb.

Initially, Alexa felt certain the rift with Shelley would mend, but it had only grown. Eventually, the Porters packed up and moved without warning. The severed friendship with Shelley broke Alexa's heart, but losing Tanya to another violent act had exposed the deep wound festering inside. She was the common denominator, and if it weren't for their association with her, Shelley would be free from mental torment, and Tanya would be alive.

Tentacles of ice felt like they had snaked out and surrounded Alexa's heart, making it impossible for Alexa to deny the truth any longer.

"This was my fault."

Chapter Two

It was almost seven o'clock by the time she arrived at her condo on the Southwest Waterfront. After taking a shower, Alexa put on a pair of lounging pajamas and ordered takeout. While waiting, she sat on the couch and jotted down the action plan for the next day. She wasn't looking forward to being in charge of packing up Tanya's apartment, but she had promised Tanya's parents she would handle it.

Lighting a few candles, Alexa sat down for a quiet meal but moved the steak salad around in the mango wood salad bowl with the Moroccan blue-tiled inlay. It was a gift from her cousin, Zane King, and one of her favorites. Unfortunately, her appetite was as absent as a good night's sleep these days.

The cell phone ringing startled Alexa. Upon seeing the caller's name, she didn't bother with salutations when she picked up.

"I wish you were here with me."

"If it weren't traveling for work, you know I would be," her cousin replied. "I know today had to be rough for you."

"Yes, it was. I've realized that I don't need to have close friends."

"What? Lex, what are you talking about?"

"Bad things eventually happen to people that I love."

"First of all, that's merely a coincidence. Besides, I'm your best friend, and I'm still here."

"Yeah, but for how long, Zane?" she cried. "Plus, you're family. Maybe you all are immune."

"Lex, that's grief and fear talking. These are mere flukes, that's all. You aren't a magnet for danger. It's unfortunate, but sometimes bad things happen to good people. It's not your fault."

When she remained quiet, Zane said, "Quit ignoring me."

"I hear you, Z."

"You say you do, but do you believe it?"

"I had a run-in with Byron," she said, changing the subject.

"What? Why?"

"He didn't take too kindly to me ignoring him and refused to leave until he had convinced me of his innocence. I told him I didn't buy his act for a second and that I'd find a way to make him pay for Tanya's death."

"Easy, cousin. Don't underestimate that man. He could be dangerous."

"I know, but I'm not about to let him get away with anything, Zane. Tanya is gone because of his violent nature."

"We don't know that for sure."

Her eyebrows shot upward. "Zane—"

"Wait, hear me out before you jump all over me. Look, I agree with you, Alexa. Byron Monroe is bad news. I'm merely suggesting that you tread lightly. We can't prove that Tanya's death wasn't an accident, and you can't convict anyone of murder due to a feeling."

"Quit worrying. I promised Mom and Dad that I would be careful and will."

Zane audibly sighed. "Good. Hey, I've got to run. I've got an early meeting. Keep me posted on how things are going, okay?"

"I will," Alexa agreed before hanging up.

IT HAD BEEN three weeks since the funeral and clearing out of Tanya's apartment. The more days ticked by, the worse Alexa became. Sleep was a foreign concept. She practically lived at work and survived on bottled water and protein bars. But the one thing that provided Alexa with a modicum of peace was laps in the condo's swimming pool. It was the only time when her mind was at ease. It was her coping mechanism.

One night after work, Alexa was about to go swimming when her father called.

"Hey, Dad," she said as she maneuvered into her suit. "What's up?"

"We have to talk, honey."

Two things tipped her off this would not be a social call—her father's gruff voice and the fact that he placed her on speakerphone. Not having time for beating around the bush, Alexa jumped right in.

"Okay, what do you two need to discuss?"

"You, Lex," her mother replied. "We're worried about you."

"I don't know why."

"Then allow me to clarify," her father replied. "You haven't been home for a family dinner in forever, you're working a minimum of fifty hours a week, and from what I hear, you look like you haven't slept in ages. I won't even mention the mini meltdown you had at work."

Alexa was shocked, but that quickly drifted into anger. "What, are you keeping tabs on me? I don't need anyone trying to micromanage me, Dad."

"Alexa, that's not what your father is doing, and you know it. You're merely deflecting because everything he's said is true."

"It may be true, but I can handle myself."

"I should've insisted on this weeks ago." Her father sighed. "Alexa, you need to take a leave of absence and get yourself together."

"Dad, that's crazy. I don't need—"

"You know what we're dealing with at work. I need you operating at one hundred percent, Alexa."

"I haven't dropped one ball nor had a decline in my performance."

"Yet," he countered. "Something could happen at any time.

That's not a risk I'm willing to take from any employee—especially not my daughter."

When they ended the call, Alexa was livid. Snatching up her bag, she slammed out of her condo and strode toward the elevator. Jamming her finger on the down button, Alexa paced in circles while waiting.

"I can't believe he benched me. Like I can't handle myself," she snapped, and took the steps down to the fitness center instead. She pushed the door open and almost slammed it off its hinges. Yanking off her clothes, Alexa tossed them on a lounge chair and dived into the cool water.

Swimming laps, Alexa lost count of how many revolutions she did. She continued until all the hurt, anger, guilt, pain and sadness had left her body, and her muscles ached with exertion.

Hovering weightless in the water, Alexa let her mind go blank and floated. Nothing mattered except the comforting silence and the next breath. Not just to sustain her life but to honor Tanya's.

When Alexa emerged from the water thirty minutes later, her skin was wrinkled like a prune, but she felt rejuvenated and lighter than she had in weeks.

"Dad was right. I'm in no shape to continue like nothing is wrong." Alexa hoisted herself out of the pool. "It's time to stop moving through life and reacting to things that happen. From now on, I have to get proactive," she said with conviction. "Everyone has a God-given talent. It's time I found mine."

ALEXA STOOD AT her parents' front door, her finger hovering over the doorbell.

"Once I do this, there's no going back," she said aloud.

Alexa had spent the last three weeks at the Serenity Wellness Center in San Jose, Costa Rica. It was a pristine white compound in the middle of a lush rainforest. It had exceeded her expectations. At the retreat, Alexa had spent the entire stay surrounded by professionals dedicated to creating a safe, welcoming environment that encouraged their guests to restore their minds, bodies and souls.

There, Alexa met Dr. Marena Dash-McKendrick, a biochemist from North Carolina. They gelled instantly and promised each other to keep in touch.

Another incredible outcome of her time at Serenity was that Alexa had discovered her purpose. It was the reason why she had come straight from the airport to her parents' without delay. Now that she had a direction, she was eager to begin her new life.

Alexa greeted her parents and eagerly discussed her trip. She answered questions and gave them gifts she had purchased on one of the group outings to town.

Now she sat perched on the edge of her favorite leather armchair in her father's office doing her best to summon the courage to jump into the abyss without a parachute.

Alexa laid out her plan in detail because Margot and Jake King were laser-focused when it came to setting the groundwork and laying out all the facts.

Once done with her well-thought-out argument, what concerned Alexa the most was that her parents just sat there staring at her in utter silence. Both were on the couch across from her with their hands folded in their laps.

After more painful seconds, Alexa felt compelled to demolish the silence.

"Dad, I know how it sounds, but I'm not crazy."

Jake leaned forward, his elbows resting just above his knees. "I didn't say you were, sweetheart."

"Well, I was thinking it," Margot snapped before turning to her daughter. "You want to be a bodyguard? Alexa, this is insane, not to mention dangerous."

"Not just a bodyguard. I did the research," she added. "I'll be a close protection officer."

Margot shook her head. "Oh, great, that's even riskier."

"I know, Mom, but it's what I want to do—what I have to do."

"Is it? Alexa, I know you feel guilty about losing Tanya, but you can't continue blaming yourself."

"It's not just about her, Mom. It's about protecting the Brendas in the world."

Margot glanced between her daughter and husband and then threw her hands up. "Am I supposed to know what that means?"

"Brenda was a woman at the retreat. She was in a horrible relationship that almost turned violent. It got to the point where she said she didn't even recognize herself anymore. There were so many similarities between her and Tanya." Alexa's voice trembled. "Family and friends begged her to leave him, but it wasn't until he threatened to kill her that Brenda found the courage to leave.

"It took a lot for her to tell her story. The counselor said that was why she founded Serenity. She felt that everyone needed the chance to open up. To release the pain holding them hostage and stealing their voice. To transform themselves no matter their circumstances. To heal. That's when I knew what my calling had to be."

"Alexa, there must be a better way to devote yourself to a cause that doesn't include peril. Why not volunteer at a shelter, or start a nonprofit? There are a million ways you can make a difference without risking your safety."

Jake turned to his wife. "Can you give us a minute, love?"

"Only if you plan on talking some sense into our daughter."

He squeezed her hand. "Please, Margot."

Nodding, she turned and strode out of the room, slamming the door behind her.

"I know Mom is upset, but I'm not changing my mind about this, Dad."

Her father stood and walked over to his desk. "I can see that, Lex. But what I need to know is if you have thought this through." He sat on the edge of the table and crossed his arms.

"I mean good and thoroughly through, Alexa. This isn't an easy path you're choosing. It's dangerous, and to become an expert, you'll have to know a great deal about many subjects. This profession is… We're talking life-and-death, but also risk assessment and mitigation, tactical, combat, movement safety—"

"Dad, we work in risk and threat assessment now. I know this job has much to learn, and I'll need specialized training."

"There's so much more to it than that, Lex. First, you'll be putting yourself in harm's way to protect someone else." Jake studied his daughter. "Do you understand the gravity of that choice? Hundreds of things could go wrong for each one that goes right in the field. Are those odds you can live with?"

Chapter Three

Alexa stood resolute in front of her father's desk. "I'm not changing my mind, Dad. I want to be an executive protection specialist to protect women who can't protect themselves. It's what I want to do. It's what I *have* to do."

Jake pinched the bridge of his nose. His stern expression echoed the gravity of his only child's decision.

"If you're sure, Alexa, and you're one hundred percent committed—"

"I am."

He shook his head. "I guess I shouldn't be surprised. When you were at the university library, you almost made that Peeping Tom eat a book on constitutional law when he got fresh with your dorm mate."

"Well, he needed to study that book anyway," she pointed out.

Unable to help himself, Jake chuckled. "Okay, Alexa. If you're dead set on this path, all my resources will be at your disposal. I have an old friend who runs a training academy with his son and a few other buddies who can help. They each have decades of experience, so you'll have the best training available."

She visibly relaxed. "Thank you, Dad. And I'm sorry about leaving you short one senior analyst."

"Don't worry about it, honey. I'll make all the arrangements."

She rushed to hug her father. "Thank you."

He returned the embrace. "The only thanks I need is you to be safe, sweetheart." He glanced into her eyes. "Do you hear me?"

"Yes," she said tearfully.

He kissed her cheek. "Good. Now I have to talk to your mother. Which isn't going to be easy." He sighed heavily.

"No, this is my decision, Dad. I'll be the one to talk to Mom."

Alexa found her mother outside by the pool in her favorite chaise longue. As was her habit, she sat by her mother's feet at its end.

The lights were on in the pool and around the perimeter. They both sat transfixed as the nighttime shadows and the shimmering blue water vied for dominance.

"I know you're worried."

"That would be an understatement," her mother murmured, never looking up. "Alexa, this is dangerous. Anything could happen."

"I know, Mom. But I can't ignore this anymore. It's eating away at my soul. I wasn't there for Shelley or Tanya. Not when it mattered. I want to help other women feel protected and safe, at least when they're in my care."

Margot turned to face her daughter. Alexa saw that she had been crying. There was also undisguised anguish in her eyes. Her mother's pain tore at her heart.

"Why is this your cross to bear, Alexa? All this guilt is misplaced. What happened to Shelley was an unforeseen event caused by a desperate man's ill-considered actions. Tanya also had a choice to make, and she made it. To her detriment. You aren't to blame for either incident."

"Mom, I'm not trying to hurt either of you—"

"I get it. You have to follow your heart. Your tenacity is something I've always admired about you, Alexa. You've always been a fighter and willing to help anyone that needed it. And as worried as I am, I know you'll do well. You're my daughter, after all."

That garnered a smile from Alexa. "I learned everything I know from my mother."

"Not everything," Margot chuckled before reaching for Alexa's hand. "Whenever you're obstinate and set in your ways, you remind me of your father."

She leaned in and hugged her mother tightly. "I love you, Mom."

"I love you, my darling daughter. I couldn't be prouder of the woman you've become. Promise me that you'll be careful and return in one piece."

"I'll do my best."

WHEN SHE GOT HOME, the first thing Alexa did was call Zane and bring him up to speed on her decision.

"I couldn't be happier for you. When do you leave?"

"What?" Alexa lay back on her bed and crossed one leg over the other. "I thought you'd try to talk me out of it, too."

"For what? It wouldn't make a difference anyway. I'm nowhere near as persuasive in arguing as your parents, so why waste my time swimming upstream?"

Alexa couldn't fault her cousin's reasoning. Not when it was true.

She went upstairs and began brushing her teeth and prepping for bed.

"You realize you're putting a damper on my social calendar, don't you? How am I supposed to hang out with my best friend if she's in— Where are you going again?"

"Colorado." She paused while rinsing her mouth. "Dad said that his buddy James Riker Sr. and his son own a facility in Pagosa Springs."

"Uh-huh. For how long?"

"Twelve weeks."

"You can't be serious," Zane complained. "Three months, Lex? That's insane."

"It's going to take time. There's so much I have to learn.

Functional movement, first aid, several martial arts disciplines, defensive and offensive evasive maneuvers—"

"While that all sounds very impressive, I'm still going to miss you."

"I'll miss you, too."

"I can't believe that Uncle Jake is arranging all of this. Who doesn't he know?"

"Seriously," Alexa agreed. "I must admit to being surprised myself. I knew Dad had a lot of connections and old military buddies, but I never knew how extensive the list was until now."

"I'm sure his contacts will be helpful later," Zane reasoned. "Count your lucky stars. You're getting the VIP treatment."

"Zane, I don't want anyone going easy on me because I'm Jake King's daughter. I plan on earning my place on my own merits."

"I hear what you're saying, but don't be crazy. It's a highly competitive world you're about to enter. You'll need all the help you can get."

"That's true."

"Lex, I'm proud of you. You're daring to envision a whole new life for yourself. You'll be making a difference in the world. Don't get me wrong, you were excellent in cybersecurity, but I'd always felt that was Uncle Jake's choice for your life and not your own."

"I loved my job, Zane. I'm not leaving because I'm unhappy with it. I'm going because I believe this will be more rewarding for me."

"I'm sure it will, Alexa. I can't wait to hear about how it's going."

"I promise to keep you in the loop on my progress."

"You'd better."

After hanging up, Alexa set her cell phone on the nightstand. Then, staring at the ceiling, she placed her arms behind her head. This was such a significant change in her life. She was excited, but she was terrified, too. Failure wasn't an option. She would go all in, and she would complete the program.

"Well, Tanya. Neither of us saw this coming."

IN THE LATE AFTERNOON, Alexa arrived at the Phalanx Training Academy in Pagosa Springs, Colorado. It was a seven-hour flight from Washington, DC, with a layover in Denver and an hour's ride from the Durango Regional Airport to the southwestern town. The academy had hired a driver to pick her up, for which she was grateful since it allowed her to stretch out after the long flight.

Upon sign-in, a young woman escorted her to James Riker's office.

When they entered, he was engrossed in paperwork.

"Ah, you must be Alexa King."

"Yes, I am."

James came around his desk and hugged her, which caught Alexa off guard.

"It's a pleasure to meet you finally. You can't imagine how your father goes on and on about you. I tell you, Jake would talk a dead man to death if you let him." He winked.

"I'm afraid Dad doesn't talk much about his military buddies other than they're his brothers for life."

"That we are. And don't you mind us old dogs. Once we get settled somewhere, we seldom visit each other, no matter how much we talk about it."

Alexa laughed. He reminded her a lot of her father. They were tall, muscular, good-looking men with infectious smiles, rich brown skin and salt-and-pepper hair that was cut close.

James took Alexa's luggage and ushered her outside to a nearby Jeep.

"Come on, let's get you settled, then I'll show you around. You'll meet my son, JJ, later. He's in the middle of teaching a class. Normally, we have a full house, but our summer session isn't as busy. He teaches several free classes if time permits. Come on, I'll give you a tour."

Alexa barely got in an "okay" before James was on to the next topic. She listened to him provide background on the academy while they drove. He reminded her of her father in many ways, just more talkative.

"We have about three hundred acres total, with a few lakes, the national forest nearby and spectacular views of the San Juan Mountains."

"It's beautiful here but kind of remote."

"That's by design," he replied. "At Phalanx, we teach many courses in ninety days. Executive protection officers put their life on the line for their principal." He turned to her. "That's the person that you're protecting. Depending on the contract, that may not be your actual client."

"I understand."

"Anyway, you must know the job's practical, functional and technical aspects. They must become instinctual, Alexa. Our reputation is without reproach because we hire the best instructors in the field, surpassing what other companies teach their students and offering continuing education to our graduates."

"I've read up on your company. You all have an impeccable track record, Mr. Riker."

"Please, call me James, or Jim."

"Okay. I wanted to say thank you for taking me on as a student on short notice."

"When your father called, I admit I was surprised by his request."

"Why? Because I'm a woman?"

"No, the number of women in executive protection is rising. It's because close protection isn't for everyone, Alexa. It takes a unique person to handle the job. It's dangerous work and solitary, with extended hours, not many holidays off or visits home."

Finally, he turned and pinned her with a stare. "You need to ask yourself if this is what you want to do in life and be clear on your answer."

"I understand."

"I don't know that you do, Alexa. I'm asking if you are willing to turn your life upside down for this program. Are you willing to put your mind and body through pain, discomfort and being pushed to the limit of what you think you can handle? This program is more than just learning new skills and carrying a weapon. It's about mind over matter. Realizing that you can do things you never thought you'd be able to do, being responsible for another human being's safety and well-being. And most importantly, ask yourself if you're willing to take a bullet for your principal if it comes down to that? Are you willing to lay down your life to protect someone else, Alexa?"

Chapter Four

After their talk, James drove Alexa to her lodgings. They pulled down a dirt road, the only one Alexa had seen for some time. It led to a circular drive and a small log cabin surrounded by trees. The red cedar home had a red tin roof with modest landscaping.

"This isn't too remote for you, is it?"

Alexa jumped down from the Jeep and looked around. The mountain vista was majestic, with not one wrong view from any direction.

James pointed toward the back of the cabin. "There's a lake just a few minutes' walk down that path. It's well-stocked, so there are a few poles and a tackle box in the shed if you're an angler. There's also an ATV. You know how to drive one of those, don't you?"

"Yes, I do."

"Great. We're having dinner at our place tonight if you're up to it?"

"Oh, yes, of course. Thank you."

"It'll be after JJ's last class. The ATV's out back. You can ride up to my office at about seven."

"Thanks, I'll see you then," Alexa replied, escorting him out.

Alexa gazed around the log cabin. It was an open floor plan with many windows to let in the natural light. The living room had a fireplace made from river rock. A well-worn maple-brown leather couch with two big pillows with an Aztec design was right across from it. A coffee table and two chairs with a side table completed the space. The decor was homey and welcoming. The wood dining room table had six chairs and was right under the window, giving guests a magnificent view of the mountains. Photographs of Native Americans were displayed proudly on the beamed walls in color and black-and-white.

Expecting the kitchen to be understated, Alexa was pleasantly surprised to find it was high-end and well furnished. The countertops were black-green granite with white and gold veins across the surface. A stainless-steel KitchenAid gas stove with five burners took up one side of the kitchen with the built-in microwave and oven nearby. In addition, there was a coffee machine, an air fryer and a slow cooker.

She ran her hand over the beverage brewing system before peeking into the metal drawer underneath that housed apple cider, coffee and tea pods.

"I can't wait to use you," she said dreamily.

The stainless-steel farmhouse kitchen sink was under the window.

"Eye candy. Just what I need while I'm doing dishes."

Next, she headed to the bathroom and gasped when she saw a large corner Jacuzzi tub in the same river rock as the fireplace. Half the wall behind it was glass. There was a separate shower, double sinks and a toilet area.

The cabin had two bedrooms that were similar in size on opposite sides of the house. Both had en suite bathrooms, a sliding door leading to a wraparound porch, window seats and huge walk-in closets.

Going back to the other bedroom, Alexa unpacked and took a shower. The hot water beating her back like a drum solo felt heavenly on her tired muscles.

Alexa chose jean shorts and a short-sleeve T-shirt to wear for dinner.

She glanced at her watch. She still had two hours before dinner. "Good a time as any to look around."

She shoved the phone in her pocket and went to retrieve the quad keys. Alexa had always been good with geography, so she confidently followed the path and her instincts to return to the main building. When she passed a break room, she spotted a refrigerator case with drinks and healthy snacks. Thirsty, Alexa retrieved an iced tea and continued down the hallway.

Rounding a corner, Alexa was about to enter James's office but stopped short at hearing raised voices.

"Since when is Phalanx a vacation destination?"

"What are you talking about?"

"Dad, I saw Jake King's note about doing him a favor and getting his daughter enrolled."

"JJ, he was talking about—"

"So, Alexa King has nothing better to do than disrupt our lives by signing up for our program she'll drop out of after two days? Can't we give her a tour and a T-shirt and be done with it? These weekend warrior wannabes are a waste of time and space."

"Don't be rude, JJ," his father snapped. "Alexa isn't here to take up space. Jake was very clear on his daughter's intentions. He assured me that she would take our training seriously, and I believe him."

"Well, I don't. We haven't had a woman complete our training program since…in forever," James Andrew Riker Jr. finished abruptly. "She could get hurt or, worse, cause someone else to be injured while she's out proving to herself that she can cut it."

"Nonsense," James dismissed. "I've met her. You haven't. She's serious about being here and deserves a chance to prove herself. So she stays. End of story. And the favor you mentioned that Jake asked me for was to *not* treat Alexa any differently than anyone else. She must earn her spot here. If she doesn't he expects her to get cut just like any other student."

His son crossed his arms. "I say you're making a big mistake. I read her application. It's obvious that Daddy gives her whatever she wants. She works for his company, went to the best schools and was a military brat."

"So were you," James pointed out.

JJ's expression darkened. "She's nothing like me, and I'm not going easy on her just because. It may be a moot point anyway. Mark my words, she'll wash out within a week and go crawling back to her fancy condo in Washington, DC."

Alexa reared back as though she had been stung by a bee. Her chest rose and fell with the pent-up energy she held in check. It was all she could do not to barge into James's office and demand his obnoxious and rude son retract every haughty accusation he'd slung her way.

Angry didn't scratch the surface of how she felt. *How dare he!*

She had no clue what she'd done to deserve this man's venom, but Alexa was determined to shove her diploma under his sanctimonious nose when she graduated.

Hearing both voices coming closer, Alexa rushed down the corridor. Unsure where to go next, she was about to head outside when another sound caught her attention. Following the noise, Alexa opened the door and went into a studio. There were several older adults in a circle on the mat. They were sparring, so she hung back not to be intrusive.

An instructor was teaching them an evasive technique. The man was wearing a protective face mask along with protective gear. His voice was calm and encouraging as he explained the moves to the students and studied their movements as they practiced.

Spotting a row of bleachers in the corner, Alexa took a seat. The man seemed kind and patient as each person had a turn.

"There seem to be some trainers here that can be professional and courteous. Shocking," Alexa snarked.

When a buzzer rang, the man announced that the class was over. The group thanked him and dissipated as another man entered from a side door and strode onto the mat. Alexa observed him with curiosity.

After patting a few people on the back, the teacher walked over to where the newcomer was standing. He was also wearing a protective helmet over his face. Some participants filed out of the room, saying their hellos to Alexa as they passed.

A woman stopped in front of Alexa. "Are you joining our class?"

"She's not old enough," a man said patiently from behind. "This is a senior citizens' self-defense class," he explained. "She doesn't look like she has an AARP card yet."

"That's true," Alexa chuckled. "I'm here for another training program, I just heard the commotion and came in to check it out."

"What do you think it'll be today?" one of the seniors asked his buddy before sitting down on the bench next to Alexa. "Sticks or swords?"

His friend shrugged. "Beats me, but it's always good. My money's on Andrew."

"Oh, great. More of that invisible money you love to bet with."

A loud crash caught her attention. Glancing up, she saw the two fighting with long sticks.

A woman nudged Alexa. "Looks like it's bōjutsu."

"What?"

"It's Japanese for staff technique. It's a type of stick fighting."

The woman had to speak loudly because the instructors were going full throttle, and the noise was deafening. Fixated, Alexa watched in awe as one man used his pole to sweep the other's feet from under him. There were several passes before they threw down the sticks and started grappling. When the man on the bottom finally tapped out, his opponent helped him up. Taking off their masks, they slapped each other on the back before walking over to join the crowd.

Alexa noted that both men were tall, and very attractive. One looked like an older, heavier version of the actor Scott Eastwood. The new guy was Black, had a muscular physique, arresting brown eyes, a mole on his cheek just under his right eye, and a scar from his bottom lip to his chin. Alexa found herself wondering how he got it. She guessed that he was either military or a former serviceman by how he carried himself. Either way, he was swoon-worthy, and she would have had to be incapacitated not to have an immediate response to his physical attraction.

She tried not to stare, but at this point, Alexa felt it would've been easier to outrun a bear while drenched in honey.

Eventually, the man's gaze connected with hers from across the room. When it did, his demeanor shifted so fast it caught Alexa off guard.

Unprepared for his outward hostility, she choked on her tea, dissolved into a fit of coughing, and then spilled her drink down the front of her clothing. She yelped as the cold liquid met her skin.

Everyone in the room turned and stared. Including the man she was just gawking at.

Though struggling to breathe, Alexa stood there dumbfounded. From the hostile way he was staring at her, and the similarity in looks, this guy had to be James's son.

Chapter Five

Mortified, she bounded out of the room and down the hallway to the break room. Grabbing some paper towels, Alexa wet them and vigorously dabbed at the front of her shirt.

What a jerk, she mused. *One minute he's smiling, and the next he's glaring like I spit in his coffee.*

"You must be Alexa King."

Alexa whirled around to find the rude man in question standing inside the doorway with his arms crossed. Despite just having had a rigorous workout, he was as relaxed as she was flustered. A towel was draped over his neck, with sweat still glistening on his face.

Well, if he thinks he's going to intimidate me, he's in for a disappointment, she said to herself. *He may be cute, but that doesn't give him a pass to be ill-mannered.*

Giving up on the shirt, Alexa threw the mound of wet paper in the trash and turned to face him like she was going into battle.

"And you must be James Riker Jr. Or should I call you JJ?"

"Andrew is fine. It's my middle name. Outside of family, no one calls me that."

He pushed off from the wall and came forward. He extended his hand. "It's a pleasure to meet you, Miss King."

Her arms stayed at her side. "I find that hard to believe given your behavior earlier," she replied with a calm she didn't feel.

That gave him pause. He lowered his hand. "Have we met?"

He may look like his father, but it was obvious he had not inherited James's easygoing nature.

"No, we haven't. Which is the reason why you dragging my name through the mud to your father was baffling."

For the first time, Andrew looked uncomfortable. "My apologies. I didn't mean for anyone to overhear."

"Interesting that you apologized for being overheard, and not what you said. Look, I don't know what your problem is, or why you've painted me with a broad brush. Frankly, I don't care. I'm not easily intimidated, Mr. Riker. Nor do I cower on command. I'm here to gain what's up there," she said, pointing to his head. "Not your approval."

"Fair enough. But I admit that I'm surprised to find you at Phalanx, Miss King. Based on your application, you don't seem the type that's interested in this kind of career."

"It would appear that you have a certain image in your mind of who I am, and what I would or wouldn't do. I can't imagine what's caused this fixation."

"Fixation?" Andrew laughed heartily. "I certainly wouldn't call it that. No, you just remind me of someone I know. She talked a good game, but in the end, she didn't have what it took for this line of work. My guess is neither will you."

"Ah. Biased and closed-minded." Her smile was as sweet as cotton candy. "Why should I be surprised based on your rudeness."

He returned the smile. Not in the least ruffled by her putdown. "Good to know. I see we're off to a great start."

"Thanks to you."

Before he could say more, Alexa turned on her heel and strode out of the room.

Andrew stood there a few moments, feeling like he'd just been dismissed. He had to admit that he was surprised that Alexa overheard his discussion with his dad. That was unexpected, and he chided himself for losing his temper at work. It was unprofessional and never should have happened. But he had seen her picture, and it had sparked a memory that wouldn't let go.

Alexa King was sure of herself. That much was obvious. And clearly, she wasn't overly sensitive because she had gotten angry instead of dissolving into tears. Andrew appreciated her spunk, but from the moment he read through her application and saw her picture, Alexa had rubbed him the wrong way. She reminded him of someone he would have preferred never to think about again. Despite that, meeting Alexa for the first time was startling. Andrew was surprised by her beauty and how she carried herself. Her photo had not done her justice.

Alexa was taller than most women he had met, with long, wavy hair that framed her face. There was a faint scar on her left cheek that made him wonder at the cause. Alexa had dimples and bright, welcoming eyes.

Not exactly welcoming, he corrected himself. Her gaze when he caught up with her in the break room was as brittle as frozen metal. Andrew could've kicked himself for stirring up this beehive. "Why did you have to look like *her*?" he groaned. Maybe Alexa would do them both a favor and quit by the week's end. *That would put us both out of our misery*, he reasoned. A man could hope.

ALEXA GRITTED HER TEETH. She was so angry at Andrew Riker that she couldn't think straight. She had returned to the cabin and pondered not going to the welcome dinner, but Alexa had given her word. And once given, she never rescinded it.

Decision made, Alexa changed into a pair of brown linen trousers, a plain white oxford shirt that was open at the neck and a pair of black block-heeled sandals.

Dainty gold earrings with a matching necklace completed the semidressy look. Next, she swept her hair up into a high bun. If she was going into battle with Andrew Riker, she wanted to look good doing it.

Confident and relaxed, she headed out. Not wanting to arrive windblown, and with bugs stuck in various places, she took her time driving the all-terrain vehicle.

THE RIKER RESIDENCE was a combination of wood and stone. Alexa marveled at its natural beauty and how large it was. She figured that it was at least six thousand square feet. A wraparound porch on the front, several rocking chairs and a two-seater swing allowed for plenty of conversation while admiring the mountainous views. By the time she parked the ATV and was heading up the steps to the porch, Andrew was already on the top step waiting.

"Welcome, Miss King. I hope you're hungry. Dad has never mastered just cooking for a small group, so there's a lot."

Confused by his congenial behavior, Alexa made an effort to reciprocate. "Thank you. And yes, I am."

"Mom died two years ago," Andrew explained. "I was hoping that Dad would take more time off, but he did the opposite. Instead, he threw himself into work and hasn't come up for air yet."

"I'm sorry to hear about your mother."

"Thanks." Andrew motioned toward the front door. "It's been rough, but we've done our best to be there for each other."

"I, um, have to ask. What's with the complete turnaround? Earlier you were—"

"Rude? Horrible? Loud and wrong?"

"Keep going, I'll stop you when I disagree."

He chuckled. "I deserve that."

An awkward silence crept into their conversation. Alexa struggled for something to say. "Do you have any siblings?"

"No, I'm an only child."

"Me, too," Alexa confessed. "You know when it's hardest to bear?"

"Holidays?"

"Yep. That's when I miss having brothers and sisters. Though I don't mind being spoiled," she joked.

Andrew stared at her for a moment. His expression darkened slightly, but it was enough for Alexa to notice.

"There you two are," James yelled from the kitchen. "I was beginning to think the guys and I would have to eat this super-scrumptious meal ourselves."

The lighthearted moment restored, Andrew looked heavenward. "He loves to brag about his cooking like some seasoned pitmaster. He just started grilling and smoking meats last year."

They went into the kitchen and greeted Andrew's father.

"I hope you two are hungry. Got enough to feed a bear."

Glancing at Alexa, Andrew mouthed the words *I told you* before saying, "Can't wait. It smells amazing in here."

The meal stretched out on the granite countertops was massive. There were six side dishes: smoked brisket, chicken and sausages, corn on the cob, potato salad, coleslaw and yeast rolls.

"Dad?" Andrew said in shock. "What in the world? You said a little something."

"Well, I got to grilling, and the grilling bug bit me, so I kept adding more stuff. Finally, I decided I'd better invite everybody." He grinned.

A woman came into the kitchen carrying an armful of folded napkins and a tablecloth. "You know how he gets once there's a burr under his saddle."

Alexa had to hide her smile as the older woman nudged past James to get several trivets from a drawer.

"Esther, this is Alexa. Alexa, this is my housekeeper and boss, Esther." James winked.

"Nice to meet you, Alexa, and don't mind him," she said, inclining her head toward James. Esther turned and handed the linens to Andrew. "Would you take care of the table while I finish up in the kitchen?"

"I'll help you," Alexa replied, and followed him into the dining room.

They worked as a team to set the table.

"Your housekeeper seems like she's time enough for the two of you."

"Esther is wonderful," Andrew agreed. "She has us toeing the line for sure. She's been with our family for decades and is like a second mother to me."

"Do you normally have students here for dinner?"

"We have a big dinner on the first night. We feel it's important that the students should get to know each other. You all will be working as a team for the next ninety days."

"Oh, I'm surprised you're not hoping I drop out long before that."

Slightly embarrassed at her guessing his thoughts, he said, "Being in the protection business isn't about being a lone wolf. It's about teamwork. Your team has to trust you, and it's the same for you. There are many moving parts, Alexa. Each must function independently but also as part of the whole. That's how you keep your principal, team and yourself safe."

"That makes sense."

When they were done, she followed Andrew back into the kitchen to help bring out the food.

James and Andrew were at ease entertaining and being cordial to their guests. Including Alexa there were twelve students, a lead trainer and several instructors who came to dinner. It was a loud, laughter-filled affair. The dinner was buffet style, so some were seated at the dining table, while others grabbed spots in the family room.

Being the only female student at dinner didn't intimidate or bother Alexa. Instead, she worked the room, introducing herself to each classmate, sizing them up as she went. Most were cordial and welcoming, but there were a few of the guys who weren't overly thrilled that she was there. One of them, Tate Bannon, was overtly hostile.

"You can't be serious," he said when she introduced herself. "You really think you're cut out for executive protection?" He practically laughed in her face.

"That's what I'm here to find out," she said, looking him straight in the eye. "This is a marathon, not a sprint, Bannon. And I plan to cross the finish line just like everyone else here."

"Wanna bet?" he remarked under his breath.

Alexa moved off before she said something to Tate that she would regret.

She wasn't about to make it easy for Andrew Riker to dismiss her. For whatever reason, both had assumed she wasn't cut out for the job. Which meant that she would do whatever it took to prove them wrong. *Loud and wrong*, she added for good measure.

LATER THAT NIGHT, Andrew sat on the wooden swing on the back porch. He was absentmindedly swaying the rocker with the heel of his foot.

His thoughts drifted to Alexa. Despite their rocky start, Andrew tried to make up for his bad behavior earlier that day. He was engaging, sought her out on several occasions to ensure she was enjoying the party and offered to drive her home in his Jeep so she wouldn't have to drive the ATV at night, but she had declined, assuring him that she would be fine.

"Glad to see you've mended fences with Alexa."

He turned to see his father coming through the screen door. James leaned on one of the porch's support beams and observed his son.

"I wouldn't exactly call it that."

"One thing you'd better call it is finished," his father warned. "There's enough to worry about with the training and coursework. I need everyone focused and with a clear head, so no one gets hurt—that includes you, Andrew."

Whenever his father called him Andrew, he meant business.

"I know," he responded. "Business is business, Dad. I'm not about to jeopardize that for any reason."

"Good. Then keep whatever hang-up you've got about Alexa to yourself. I don't want it affecting your work, or her learning."

"It's not a hang-up," Andrew countered. "But come on, Dad. Don't tell me you don't see the resemblance."

"What I *see* is you stirring up trouble where there is none. And that's not something we can afford."

After a few moments, Esther joined them on the porch.

"It's a beautiful night," she breathed.

"Yes, it is," James replied, stepping away from the railing. "How about a stroll? Something tells me that my son here could use some alone time."

Andrew knew his father was right. He would do his job and train Alexa just like any other student. If she decided it was too much to handle and quit, that would be one less potential crisis later.

Chapter Six

The next few weeks were grueling for Alexa. She loved every minute. After the preliminary introductory coursework, filling out a guard card application and other required documents, they watched videos on executive protection, legalities and government policies. From there it was straight into hands-on and practical applications. An entire world opened up before Alexa, and she embraced it wholeheartedly.

That afternoon's sessions were all about strength, agility and endurance. Their instructor drilled them on functional movements to help improve flexibility and speed.

Alexa's muscles were sore when they were finished, but she kept it to herself since no one complained about their workout.

One of her classmates waved. "See you tomorrow, Amazon."

Alexa waved back. Everyone in class had a nickname, and Alexa's was Amazon. She was hoping it would wear off after a few days, but no such luck. It had stuck, so she embraced it. Upon reaching the cabin, the first thing she did was run a hot bath. Scouring the linen closet, Alexa almost whooped for joy when she found another box of Epsom salts. While the water was running, she called her parents to catch up.

"I was beginning to think you'd forgotten our telephone number," Jake teased.

"I'm sorry, Dad. It's been hectic this week. And we had functional movements and hand-to-hand combat training all afternoon. I'm spent."

"Did you have Dixon?"

"Yes." She grimaced and instinctively massaged her arm.

"He's a machine. He's going to put you through your paces, Lex."

"I can see that," she grumbled. "I'm running an Epsom salt bath as we speak. It's the third one this week."

Her father laughed. "Get used to it, Booba. There'll be plenty more in your immediate future."

She grinned at hearing the nickname that only he used. "I know, Dad. Gotta take the bad with the good, right?"

"You got it, kiddo."

"Speaking of much-needed pain relief, I have to run. My tub is almost full. Say hi to Mom for me. I'm sorry I missed her."

Jake chuckled. "She will be, too, sweetheart. And take it easy. You're the only daughter we've got."

"Don't worry. I plan to return in one piece."

A WEEK LATER, Andrew was in his office working on a lesson plan when his father came in and sat down.

"Hey, Dad. What's up?"

"Just wanted to check in and see how things are going with Alexa?"

Leaning back in his chair, Andrew crossed his arms. "She's doing great. Her firearms instructor said she's at the top of the class and is an excellent marksman." He caught himself. "Markswoman. She's inside the eight rings every time. She's got the aptitude for mastering the fundamentals, and Alexa is acing all her written exams and holding her own in the simulations."

James nodded. "But?"

Andrew frowned. "But something is holding Alexa back. The mechanics are there, but the passion isn't. Her focus is split, and that keeps her from giving it her all. From being in the zone, you know?"

"Does that have anything to do with Tate Bannon? From

what I've seen, he enjoys giving her a hard time. A few of them do."

"I don't think so. Alexa seems like she can handle it. She can give as good as she gets."

"Still, keep an eye on that," his father warned. "Competition and ribbing go with the territory, but I want to make sure that's all it is. This is no place for bullies."

"Understood."

His father got up. "Whatever is going on with her, you'll have to find it, JJ, because we're getting to the drop-off point, and Alexa needs to make it over the hump, or she's done. And I'd hate to tell Jake King that his daughter washed out of the program at this stage in the game."

Andrew tapped his pen absentmindedly on his desk. "I know."

That afternoon, the students were taken a few miles away to a practice center. The group was split into two teams for tactical maneuvers. Their assignment was to find the hostage in an abandoned building and get them to safety while eliminating any threat. Everyone was required to wear tactical gear, but they would be using practice ammunition. Alexa's team was first up. Headsets allowed them to keep in contact as they fanned out. The building was dark and musty, and visibility was poor, so Alexa stuck to the walls as she made her way across the space toward the steps.

"Watch your backs," their instructor cautioned. "Anything could be a potential threat."

Alexa made her way up the stairs. Her heart was hammering inside her chest, and she felt the sweat gathering at the nape of her neck. The gear was heavy and the heat stifling. She took a few deep breaths to calm herself before proceeding to the second floor.

The sounds of gunfire and yelling erupted in the silence. Glancing over at her partner, he motioned for them to get moving. Following his lead, Alexa hurried up the stairs. At the top, she melted into the wall and followed it down the corridor. Her eyes were burning from the perspiration that ran off her forehead. She took a second to swipe it away before they were under fire.

Dropping down to make herself small, Alexa's partner spun around to return fire before yelling, "Move," over his shoulder.

She was running down the hall now with him right on her heels. Alexa entered the first door she saw and barely had time to duck as something whizzed past her head.

Crouching down, Alexa saw two figures in the far corner.

"Help me, please," a woman cried out.

Alexa raised her weapon. "Let her go," she demanded.

A man had one arm around her neck while the other was holding a pistol straight at Alexa. "I don't think so. Drop your weapon, or she's dead."

Dozens of scenarios rushed through Alexa's brain as she struggled to keep her wits about her. Adrenaline coursed through her body, causing her to feel nauseous, but she ignored it.

"Do you have a clear shot?"

"Negative," her partner replied.

Before she could react, the kidnapper opened fire before dragging the hostage out a rear door. Alexa hit the floor before returning fire. She heard her partner yell, "I'm hit!"

Alexa turned around and saw that her teammate had a huge bright yellow spot on his chest.

She rushed after the kidnapper.

"Wait," her partner called after her. "Shouldn't we wait for backup?"

Alexa pulled him farther into the room and slammed the door. Grabbing a turned-over chair, she wedged it under the doorknob. "There's no time. We're not losing this exercise. You're fine," she said, checking her ammo. "Stay put. I'll go."

It was eerily quiet as Alexa ascended the stairs in front of her. The radio chatter in her ear confirmed that there was only a handful of students from both teams still left in the maneuver.

Crouched low, Alexa cautiously opened the door and proceeded into the room. Boxes and junk were everywhere. The rest of the area was cast in shadows, with only one window providing light. Recalling her training, she stuck close to the wall as she moved.

Someone jumped out from behind a box with a gun pointed at Alexa. She fired without hesitation. As she ran past, another assailant grabbed her from behind. Her rifle fell to the floor. Alexa barely dodged a blow to the gut. She took a swing, but it was deflected, and before she could recover, the man snaked an arm around her neck and tried to pull Alexa off her feet.

"Give up," the man growled in her ear. "You're not cut out for this. Just admit it."

"Not happening," she gasped, trying to break his hold.

"One day you'll be in over your head and cost someone their life, King. And you'll be powerless to stop it."

That got under Alexa's skin. She paused for a split second, but it was enough.

Her opponent flipped her, and she landed hard on her back, knocking the wind out of her. Alexa turned on her stomach. Slow to get up, she mumbled something.

"I can't hear you," he taunted. "Do you give up?"

Spinning around, there was a pistol in Alexa's hand. She fired at point-blank range. A yellow paint splatter surfaced across the man's middle section before he hit the ground with a groan.

"I said, not today."

Retrieving her rifle, she spotted the target running toward a narrow plank, pulling the hostage behind him. Alexa raced across the space, and when everyone was clear, she launched herself at the man and victim, knocking them both off-balance. With the assailant effectively separated from the woman, Alexa jumped to her feet ready to engage the man when the crack of a pistol shot rang out. She felt the bullet connect with her chest a second before the force of impact knocked her backward and sent her crashing into a stack of crates.

Chapter Seven

"Alexa? Alexa, can you hear me?"

She felt something tugging at her and a cacophony of sounds overhead. Alexa tried again to drag herself out of oblivion and back to consciousness, but it was useless.

"She's out again," the facility's doctor confirmed.

"How did this happen?" Andrew snapped.

Before anyone could answer, he continued his rant.

"Someone better tell me how in the world someone's gun had live ammo," he yelled as he paced. "We're supposed to have safety protocols in place to ensure that nothing like this ever happens. Alexa could've been killed."

Several of the instructors were hovering just inside the treatment room in the infirmary. Each looked incredibly worried, and nervous.

"We have our team looking into it," one of them replied, his face a mask of concern. "It was clearly an accident."

"An accident I can't explain," another man chimed in. "I double-checked all the equipment last night before locking up."

"Obviously, something was overlooked."

Everyone turned at the irate voice behind them.

The men scattered as Andrew's father rushed in and went straight to the hospital bed. He peered down at Alexa and then at the doctor treating her.

"How is she?"

"She'll feel like she got run over by a dump truck and likely have one heck of a bruise, but she'll live."

"I want a report on my desk in an hour—including a statement from the student who shot her."

Andrew didn't bother looking up to see if his employees acknowledged his command. The two teachers nodded to no one in particular before rushing out of the room.

Andrew sank into the chair next to Alexa's bed. He ran a hand over his face.

"This could have been so much worse, Dad."

"I know, JJ." He clapped Andrew on the back. "We'll get to the bottom of this."

"She could be out for a while," the doctor informed them. "I can call you when she comes to."

"You go ahead," Andrew told his father. "I'm going to stay."

James took Alexa's hand and squeezed it. "Okay. Let me know the moment you hear something."

"Roger that."

IT WAS ALMOST midnight before Alexa came to. Andrew was leaning back in the chair asleep with his arms crossed and legs stretched out in front of him. His eyes snapped open when he heard Alexa moan.

"What happened?" she asked. Her voice sounded like tires rolling over gravel.

"You had an accident," he confirmed. "Hang on a second."

He hopped up and went to get the doctor. They both returned less than a minute later. Andrew hovered while he examined Alexa and asked her a few questions.

"I'll give you something for the pain," he said as he injected her with medicine. "It will also help you sleep."

Alexa's worried gaze connected with Andrew. "I don't remember anything."

"Don't worry. Try to rest, Alexa. I'm sure it'll come back to you soon."

Her eyes drifted shut and seconds later she was asleep.

"You should call it a night, Andrew. She'll be out until morning."

He nodded and headed for the door. "I'll be back first thing."

Andrew glanced over his shoulder at Alexa. His expression was grim as he watched her chest rise and fall several times before he left.

Walking the short distance back to the house, he was grateful when he arrived to find it quiet and everyone gone to bed.

Silently, Andrew climbed the steps to the second floor. He was careful not to make noise as he headed to his bedroom. He was exhausted and had a pounding headache. The last thing he felt up to was a lengthy conversation with his father.

Aside from the clock on his nightstand, the room was pitch-black. The darkness was soothing to his head, so he moved around without light. Kicking off his shoes, Andrew stripped and dumped his clothes in the hamper just inside the bathroom before turning on the water for a shower. He placed a towel on the bronze hook on the wall outside of the shower and climbed in.

He welcomed the pounding hot water beating into his tired muscles.

While he soaped up, Andrew replayed the events of the day. He couldn't wrap his head around how a gun containing real ammo was used in one of their training exercises. In the history of their school something like this had never happened before.

If Alexa had not been wearing a bulletproof vest for precaution, she would have died.

That thought flooded him with anger, which was quickly replaced with remorse when he recalled his treatment of her when she had first arrived.

Andrew turned the water off and stepped out of the shower. As he dried off, his mind ran through various scenarios of how such a momentous mistake could have happened.

What if it wasn't a mistake? What if Alexa's accident was intentional?

Still moving around in the dark, Andrew retrieved a pair of pajamas from his dresser and put them on. When he was done, he settled into bed.

After a few minutes of trying to go to sleep, Andrew rolled onto his back and placed his arms behind his head. He pondered several of his students who hadn't warmed to Alexa and had on occasion given her flak.

Tate Bannon was at the top of this list. It was no secret that he didn't want Alexa in the program and had even gotten into an argument with her after she bested him sparring during a martial arts class.

That thought made his jaw clench. If one of his students had purposely endangered another student's life, it would be grounds for expulsion. And Andrew wouldn't hesitate to nail whoever was responsible's butt to the proverbial wall. He wasn't about to risk Phalanx's reputation on a student's prejudices, no matter who it was.

LATER THAT MORNING, Alexa was sitting up in bed when the doctor came in.

"And how are you feeling, Miss King?"

"Like an elephant sat on my chest all night."

With a smile, he examined his patient and then scribbled a few notes into her chart.

"I want you to take it easy for a day or two. And no physical exertion until you're feeling better."

"Thank you for taking good care of me."

"My pleasure, Miss King." His blue eyes twinkled as he wrote her discharge orders. "Try not to get yourself shot again, okay?"

"Believe me, it's the furthest thing from my mind, Doc."

"Glad to hear it," Andrew replied as he strolled into the room.

The doctor repeated her discharge instructions and then excused himself. Andrew observed Alexa, who was attempting to put on her shoes.

"Here, let me help."

He rushed over and helped tie up the laces.

"Thank you, for the change of clothes," she replied congenially.

"You're welcome. Though I admit I thought you were going to challenge me and say that you could put on your shoes yourself."

"I would have, but I'm too tired."

Alexa tried to sound lighthearted, but it came out sounding like she was exhausted.

"Let's get you up," Andrew replied, helping her to stand.

Alexa gritted her teeth against the soreness in her chest.

After helping her into his Jeep, Andrew hurried around the side and jumped in.

A man watched the sport utility vehicle drive down the dusty path toward Alexa's cabin. Retrieving the cigarette from his lips, he dropped it on the ground and stamped it beneath his boot.

"Close call, Miss King. Next time, you won't be so lucky."

ALEXA HAD FALLEN asleep a few minutes after Andrew helped her to bed. When she woke up, the sun had almost set. She blinked a few times and cautiously raised herself up on the pillows strategically placed behind her head.

"Take it easy," Andrew said, popping up from his chair and rushing over.

"I'm fine," she replied after making a bit of an adjustment. She sighed with relief because it had not hurt as much as she had anticipated.

Esther came in an hour later.

"Changing of the guard," she announced before setting the tote bag she was carrying on the bench at the foot of Alexa's bed.

"I've got cards, movies and magazines in case you get bored."

"Esther, I'll be fine tonight. There's really no need to stay."

"Nonsense," the older woman dismissed. "The doctor told

you to rest, and that's what we're going to ensure that you do. Now, how about one of my homemade lemon bars?"

Andrew leaned over Esther and retrieved a sugary treat. He took a bite and sighed blissfully. "These are the best, Esther. You ladies have a good night. I'll check in first thing in the morning."

Ensuring the house was locked up tight before he left, Andrew drove back to his office to retrieve the requested report. He was sitting at his desk with his feet up, poring over the document, when his father came in and sat down. "Anything of import?"

"No. Velasquez confirms that all the weapons had dummy ammo when he transported them to the building."

"Then who secured them once they arrived?"

"Roberts did, but admitted there was a window of about fifteen minutes when he was instructing the class that his eyes weren't on the equipment."

James frowned. "So we've got nothing."

"Not yet. But I'm not about to let this go until we find our culprit. My gut tells me someone was deliberately targeting Alexa."

"How? No one knew who would get each weapon."

"That's not exactly true. The gear was all separated out by the time the students arrived. We started the maneuvers shortly after that."

"So it couldn't have been a student because they were all accounted for and receiving instructions," his father reasoned.

"We only had two teams there for manuevers, but other training sessions were going on that day. Anyone could've had access during those fifteen minutes where the weapons were unattended."

"I don't like this one bit. We need to find this guy, Andrew, before anything else happens. Alexa shouldn't be fearing for her safety."

"I'll get to the bottom of this, Dad. Rest assured, this won't happen again."

Chapter Eight

"A perfect way to start the weekend," Andrew said as he set his helmet on the seat of his ATV and walked over.

"I thought so," Alexa replied.

"How'd baton training go?"

Her face lit up. "Loved it. They had me sparring against Big Mouth. I took great pleasure in sweeping his legs from under him—again."

Andrew laughed at the thought of Tate Bannon being bested again by Alexa. Getting behind her, he pushed the swing. He expected Alexa to protest, but when she didn't, he continued.

"I haven't been on a swing since middle school."

"Just like riding a bike," Andrew countered.

"I suppose you're right."

He pushed Alexa higher and higher until she laughed so hard she started hiccuping.

"Get me down," she yelled between gasps of air.

"Not until you say the magic word."

"Embussing."

"Nope."

"Cover fire?"

"Not even close."

"Chase car?"

It was Andrew's turn to laugh heartily. "You're terrible at this game."

"Andrew, please let me off."

Immediately, he took hold of the swing and began slowing her forward momentum until she came to a complete stop.

Alexa placed her feet on the ground, and Andrew extended his hand. She put her fingers in his firm grasp. When she stood up, she pitched forward into Andrew's chest. He wrapped an arm around her waist to keep her steady.

"Are you okay?"

"Yes, sorry about that," she said when she could steady herself. "Got a bit dizzy. So, what was the magic word? Please?"

"No," he said with a devilish grin. "It was Andrew."

"Andrew," she repeated slowly.

Gazing into his eyes, Alexa stood rooted to her spot, which meant there were mere inches between them. Andrew's arms were still wrapped around her waist. It hadn't dawned on him yet to remove them. Instead, the blush that inched up her neck and splotched its way across her face had him riveted.

He stared at her intently. His hands caressed her back before he moved one hand up to catch a wisp of her hair blowing across her face. Andrew twirled it between his thumb and index finger before placing it behind her ear and resting his hand on the side of her cheek.

"You scared me to death. Do you know I've barely thought about anything else but you since the accident?"

Alexa peered up at him. Whatever she expected Andrew to say, this wasn't it. Nor was the expression on his face that made her skin tingle.

"That wasn't my intention," she whispered once she could speak.

"Mine, either," Andrew said absentmindedly as his fingers outlined the curve of her face. "Yet here we are."

For a moment, Alexa gave in to the fascinating tingling she felt unfurling inside of her and leaned into his touch. When his gaze moved to her lips and his head lowered, Alexa closed her eyes in anticipation of a kiss she hadn't dreamt of wanting until this moment.

"Andrew."

A noise behind them broke the spell.

Alexa's eyes flew open. The shock of what had almost happened was enough to bring her back to her senses.

"Andrew, I'm sorry. I shouldn't have... This can't happen," she blurted out before backing out of his arms with such force she almost toppled over. "I had no right to lead you on like that. I'm—"

Andrew reached out to steady her before returning his arms to his sides. "Married?"

Alexa's face scrunched up in question. "No."

"Oh, you have a boyfriend."

"No," she repeated. "I'm not seeing anyone. I just can't get involved with anyone. I don't do relationships. It's dangerous to be near me."

His eyebrows shot up in surprise. "What?"

"I'm sorry, I didn't mean to be precipitous. What I should have said was—"

"I got it," Andrew cut her off. "Strictly professional. I shouldn't have tried to kiss you. The last thing I want to do is make things awkward between us."

For a moment, his expression was unreadable, but eventually, it returned to neutral and he offered up a reassuring smile.

Alexa wasn't making sense to him right now, but he understood that she had drawn a line between them, and he would respect it.

Though there was some chemistry there, Andrew had learned from past disasters that all endings weren't happy. It was a lesson that almost cost him everything and not one he would ever repeat. Not even for Alexa.

"Thank you," she said before putting some space between them. "That was fun."

"You're welcome." It took Andrew a moment to remember why he'd come over in the first place.

"Fishing," he finally blurted out. "How about going fishing with me? There's a stream not too far from the house."

"Sounds good. How about you get the equipment, and I'll be back in a few?"

"Sure," Andrew agreed.

Waving, Alexa disappeared into the house. She hurried to the bathroom and doused her face in cold water.

"What was that?" she said, staring at herself in the mirror. "You can't afford distractions, King—of any kind."

There was no doubt that Andrew Riker was good-looking with an enigmatic air about him, but that was no reason for Alexa to get off track. She didn't have time for playful banter or harmless flirting. She was there to learn her trade and that was it. *So how is fishing work-related?* Alexa asked herself.

"Good point," she said aloud. Brushing her hair, Alexa secured it into a bun at the top of her head. She retrieved a sun visor from the closet in her bedroom and then rushed outside to meet Andrew.

Alexa carried the fishing poles while Andrew took the tackle box and a bucket. He had tried to bring everything, but she refused.

"Do you have to do everything yourself? You know it's okay to get help sometimes, right?"

"I was raised to be self-sufficient," she replied. "My parents thought it was important to rely on your abilities to get things done. So I had my first job at six."

He looked surprised. "Doing what, a lemonade stand?"

"No, a cleaning business."

He arched an eyebrow. "Are you serious?"

"Yes. My friends would pay me to help them clean up their rooms."

Andrew shook his head. "Somehow, I can see that."

Reaching the stream, they set up and then searched for worms.

"These lakes are stocked with catfish, panfish, perch and bass, so we should stand a fighting chance of catching something for dinner."

"This is the perfect time to come," Andrew said after they'd cast a few times with no luck. "Early morning or late evening is ideal."

As if to prove his point, Alexa got a hit.

"I've got a bite," she said eagerly. She waited until the third hit before reeling it in.

"That's a decent-sized yellow perch," Andrew remarked before dropping it into the water-filled bucket.

They chatted as they fished, and by the time the sun started setting, Alexa was bragging about her superior fishing skills as they packed up and returned to the cabin.

"Uh-huh. How about you save that boasting for when it's time to clean fish?"

"Please," she scoffed. "I slay at that, too."

Andrew burst out laughing. "The, uh, fish slayer?"

She joined in. "Now, doesn't that have a ring to it?"

Working together, it didn't take long to clean and prep all the fish for frying.

At dinner, Andrew took a bite and smiled. "This is delicious. You did a great job on the fish. Is there anything you can't do?" he teased.

"I'm not too good at relationships," Alexa replied, but clammed up. She was surprised that she had even said it aloud.

There was an awkward silence where the statement drifted in the air like an airplane circling the runway.

"Why not?" Andrew asked before he could think better of it.

Alexa was quiet so long that he looked up.

"It's a long story that I'd rather not go into tonight," she finally answered. "Suffice it to say, I've been known to have trust issues."

"You've been hurt before?"

"You could say that. I had a best friend that was in a toxic relationship. I saw firsthand how deadly the consequences can be. It's not something I'd ever want to experience."

Andrew's eyebrow rose at that. "Alexa, not every relationship is like the one you described. Look at your parents. They're still married. You've got a decent blueprint for relationships that do turn out well," he reasoned.

"True, but I've never known that kind of happiness. The boyfriends I've had were few and nothing memorable. It's better if I'm alone because at the end of the day, I'm just not willing to risk it."

He glanced over. "Risk what?"

"My heart."

"Well, in this line of work, you miss all those important get-togethers with your significant other. Like birthdays, anniversaries, holidays. It's hard on relationships."

"As I said, I'm not interested in a love life."

"Then you'd be the first woman I've ever encountered that wasn't."

Alexa cut her eyes at him. "I always say what I mean. I never lie. You think every woman is just waiting around to get swept off her feet by a man?" Before he could answer, she continued. "Well, not me. I'm good."

Andrew digested that information. Alexa may not lie, but something was lurking under the surface that she wasn't sharing, affecting her performance. *Don't worry, Alexa*, he said to himself. *Whatever it is, I'm going to find it.*

"Are you okay?"

He glanced up. "Yeah, why?"

"You have this intense look on your face."

"It's nothing, just an issue at work that I'm trying to solve."

"I'm sure you'll work it out. You seem to be resourceful."

Andrew grinned. "Careful, Lexi, that sounds pretty close to a compliment."

She paused. That was the first time he'd called her by a nickname.

Alexa made a face. "Oh, so we're friends now?"

He sat back and regarded Alexa. "I thought you weren't good at relationships?"

"I meant the romantic kind, and you know it."

Andrew stood and began clearing the dishes from the table. Alexa followed suit.

"Well, now that we have that cleared up," he teased as he placed the dishes in the dishwasher while Alexa put the rest of the food away.

Suddenly, he stopped and turned around.

"Yes, Alexa. I'd like it if we were friends." Andrew leaned closer. "That doesn't mean I will take it easy on you."

"The thought hadn't crossed my mind," she shot back before resuming her task. After a few minutes of working in companionable silence, she glanced at Andrew over her shoulder. "Besides, I'd be disappointed if you did."

Chapter Nine

Alexa was slammed back into the wall, and her opponent brought his arm to her neck.

"Get your back stabilized, Alexa. Break the hold before he chokes you out," her instructor cautioned. "And don't try to pry his arm away with your hand. You won't win just trying to go strength against strength."

Using the palm of her hand, Alexa struck the man she was fighting against in the face, but he didn't budge, so she did it again.

"If he doesn't drop his arm, what do you do? Come on, think. The average person is unconscious from lack of oxygen in six seconds."

She immediately used her fingers to simulate an eye gouge, took her other hand, shoved his arm away from her neck, wrapped it around his face, and pushed him up against the wall before following up with a knee kick to his middle.

In the following exercise, Alexa went for a strike, but it was blocked, and she was thrown to the mat so hard that it took her a moment to recover.

"You okay, Amazon?" her classmate laughed. "You gotta learn to take a punch."

"Knock it off, Bannon," her instructor warned before pulling Alexa aside.

"King, you're not concentrating. Try it again. This time, think about how you're going to take out a hostile that's bigger and taller than you. Sometimes an obvious response may not be the best—you need to improvise."

"Got it." Alexa returned to her place on the mat. This time she evaded Tate's frontal attack and responded with a combination of hits before taking him down to the mat and following up with a blow to the gut and the jaw.

She jumped to her feet. "You're right," she said, breathing heavily as her opponent slowly got up. "I gotta learn how to take a punch."

"Good job," a few of her fellow students remarked as she walked by.

"Okay, class. Hit the showers and report back in an hour. Your tactical mobility instructor will meet you out front."

Alexa left the training room and hurried to her ATV. The last thing she wanted was to have a classmate stop her for a chat. The instructors were sticklers for time, and anyone late usually got called on the carpet for tardiness.

At the cabin, Alexa went straight to the kitchen cabinet and retrieved a bottle of ibuprofen. It was hard to open the bottle because her hand was slightly shaking from exertion. It took some effort, but she got the bottle open, took two pills, then a swig of water from her bottle. Finally, she took a minute to sit on the couch and regroup.

When her cell phone rang, Alexa glanced at the table.

"You're lucky you're this close," she said tiredly before reaching for it.

"Hey, Lex," Zane said when she answered. "I haven't heard from you in a while and thought I'd check in to see how it's going?"

She leaned back and closed her eyes. "It's going. I'm just not sure in which direction yet."

"You sound horrible. Uncle Jake and Aunt Margot said they haven't heard from you in over a week, and before that, it was only ten minutes."

"I know. We've had a lot of work to do, Zane. There are

only a few weeks until the course is over. So the pace has been pretty intense."

"Lex, are you sure this is still what you want?"

"Yes—one hundred percent. Training is insane, but I've never doubted that this is what I want to do with my life."

"Okay, just checking. I'd be a horrible cousin and best friend if I didn't ask, right?" He chuckled. "So, is there anyone you want to take to the mat yet?"

"Not on your life. I'm here for business, not to fill my social calendar. But there's one superhot commando teaching us tactical and combat training and—"

"Wait, did you say superhot? Sounds like you're mixing a bit of fun and pleasure with all that business. I'm surprised at you, Lex. I didn't know you had it in you," Zane joked.

"What? No, it's not that at all. We're not— Nothing is going on. I meant cute in the loose sense of the word."

"Nice try, but I know you better than that, cousin. You meant it exactly as you said it."

"Since you *know* me, you know that nothing will come of it. I'm merely pointing out the obvious. Andrew is good-looking and knows his stuff."

"Alexa, you know it's possible to talk and chew gum simultaneously, right?"

"Not for me. I have a plan, Zane. After I graduate, I'll learn the ropes, build up my experience and eventually open an agency of my own. The dating game doesn't factor into my plan."

"I hear you chirping, Big Bird," he teased. "But life has a way of throwing curveballs we didn't expect. You should know that more than anyone."

She thought of Tanya and felt guilty for being so busy that she hadn't thought of her friend sooner. She was one of the main reasons she was there.

"Thanks for calling, Zane, but I have to go. I still have to shower and get ready for the next session."

"Okay, but call your parents sometimes, please. Of course they'd never say it, but they miss you, Lex. A lot."

"I miss them, too, and I will. Thanks for calling, Zane. It's good to hear your voice."

"Likewise, kiddo."

Alexa hit the shower when she hung up. She still had thirty minutes left when she finished, so she took a quick twenty-minute nap. It wasn't much, but it helped her refocus.

Defensive and tactical driving were two of Alexa's favorite classes. Unfortunately, the instructor announced that today's training was at a different facility, so a shuttle drove the group to a closed course.

"Your job will take you worldwide, so we don't want to assume that you'll only be driving in urban areas," their instructor reasoned. "For example, you may protect principals in Europe, where driving conditions may not be as congested as in the United States. Some maneuvers you'll learn, like a J-turn, barricade breach and pendulum turn, better known as a Scandinavian flick, will come in handy."

The drivers had radios in their helmets for close contact with their instructor.

"What we're going to practice in this turn is front and rear weight transfer and side slides. This maneuver is perfect if you find yourself on the wrong side of the road and need to bring your vehicle under control. You will be using both feet. The left for braking, and the right for the throttle to help shift the car's weight. With practice and calm, you'll be able to do this on multiple road surfaces and at speed."

After discussing the fundamentals, the instructor said, "King, you're up."

"Yes, sir."

Alexa got into the vehicle, secured her seat belt and took off. She executed the pendulum turn and skidded sideways around the curve without error. Alexa felt excitement as the car handled as she'd expected.

"Well done, Miss King. Try it again—faster."

This time, Alexa went through the course at a greater speed. Her face was a mask of concentration while she maneuvered the car through the turns. As she was coming out of a turn, Alexa went to hit the brake. The pedal went all the way to the floorboard.

Alexa tried it again, and it occurred a second time.

"My brakes are out," she said calmly into her headset.

"Don't panic," her instructor replied. "I need you to carefully engage the emergency brake."

"That doesn't work, either," Alexa confirmed after following his instructions.

Downshifting to a lower gear, she was coming up fast on the next turn. Alexa hugged the outside lane not just to shave off some speed, but to keep the car from sliding or rolling.

"You need to cut more speed," her instructor advised.

Easing the two right tires off the road and onto the shoulder slowed the car down even more. The car careened off the road and down an embankment, but it did not flip over. Eventually, the vehicle rolled to a complete stop. Her hand was shaking so bad that it took a few moments before she could put the car in gear and shut the engine off.

"Well done, King," her instructor said in her ear. "Hang tight. We're sending help to come get you. We'll tow the car back so that we can check her out to see what happened."

"Roger that." Alexa heaved a sigh of relief. Her hands shook as she removed her helmet. "It's going to be okay," she told herself several times while she tried to fight back tears.

UPON RETURNING BACK to Phalanx, the class was invited to a picnic and given the weekend off from studies since Monday testing would commence. Alexa was still shook up by the incident and decided that she needed some time to compose herself. Back at her cabin, Alexa pondered whether she would go to the picnic.

It was a harrowing experience, but she did not want to appear antisocial or as though she was still spooked from the incident at the driving course.

Alexa was putting the finishing touches on her outfit when she heard a knock at her front door. When she opened it, she was surprised to find Andrew on the other side.

For the first time since she arrived, Alexa was wearing a sundress. It stopped at her knees and showed off her shapely brown legs. She was wearing platform sandals, and her hair was still wet from the shower and slicked back in a high ponytail. The natural curls cascaded behind her, stopping just above her shoulders.

He stared at her for a few moments before saying, "Are you okay?"

Oblivious to the shift in the air, Alexa stepped aside and let Andrew enter.

"Would you like some iced tea? Or I've got lemonade?"

She would have walked by, but Andrew took her by the shoulders and turned her to face him. His expression was a mask of concern.

"Are. You. Okay?"

She took a moment to study Andrew's face. His eyes were wide, and his face was taut with worry. She could feel every point where his fingers connected with her arms.

Her stoic expression slipped. "No. Not really."

The words were coerced from inside Alexa as fluidly as a snake being propelled out of a basket by a snake charmer.

Before she could elaborate, Andrew swept her into a hug. After a moment's hesitation, Alexa relaxed into the embrace and held on tight.

"It's okay," he said softly. "You did everything right."

The tears fell faster than she could stop them. "I'm sorry. I'm here bawling like a baby."

"Shh," he soothed. "You're entitled."

Andrew swiped the tears from her cheeks with his thumbs. Before he could stop himself, he leaned down and kissed her.

Chapter Ten

Though his face was mere inches away, Alexa was shocked when Andrew's lips touched hers in a tentative kiss. Shock soon gave way to a rush of desire so unexpected and powerful that Alexa had to hold on to him for support.

The caress grew more intense by the second, making Alexa oblivious to anything but the warm feel of Andrew's lips moving possessively against her own.

This can't be happening, she chided. *This is too dangerous, and you need to stop.*

She heard the warning in her head and knew that no good could come of it, but at that moment in time, Alexa was oblivious to anything but the feel of Andrew's body. The scent he wore was the perfect blend of sexy, spicy and woodsy. Its distinct notes overloaded her olfactory receptors, making it hard to concentrate on anything but Andrew Riker and the sensations he evoked.

Somewhere in the distance, Alexa detected a ringing sound. For a moment, she thought it was her own ears, but eventually realized it was her cell phone.

It could have gone on ringing for an eternity for all she cared, but it was enough of a distraction to yank them both out of the haze of yearning they were caught up in.

Alexa came down as sharp as an elevator lurching to a stop. It was jarring.

"I'm… I'm sorry," she said, trying to find her bearings.

"No, I'm at fault. I promised I wouldn't cross a line and I did."

His breath sounded so ragged that it gave Alexa a start.

"We both got caught up in a moment," she murmured.

"You had a harrowing experience, Alexa, that would've upset anyone."

She smoothed her dress and tried not to focus on her shaky hands.

"Yes, but it's part of the job. I should learn how to handle the unexpected better than this."

A sheer look of discomfort passed across Andrew's face. He ran a hand over his jaw and cleared his throat. "It wasn't an accident."

She stared at him. "What?"

"The brakes on the car you were driving didn't just go out on their own. It was sabotage."

"But why? Who would've done something like this?"

With his faculties back under control, Andrew focused on the imminent danger from the attacks on Alexa as opposed to the way that brief interlude had made him feel.

"I don't know, but I promise you that we'll find out. Until then, it's probably prudent to suspend your training. I don't want any more accidents. Thus far, you haven't been seriously injured. I don't want to keep putting you in scenarios that will push the envelope."

She nodded and began thinking over run-ins that she had encountered with different classmates. There had only been three of them, but which one was responsible?

"Please stop doing that."

Startled, Alexa glanced up at Andrew. "Doing what?"

"When you're hyper-focused on something, you bite your lip. It's distracting."

Her mouth dropped open. She had not known that. By the intense way he was staring at her, it was a habit Andrew was trying his best to ignore.

"We should go."

"Sure, I'll just get my purse."

She hurried into the bedroom to retrieve her pocketbook from a chair. When she returned, the front door was open and Andrew was waiting on the porch. He held the door open as she stepped through it. Locking it behind her, Alexa dropped the key into her purse and followed him down the steps.

"Your dress is pretty."

"Thank you. I threw it in at the last minute. I wasn't sure if I'd even have an opportunity to wear it."

"You'll make quite an impression on the guys."

"Hardly. Most of them don't even notice me. Which is just fine," she added quickly. "I like being just one of the guys."

Andrew's step faltered. He waited to see if she was kidding, but Alexa looked like she believed what she'd just said. So, as crazy as it sounded, he decided not to point out that there was no way any man considered Alexa just one of the guys. Especially him.

Walking around to the driver's side, Andrew had to take a minute to compose himself. Alexa was wreaking unexpected havoc on his system. Was she oblivious to her effect on him and several other students at Phalanx? Everyone respected Alexa in class, but even Andrew noticed a few appreciative glances as she walked into a room. He caught a few men staring too long and gave them a look.

Not that he was trying to stake a claim or anything. They were just friends, and though he was attracted to Alexa, he would never take it further than that kiss. It shouldn't have happened in the first place. The last thing anyone needed while learning extensive training was distractions. Everyone's head had to be in the game. Mind-wandering could get someone injured or worse.

Besides, Alexa had made it clear that she wasn't open to a relationship. And as much as he had enjoyed that kiss, she was right. He wasn't up for getting his heart battered and ripped to shreds again, either.

Just friends. Yeah, I hear you, Alexa. Andrew smiled back. *A wise decision for both of us. Let's pray it lasts.*

"So, TELL ME some things about you that I don't know."

"Really?"

"How else is our friendship supposed to grow?" he countered.

After eating at the picnic, they decided to take a walk down to the lake. They had strolled in companionable silence before Andrew posed the question.

She glanced over at him. "Fair enough. I worked as a senior cyber threat analyst for my parents' company. I loved my job. I enjoy a wide range of movies, music and books. Except for horror movies—I never could get into them."

"Let me guess. You sleep with the light on after watching?"

"Uh, I so do," she laughed. "I enjoy being out in nature—always have. My favorite food is nachos, and sweets are my go-to food when I'm stressed."

She stopped walking. Andrew halted and turned around.

"What's wrong?"

"I've had two worst days in my life. The first was when my best friend, Tanya, died a few months ago. The second day was at a park in Great Falls, Virginia. I was a teenager at the time. My friend Shelley and I got attacked while hiking on a trail."

Andrew's expression turned somber. "I'm so sorry, Alexa. I can't imagine how you must've felt in both situations."

She stared off into the distance. "It took a long time for me to come to terms with losing them. They were my best friends."

Andrew placed a hand on her shoulder. "You're still not over them, Alexa."

Their gazes locked. Sadness waded in the depths of her eyes, replacing the happiness that occupied them only moments before. She absentmindedly ran a finger along the scar on her cheek.

"No, I guess I'm not. But I try not to let the pain of losing my best friends engulf me. Instead, I try to focus on ensuring that Tanya's death and my lost friendship with Shelley weren't in vain."

He stepped closer. "Alexa—"

"Let's not," she cut him off. "I don't want to get melancholy and spoil this amazing day."

Her body language was a clear sign that those walls of protection were back up, so Andrew didn't push. Instead, he placed her hand on his forearm and guided her down the path.

"What you need right now is a distraction."

She beamed with excitement. "Then lead the way."

IT HAD BEEN ages since Alexa had enjoyed herself this much. Andrew had taken them to the other side of the lake with a paddleboat. As they moved around on the water, he told her a stockpile of funny stories that kept her laughing. It was hard to feel down around him, and she appreciated getting to know him better.

"You know, after Shelley and Tanya, I didn't think I'd meet anyone again. Now I've got two great friends in my life. You and Marena. It makes me…" She stopped suddenly.

"What were you going to say?"

"It makes me less hurt over the two I lost."

Reaching out, Andrew grabbed her hand and squeezed.

"Alexa, you aren't alone. I'm here if you need me—anytime."

Andrew knew it was true the moment he said it. He may not be able to connect with anyone again on a romantic level, but he could offer Alexa friendship. That was safe and predictable, and wouldn't break his heart. He was also recovering from a relationship that had left him in pieces. For Alexa, it was violence and grief that kept her at arm's length. For him, it was an overambitious ex-girlfriend who loved power, connections and prestige more than him.

"Thanks, I appreciate that." She closed her eyes and released a breath. "This day was exactly what I needed. You must read minds, too."

Andrew shrugged as he continued pedaling. "What can I say? It's a gift."

The two sat in silence for a long time and enjoyed their surroundings. Andrew studied Alexa when she was soaking up the sun. Then, as if sensing his scrutiny, she opened her eyes.

Watching her sunbathe brought back a similar outing. It started out as a wonderful day but had turned into a huge blowup faster than a summer rainstorm in Florida. Just thinking about his ex-girlfriend instead of the great time he was having with Alexa made him feel out of sorts.

She touched his arm. "Are you okay?"

He shook himself out of the memory. "Yeah, I'm fine. I guess it's time we headed back."

"Oh. Yes, of course." Alexa helped him paddle back to the other side of the lake.

On the way back to the cabin, Alexa tried not to ask about Andrew's sudden mood change while they drove home. He turned on music, but she remained quiet other than asking about an occasional song.

When he pulled around the circle in front of her cabin, Alexa unbuckled her seat belt and turned.

"Andrew, is everything okay?"

"Yes, of course. I'm sorry, Alexa. I was just thinking about some work I must complete tomorrow."

"Tomorrow's Sunday. I thought you were off the entire weekend?"

"That was the plan," he replied. "Until I remembered some tests I have to grade and post."

"Okay."

Before she could say anything else, Andrew jumped out and walked around to her side. He opened it and helped her out.

"Thank you."

"My pleasure." He followed her up the steps.

"I had a wonderful time today," she said after unlocking the door.

"I'm glad you enjoyed it."

She shifted from one foot to the other. Finally, she said, "Have a good night."

"You, too, Alexa."

Andrew watched her walk in and didn't move until she'd shut the door.

By the time she peeked out of the window, he was already in the Jeep and pulling off.

"What was that about?" she wondered aloud.

Chapter Eleven

Jake King was in his study reading when his cell phone rang. Glancing at the screen, he set his book down and grabbed the phone.

"Alexa." He sighed with relief. "Are you okay, sweetheart?"

Alexa settled back onto the pillows. Hearing her father's voice caused a rush of emotion. She forced herself not to cry. "Just fine, Dad."

Standing, Jake moved to the couch. He sank into the buttery soft leather cushions, his legs stretched in front of him.

"Andrew said it'll be nose to the grindstone until graduation."

"Are you talking about JJ Riker?"

"Yes, everyone but James calls him Andrew."

"Got it," her father chuckled. "He seems like a very accomplished young man."

"He is, Dad. He's very knowledgeable on a lot of subjects. He's smart and very caring."

Grinning, Jake reclined farther into the plush cushions. His gaze traveled to his bookcase, where there were pictures of his daughter in various stages of her life. His favorite was one with the three of them after falling into a mound of leaves they had just raked. He missed his daughter's light, carefree nature. Listening to her talk in such an animated way provided a glimpse of the old Alexa. It warmed his heart.

"Sounds like you two have hit it off."

"We have. The Rikers have been wonderful hosts."

"Glad to hear it," her father said approvingly before leaning forward so his elbows rested on his thighs. "So, when were you planning to tell me about the accidents?"

There was a long pause. So long that Jake said, "Before you deny it, I should mention that James called me to tell me about both training incidents."

"He shouldn't have done that."

"Lex, it's obvious from the sounds of it that you weren't planning to tell us."

Alexa got up out of bed and started pacing. "That's because there's nothing to tell, yet. The Rikers are investigating what happened."

"Booba, I can—"

"No, Dad. You've done enough—and I mean that in a good way. There haven't been any incidents in the last week. Plus, I can handle myself."

Before her father could respond, Alexa heard a commotion and then her mother's voice in her ear. "We know you won't let anyone push you around, Alexa."

After ending the call with her parents, Alexa was too wound up to sleep. She decided to go for a walk outside. Changing into a pair of shorts, a T-shirt and sneakers, Alexa left out the back door. The landscaping and floodlights provided some illumination as she walked down the path toward the old wooden swing.

Alexa could hear crickets and the occasional woodland creature as she continued her stroll. The last thing she wanted was her father intervening to discover who was behind the attempts to scare her.

Was that all it was? she pondered. *Some person with a bone to pick? How is that even possible? I don't know anyone here.*

Sitting on the plank, Alexa pushed off so that she could gently sway to and fro. She thought back to the last time she was out there with Andrew.

Closing her eyes, she recalled their playful banter and the heightened awareness of him.

"He's a complication you just don't need," she whispered aloud.

Suddenly, Alexa stopped in her tracks. The hair on the back of her neck shot up and she had an uneasy feeling that she was being watched.

Turning to the left and then right, she attempted to hear anything that might give her a clue what was out there.

What if it was a bear? Or some other dangerous animal? Alexa was defenseless against that kind of attack. Her eye caught something at the base of the tree anchoring the swing. She stared at it for several seconds. There were several cigarette butts scattered on the ground.

That's when she heard the distinct sound of movement to her right.

"Who's there?" she yelled.

Silence.

It was too dark to make out a target, and with no weapon, she didn't stick around to investigate. Alexa jumped off the swing and took off running in one motion. Air filled her lungs and fear propelled her forward. Not once did Alexa slow down or look over her shoulder. Only when there was a door safely between her and the outside did she look back. There was nothing there.

Locking the door, she rushed to the front door and checked the bolt. Next, she checked each window latch. Everything was secure. Arming the alarm, Alexa should have felt safer, but she didn't. She was still plenty freaked out.

She glanced at the clock on the mantel. It was one thirty in the morning. She thought about calling Andrew. She knew he would come, but she didn't want to disturb him. For now, she was safe and in no danger.

Going into the kitchen, Alexa made herself a cup of tea, hoping it would calm her nerves. She was still in fight-or-flight mode and felt jittery.

She sat on the couch and tucked her legs under her. There was no way sleep was coming anytime soon.

"WHAT WERE YOU THINKING? You should've called me, Alexa." Andrew knelt and examined the used cigarettes littering the ground. He used a plastic baggie to scoop them up. Turning it inside out, he secured the bag and placed it into his pocket.

"I don't care what time it was, you should've let me know what happened."

"I was fine," she countered stubbornly. "There was no reason to wake you in the middle of the night. I made it back to the house, everything was locked up tight and I turned the alarm on. Nobody was getting inside."

"Unless they wanted to," he pointed out before striding off toward the house.

Alexa fell into step beside him. "Okay, next time, I promise to contact you the moment something strange happens."

"There won't *be* a next time," he ground out. "Whoever the culprit was did a pretty good job of hiding his tracks. Until now. Your coming outside was unexpected. It startled him, so he took off to avoid being discovered but left these." He patted his pocket. "There will be mucosal cells on the tips of his cigarettes. I have a friend at the FBI that works in the lab. He'll get these analyzed. If your assailant is in the CODIS database, my buddy will find him."

"CODIS?"

"It's the FBI's Combined DNA System, which is a DNA database. It has multiple tiers, criminal, federal, local and international, that can be accessed to track anyone who has been entered into the system. If he's a student of ours, he doesn't have a criminal background, or he wouldn't have been accepted. So what we're looking for is anyone who has a reason to have their DNA samples in the database. Likely a state or federal employee."

"Will that take long?"

"Likely a few days. Depending on how many tiers have to be searched. In the meantime, you're coming back to the main house with me. It's not safe for you to be out here by yourself until we have the culprit."

"Andrew, is that necessary? I have the alarm, and I'll be careful."

"We're not taking any chances, Alexa. This could've gone differently last night. I'm not about to give him an opportunity to come at you a third time. Let's go pack your gear and get going."

Realizing he wouldn't be swayed, Alexa nodded and went to pack her belongings. When they arrived at the house, James and Esther were on the front porch.

"Everything taken care of?" James asked his son.

"Yes, the house is secure, and the alarm is on."

"I'm sorry to impose," Alexa began.

"Don't be silly," James replied. "We are here to ensure that our students are safe. We take that responsibility seriously, Alexa."

She nodded. "Thank you for your hospitality."

"Of course," Esther replied, taking Alexa by the arm. "Come on inside and let me show you to your room."

Andrew hung back with his father.

"How soon can we get the results?"

"I called in a few favors to get it rushed, but it depends. It could take a few days or a week or so. I'm driving into Pagosa Springs shortly, where my contact will be waiting. He'll get the samples to my friend at the FBI."

James held the door while Andrew took in Alexa's luggage.

"I want a lid kept on this. I won't risk Phalanx's reputation on some crazy with a personal grudge against one of our clients."

"I'll handle it," Andrew said tersely. He moved off to take the bags upstairs, but James stopped him.

"Hey, what's going on?"

"Nothing."

James stepped into his son's path, crossed his arms and waited. "Andrew."

Blowing out a harsh breath, he dropped the bags he was carrying.

"This shouldn't have happened. I let myself get sidetracked.

If I'd followed protocol like I should have, I'd have continued the investigation after the first incident. Now we almost had a third occurrence. Alexa could've been accosted, or worse. This is unacceptable, and I'm not just talking about for our company's reputation. She could've been killed, Dad."

"I agree. How did you let yourself get sidetracked?"

Andrew frowned. "What?"

"You mentioned that you let yourself get sidetracked. How?"

He ran a hand over his stubbled jaw. "By Alexa. I've been spending time with her lately and—"

"And that's a bad thing?"

"Yes," Andrew countered. "If I'd been doing my job instead of getting to know her better, we may have caught this guy by now."

"Do you have a Magic 8 Ball or something?" James chuckled.

"I'm serious, Dad. I should've stuck with my original instinct and just stayed clear of Alexa King. She's all over the place, and I still get the feeling that she's holding something back. If she's not one hundred percent committed to this career it could cost someone their life. Plus, you'd think her reminding me of Olee would be enough of a warning. I should've listened to my gut and steered clear of her."

A gasp overhead drew both men's gazes upward. Alexa and Esther were standing in the interior balcony. Holding on to the rail, Alexa's face was flushed red with embarrassment. Realizing that she'd been discovered, she excused herself and rushed down the hall. Seconds later, the bedroom door slammed. Esther tsked and shook her head before following Alexa.

James scowled at his son. "And what does your gut say now?"

Andrew closed his eyes and shook his head. "That I've just made a monumental mistake."

Chapter Twelve

For the next week, Alexa and her classmates didn't have time to come up for air. Instead, it was nonstop training and testing for the group. For her, the days began to blur together. She hadn't seen Andrew at all outside of his teaching capacity. He had attempted to knock on her door and apologize afterward, but she ignored him.

After a few days it had become weird. Alexa decided to confront him about what she had overheard, but he was gone by the time she got up, and not home by the time she went to bed. James and Esther had done their best to compensate for Andrew's absence and were model hosts. Alexa let it go. She was under a lot of stress getting ready for finals, and the last thing she wanted to do was increase the weirdness between her and Andrew.

In hindsight, Alexa would later recall that things being just weird would've been a cakewalk compared to the full-blown disaster that was about to occur.

After class, she went looking for Andrew.

"He left a while ago," James told her when she poked her head into his office. "Had a burr under his saddle about something. Try the sparring room. JJ usually goes there when he needs to blow off steam."

"Okay, thanks."

"My pleasure, kiddo."

Alexa found Andrew in the studio practicing on the Wing

Chun dummy. The wooden athletic instrument cultivated fighting skills and chi in Chinese martial arts training.

Not wanting to interrupt him, she sat at the back of the room and watched.

It was some time before he stopped and said, "What's up, Alexa?"

Surprised, she said, "Sorry, I didn't mean to disturb you."

"I saw you when you came in."

Alexa thought Andrew must have used peripheral vision since he hadn't looked up once since she'd arrived.

She got up and walked over to the edge of the mat.

"Don't you think it's time we cleared the air?"

"What are you talking about?"

"About what I overheard and how absent you've been since then."

"I've been busy. This is the last week of the program, so it's been hectic."

"Yeah, you mentioned that before. I just wanted to let you know that it was never my intention to cause problems for you. I don't know who Olee is, but clearly whoever she is, being compared to her wasn't a compliment."

Andrew stepped away from the testing equipment and faced Alexa. He opened his mouth to say something but then stopped.

"What?"

"Nothing."

"Andrew, I know something's up. Even your dad said something's on your mind, and you're distracted. Please, just tell me what it is."

"Why do you want to be an executive protection officer?"

Her eyebrows shot upward. "What do you mean? I thought I'd already answered that. I want to help protect people. Especially women."

"I know what you said. I just question your motivation."

Alexa frowned. "What, you think I'm lying?"

"That's not what I'm saying," he countered. "You said you want to help women. So why not volunteer or work with already established organizations back home? In comparison, being someone's bodyguard and protecting someone's life with your own seems excessive."

"I want to help women in danger, whether from a person, a hostile situation due to work, or external forces."

"That's the *what*, Alexa, not the *why*."

She blew out a breath in frustration. "I don't know what you want from me, Andrew."

"The truth."

"You got it."

Without warning, Andrew grabbed her and spun her around so that his arm was around her neck. Caught off guard, Alexa struggled against him.

"You're the only one keeping me from getting to your principal and doing whatever I want. So what are you going to do to stop me?"

Immediately, Alexa used a jujitsu defense to break his rear choke hold. She tucked her head slightly, grabbed his arm, and pulled down heavily on it before wrapping her leg behind the calf of his leg. Then, she dropped her base and spun one hundred and eighty degrees before pushing against her blocked leg, causing Andrew to lose balance and hit the floor. In seconds he was up and coming after her again.

He tried to swing at her, but she blocked his arm and pushed it away from her face.

Alexa backed up to give herself some distance. She was baffled as to why he was forcing this fight, and she was getting angrier by the minute.

"Andrew, what are you doing?"

"Why, Alexa?" he asked as he moved to take her down again. "Tell me what's really at the heart of it?"

She evaded his takedown and countered with a blow to his midsection. Andrew doubled over. Sweat was dripping from his forehead now.

Alexa was getting angry at him. He could see it in her stance, in the way her chest heaved with exertion and by her expression. Behind the confusion at what prompted the altercation, she was mad. Good. It's the reaction that he was after. Irate people were more concerned with being irritated than hiding the truth.

"I don't know—"

"You're lying," he snapped before coming after her again and again.

"I told you that I don't lie," Alexa snapped back.

Andrew had gotten under her skin in a way that no one had before. Alexa's eyebrows scrunched together in concentration as she looked for weaknesses in his attack. Her nostrils flared from the anger rushing throughout her body. "Then tell me."

This time, it was he who was on the defensive as Alexa tried to back him into a corner. But her triumph was short-lived because Andrew countered the maneuver and knocked her off-balance. Alexa crashed to the floor. Her body protested in pain, but anger was a powerful strength booster. She was back on her feet in seconds ready to lunge at him again.

"What are you hiding, Alexa?"

The question caught her unawares, and was just the push he needed to cause her to erupt.

"I couldn't protect them," she yelled. Her face contorted with rage. "I couldn't stop us from being attacked at the park. Is that what you want to hear? Fine, I wasn't strong enough."

Frustrated, Alexa threw a punch at Andrew, but he used his hand to push her fist slightly past so that she missed the mark. She tried again, but he rotated his body to avoid the hit, countered and knocked her to the floor. She let out a howl of frustration. Next, he set up a mount.

"You said 'us.'"

"No, I didn't."

"Yes, you did. You said 'I couldn't stop *us* from being attacked.' This isn't just about your best friends, Alexa. Your decision to be a CPO is also about *your* need to feel safe and in control."

Setting up a guard using her forearm, Alexa placed her other hand across her wrist to keep him from moving higher up her frame. "No, it's not," she gasped, struggling.

"It is. The man in the park took something from you, didn't he? Your innocence? Your feeling of safety and security? Losing Tanya took something from you, too. You've spent all this time trying to get it back. Trying to make yourself whole again, but deep down, you're the one needing protection—aren't you?"

"You don't know anything about it," she roared. Grabbing his hips, Alexa used the force of an upward thrust to launch Andrew off to the side before rolling out of his grasp and vaulting to her feet.

"Shelley's whole life has changed. She's a shell of the person she once was. And Tanya shouldn't have died. She'd be alive today if it weren't for her abusive boyfriend."

"How is that your fault?"

"I begged her to leave him, but she didn't listen until it was too late. So spare me your sympathy, because you have no idea how I feel—what I lost."

Andrew stood. "I do," he shot back. "I know what it's like to lose someone you loved and be helpless to stop it. I've felt the pain and guilt eating you from the inside out. It's all-consuming, and you'd do anything not to feel it—to be able to escape."

Andrew's voice broke. "Alexa, you have to let the baggage go." He placed his hands on both shoulders to keep her in place. She tried to pull away, but he held tight.

"Let me go."

"It's affecting your focus, and that's not good for you or your clients. You can't let anything distract you in the field. If you let your emotions lead, you'll make a mistake that can get you both killed." Andrew dipped his head so that they could make eye contact. "Do you *hear* me?"

"That won't happen because I'll never let my feelings jeopardize a mission."

"You can't say that," he countered. "One day, an enemy may discover who you care about and exploit that."

"Not if I've stopped caring."

Andrew stared at her a moment. "What does that mean?"

"Aside from my family, the people I love tend to sever contact or die, so now it's easier not to let anyone into my heart anymore."

"And you think you can just turn off your emotions?" Andrew said incredulously. "Alexa, that's not sustainable."

Exhausted from the sparring, she leaned over to try and catch her breath. Tears flowed down her face, making her gaze blurry. She blinked several times to clear her vision but eventually wiped her hand across her face as if the tears were an annoyance. "Loving people is a liability I can't afford," she said tiredly.

He loosened his hold but didn't let her go. Instead, he pulled her into his arms.

Alexa tried not to cry more, but it was pointless. She was too overwhelmed, so the tears just flowed.

"While I may not agree with your logic, I get it, Alexa."

"Who was it?" she finally murmured into his shirt a few minutes later. "The person you lost?"

His eyebrow arched in surprise. Olee came to mind, but he tamped that memory back down where it belonged. That betrayal was too raw to voice. "One of my buddies in the field," he whispered. "He was my best friend and was killed in the line of duty. I wasn't there when he died."

She raised her head to look at him. "I'm sorry, Drew."

He nodded. "It took me a very long time to get past it. Past the anger and the guilt over losing him."

"Of being spared?"

"Yes."

"I know how that feels."

He smiled. "Did you just call me Drew?"

"Yeah, I guess I did. Do you mind?"

"No. Can I call you Lexi?"

She scrunched her face up. "If you must."

Andrew laughed. "Does anyone else call you that?"

"No."

"Then I must."

She burst out laughing. He soon followed suit.

Suddenly, Andrew sobered.

"Alexa, I'm sorry about what I said last week. It wasn't about you. Well, not completely. I was feeling out of sorts because of what happened. It caused me to remember another time when I was in a situation where I didn't feel in control of what was happening around me. Let's just say I learned a painful lesson that I don't ever want to repeat."

"Thank you," she murmured.

Andrew's thumb brushed away the tears under one eye. "You're welcome."

"Are you ever going to tell me what happened with this mysterious woman from your past?"

Andrew looked like he'd just been sucker punched. "How did you—"

"You may not have provided details, but it's written all over your face."

"Maybe someday," he reluctantly admitted. "But not now."

"This," she said, waving her hand around the mat, "was you trying to find my Achilles' heel, wasn't it?"

He nodded. "The scab had to be removed so that the wound you're still carrying can heal."

Alexa inched closer. "Thank you."

Standing on her tiptoes, she pressed her lips against Andrew's mouth without warning. It took a moment before his arms wrapped around her waist to hold her tight.

A purr of contentment drifted out of her mouth before she grasped his shoulders like she was drowning and Andrew was the only life preserver for miles.

Eventually, Alexa pushed against his chest, and Andrew released her immediately. It was so sudden that the momentum propelled her backward. He reached out to stop her from falling.

"I'm sorry. I shouldn't have kissed you like that," she squeaked, moving away. "That's not exactly the kiss that friends give each other."

"Depends on the friends," he teased.

"Andrew, I don't want to complicate things. We're friends. We need to stay that way. Anything else would just get awkward."

His expression turned incredulous. "Kind of late to put that horse back in the barn, don't you think?"

Chapter Thirteen

"We have to," she replied. "I just poured my heart out to you about why I don't do relationships. I'm sorry."

She hurried across the mat.

"Alexa, wait," he called out.

She turned but remained where she was. "Thanks again for helping me, Andrew. And I want you to know that I heard you."

He observed her from across the distance.

"I meant every word, Lexi," he replied. "Including the unspoken ones laced in that kiss."

She rushed out of the room and didn't look back. It was hard for Alexa to think of anything on the ride home except the feel of Andrew's mouth covering hers in a kiss that ignited every dormant area of her body like an accelerant. Now Alexa felt like she was blazing out of control.

"What were you thinking?" she accused herself. "This is a disaster."

The move was reckless and crazy, yet at that moment, it was impossible not to do what she had been fantasizing about for a long time. The wonder of kissing Andrew had overridden all her carefully erected boundaries and common sense.

Parking the ATV, Alexa went inside and headed straight for the shower. As the hot water pounded against her back, she realized why she needed to forget Andrew Riker's mischievous smile and smoldering eyes.

"Because no good can come of it," she scolded, but then

her thoughts of the kiss they shared caused Alexa to switch the hot water to cold.

Desperate for a voice of reason, Alexa called her cousin when she was finished.

"Hallelujah. It's about time," he said after hearing the account of what happened.

"Zane, this is no time to joke."

"You thought I was? Lex, what's the big deal? You like him, and clearly, the feeling is reciprocated, so why not see where it goes?"

"I'll tell you where it's going," she groaned. "Straight into a bona fide disaster."

Sitting on the bed, Alexa spun around until she was lying on her back with her legs stretched out on the headboard. "I'm not about to see that happen. I need Andrew in my life."

"You're telling me."

"As a friend," Alexa clarified. "He's important to me, Zane. I can't risk losing that."

"You realize you're overthinking this, right? By a lot."

"I'm being cautious."

"No, you're being crazy. You haven't talked like this about a man in eons."

"That's because work is my life."

"It's not your life, Alexa. It's your camouflage."

She turned right side up in the bed. "What is that supposed to mean?"

"You're hiding in plain sight, cousin, under the guise of socializing and spending time with people, but in truth, you're scared to have anyone get too close to you because you're afraid of what that kind of closeness could mean if things go pear-shaped."

"Zane, that's not true. I'm friends with Marena, and everything is going just fine."

"We both know that's because she lives in North Carolina, far away enough to keep her at arm's length. It's safe."

An uncomfortable silence descended on the telephone line.

"You may be mad at me for what I've said, but you know that all of it is true. I love you too much not to point out that you're self-sabotaging your life, Alexa. Our hearts aren't designed to be encased in plexiglass for fear of being broken. That's not how life works. Risking pain and heartache comes with the territory. It's time you came back to the land of the living because you can't spend your entire adult life waiting for the other shoe to drop."

After hanging up, Alexa recounted the conversations with Andrew and Zane. She didn't feel like she was self-sabotaging. In her mind, it was self-preservation. It was time for her to fess up about why she didn't let anyone new in too far past her defenses. It was simple. Her heart couldn't take another break regardless of Zane's statement about living without the plexiglass. After having two best friends ripped from her life, she wasn't strong enough to have it happen again.

So if that meant living the life of a hermit and only experiencing life on the periphery, one step below loving someone, then so be it. No one would end up hurt, damaged or dead. "I'm fine with those odds," she said before propping her arms behind her head and staring into the dark. Thoughts of what Tanya would say to that drifted into her mind.

Lex, quit pretending to live and live.

The expression on Tanya's face and the intonation in her voice played out in her head.

"Oh, Tanya," she cried softly into the soundless room. "I miss you. If ever I needed your advice about what to do, it's now, because I'm scared to death."

"YOU WANTED TO see me, sir?"

Andrew and his father glanced up as one of their students entered the office.

"Yes, Jeffries. Take a seat."

James grabbed the folder sitting on his desk. Not one to mince words, he got straight to the point.

"You're expelled, Mr. Jeffries."

The young man's eyebrows shot upward. "Excuse me?"

"This can't be a surprise," Andrew replied in a clipped tone. "You were behind the attacks on Miss King. Are you going to make us go over the evidence?"

He shifted in his chair. "What evidence? I haven't done anything that warrants you kicking me out."

James opened the folder and retrieved a document. He tossed it across the desk.

"We retrieved all the shell casings from the training exercises. Each student has color-coded ammo so that we can track their fire patterns and how well they did in the assignment. Your count was off by two rounds. Which, subsequently, was the number of live rounds fired at Alexa. In your statement, you said that you were nowhere near Alexa during any of the exercises that day, but surveillance cameras show you and Miss King engaged in hand-to-hand combat prior to your shooting her in the chest. She struck you in the face, after which your blood splattered onto her tactical gear. We had the sample analyzed, and you are a match."

His gaze shifted from Andrew to his father. "That was an accident," Jeffries stammered. "You can't be suggesting that I would purposefully try to harm her?"

"I'm not suggesting anything," James said curtly. "I'm flat-out saying you did it. We can't place you at the scene when her brakes failed, but it was you outside of her cabin smoking the cigarettes that you so carelessly left."

"So? I was merely watching her. That's not a crime," he shot back.

"Stalking is an escalated crime. And the DNA left on the cigarettes also points to you, Mr. Jeffries. Add the training incident, and it's enough to have you arrested and charged," Andrew informed him.

Edgar shot to his feet. "I wasn't trying to harm her," he repeated. "I was only trying to scare her. I wanted to prove that she'd crack under pressure. She doesn't deserve to be here, and everyone knows you all gave her preferential treatment. Just ask Tate and a few of the other guys. After a few mishaps the plan was she'd quit and prove my point."

Andrew glared at him. "Then you're as stupid as you are careless. Alexa is highly qualified and earned her spot—you just lost yours."

Two police officers entered the room to take him into custody. When he saw the cops, he tried to make a run for it, but didn't get far. Andrew anticipated his resistance and grabbed him.

"You can't do this," Edgar yelled, trying to break free. "My father has connections—"

"So do we," Andrew countered before shoving him in the direction of the two officers. "Get him out of here."

Edgar's face was contorted with rage as he fought against the police officers. The vein in his forehead bulged against his skin as he was dragged out of the room.

After the three men left, Andrew sank into an armchair. He pinched the bridge of his nose. "Glad that's over."

"Me, too," his father agreed. "Now Alexa is safe from that nitwit's schemes."

THREE DAYS LATER, the Phalanx students graduated. Everyone was dressed to impress in dark suits for the ceremony and could barely contain their excitement. Hearing her name, Alexa got her certificate and shook hands with James, Andrew and the instructors. It was their last night at the training academy, so the Rikers threw a party. Alexa stayed for about an hour but decided to call it quits. She said her goodbyes and was headed out when Andrew called her name.

"Leaving so soon?" he asked when he reached her side.

"Yes," she told him. "I'm headed back to the cabin to pack."

"Then allow me to give you a ride."

"No, thanks. It's a beautiful night out, so I'll walk."

Without another word, Andrew fell into step beside her.

It was dark out, so he retrieved a flashlight from his car.

While they walked, Alexa gazed at the starry sky. "I'll miss it here."

"Me, too."

She looked surprised. "You're leaving?"

"I've taken a consulting job in Dubai. I'll be gone for a few months."

A frown wrinkled her forehead. "Oh. Well, I wish you all the best, Andrew."

"Thanks. You, too."

Alexa stopped suddenly and faced him. "I want you to know that I appreciate everything you and James have done for me. This has been the most amazing time of my life, Andrew. I'm a better, stronger person because of you."

"We just laid the foundation, Alexa. The motivation and raw talent were already there."

Shaking her head, she resumed walking. "Can't you take a compliment?"

"I'm just saying that you did a fantastic job."

"Drew."

"Okay, okay," he laughed. "Thank you."

By the time they reached the door, they were laughing and joking like old friends.

She unlocked the door and turned to Andrew. "Would you like to come in?"

He stepped forward until he was mere inches away. "I would, but I think I'd better go."

They stood rooted to their spots for a few moments staring at each other. They were so close that their breaths mingled. Finally, it was Alexa clearing her throat that severed the connection.

"Well, I'd better go in before we get attacked by mosquitoes." She hugged him. "Thanks for everything, Andrew."

He held her tight for a moment before letting her go. "My pleasure, Lexi."

Andrew searched her face a moment, committing it to memory before he leaned down and kissed her. It was meant to be a light, quick action, but it quickly morphed into something hotter than he had expected.

Alexa's arms slipped around his neck, prompting Andrew to back her up against the side of the cabin and deepen the kiss.

Moments later, their embrace ended as abruptly as it began. He released Alexa.

"I'm sorry. I should not have done that."

"It's okay," she said quickly. "No harm done."

The sudden loss of shared body heat made Alexa shiver. She rubbed her arms to warm up. Everything in her screamed out to stop him. To not walk away without coming to an agreement, but Alexa ignored her own longing. Her stomach was tied up in a ball of knots over the decision. Feeling a sudden emptiness, she forced herself to back away. "Take care of yourself, Andrew."

He lingered for a moment, but then stepped back, too. His face showed his resignation. "You do the same."

She watched him head back down the path before turning and going inside. After she shut the door, Alexa leaned against it. Her heart was racing, and her lips tingled from their explosive kiss. She missed him already. "I have to walk away," she said aloud. "It's better this way because if anything happened to you, Andrew Riker, I might not survive it."

Chapter Fourteen

Three years later...

Alexa placed her SIG Sauer P365 handgun in its holster and slid the navy blue suit jacket over her white blouse. After fastening the buttons, she retrieved a dragonfly lapel pin from her jewelry box. Its wings were gold, and the body was garnet. She secured it to her lapel and then put on diamond stud earrings before sweeping her hair up in a chignon bun at the base of her neck.

Picking up a pair of glasses from her nightstand, she put them on and headed downstairs.

Before she had reached the bottom of the steps, her cell phone rang.

"Alexa King?... Yes, I'm heading out now."

She hung up the phone, grabbed her luggage and purse, and left.

There was a black Mercedes S-Class sedan waiting for her at the curb. When she reached the bottom step, a woman had exited the passenger seat and opened the back door.

"Thanks, Miranda."

"You're welcome, Miss King."

"Good morning, Valerie."

"Good morning, Miss King," her driver replied.

Her assistant handed her a gold folder.

"Is everything in order, Miranda?"

"Yes, ma'am. Your gear is in the trunk, the advance team has scouted out the route and car two is in place. Everything is green."

"Good. And how was your date?"

Miranda blushed. "It was great! Things are going along well. His name is Apollo Hayes. He's tall, handsome and so attentive. I can't wait for you to meet him!"

Alexa's assistant was a stunning petite Hispanic woman. At five foot four, she stood below Alexa's shoulders. Miranda had long black hair and brilliant brown eyes and dimples. Her family was from Houston, Texas, and they were very proud of her moving to Washington, DC, and landing her dream job. Miranda was passionate about learning the ropes and working her way up the ladder at Dragonfly International. Her goal was to eventually become a close protection officer, and she relished the opportunity to learn and work under Alexa. To her, her boss was strong and smart, and cared about everyone around her. She looked up to her and was inspired by Alexa's strong work ethic.

"I'm glad you had a good time. Bring Apollo by the office sometime. I'd love to meet him," Alexa replied before she turned her attention to a file she needed to review.

Alexa's condo was a quick drive to the Salamander hotel on the Southwest Waterfront to pick up their principal.

When they arrived, Valerie pulled up to the front of the hotel. Alexa got out and walked into the opulent lobby. Spotting her CP officer, Dyan Grayson, standing to the side while her principal checked out, Alexa walked over to her operative.

Dyan was one of Alexa's good friends. They met when Alexa was just starting out. Both had worked at the same firm while on assignment and had hit it off. Dyan was five foot eleven, and had a strong, muscular physique. She had smooth, dark brown skin and vivid gray eyes. Most people who saw her became mesmerized. They often mistook her for a model. Which Dyan would graciously deny and keep moving. Occasionally, she would wear contact lenses in the field to allow her to blend into the background when needed.

As serious about exercising and weight training as she was about protecting her clients, Dyan was always training. When Alexa decided to start her own agency, she instantly gave her notice as well, telling Alexa that it wasn't even a question of if she were coming to work for her.

"How is everything, Dyan?"

"Uneventful night, Miss King. The principal had an early dinner, worked until about eleven thirty and then called it a night."

Alexa nodded. "I'll see you on the plane."

"Yes, Miss King," she replied before her team walked past Alexa and left.

Dyan was a regimented person and never called Alexa by her first name when they were in mixed company. Alexa knew she wasn't going to budge on that, so she did not try to dissuade her.

A woman in a red pantsuit turned around. When she saw Alexa, she smiled.

"Thank goodness you're here, darling. Dyan is nice, but she never lets me have any fun."

"Good morning, Mrs. Crawley. I'll be sure and speak with her as soon as we're wheels-up."

As they walked to the car, Alexa had to smile. Veronica Crawley was an heiress to a large private equity firm in Zurich, Switzerland. She was one of Alexa's top clients.

She guided her principal out of the door and into the Mercedes.

"I hope you've packed evening wear, Alexa. I've been invited to several parties while in Chamonix."

"Of course, Mrs. Crawley."

"Good. It will be good to get back to Beauté Majestueuse."

"Yes, ma'am, it will."

The chalet Beauté Majestueuse was one of her client's residences. It was in the luxurious resort area of Chamonix-Mont-Blanc at the junction of France, Switzerland and Italy. A gift from her late father, the seven-thousand-square-foot villa with six bedrooms and seven bathrooms boasted picturesque views of the Alps.

Alexa watched the scenery whiz by on the way to Washington National Airport, also known as Ronald Reagan Washington National Airport. She glanced at her watch. Unfortunately, Alexa would not get a chance to let her parents know she would be on an assignment out of the country. Typically, they preferred a phone call instead of texting if she traveled, but Alexa was pressed for time, so she typed out a message on her cell phone.

A few seconds later, her father responded with a frown emoticon. Since she and Shelley got accosted years ago, her parents' protectiveness was expected. When she pointed out that she was in her thirties now, her mother replied that she failed to see the relevance of that argument because she would always be her daughter.

Alexa wondered if her grandmother acted like her mother but refrained from asking. She didn't have time for one of her mother's lengthy rants.

When they arrived at the airport, Alexa thanked her driver before her team of close protection officers headed to Mrs. Crawley's private jet. Their client received numerous death threats and required around-the-clock detail when she traveled. As a result, several bodyguards and close protection agents worked directly for Crawley's company. Still, Veronica preferred that her immediate detail be all women, so Alexa and her team were on point with the others as secondary protection.

Once they were wheels-up, Alexa and her associates reviewed their operations plan. It listed everyone's assigned roles. For example, the drivers, surveillance officers and personal escort section all played a role in protecting Veronica. Alexa was the primary protection officer, also called PPO, and once she was satisfied that everyone was up to speed on all the plans, safe houses, maps and multiple routes reviewed, she allowed her team to take a break and relax for the remainder of the flight.

"What's troubling you?"

Glancing up, she saw Dyan take a seat across from her chair. "Nothing. Why?"

Dyan secured her seat belt and then relaxed into the plush leather.

"You look a little edgier than usual."

Alexa shrugged. "I don't know why. I'm fine."

"You know Clive likes you."

"Say what?" Tilting her head to the left, Alexa briefly observed him. He was one of her client's main bodyguards. He was a mountain in a single-breasted suit.

"No, I didn't know that," she said dismissively. She did, but she wasn't about to tell Dyan that. Ever the romantic, her colleague would try to read more into it than there was.

As far as Alexa was concerned, Clive was efficient, professional, he knew his stuff, and he could keep a cool head in a crisis. She wasn't interested in him for anything more than that, so personal details about him were irrelevant.

The look Dyan gave her said she didn't believe her. Alexa shrugged, almost as if Dyan had voiced her opinion aloud.

"I'm going to get some sleep," she announced, stretching her legs and getting comfortable.

"You just don't want me plying you with questions about Clive," Dyan mumbled.

"You're right. I don't. Besides, there's nothing to say on the subject. I don't date. End of discussion."

"Alexa, there's no reason you shouldn't entertain the idea of having a relationship with someone. It might be good for you. You know it's good to have a work-life balance—not to mention a horizontal workout now and then."

Opening her eyes, Alexa pinned Dyan with an annoyed glance. "Why this sudden interest in my love life?"

Her friend took a sip of her hot chocolate. "You mean besides the fact that you don't have one?"

"I don't have one because I don't *need* one," Alexa countered. "So quit worrying about me, please. I'm fine—couldn't be better."

"What couldn't be better?"

Both glanced up to see their topic of discussion hovering over their seats. He leaned in as if waiting to hear the punch line of a joke.

"Not what. Who." Dyan smiled sweetly and waited for Alexa to answer.

Letting out an exasperated puff of air that could have leveled a tree, Alexa scowled at Dyan before turning her attention to Clive.

"I was just telling Dyan here that I don't have the time, or the inclination, to date."

"Oh," Clive replied, relaying his disappointment at her news.

Alexa didn't want to, but she couldn't help gazing at Dyan. Her smug look said *I told you so.*

"Yeah, I get that," Clive said, finally rallying to offer a reply. "This line of work is all-consuming."

"Exactly what I've been saying." Alexa nodded in agreement. "We have enough to tackle without worrying about missing date nights or forgetting your significant other's birthday or anniversary. There is no way I'd want to deal with that kind of pressure."

"Unless the man was extraordinary," Dyan remarked.

"He'd have to be."

At that, Clive bowed out under the guise of getting some food.

When he left, Dyan observed Alexa so long that she shifted in her seat.

"What?"

"You've never been in love."

Alexa scoffed. "First of all, that's private."

"And true."

"Okay, I've never been in love in the romantic sense." Alexa stared out of the window. "I've never met a man that I wanted to get close enough to in order to develop those kinds of feelings.

Well, at least not someone I would turn my life upside down for, put him first above everything else and sacrifice my life for."

"Well, at least?" Dyan said, homing in on the statement with zeal. "So, there was someone."

It wasn't a question.

Alexa remained tight-lipped, but Dyan crossed her arms and waited.

"Okay, fine," she replied, admitting defeat. "Yes. There was someone that I was attracted to, but the timing was wrong. I was just starting my career and had a plan to follow—it didn't include a serious relationship."

"Or any relationship from the looks of it," Dyan snickered.

"Exactly."

"Alexa, it's been three years. Dragonfly International is thriving. You're one of the top woman-owned businesses in our field and on the Top 10 Executive Protection Companies list this year. Business is beyond great, and you've garnered respect in what was once a strictly male-dominated field. So I think you can stop and smell a rose or two. Or should I say a man's cologne?"

Reluctantly, Alexa had to laugh at that one. "Dyan, I know you mean well, but I love my life the way it is. So for now, Dragonfly is my top priority and the only thing on my mind."

"It's not your mind that I'm trying to help out."

Shaking her head, Alexa decided to get some sleep. But before she drifted off, Andrew materialized before her eyes. He was smiling at her with his usual self-assured air. Next, she pictured how soft his mouth would feel at the base of her neck.

That thought jolted Alexa upright. Her gaze darted around as if she expected Andrew to be sitting across from her with a smug look on his face.

"No, no," she whispered before wiping her face, simultaneously feeling hot and cold. Why did Dyan have to talk him up? Alexa had been doing well for years without thinking about what could have been. He was a friend and a colleague. Nothing more.

It didn't matter how tall, well-built and incredible he was or what he did to her blood pressure. Andrew Riker was a heart-throb of a distraction Alexa simply couldn't afford.

Chapter Fifteen

Andrew sailed through the air. Seconds later, his back connected with the training mat. The dull thud from his body coming in contact with the thick padding ricocheted around the room.

"Dude, you're not concentrating. Do you want to spar, or don't you?"

Andrew's eyes shut, and his face wrinkled as he tried to work through the pain in his midsection. He could've kicked himself for not being ready to absorb and redirect the energy of that punch.

Slowly getting to his feet, Andrew tightened the belt on his gi. "Sorry, man." He returned to his position. "Let's go again."

This time, Andrew anticipated his friend's moves and did well to counteract them and deliver blows until he got caught with a roundhouse kick.

"Okay, that's it for today."

A bit slower getting up this time, Andrew bent over and took a moment to even out his breathing. "I'm fine."

"Come on, man. Where's your head at today?" Sanjay Kholi groused. "You could've easily dodged both those shots."

"I know." Andrew went to grab a towel. He dried his face and neck and then drained half his water bottle. "Seems I'm a little preoccupied today."

"How many times have you told me that split focus gets you killed or worse—"

"Puts your asset in danger," Andrew finished for him. "You're right. I have no defense for not concentrating."

"I'm not looking for a defense, my friend. More like an explanation."

Sanjay followed Andrew down the hall to the men's locker room. They both stripped and headed for the showers.

"It's Alexa," Andrew finally announced over the loud whooshing of water barreling out of the showerhead.

"What about her?"

"I can't get her off my mind. Especially lately."

"What's that got to do with it?"

It was hard for Andrew to explain something that he didn't understand. On occasion, they ran into each other, and Alexa had always been cordial and happy to see him, but something was off. It was as if they both were waiting for something. He couldn't call it mixed signals, because she had always been clear on not wanting to be anything but friends. Still, there were moments when she'd call to ask his advice about something and they would... Andrew paused to find the right word.

"Linger," he finally said.

"Who's lingering where?" Sanjay roared.

Andrew shut the water off. "It's nothing."

"You aren't making any sense, my friend."

He snatched the towel from the peg outside the shower and dried off before securing it around his middle.

"Tell me about it," Andrew muttered. "I need to forget about it."

Sanjay looked confused. "About lingering?"

"About Alexa," Andrew clarified.

"Oh. If she causes this much dismay, my friend, that would probably be wise."

Sanjay was right. He knew it. It was time to let Alexa go. No more wishing things were different. They weren't, and it was time he stopped wishing things would change and accepted the reality of how things were.

"You're right. Time to quit pining."

Decision made, Andrew felt lighter than he had in months. He whistled a cheerful tune while he dressed. Then, after bidding his friend goodbye, he went home.

"JJ, I need you," his father called out from his study not even a minute after Andrew came through the front door.

When Andrew poked his head in the doorway, his father motioned to the chair across from his desk.

"Sure, what's up?"

"There's a security consulting assignment for an old client. But, unfortunately, I've got a scheduling conflict that's come up, or I'd go myself."

"No problem."

James glanced up from reviewing the contract when his son didn't continue. He eyed his son curiously. Then, with a slight nod, he sat back in his chair.

"Okay, what's going on?"

Andrew's expression turned quizzical. "I'm not sure what you mean."

"This is the first time you've agreed to cover an assignment for me without asking for a whole heap of details."

"Does it matter? You asked me to help."

"And I appreciate it," his father acknowledged with a wide smile. "But this isn't like you, son. I'm just wondering why the change-up?"

Andrew crossed his leg, resting his ankle on his knee. "Just feeling the need for a change of scenery lately. Something to take my mind off a few things. Besides, we're on a break, so now's a great time to go."

"A few things, or one specific thing?" James inquired. "Or should I say someone?"

"What do you mean?"

"Come on, JJ, I'm your father. And even if I weren't, I'm still a very observant man. You like Alexa, and you've been on a slow burn since you met her. So I say it's time to stop dragging your feet before someone else stakes a claim."

"Dad, first off, I'm not discussing my love life with you—"

"Good, because it's hard to talk about what you don't have."

Andrew shook his head. "Second, stake a claim? I'm not prospecting for gold. Besides, we're just friends. I can't make her interested in more than that. She's been clear since the beginning on how she felt. So there's nothing more to do."

"Balderdash," James replied, then stopped short. "Are people still saying that?"

Andrew snorted. "No one under eighty."

"I've seen you two together. And the fact that she is still in your life tells me that you've gotten past her looking like—"

"Don't say her name," Andrew warned. "It's better if you don't talk natural disasters up."

"I hadn't planned on saying it," James countered. "I was merely going to say that whatever hesitations you seem to have had early on seem to have resolved themselves, no?"

"No. There's still the very big hurdle of Alexa herself. Like I said, she's made herself crystal clear."

"Alexa likes you, son. Regardless of what she says."

"I'm sure she knows her mind, Dad," Andrew countered. "Not that it matters. I will be on assignment, and I'm sure that wherever Alexa is, she's working. So, let's forget it."

"Consider the matter dropped." Then, handing his son the client folder, James waited until Andrew left before relaxing into a smile.

"Molasses may not be the best way to catch this particular dragonfly. Time to shake things up for you and Alexa, my boy, and see what happens."

Five days later...

ANDREW ADJUSTED THE black bow tie until he was satisfied. He glanced in the mirror before sliding on the midnight blue tuxedo jacket. The black satin lapels provided a subtle contrast between the two. He retrieved his pistol from the nightstand and slid it into his gun holster before buttoning up the jacket.

There was a quick knock at his bedroom door.

"Coming." Andrew strode across the room to open it.

"Good evening, Mr. Riker."

"How are you, Etienne?"

"Very well, sir. Mr. Simms is ready."

He followed the butler downstairs to the group assembled in the foyer.

"There's my security expert," Mr. Simms's voice boomed. "I told a few of my colleagues that you're here to revolutionize my security detail."

"Thank you, sir. I'll do my best."

"Now you're just being modest," Mr. Simms replied. "Phalanx is one of the best in the business, and you know it. That's why you're here." He pulled Andrew to the side.

"I'm sure you heard about that unfortunate mishap a few weeks ago. One of my men got sloppy, and some disgruntled former employee almost caused a scene. Unfortunately, incidents like that tend to have a snowball effect. I can't shake my stakeholders' faith in my abilities to lead or tarnish my company's reputation."

"No, of course not. I intend to observe your team and provide any necessary alterations to processes. You understand that may result in additional training or even staff changes?"

"Whatever you need to do. You have complete operational control, Andrew. I've known your dad for years, so I know I'm in great hands. James didn't even rake me over the coals for not hiring Phalanx in the first place." Mr. Simms chuckled. "I wouldn't have blamed him in the least."

"Don't worry, sir. We'll get things back on track."

He clapped Andrew between the shoulder blades. "I don't doubt it."

Several Range Rovers were on hand to transport the businessman's entourage to the nearby chalet for a formal charity event. Andrew was there strictly for observation of his client's team.

When they arrived, there was a reception already in progress. Andrew's gaze roamed the luxurious great room, taking in the immaculately dressed guests and uniformed waiters serving drinks and canapés. Before they had come, Andrew sat in on the operations meeting for Mr. Simms's protection officers. The chalet Bruyère was at the foot of the Alps. The residence belonged to one of his client's business partners, and while the view was spectacular, the team was more concerned about entry and exit points, the guests attending and safe houses along the route.

Keeping a low profile, Andrew waved off the flute of champagne a waiter had offered him. He didn't drink while on duty, so he asked for a glass of club soda instead. More to have something in his hand while walking around. When on assignment, Andrew worked hard to blend in. Granted, he was in the Alps and noticed the only people of color at the event were on Mr. Simms's security detail, so there wasn't but so much being a wallflower he could do. That thought made him chuckle.

He was about to take another sip of his drink but stopped. A weird feeling settled into the pit of his stomach. His body's early detection system that something wasn't right.

When Andrew got these hunches, he never ignored them. Instead, he paid close attention to everything happening around him.

That's when he saw it. There was nothing unusual to the untrained eye about the two elegantly dressed people standing there talking, but Andrew could tell the man was upset by his body language. The woman's back was to him, but he saw her leaning into the man to speak with him. Then, when the man tried to step around her, she placed her hand on his biceps and guided him down the corridor.

Before he'd even registered, Andrew was moving to follow them. He set his drink down on the table along the way. He spotted them moving away from the guests and down a flight of stairs. Glancing around, he confirmed that everyone was engaged and enjoying the party.

Silently, he crept down the stairs. At the bottom, Andrew

walked into a wood-paneled theater room with two large couches, several plush beanbags and a large projection-screen television. Continuing down the corridor, he poked his head into a sauna and the adjacent steam room.

Where could they have gone? he questioned himself. That's when he heard two muted voices. Silently, Andrew strode toward a room at the end of the hall. He could hear the raised voices and see that the once-agitated man was flat-out belligerent.

"No, I will not calm down. I have every right to talk to her. This is a free country, you know. You can't prohibit me from speaking to whomever I please. Now step aside."

The woman remained planted in front of him. Nothing about her body language seemed excited. Instead, she appeared calm and spoke to the man slowly, soothingly.

"I'm sorry, sir, but Mrs. Crawley is here to enjoy the charity event. If you would like to give me your name, I would be happy to relay any message you have for her tomorrow."

"And I said I'm not doing that. I am going to give her a piece of my mind. I was a good employee. I didn't deserve to get fired over some stupid misunderstanding, which she'd know if you'd let me speak to her. But you know what, why am I wasting my time with you? I don't know who you are, but this conversation is over. Now move."

He reached out to shove the woman out of his way. Andrew watched in growing amusement as she used the man's momentum when he tried to grab her to flip him to the floor by the arm. Before he could utter a word, she hauled him to his feet and grabbed him by the scruff of his collar. When she turned around, and they saw each other, both froze.

Alexa and Andrew were speechless and stood rooted to their spots. Her aggressor tried to use the opportunity to make a run for it, but she was still holding his collar, plus Andrew was blocking their path.

"Andrew?" Alexa said when she'd recovered herself. "What are you doing here?"

He grinned. "You know me. I have a habit of turning up where I'm least expected."

Chapter Sixteen

Alexa crossed her arms. "I'm serious."

"I'm here on business," Andrew explained. "So, how are you, Lexi?"

"I'm doing great—and you?"

Alexa's detainee was incredulous. "Who cares how he is? Let go of my neck."

"Shut up," they both said in unison.

Andrew's gaze returned to Alexa. "Of all the places we could've run into each other."

She nodded. "Who'd have guessed Chamonix, France?"

"Not me." He turned to the man struggling to get free. "I see you're on duty?"

"Yep. I have a client here for a few weeks. And you?" she inquired.

"I'm doing some security consulting."

"Well, that's exciting."

"No, it's not," her captive groused.

"If I have to tell you again to stop talking, you'll be walking home with a limp," she promised.

The man snorted. "And I'll sue that sequined dress off your body."

"How do you stand it?" Andrew asked seriously. "I've only known him two minutes, and I'd love to deck him already."

The man went to say something, but Alexa cut him off.

"You've tried to threaten and intimidate my client, and

you took a swing at me, so by all means, call your lawyer," she countered.

He grumbled but remained quiet.

Escorting him through the patio door, Alexa guided him along the wooden deck to the front of the house. Then, spotting one of her employees, she headed his way.

"Is the principal on the go?"

"Yes, Miss King. Dyan took Mrs. Crawley in the lead car. We left car number two here for you."

She nodded. "Escort this gentleman to his vehicle and see that he leaves the premises."

"Yes, Miss King."

When her employee left, physically pulling the protesting man behind, she turned to find Andrew standing with his arms across his chest.

Shaking her head, Alexa went up to him. "Enjoying the show?"

"Oh, yeah," he laughed. "You were impressive, Miss King."

"Thank you, Mr. Riker. Fishing for compliments considering Phalanx taught me everything I know?"

Andrew fell into step beside her. "Not at all. I'm pleased you're doing well and Dragonfly International is thriving. You've made a solid name for yourself in our community, Alexa. That's all my dad and I ever wanted for you."

"Thanks, Andrew. That's high praise coming from you. And it's good to see you."

Their shoes tapped out a staccato beat on the wood decking as they returned to the entrance at the back of the house.

"It's good to see you, too, Alexa."

When they went in, Andrew noticed the slightly blue tinge to her lips and her shivering. Rushing to the couch, he grabbed one of the thick sherpa throw blankets and draped it over Alexa's shoulders.

"Thank you," she said through chattering teeth.

"You're freezing. Why didn't you say something? I could've escorted the whiner outside to your team."

"That's my job, and I'm fine," she retorted.

Andrew studied the floor-length V-neck sequined gown that she was wearing. The flutter sleeves and slit above her right leg exposed some of her skin to the elements.

"Alexa, your lips almost match the gray of your dress. If you don't warm up soon, I will be forced to escort you to the sauna. Better yet, that might still be a good idea."

"Don't you dare," she cautioned before a shimmer of a smile peeked through a stern frown.

He helped her sit down on the couch closest to the fireplace before he flipped the switch to turn it on. At the same time, Alexa rubbed her shoulders vigorously, trying to warm up. Finally, the gas ignited with an audible whoosh, and flames shot to life.

Andrew sat as close as he could to help with the transference of body heat. He placed an arm around her shoulder and drew her close. Her body wasn't shivering as much as before.

"You'd better not catch pneumonia."

"That's not in the schedule."

His chest shook with delight while he rubbed his hand up and down her blanketed arm. Andrew was startled when Alexa moved closer, resting her head on his shoulder.

The room was eerily quiet save for the occasional muffled voices and footsteps coming from the first floor.

"Always by the book, huh, King?"

"It's easier that way. Everything is predictable—no surprises."

"Yeah," he agreed. "But where's the fun in that?"

It was two days later when Alexa received a text from Andrew. Both got a break in their schedules, so they decided to meet. Dyan was on point as the CPO for the day and took Mrs. Crawley to the spa.

"So, where's he taking you on your date?" Dyan had said when she heard about Alexa's plans.

"It's not a date. We're simply two friends getting reacquainted on our day off."

Dyan pulled out her phone.

"What are you doing?"

"'A date is time spent with another person that is enjoyable and allows you both to grow closer.'"

Alexa's mouth dropped open. "Did you just google that?"

"Yes, I did. And as you can see, by definition, you two are on a date."

Alexa's eyes shot heavenward as she excused herself to go and get ready.

The forecast was for a clear day with a high temperature of forty-seven degrees. Alexa didn't know where they were going. Andrew suggested that she dress comfortably and in layers, so she wore black stretch leggings, hiking boots, a fleece jacket and a long-sleeve Henley shirt. Pleased with her appearance, Alexa grabbed her coat, hat and gloves and headed to the family room to wait.

When the butler announced that Andrew had arrived, Alexa followed him outside.

Several of Alexa's team were walking the perimeter of the house. Each looked surprised when she and Andrew walked by but refrained from comment. The snow was piled high on either side of the shoveled driveway. Andrew's car was toward the entrance of Beauté Majestueuse, so they walked down the road. While they strolled, Alexa took in the snow-covered trees and glorious mountain view. Retrieving her cell phone from her jacket pocket, Alexa took pictures of the snowy scene and a few of Andrew. "How are you this afternoon?" he greeted her, opening the silver Range Rover door and helping her climb up.

"I'm wonderful."

She waited while Andrew walked around to the other side. Then, when he slid behind the wheel, Alexa said, "Okay, so where are we going?"

"Come on. I can't tell you yet. Then it wouldn't be a surprise."

Andrew started the car and entered an address into the GPS.

He used his hand to block the screen from her view, which caused Alexa to arch an eyebrow.

"Yeah, about that. I'm not big on surprises, Andrew. It helps when I'm prepared and—"

"Uh-uh," he interrupted as he pulled off. "You're not working today, so come back off high alert. Besides, you'll like this surprise," he said confidently.

Alexa couldn't argue with his logic. She nodded her agreement and allowed Andrew to continue with their journey while she enjoyed the scenery.

They chatted as he drove. "How are your parents?"

"Doing well. Not happy I'm over four thousand miles away," she explained. "But they're supportive of my career. They always have been."

"That's valuable to have."

"Don't I know it," Alexa agreed. "Our family isn't that large, so it's always special when we get together."

Andrew parked and cut the engine when they pulled outside their destination.

"Where are we? Come on, now is a great time to fill me in."

"Fair enough. We're going skijoring."

Her expression was blank. "What?"

"It's a winter sport that means ski driving, and you're pulled along on skis behind a horse." He stopped. "You can ski, can't you?" Andrew frowned. "I suppose I should've asked before now."

"Yes, I can ski," Alexa responded with a laugh. "This sounds like fun. I'd love to try it."

Thirty minutes later, Alexa was holding on tight as a horse gently galloped through the snowy trails. Her cheeks were hurting, not from the cold but from all the laughing and smiling.

Eventually, their guide led the horses back to the stables.

When they turned a corner, Alexa lost her grip and her balance. She went careening off the path and into a snowbank.

"Alexa," Andrew yelled as he let go of the harness. He

came to a complete stop before he undid his skis and went after Alexa.

"Hey, are you okay?" he said with concern.

"Fine," she giggled. "Except for the fact that I'm stuck."

"Here, let me help you."

"No, I've got it," she said quickly.

He watched her attempt to stand twice before going over and grabbing her hand to hoist her up. Off-balance, Alexa was stable for a few moments before the skis began to slide.

"Wait, I've got you," he said, trying to keep her steady.

Before either could stop it, Alexa fell backward, taking Andrew with her.

He lay sprawled on top of her in a tangle of limbs. Once Alexa recovered, she started laughing so hard she began hiccuping.

Unable to stop himself, Andrew joined in.

They finally sobered. He gazed down at her. Suddenly, he lifted his gloved hand and moved a wisp of Alexa's hair out of her face.

She stilled.

"Why do you do that?"

A look of confusion crossed her face. "What?"

"Never accept my help? Or, as far as I know, anyone's help?"

"I like doing things myself. It's better that way."

He touched her cheek. "Better or safer?"

All of a sudden, the air between them grew dense with tension. Andrew's face was mere inches away. Alexa could feel his breath mingling with her own, and his eyes were intense, as if he were trying to peer into her soul. She worried that he could hear the hammering of her heart. Alarm bells went off in Alexa's head. Every inch of her warned that this was dangerous. That *he* was dangerous. Her gaze drifted to his lips. His upper lip was a cupid's bow and matched his full lower lip perfectly. There was a bit of razor stubble along his jawline, and the scar from his lip to his chin still mesmerized Alexa.

They were so close that all she needed to do was tilt her head up, and their lips would be locked in a kiss.

The moan that drifted between her traitorous lips left her mortified.

She tried to push him off, but his body weight held her firmly in place.

"Andrew, I think we'd better get up," she said, still struggling to free herself.

"Answer me, Lexi."

She blinked several times. She was so affected by his proximity that she had forgotten the question.

"What?" she said, trying to stall.

"Why do you keep me at arm's length?"

"You don't appear to be at the moment, do you?"

"Alexa, what are you afraid of?"

Before she could respond, their guide called out from about one hundred yards away.

It was the proverbial splash of cold water needed to break the connection. Andrew glanced at her a final time before he got up. This time when he held out his hand to help Alexa, she accepted it.

"There you are," the worried man said when he reached them. "Is everything okay?"

Andrew glanced at Alexa with a heated look so intense that it took her breath away. She could only nod her head in response.

Chapter Seventeen

When they returned to the stables, Andrew unsnapped his snow boots from his skis. He turned to help Alexa, but she was already undoing her boots.

One of her buckles was stuck, so Alexa tugged on it sharply. "Here, let me."

She started to refuse but stopped. Instead, she gave him a demure smile. "Thank you for bringing me. It was a great surprise, Andrew."

The mutual attraction still hummed between them like a powerline, but for now neither acknowledged it.

He grinned. "Glad you liked it," he replied as they returned their gear. "But the day isn't over. How about some lunch?"

"Are you kidding? I'm starving. Lead the way."

ANDREW CHOSE NEOPOLIS, an Italian restaurant in the Centre Commercial Alpina in Chamonix city center with an impressive view of Mont Blanc and the banks of the Arve river.

The restaurant was cozy, with wood tables and brown leather chairs. White walls were decorated with paintings, and wood ledges held carafes, baskets and other artifacts from bygone eras.

Alexa ordered the capricciosa pizza while Andrew ordered the spaghetti Bolognese. The restaurant was busy, making intimate conversation difficult, but they enjoyed being there and eating delicious Italian food.

A walk along the river followed lunch, which allowed them a chance for quiet conversation.

"I've enjoyed my day, Drew. Thanks again for suggesting it."

"My pleasure, Lexi," he said, grinning.

Alexa observed the shops as they walked by. Eventually, she said, "To answer your question, it's safer."

Andrew didn't stop walking. After a moment, he said, "You are always safe with me, Alexa. Don't you know that by now?"

Alexa's cell phone chirped. She checked her text message and frowned.

"What's wrong?"

"That's Dyan. We have an issue with the driver in car two. He ate something that didn't agree with him and was forced to make a pit stop."

Andrew nodded and ushered Alexa back to the Range Rover.

"Where's your backup team?" he asked along the way.

Alexa's stride was almost as long as his as they rushed back to their parking space. Andrew's mind was racing with possible scenarios.

"They're en route."

When they got to the SUV, Andrew started the engine and turned to Alexa.

"Where's the lead car?"

Alexa tapped out a message to Dyan and waited.

"On la Mer de Glace," she finally said.

Andrew looked at the navigation system. "That's only four minutes from here. We can intercept them."

Dyan gave Alexa their coordinates, and she added them to Andrew's GPS.

It didn't take long to spot the lead car, but Alexa pointed out a black BMW 7 Series that had pulled up parallel to Dyan's car. They gave it a few moments, but when the other vehicle matched their speed, Alexa turned to Andrew.

"I see them," he said before she could say a word and sped up to intercept the chase car.

Alexa called Dyan's cell phone. "We're right behind you. Have the driver execute maneuver E."

"Will do," Dyan replied before hanging up.

"The driver will speed up so that you can take his place and deal with the other car," Alexa explained.

"Got it," Andrew replied.

Both were all business as they worked together to deal with the immediate threat to Alexa's operation.

He sped up and got behind Dyan's car so that when the driver hit the gas and took off, they quickly slipped in to deal with the BMW. Alexa used the time to write down the license plate number.

The other car sped up to pass, but Andrew's Range Rover connected with the left panel of the vehicle and pushed it to the right. The BMW veered sharply and ran off the road. Andrew shot past to catch up with the principal's car.

"Alexa, are you okay?"

"Yep, I'm fine. Great driving," she replied with a smile.

Andrew caught up to Dyan's car and dropped behind her while Alexa called to check on their second car's driver and let the backup car know that she and Andrew were following the lead.

She ended the call and turned to Andrew. "He has food poisoning."

"Coincidence?"

"Unlikely. He ate the same meal as the other CP officers, and they're all fine. I'll check it out when we get back and my principal's secure."

The two cars pulled into the driveway at Beauté Majestueuse, and Dyan assisted Mrs. Crawley into the house. Alexa and Andrew got out of the car, and he checked the damage on the rental car.

"It's not too bad."

"I'm glad. Thanks for helping me out today."

He grinned. "My pleasure. Never a dull moment, hey, King?"

"That's true," she replied. "Which is one of the things I love about my job."

Andrew nodded. His smile was brilliant. "Thanks for a lively day."

"That it was," she agreed. "I enjoyed the food, skijoring, the walk along the waterfront and the car chase."

Andrew laughed. "Of course."

There was an awkward pause before she said, "I'll see you later?"

He nodded. "I'm headed to Geneva tomorrow, but it'll only be a two-day trip."

Alexa frowned before she caught herself. "Oh. Then safe travels, Drew."

"Thanks. I know you'll hold the fort down, Lexi."

She chuckled. "Always do."

Turning, she strode into the house to find her team waiting in the living room. She returned to all business.

"How's the principal?"

"She's fine," Dyan replied. "Most of the time, she was on her phone conducting business and wasn't paying attention to her surroundings."

Alexa pinched the bridge of her nose. "I'd like an incident report in thirty minutes on what went wrong, how this could've been avoided and what steps we'll take to ensure that things go smoother next time. If Andrew and I hadn't been close, this could've had a different outcome."

Her team agreed and dispersed, giving her time to return to her suite to shower and change clothes. When she returned thirty-five minutes later, everyone was at the dining table waiting.

"Okay," Alexa said, claiming the spot at the head of the table. "Let's begin."

A FEW NIGHTS LATER, Mrs. Crawley hosted an intimate dinner party for some friends. There were various glass jars and vases filled with water, cranberries, green twigs and floating candles placed as centerpieces on the table and around the room. The warm glow of the candles replaced the bright overhead lighting that illuminated the dining room and complemented the solid custom acacia wood dining table and chairs. There was a runner on the table that included winter touches of evergreens, pine cones and holly. The red and green were a beautiful contrast to the cream-colored china plates with gold chargers and crystal glasses.

Alexa was the CP officer on duty and remained at a distance from her principal for the entire evening. Since they were in a controlled environment and had cleared the guest list, Alexa gave a few of her team the night off. The remaining employees were strategically placed around the chalet to avoid drawing attention. To anyone observing, she was merely one of Mrs. Crawley's employees.

Alexa had her laptop out and appeared to be working, but she observed everyone attending the party to ensure there were no surprises and that the night ran smoothly.

Her cell phone vibrated. Alexa glanced at her principal before she checked it.

How's everything?

She smiled, and her heart fluttered. *Andrew.*

Great. Principal is having a dinner party. Pretty sedate. How's Geneva?

I just finished a training session. Have some paperwork to do, and I owe Dad a call.

I do, too. My parents get antsy if I don't check in often on assignments. You'd think I was still a teenager.

You, too? LOL. How about dinner when I return? I promise it'll be a less hectic day. No car chases or overzealous fans.

Don't make promises you can't keep.

That garnered her a smiley emoji from Andrew.

Fair enough. There might be some chaos and mayhem involved.

That's more like it.

Can I ask you a question?

Sure, Alexa replied.

Did you smile when you saw it was me texting?

Alexa's cheeks flushed with excitement. She pondered if she should be truthful or not. Finally, she typed her answer.

Yes, I was happy to see it was you.

So, you miss me?

Alexa pondered his question. Try as she might, she couldn't deny that she had been thinking about Andrew a lot since he had left. Their ski outing played nightly in her dreams. Each time, they ended up kissing. It was hot and explosive, and always left Alexa wanting more when it was over. Each time she woke up feeling strung tighter than a violin string. It was disconcerting to her. She was placing her toe in water that was sure to burn.

Are you there?

She glanced down at the screen before turning around. Alexa noticed that everyone was enjoying the party and not minding her.

Yes, I miss you. I enjoyed spending time with you, Andrew. It has been a pleasant surprise.

How pleasant? he texted back.
Alexa almost grit her teeth in frustration.

Andrew, why are you fishing for compliments?

I'm not. Merely seeing how truthful you'll be in answering my questions.

I told you that I never lie.

We'll see if that's true when I return and I'm standing right in front of you.

Alexa felt her body growing warmer just recalling the last time Andrew was so close.

Andrew, I have to go. It looks like the guests are leaving.

Duty calls? Fair enough. We will continue this conversation later. Good night, Lexi. Sweet dreams.

There was no doubt that her dreams would be even more intense thanks to him.
Alexa shifted in her chair, suddenly feeling the need for some fresh mountain air. It was time to admit the truth. She was falling and there was no way to stop it.

Good night, Drew.

Chapter Eighteen

Alexa had off the next day, so she went into Chamonix and treated herself to a spa day at one of the luxury resorts. She had received a bamboo deep-tissue massage, followed by a detoxifying body wrap, a eucalyptus steam room session and a few minutes in the hot tub. While she was getting a deluxe pedicure, she called her friend Marena to catch up.

"Alexa, it's been forever since we've spoken. Bring me up to speed. What's been going on with you?"

She watched as the woman sitting on a stool at her feet massaged a cold, blue-green invigorating scrub into her legs. The rhythmic motion lulled Alexa into a further state of relaxation. Alexa leaned back into the soft white leather massage chair and pressed a button to start a combination of rolling and kneading her muscles. A blissful sigh escaped her lips.

"Well, I've been in Chamonix, France, for a few weeks. I leave for home in a few days. Let's just say this assignment has been full of unexpected surprises."

"Really," Dr. Marena Dash-McKendrick remarked. "And what do you mean by surprises?"

"Not all what," Alexa replied, feeling so relaxed that she yawned several times. "Some are a who."

"You don't say? Would one of those whos be Andrew Riker?"

"Yes." Alexa tried not to gush, but it was hard to do with

the smile encompassing her whole face. "He tops the list, yes. I mean, figure the odds of us running into each other in France?"

"Seems predestined if you ask me."

Alexa choked on the seltzer water she had been offered. "Predestined? That's laying it on a bit thick, isn't it?"

Marena snickered.

"Oh, stop. It's not all dreamy. We just reconnected, and we're simply getting to know each other better."

"And has this time playing twenty questions changed your opinion of him?"

Alexa paused before she answered that. "No. Quit reading more into this than it is. We're still just friends."

"You're a terrible liar."

"Now you sound like my cousin, Zane."

"He's not wrong. Besides, I can hear what you're still trying to deny in your voice. You *like* him."

"Okay, yes, I do like Andrew. But there's so much going on with work, I can't afford to split my focus," Alexa dismissed. "Before I forget, we have a new client, Ruben Tyndale, who will come in shortly. A very VIP client, I might add."

"Congrats, Lex. I'm glad business is doing so well. Oh, Lucas is here for a visit. He wanted me to make sure I told the 'Amazon' hello."

Alexa laughed. "And how is your brother doing? I knew I shouldn't have told him my nickname when we were on that mission in London."

"Oh, you're never going to hear the end of it. Lucas said it suits you too much. And he's well. He and Coulter have decided to build me a larger workspace in the backyard for all my inventions."

"Speaking of which, anything new that Dragonfly can acquire?"

"Of course," Marena said gleefully. "I'm working on a ring that shoots out a burst of a sleeping agent."

"I know of a few people I'd love to put to sleep," Alexa joked. "If you need someone to test the prototype—"

"Don't worry, I'll send it as soon as it's done. And don't get too excited. It doesn't last that long," Marena added. "Now, back to my original question before you decided to redirect."

The woman doing her feet was rubbing hot stones on her legs. Alexa sighed blissfully. "I wasn't redirecting," she finally managed to say. "And business has been booming. Dragonfly has had steady repeat business and word-of-mouth recommendations. And now that we're about to sign this new client, we're finally out of the red."

"I'm happy for you," Marena exclaimed. "You deserve it."

"Ruben mentioned the person we would be taking on is an ultra-high net asset. We'll go over the details in our operational meeting when I return home. First, we'll determine why the principal needs protection and how long. Is it because of a digital stalker, angry ex-lover, corporate espionage, or if it's for business travel—"

"You know I'm not applying for a job, right?" Marena laughed.

"Oh, am I boring you?" she countered while accepting a proffered glass of sparkling water with lime.

"To death."

"What? The world of close protection is so exciting," Alexa gushed while adjusting her massage chair. "It's amazing that you never do the same job twice. Every client and operation is different. You know, like when you're making serums in your lab, designing tech gadgets or antidotes to save your husband from certain death by poison."

"Touché," Marena replied. "So what's Zane's take on your latest client?"

Alexa chuckled and pointed to the nail polish swatch that she wanted. "You know Zane. He's betting whatever Ruben Tyndale wants to discuss involves some supermodel with a stalker."

"He would pick the scenario with a supermodel.

"Speaking of people we love to look at, tell me more about Andrew. Has he come to Washington to visit?"

"Uh, segue much?" Alexa teased. "And no, he hasn't come

to DC. He's been tied up with work lately, too. He's in Geneva right now but will be returning to Chamonix. I'll get a chance to see him before I go."

"I bet he'd come if you asked him."

"Marena."

"Okay, okay. I'll let it go—for now. But only because I've got to run. Congrats again on landing the new client. Let me know how it goes."

"Thanks, and will do," Alexa promised.

Alexa hung up and had to laugh at her friend. Marena hadn't changed since they met at the retreat years ago. *The one that changed my life. Who would have thought I would decide on this career after going to a transformational retreat that Tanya had suggested?* Her mind drifted to Andrew again. Yes, life did have a way of trying to throw curveballs.

ANDREW ENDED UP detained and made it back on Alexa's last night in France. They dined at Le Matafan in the heart of Chamonix. It was a relaxed atmosphere with primarily wood decor with bright red as an accent color used in the tableware, lighting and seating.

Alexa marveled at the hundreds of pieces of wood logs flush on accent walls around the restaurant. It was unique and, paired with the fireplace, added to the romantic flair.

While they dined on pumpkin gnocchis with butternut cream, and octopus cooked in bouillabaisse, they talked about their upcoming assignments.

"It sounds like a wonderful opportunity to showcase Dragonfly. I wish you all the best. Let me know if you need anything."

"I will," she promised. "What about you? Thailand sounds exciting."

"I've been there a few times, so nothing out of the ordinary. Just babysitting a few businessmen for a summit."

"And what's next after that?"

"That would depend on you."

Alexa was about to take a bite of her gnocchi and stopped. "Me?"

"Despite your dire warnings as to why we wouldn't work together, Alexa, I get the feeling that you're not so sure that still rings true."

"Andrew—"

"Before you deny what I know as facts, hear me out. I propose a trial."

Her mouth dropped open. "A what?"

"When our assignments are over, let's schedule some time together. Uninterrupted time to get to know each other better. Without work getting in the way."

"Andrew, I—"

He took her hand, turned it over and kissed the pulse point of her wrist. Instead of releasing it, he held her hand captive, caressing her fingers with the pad of his thumb.

"Don't think. Feel, Alexa."

At the moment, Alexa could barely breathe. She stared at Andrew stroking her hand as if she had just grown the appendage out of thin air.

"That's a good sign."

Alexa felt warm and tingly all over. "What is?"

Andrew leaned in closer. "The fact that I'm not on my knees in a headlock right now." His gaze held a hint of playfulness. "I'd say you're at least amenable to my proposition."

Truthfully, Alexa's answer was yes the moment he suggested it. She'd find a way to deal with those subconscious worries later. For now, there was no way she was refusing anything this man offered.

Alexa leaned in to give him her full attention. His cologne wafted into her nostrils. The woody, masculine scent was heady and lulling her like a seductive siren song.

"Andrew?"

"Yes?"

"I don't like you."

His expression was so intense his gaze could have melted cheese without a fondue set.

"I'm glad. Because I don't like you, either."

Chapter Nineteen

A week later, Alexa was in her office reviewing the operational manager's detailed report on Ruben Tyndale and his company, Tyndale Global Holdings. Their latest annual report was quite impressive. Tyndale had business ties in entertainment, fashion, media and banking.

She was making discussion notes when her administrative assistant buzzed her office to let her know Mr. Tyndale had arrived.

"Thanks, Miranda." Standing, Alexa smoothed her dark gray pantsuit and ran her tongue over her teeth. Seconds later, the door opened, and he was ushered into her plush office.

"Good afternoon, Miss King," Ruben said as he strode across the room.

"Hello, Mr. Tyndale." They shook hands before Alexa motioned for him to be seated.

"Let me start by saying how thrilled I am to meet you finally. Your track record is stellar, Miss King, and I need the best."

"Thank you, Mr. Tyndale. We appreciate your business."

"Please, call me Ruben."

"If you'll call me Alexa," she returned. "Now, how can Dragonfly be of assistance?"

He shifted in his chair. "It's not for me—at least not directly. I have a high-profile business partner and client who needs your company's specialized protection. She's a young lady whose career has taken off. She owns very successful jewelry, makeup line and fashion accessory businesses and recently made the Forbes billionaires list. She will be traveling to several shows in the US and Europe, so I want her safe—especially from her boyfriend."

Alexa sat back in her chair. "Mr. Tyndale, while this isn't outside my company's skill set, I'm curious why you didn't mention to our operational manager that you aren't the principal?"

"Miss King, it's a rather delicate situation, and I didn't—"

Before Ruben could explain, a tall woman burst through the door. She walked in like it was her office. Her winter-white wool pantsuit was adorned with a diamond-and-gold belt. Her bracelets, earrings and necklaces were gold as well. The black suede red-bottomed ankle boots were devoid of adornment, as was the black suede handbag providing an understated anchor to the opulence of her ensemble.

"I'm sorry for the intrusion, Miss King," her assistant, Miranda, said, rushing in behind the woman. "I told her that you were in a meeting, but—"

"It's okay, Miranda," Alexa said, rising out of her chair.

The woman stopped in front of her desk. "Whatever Ruben has arranged, you can forget it. I have no intention of going along with this insanity." She scowled at him. "There is nothing that I'd ever want from this woman."

Before Alexa could reply, the woman removed her black sunglasses and glared back.

The color drained from Alexa's face, and it took several moments for her to recover from seeing her ex–best friend Shelley's baby sister. "Sophia?"

"So, you remember me," she said with a mocking smile. "Good. Then you know that there's nothing I'd ever want from you after what you did to my family."

Sophia spun around and pierced her business partner with a murderous glare. "Ruben, I don't know what you thought coming here, but I don't need *her* help. Nor will I ever need anything from Alexa King. I'm leaving."

"No, you're not," he countered. "You will stay here, and we will work this out."

"How could you?" Sophia accused. "She left my sister to die at the hands of some madman while she saved herself."

"You know that's not true," Alexa shot back. "I went to get Shelley some help. She's here today because of me."

Sophia leaned over Alexa's desk. "You mean she's psychologically damaged because of *you*."

Ruben bolted up and took hold of Sophia's arm. "Okay, let's calm down, ladies. Sophia, this isn't getting us anywhere. I'm sure we can find a way to—"

"Don't you even act like I'm the one being unreasonable when you've blindsided me like this." Sophia yanked her arm away.

"I'm sorry, Mr. Tyndale, but under the circumstances, I don't think this is going to work," Alexa said firmly. "I'll be happy to recommend another—"

"Excuse me, Miss King, can I have a word?" Dyan called from the doorway. "We have a situation regarding a client that I need to speak with you about."

Alexa hesitated.

"It's imperative."

"Certainly, Dyan." Ignoring Sophia, she turned to Ruben. "Please excuse me for a moment."

"There she goes running away again. Typical."

Alexa forced herself to refrain from commenting as she strode to the door. Instead, she turned her attention to Dyan when she got on the other side.

"Okay, what's going on?"

"That's what I'd like to know. So, because of a principal's temper tantrum, you're about to blow a ridiculously lucrative contract for us?"

That brought Alexa up short. "Potential principal. And you interrupted a client meeting for this?"

"He's already paid a retainer fee, and a screaming match was more like it," Dyan retorted. "Alexa, this isn't like you. You can get along with anybody. I've seen you do it."

"This is different," she shot back. "This is Shelley's younger sister. I'll add who is just as vicious now as she was almost fifteen years ago." Alexa stopped talking and sat down at Miranda's desk. She searched through a few drawers before pulling out a bag of chocolate chip cookies from the numerous snacks her assistant kept in her desk. Ripping open the foil bag, Alexa popped a few into her mouth. Closing her eyes, she chewed in blissful silence. Then, almost as an afterthought, her eyes flew open to find Dyan staring at her in stunned silence.

"Stress eating?"

"It's warranted," Alexa countered. "Dyan, you have to understand, there's no reasoning with Sophia about anything. She thinks I'm fully responsible for Shelley's deterioration." She ate a few more snacks before saying, "Maybe she's not wrong."

Dyan leaned against Miranda's desk. "You know that's not true. You told me you were teenagers at the time. I know you did the best you could because you're a fighter, Alexa, and you don't give up. Yet you're ready to throw the towel in now and walk away from a contract with Tyndale Global? Boss, think about it. Anything they touch skyrockets to the top, and regardless of how annoying she is, Sophia Porter has the Midas touch right now. If everything goes well, Tyndale's referrals and possible follow-up work could be phenomenal. It's just the exposure we need."

Leaning back in Miranda's chair, Alexa stared at the ceiling. Her ragged sigh ricocheted around the quiet space like a Ping-Pong ball. "Dyan, this dredges up so much from my past," she said softly.

"You can handle it, Alexa. No one I know is stronger than you when you set your mind to something."

Her friend stood there and waited. Finally, Alexa stood.

"You're right. If Ruben still wants to hire Dragonfly, we will do it. One thing I won't do is let Shelley's sister cost my company a contract. I'll do whatever is necessary to make this work."

Dyan touched her boss's shoulder. "That's the Alexa King I know."

Alexa smiled and threw the empty bag in the trash. She rose and smoothed her suit before turning on her heel to head back to her office. She stopped and glanced over her shoulder. "Dyan?"

"Yes?"

"Can you get a replacement bag of cookies for me? And go find Miranda? She's probably hiding in the break room. Tell her that I'm not mad about Sophia barging into my office. It wasn't her fault. Sophia Porter is like unstable air moving over warm water in September on her best day. At some point, you realize that a hurricane is imminent."

Stifling a chuckle, Dyan agreed and went off to find their younger associate.

When Alexa strode through her office double doors, it was to find Sophia sitting in a chair next to Ruben. The barely controlled anger was emanating from her body like a force field. Alexa ignored the invisible daggers being thrown her way and turned her attention to her client.

"I apologize for the interruption. Unfortunately, it couldn't be helped."

"No problem at all, Miss King. At best, I know this is a tenuous situation, and I apologize for not providing you with advance notice."

"Mr. Tyndale, crisis management is where we excel." Alexa smiled and returned to her desk. "Now, I believe we were discussing why Miss Porter requires protection?"

"That's funny. I thought we were at the point where Ruben and I leave, and you return to your miserable little existence?"

Ruben paled. "Sophia!"

Alexa dug deep to generate a serene demeanor. "But that doesn't solve your security problem, does it?"

"Fine," she capitulated. "But if you ask me, Ruben is being paranoid. I'm in no real danger. Nico likes to be a drama king at times. He and I argued, but it isn't like we don't always kiss and make up."

"Over what?"

"Excuse me?"

"What did the two of you argue about?" Alexa clarified.

"That's none of your business."

Alexa grabbed a pen and Ruben's contract, signed it and then set it aside.

"Now it is. I've been hired to protect you from this day forward. Every move you make is my team's business, Sophia."

She placed her feet up on the coffee table. "Fine. We fought about some stupid investment. Nico wanted me to be a silent partner in some club he's trying to buy with a few friends. I think his friends are useless, and I wasn't about to go along with pouring my money down a bottomless drain, so I told him I wasn't interested. Especially not with the wastrels in tow.

"I've declined business ventures with him before, but this was different. He blew up and threatened that I'd regret my decision. A few days later, one of his friends cornered me at an event and thanked me for changing my mind and bankrolling Nico's portion." She glanced up at the two of them. "I didn't."

Alexa made some notes on her tablet. "What happened next?"

"Nico left for Portugal, and I flew back to the States for a fashion show. I haven't seen him since."

"Do you have arguments often?"

Sophia shrugged.

"Has Nico ever become physical with you?"

"Not if he values breathing."

"Good to hear," Alexa replied, making more notes. "Did you tell him about your conversation with his business partner?"

"No, not yet."

"We'll need to drill down further into your daily schedule, the places you go and the people you meet. The process will take a few hours, so you'll meet with a member of my logistics team."

"Fine. Are we done?"

"For the day, yes."

"I'll be in the limo, Ruben," Sophia replied. She turned to glare at Alexa.

"I'll work with you because I have to, but that doesn't mean I'll ever forgive you for your part in Shelley's issues."

Without another word, Sophia stormed out.

The room was draped in awkward silence.

"I'm sorry about her behavior, Alexa," Ruben said quickly. "Of course she'll never say it, but this latest falling-out with Nico is more significant than Sophia lets on. He's made more than a few missteps concerning business ventures, making me fearful of her getting involved in his harebrained schemes."

"Do they have any joint accounts?"

"Yes, but I don't think it's a significant amount that she keeps in the accounts she shares with Nicholas, but I can't be sure."

"I understand. Dragonfly is on the clock now, Mr. Tyndale—Ruben. We have a team of forensic accountants, so we'll check everything. Rest assured, we'll have a full picture soon."

Her client visibly relaxed. "Thank you, Alexa."

She stood up and walked around her desk to shake his hand. "My assistant, Miranda, will contact you when we have created our operational plan for Miss Porter's protection."

Her client nodded. "I appreciate you continuing with the contract. I know she can be caustic, but I care about Sophia like a daughter. Her father and I are old friends, and with Ralph and Carol wanting to stick close to Shelley, I promised I'd look out for Sophia. Her brand has expanded exponentially, and some might look to exploit her however they can."

"Ruben, I assure you that regardless of our personal history, while in our care, Sophia Porter will have every resource at our disposal to ensure her safety."

Satisfied, he bid Alexa goodbye and left. When her doors shut behind him, she sank to the sofa, flicked off her heels and placed her stocking feet on the coffee table. The surprise encounter left her utterly exhausted. Unable to help herself, Sophia's accusations came to mind. The years had done nothing to temper the sister's animosity. Clearly, she was still to blame for Shelley's plight as far as the Porters were concerned.

There was a lot at stake with this contract, and the earlier bravado about being able to work with Sophia fizzled out like a bottle of sparkling water that sat out too long.

Then, thoughts of her long-lost friend came to mind as if summoned. From Sophia's rant, Alexa surmised that Shelley was still having problems.

That thought didn't sit well with her, and she burst into tears before she could stop herself.

Chapter Twenty

Nicholas Michaux settled on the black leather sofa in the dimly lit club. The electronic dance music summoned many beautiful people to the dance floor like a beacon. He toyed with the drink in his hand, swirling the amber liquid around in the glass tumbler, but it remained untouched. Usually, he'd be out there dancing and feeding off the crowd's energy, too. Lisbon was famous for its nightlife, and he enjoyed partying with the best of them, but tonight he had more significant problems. Life-and-death problems.

Nicholas shifted uncomfortably. The venue was suddenly too everything. Too hot, claustrophobic and loud. Slamming the glass on the table, he bolted up from his seat. The need for air drove him past the packed space to the second floor. Once he made it down a dark hall, Nicholas turned a corner and headed up another flight of stairs to the club's rooftop. Thankfully, it was empty.

He walked over to the edge and stood there, hungrily inhaling the cool night air while trying to gather his thoughts.

Nothing was going according to plan. Nicholas had suffered countless setbacks, starting with his father's refusal to bankroll his latest project and Sophia pulling out of partnering with him for a nightclub venture with his friends. Both denials were unexpected. He'd made dicey moves to get his portion of the money, and if any of those markers came due before he convinced Sophia or his father to reconsider, he was a dead man.

The picturesque skyline was lost on him as he stared at the brilliantly lit night with unseeing eyes.

"Enjoying the evening?"

Nicholas froze. His jaw clenched in annoyance at the intrusion. "I was."

"She wants to see you."

"She who?"

Turning, he found two well-built men in black suits directly behind him.

"The Siren."

He shook his head. This was not how he envisioned his evening shaking out. "Sorry, fellas, but I don't know who that is."

"She knows you, so let's go."

"I'm not about to go off with two goons I don't know to speak to some woman I've never met."

"When my boss wants to see you, you go."

"Maybe I didn't make myself clear. I don't respond to a summons from some stranger like a trained seal."

The man nodded. "Maybe I didn't make *myself* clear. You, Mr. Michaux, don't have a choice in the matter." He patted his right jacket pocket. "Not if you want to live."

Livid, he motioned for them to proceed. One man took the lead while the other fell into step behind Nicholas.

"I don't need an escort," he snapped. "I'm capable of getting there on my own."

"Our orders were to bring you to Torre de Pérolas, which we're going to do. So quit stalling and get moving."

Nicholas was ushered outside and into a diamond-white Mercedes G 550 SUV.

Torre de Pérolas, the "Pearl Tower," was located in Torres Vedras, a municipality almost an hour's drive from Lisbon. Thankfully, the silence was as luxurious as the vehicle. He was not in the mood to make small talk when his life could be on the line. He hadn't been entirely truthful. He had never met her, but everyone in his circle knew of the Siren.

An arms dealer, a procurer of stolen art and a thief, Siren

had several illegal and legitimate enterprises. Not one to be crossed, it was well-known that she had a penchant for setting examples. Nicholas wasn't sure how he had stumbled onto her path, but being known by this dangerous woman was not good.

"We're here," the passenger called from over his shoulder.

Even in the distance, Torre de Pérolas was impressive. The uplighting around the white mansion only added to its stately appearance. Nicholas heard rumors that Siren conducted all her business at the Pearl Tower.

The main house was over ten thousand square feet and sat squarely in the middle of a massive acreage. It was a working farm with stables, a vineyard, several outbuildings, a pool, multiple gardens, a winery and an impressive turret with a wraparound balcony on the back side of the house. It was also well fortified with guards, and word on the street was that the tower was equipped with prison cells.

The car pulled into a circular driveway, stopping at the front door. His escorts got out, with one holding the door open for Nicholas, who didn't bother to thank the man as he exited.

The three men went through the massive wooden door and walked down several corridors. Nicholas checked out the interior on the way. The walls were white except for a great room with a stone fireplace.

Ushered down a floating staircase to a lower level, Nicholas found himself at the entrance to a modern dojo.

"Take off your shoes and follow me," one of the men said.

It was a stark contrast to the warm and homey feel from upstairs. However, the decor was still luxurious, with red-painted accents, rich wood walls and floors with Japanese tatami mats around the room. In addition, there were wall shelves that held swords and other sparring weapons and black lacquer room divider screens. The space exuded controlled power.

At the end were several chairs on a raised dais. The one in the middle was more impressive than the others. A woman was in the top spot, looking very relaxed and at ease. She was an older white woman with flaming red hair swept into a tight bun. She wore black leather pants, matching knee-high boots, and a long silk balloon-sleeve floral duster in turquoise, gold and black paisley. She sipped a cup of what he assumed was tea with the exaggerated slowness of someone who has the luxury of time.

"Good evening, Mr. Michaux. Welcome to Torre de Pérolas," the woman said.

"I would say thank you, but I don't know why I'm here."

"Have a seat." She signaled for one of her employees to bring a chair.

After sinking into the comfortable black lacquer chair, Nicholas turned to his host.

"Come now, Nico. You can't be oblivious to why you're here?"

He frowned at her use of his nickname. "I don't have a clue. And you have me at a disadvantage, Miss…?"

She chuckled. "Come now, don't pretend you don't know who I am." The Siren sat back and crossed her legs. "Does Gates Budreau ring a bell?"

His jaw ticked. *Yep. You've got a clue now,* he told himself.

"I can tell by your expression that you do indeed know my colleague. Lovely. That saves us some time. Now that your memory has been restored, where is my eighteenth-century Bellasini emerald, ruby and sapphire bracelet?"

Nicholas shrugged. "I'm sorry, but I don't have it. Gates showed it to me one time, but that's it."

"Mr. Michaux, everything you've heard I'm capable of is grossly underestimated. I assure you that I'm much more dangerous than you realize. Now, I want my sixty-three-thousand-dollar bracelet you stole from Gates before I carve you up like a Christmas turkey."

Shifting in his chair, he held her gaze. "I promise you that I don't have your bracelet. I never stole anything from Gates."

"Your *promises,*" she sneered, "are of no consequence to me. He said you have it, and I want my jewelry."

Her bodyguards yanked Nicholas from his seat and forced

him to kneel while Siren strode over to the wall and retrieved a katana sword from its holder. She swung it through the air in graceful yet powerful movements.

"Whoa, wait a minute," Nicholas said quickly. He attempted to fight against his captors. "I'm not lying. I didn't steal anything from Budreau. Ask him yourself."

Siren walked toward him. "I'm afraid he won't be talking— or eating solid foods for quite some time. No one steals from me and doesn't face the consequences, Mr. Michaux. It's a lesson you're about to learn. The hard way." She smiled.

Widening her stance, she was about to swing the blade at Nicholas when he screamed, "Stop! I know where to get it."

She paused. "Ah, motivation does work. Tell me where, and I suggest you hurry, because my patience is wearing thin, Nicholas. The next time I swing, my blade won't be halted."

"A friend of my girlfriend, Sophia, has it," he said in a rush. "Gates sold it to them, and I was just the middleman that delivered it. Just give me some time, and I swear I'll get it back to you."

"If you're double-crossing me—"

The burly man released him suddenly, causing Nicholas to pitch forward. His hands flew out to keep from face-planting on the wooden floor. Then he wiped the sweat from his brow with a shaky hand before rising cautiously. "I would never do that," he said hoarsely.

Siren handed the weapon to her bodyguard and then embraced Nicholas. "See that you don't," she whispered before nibbling on his earlobe. "Or I promise you my face will be the last thing you see."

ANDREW WAS AWAKENED by the vibrating sound of his cell phone. When he was on duty, he never turned it off. He glanced at the time and groaned aloud. It was two in the morning. He had just gotten to sleep two hours before thanks to a six-foot, deliciously sexy protection officer who periodically occupied his waking and now unconscious hours.

Grasping the device, Andrew lay back against the pillows. When he saw the phone number, sleep left him faster than water circling a drain.

It was Alexa. The object of his desire and the disruptor of his sleep.

Got a minute?

Yeah, sure.

Sitting up in bed, Andrew wiped his hand across his face and took a sip of the bottled water on the nightstand before pressing a speed-dial number.

"Hi," Alexa replied after picking up on the first ring. "I'm sorry to disturb you, but I could use a friend."

"No, it's fine. Alexa, what's wrong?" Andrew bolted upright. "Are you crying?"

"Something happened today," she sniffed. "It was unexpected."

"Where are you?"

"At home."

"What's wrong?" Andrew immediately started calculating how fast he could get there.

ALEXA RELAYED HER encounter with Sophia. Andrew remained silent while she spoke. Most of the time he spent trying to calm down. Her waking him up in the middle of the night and crying put him on edge. Before he had heard the cause of her distress, Andrew was prepared to land on her doorstep ready to do battle if necessary.

It wasn't a matter of if Alexa King was under his skin; he'd made it clear in Chamonix that she was.

"Well, that's a surprise," he replied when she'd finished.

"Tell me about it," Alexa muttered before blowing her nose. "Andrew, I don't think this is a problem I know how to handle."

He smiled at that. "I disagree. Alexa, you deal with split-second decisions, danger and life-and-death situations daily. This assignment would be no different."

"But it *is* different."

"Alexa, you're trained to compartmentalize your emotions and face them later. I know this is childhood trauma that you're dealing with, but you've learned to categorize your feelings. There are exercises we can go over to reinforce it. Don't worry. You can handle this."

She blew out a breath into the phone. "I don't think I can."

"Why not?"

"Because this is personal. Sophia gets to me, Andrew. I don't know why I ever agreed to do this," she cried. "Nothing good can come of it. She's like a walking day of reckoning that I can't escape."

Andrew swung his legs over the side of the bed.

"Listen to me. I've watched you over the years. I know how you think, how you move, and what you can accomplish when you get your mind, body and soul behind it. Lexi, I know you're scared, but you can do this. I have faith in you."

The line went silent for a few moments before Alexa said, "Why? Why do you have such faith in me when I can't even muster up enough for myself?"

"Because I care about you," Andrew replied simply. "And I'm your friend, remember?"

Alexa's silence tore at Andrew in a way that was unfamiliar to him. It made him feel utterly helpless, and that was something he wasn't used to. He also wished he were there with her in his arms instead of thousands of miles away.

"Alexa, if you need me, say the word and I'm there."

"I know. Drew?" she choked out.

"Yes, Lexi?"

"Thank you." Her voice trembled. "For being here when I needed you."

"You're welcome." For now, Andrew would let Alexa set the pace between them. However long it took, he wouldn't rush her. Now that he had acknowledged wanting their relationship to move forward, he was all in.

"I don't know what I'd do without you in my corner."

He chuckled. "Then I guess it's a good thing you'll never have to find out."

Chapter Twenty-One

Alexa climbed up the steps of Ruben Tyndale's private jet. It was a Gulfstream G550 business aircraft that was as elegant as it was functional. The interior had six well-padded cream-colored leather captain's chairs in the front, and a tan suede sofa with cream-and-brown silk accent pillows. The plush rug was off-white in a geometric design. At the far end of the room was a large table with two of the same chairs on each side. The walls were white with the darker cream inlay around the windows and a rich mahogany on the walls separating the seating areas. There was also a bedroom and bathroom.

Handing her bag to the flight attendant, she kept her briefcase with her and headed down the aisle. She greeted several team members before walking to the back of the plane. Then, taking a seat, she secured the seat belt.

"What are you doing?"

Sophia barely glanced up. "What do you mean? I have a flight to Los Angeles, and I'm on it."

"No, *we* have a flight. As in you and your security detail," Alexa replied as calmly as she could.

"Look, they were taking too long. I got tired of waiting around, so I left."

"We've been over this before. You don't get to leave whenever you feel like it. That's not how protection works, Sophia."

"Like I care," the younger woman groused. "I can't help it if your guys can't keep up."

"Can't keep up? You climbed out a bathroom window at the fashion show. But, trust me, if you want us more up close and personal, we will accommodate you."

"Hey, I didn't ask to be here."

"Neither did I," Alexa snapped before she could catch herself. "But for better or worse," she continued, "you are under my company's protection as long as there's a threat. So I need you to cooperate and stay with your detail. Is that clear, Sophia?"

Sophia yawned and lightly nodded. Alexa caught the barely-there agreement, so she let it go. She missed Sophia's smirk.

Alexa reached into her purse and retrieved a pendant. "Here." She handed it to Sophia.

"What's this?"

"It's a dragonfly pendant."

"I can see that, but why are you giving it to me?"

"Because I need you to wear it. It's for security. If there's ever an emergency and you need me, press the wings together for five seconds and release. That activates the emergency beacon, and I'll be able to find you anywhere."

Sophia examined the diamond dragonfly with the emerald wings. "This is so lame," she complained, securing it to her jacket. Her fingers ran over the wings. "Not bad for an imitation."

Alexa shook her head before turning her attention to some briefings she needed to review.

Sophia had several business engagements in Los Angeles and was a guest judge at a contest for aspiring jewelry designers. After landing, Alexa's local team waited to escort them to the Beverly Wilshire hotel. The competition was held in the Burgundy meeting room. Afterward, several fans asked for a picture with Sophia or her autograph. To Alexa's surprise, they stayed until she was done with every fan's request.

"It's time to go," Alexa gently reminded her. "The club opening is soon, and we still need to change."

Sophia was attending a friend of Ruben Tyndale's grand

opening for his new nightclub, so they stayed at a guest house in Pacific Palisades that belonged to Alexa's colleague Alejandro "Dro" Reyes. He owned a crisis management company in Chicago. The two often collaborated on assignments with Dr. Marena Dash-McKendrick. Alexa was thrilled to see them working with her. In the field, Dragonfly operatives relied heavily on Marena's tech inventions, while Alejandro's network of global assets provided them with an edge.

Alejandro's house was in a quiet neighborhood, far from the street, and had a fenced backyard that aided in privacy.

Alexa's room was next to Sophia's, making it easy to watch the headstrong young woman. Or so Alexa thought. When it was time to go, Sophia could not be found.

Alexa's team scrambled to locate her and was about to go on a massive search when Alexa's communication manager alerted her that she had spotted a post of Sophia on her social media page from outside by the pool and grotto.

Taking a deep breath, she counted to five. "Go retrieve Miss Porter," she quietly informed one of her officers.

THE DANCE CLUB was packed by the time they arrived. Sophia was ushered to a VIP area at the back of the club that Alexa was happy to see was away from the heavily populated main dance floor. It was a younger crowd, so Alexa chose younger-looking operatives who were easily able to blend in. The club was U-shaped, with bars set up around the perimeter of the room and the dance floor in the middle. Strobe lights danced off every surface, along with the DJ's light show that was synced with the music he played. The repetitious thumping of the club music made it difficult to carry on a conversation without having to yell.

"Stay sharp," she cautioned her team before escorting Sophia to her table.

Sophia didn't take long to announce that she wanted to dance. Alexa allowed it but had several people placed strategically around the dance floor, watching their principal's every move. The man Sophia was dancing with kept putting his hands on her rear end, which she kept moving.

Finally, he got tired of that and attempted to wrap his hands around Sophia's shoulders to pull her close. Alexa saw Sophia struggle against him and rushed to her side. In one fluid motion, she maneuvered herself between her protectee and the dancer.

He reared back in surprise. "Hey, what is this?" he demanded. "I'm dancing with what's her name, not you."

"I'm afraid your time's up," Alexa replied with a smile. "I suggest you find someone else to occupy your time."

"I don't think so."

He went to step around Alexa, but she shifted until she was in front of him again. He was shorter than she was, so he had to glance up when he spoke.

"What are you doing?" he complained. "Look, lady, you're pretty, but I'd have gone outside if I wanted to climb a tree."

Alexa smiled. "Why, thank you. Pick a new dance partner."

He stood his ground. "I don't think so. I like the one I have. This chick is hot."

He tried to force Alexa out of the way, but she grabbed him as if she would hug him. But instead, she grasped his wrists, twisted them around so they were facing upward and applied pressure.

"Ow, that hurts," he roared over the music thumping around them.

Alexa smiled sweetly. "It's supposed to. Now get lost."

She passed him off to another agent and went to Sophia's side. "We're leaving," was all she said.

"But why? The night's still young, and I'm having a good time. Well, I was until that man couldn't take a hint."

"Sophia, that's not likely to improve the longer people drink."

"Well, you handled him, didn't you? So what's wrong with me staying? You seem to have everything under control."

"Yes, and I'd like it to stay that way."

After escorting Sophia back to the car, Alexa held the door

while she got in, then slid onto the seat next to her charge. During the ride, the only thing that could be heard was Sophia's music playing on her cell phone. Eventually, she turned that off and faced Alexa.

"Are you planning to sit and not talk the entire ride home? Is that supposed to punish me? If so, you're falling a little short."

Alexa didn't bother to reply. Instead, she focused on the passing scenery.

Sophia kicked off her shoes and pulled her legs up under her. "I just wanted to enjoy myself without the entourage in tow."

Praying for calm, Alexa said, "You can do that after the threats have ceased. Ruben hired us for a reason—remember?"

Sophia snorted and began to flip through the pictures on her cell phone. "How can I forget? My style has been permanently cramped ever since."

Incredulous, Alexa turned to face her. "And isn't your life worth a little inconvenience?"

That gave her pause. Sophia instantly looked contrite. "You're right," she said grudgingly. "I apologize."

Satisfied, Alexa added, "Make sure you relay that to those officers that you ditched. They're the ones who got reprimanded for your disappearing act."

"Alexa, we have a challenge car." Her driver glanced at his rearview mirror again. "Two cars back on the right. At five o'clock."

Turning around, she spotted the dark sedan. "I see it, Anthony. Where is car number two?"

Dyan got on the radio. "Stuck one light back," she reported after a moment. "ETA five minutes."

She turned back around. "We need some air, Anthony."

"Yes, ma'am."

The twin turbo engine roared to life as the driver sped up to put some distance between them and the other vehicle.

"Who is it?" Sophia kept glancing back over her shoulder.

"We don't know yet," Alexa replied. "Don't worry. We'll lose them."

The BMW 750i cornered well as Anthony maneuvered in and out of traffic.

"Time?" Alexa asked.

"They're coming up now," Dyan confirmed.

Their second car, a Cadillac Escalade ESV, dropped in behind them and stayed at a safe but close distance.

Heading west on Interstate 10, Anthony used the opportunity to whip past a few slower-moving cars. Then he hit the gas, and the powerful sedan roared to life and took off down the highway. Traffic wasn't heavy, so they made it home in twelve minutes.

They drove up the long driveway and parked out front. Team members were waiting to assist. One opened the back door for Alexa. She got out first, then escorted Sophia inside and straight to her room.

"What was that all about?" Sophia inquired.

"Don't worry, we'll find out," Alexa assured her. "Get some rest. I'll see you in the morning."

Returning downstairs, Alexa entered the kitchen and got some hot tea. Dyan was already there.

"The passengers in the sedan following us were some over-zealous fans. They were trying to get close enough to get some photos of Sophia."

"They were being reckless and dangerous," Alexa argued. She chose a tea pod, dropped it into the brewing machine and pressed the button. "They could've caused an accident—or worse."

Alexa rubbed her shoulders while she waited for her cup to fill.

"There's something else," Dyan replied, scanning over her notes. "It may not be anything, but one of them had a tattoo on his hand that I've seen before."

Opening the pantry, Alexa glanced around for a snack. "Tattoos are pretty common."

"Not this one. Let me do some research, and I'll let you know."

Finding a pack of Pepperidge Farm Chessmen cookies,

Alexa picked up her mug and took a seat at the table across from Dyan.

"Have we found her boyfriend yet?"

"No, but we did a preliminary report and background check on Nicholas Michaux. We're still waiting to hear back from the forensic accountants."

"Thanks, Dyan. Keep me posted."

Alexa's cell phone rang. "Sorry, I've got to take this," she said before answering.

"No problem." Dyan got up and waved goodbye on her way out.

"Hi, Dad."

"Hey, Lex. How's everything? You haven't called in a while, so I wanted to check in to ensure everything is okay?"

"We wanted to check in," Margot corrected over speakerphone.

Picking up her snack, Alexa moved into the living room and sat down. "It's good to hear both your voices. I've missed you."

"We're only a phone call away, honey," her mother replied. "So what's got you so tied up that you can't call home?"

Taking a sip of tea, Alexa closed her eyes and leaned back against the plush cushion. "Not what, who. I've been hired to protect Sophia Porter."

There was a considerable pause before her parents spoke.

"Are you serious? After all that's happened, you've taken Sophia on as a client? Lex, what were you thinking?" her mother hissed. "That family has caused you nothing but pain."

"Mom, I didn't know she was the client when I took the contract."

"Well, now you do, and you can recuse yourself."

She sat forward. "Dad—"

"Alexa, I'm with your mother on this one. Why put yourself through this?"

"Because it's my job," she countered, pinching the bridge of her nose. "Regardless of my feelings, I was hired to protect Sophia. Which I'll do to the best of my ability."

"You're asking for trouble," Margot interjected. "Sophia Porter is selfish and cruel, and tried to make your life a living hell after the attack. And if I know Carol's daughter, she's probably still trying to make you suffer."

Chapter Twenty-Two

Andrew drove up to the Capital Grille, an upscale steakhouse on Pennsylvania Avenue in Northwest Washington, DC. Across the street from the Federal Trade Commission and the National Gallery of Art, the well-known restaurant was also in view of the United States Capitol and a regular haunt of the District of Columbia's political and business scene. After getting out, Andrew adjusted his suit jacket, handed the keys to the valet parking attendant and went inside. Rich African mahogany paneling and art deco chandeliers were an apropos backdrop to the dark leather chairs and stark white linen. The superlative service was to be expected from a restaurant that was famous for its dry-aged steaks, fresh seafood and worldwide acclaimed wines. While he scanned the interior, he tried to contain his excitement. He would be meeting Alexa for dinner.

The hostess escorted Andrew to a booth at the back of the main dining room. Alexa stood and enveloped him in a hug. His arms encircled her waist as he returned the embrace.

"Welcome to DC, Drew."

"Thanks, Lexi," he replied warmly before sliding into the booth. "I was pleasantly surprised to receive your invitation."

"Why surprised?"

"Well, as busy as you've been with your new client, I thought you'd be tied up until further notice."

She placed the napkin back in her lap and took a sip of her water with lemon.

"Dyan's with Sophia for the next few days at another event."

"She seems to be keeping you busy."

"That's an understatement," Alexa replied. "When we're not arguing over her intense dislike of me, we are working overtime to keep her out of trouble. She enjoys trying to find new ways to ditch her protection detail. I swear sometimes it's like guarding a toddler."

He grinned. "Sophia Porter sounds like the perfect assignment to test your mettle."

"That's an understatement," Alexa shot back.

After the hostess had provided their menus and departed, he turned back to Alexa. "I must admit that I was surprised to get your invitation."

"Well, you did say you wanted us to get together soon."

"True," Andrew agreed. "But a weekend at your parents' house? Won't that send the wrong message?"

"Of course not. They've been briefed," she explained. "And they're fully aware that we're the best of friends without any romantic entanglements."

A humorous expression jetted across his face. He refrained from pointing out that they were way past the "just friends" stage, but he merely said, "Sounds good."

The waiter arrived to take drink and appetizer orders.

Alexa chose the lobster bisque and a glass of chardonnay.

"I'll have an iced tea and the calamari," he said, handing back the menu.

"So, how's work?" she asked when they were alone.

"Busy as usual, but I can't complain. With Dad scaling back on his hours, I've been interviewing for a director of operations at Phalanx."

"Married life must be treating him well if he's reducing his workload."

"I think everyone is shocked at him and Esther deciding to elope. The way he tells it, they didn't have time for a long-drawn-out wedding."

"Hey, there's nothing wrong with wanting the rest of your

life to start sooner rather than later after declaring your feelings to the one you love. On the contrary, I think it's romantic."

"At least there were no whispers of a shotgun wedding," Andrew joked.

Alexa almost choked on her water. "Yeah, I think that ship has sailed."

"Seriously, though, I couldn't be happier for them. I'm glad that Dad put himself out there. It's been so long since Mom died. I didn't think he'd find that type of connection again, but Esther is a wonderful woman, and I'm pleased to call her my stepmother."

"She is exceptional. When I was there for training, I remember how warm and welcoming she was to me—to everyone."

"At Phalanx, Esther is everyone's mother. That's one of the things that makes being there special," Andrew pointed out. "She helps keep the trainees from being homesick."

When the waiter delivered their food, they lapsed into companionable silence while they ate.

"Oh, thank you for introducing me to Marena," Andrew said between bites. "Her devices have come in handy on several occasions."

"You're welcome, and I'm glad. She's so talented and has made my job much easier."

"Don't I know it," he agreed. "I've already used one of the cuff links that can be used as an infrared device."

"I've got a compact that does the same thing," she said excitedly. "And I've had to use it twice already."

"I think Marena will never be at a loss for business."

"Don't I know it," Alexa laughed. "But I've already told her she must continue using Dragonfly as her proving ground."

"Oh, she needs to add Phalanx to that list!"

Andrew was interrupted by a cell phone call. It was work, so he excused himself to take it. Alexa watched him walk away. She took a moment to appreciate how good he looked in the dark gray suit and a black shirt unbuttoned at the neck. The cut of his jacket accentuated his broad shoulders. Watching him made Alexa flustered to where she took a healthy sip of ice water.

It was getting difficult for her to deny that thoughts of Andrew had been plaguing her lately. So much so that she'd invited him to DC to her parents' Winter Serve Weekend on a whim. She hadn't thought he'd say yes, and when he did, it filled Alexa with excitement that he was coming and trepidation that her parents might bombard him with questions all weekend.

It was a family tradition they had been doing since her grandfather's time. Friday, guests would arrive and get settled. Saturday, her family would spend an afternoon passing out winter coats and supplies at the homeless shelters, followed by a black-tie fundraiser event at a country club in Upper Marlboro, Maryland. Sunday was church service followed by an afternoon of board games. Alexa's family was competitive, which she'd warned Andrew about in advance. He merely smiled and assured her that he would be fine. *Famous last words*, she thought to herself.

They headed to her parents' house after dinner. Alexa had been dropped at the restaurant by a rideshare service so that she could go back with Andrew. She was excited to use the drive home to spend some alone time with him before her parents swooped in to bombard him with questions and likely embarrassing stories of her childhood. She loved them dearly, but they could go overboard at a moment's notice.

When he got into the car, he grunted. It caught Alexa's attention.

"Are you okay?"

"Yes, for the most part."

She turned in her seat. "What does that mean?" she said warily.

"I hurt my back a few days ago. Sometimes it flares up when I move wrong."

"Oh." Concern for him caused Alexa to reach out and touch the back of his head before resting her hand on the nape of his neck. "Did you get injured during training?"

"No."

"On assignment?"

"Sort of."

She let out a frustrated sigh. "Drew."

"Okay." He chuckled while keeping his eyes on the road. "I was trying to break up a fight, and a large, angry woman decided to use me to break her fall."

Alexa tried to hold in her laugh, but it was pointless. Instead, she dissolved into a fit of giggles.

"I'm glad my hernia amuses you," he said dryly.

She wiped the tears from her eyes with the back of her sleeve.

"I'm sorry, I just... I can see the visual in my mind and can't get rid of it."

Despite his stern expression, Andrew eventually shared in the laughter.

When they arrived, Alexa directed him where to park. After opening her door, he retrieved his bag from the trunk.

"If you'd rather sit out on some festivities, I completely understand."

"No way," he said as he walked with Alexa to the door. "I've carried a wounded, unconscious woman on my back for miles. I think I can handle a little muscle strain."

"Very funny," she shot back. "And it wasn't miles."

"How would you know?" he countered. His eyebrows arched with merriment. "Weren't you passed out?"

Alexa found out after the shooting incident that it was Andrew who'd rushed her to the on-site infirmary after Edgar Jeffries had shot her during the training exercise.

With an indignant huff, Alexa glided past him and went to open the front door, but her father beat her to it.

"Perfect timing," Jake King announced as he stepped aside to allow them to enter. "Everyone just arrived."

Margot joined them in the vestibule. She hugged her daughter.

"Hello, sweetheart."

"Mom, Dad, I'd like to introduce you to Andrew Riker."

"The last time we met, I believe you were seven," Jake replied, shaking his free hand.

Andrew set his bag down. "It's been a while, sir."

"Welcome to our home," Margot enthused before giving him a big hug. "I hope you don't mind, but we're huggers," she explained.

"I don't mind at all." Andrew returned the embrace. "Thank you for having me."

"Of course," she replied before eyeing her daughter. "Any friend of Alexa's is a friend of ours." She turned to her husband. "Jake, this is a precedent, wouldn't you say?"

"Mom," Alexa hissed.

"What?" her mother responded sweetly. "I know you didn't expect us to fall for that 'we're just friends' thing, did you?"

Alexa closed her eyes and tried to remain calm. "It's not a thing. It's the truth."

"Andrew," her father said quickly. "Come on in and make yourself at home. Don't worry about your luggage. We'll take that upstairs later. My brother Curtis, his wife, Ernestine, and my nephew, Zane, arrived not too long ago and are all dying to meet you."

The moment the two men headed down the hall to the family room, Alexa spun around to face her mother.

"Did you have to blindside him two seconds after we stepped through the door?"

"That's not what I did."

"Mom, it's exactly what you did."

"Honey, your boyfriend will be fine. You know it's trial by fire around here. Can I help it if you didn't warn him?"

"He's not my… I already told you both that Andrew and I are just friends."

"I'll reserve my judgment for later," her mother replied before hooking her arm through Alexa's and heading to the family room. "Do you *really* want him to have a separate bedroom, or was that just for show?"

Before Alexa could open her mouth to protest, her mother chuckled. "Did you know that your right eye still twitches when you're about to have a conniption? Oh, Lex, this will be such a fun weekend!"

Chapter Twenty-Three

"Gates, I don't know where you are, but you need to call me ASAP!" Nicholas snapped before pressing the end-call button on his cell phone.

This is insane, he told himself. *How could Gates set me up like this?* This wasn't just a simple misunderstanding. If he didn't find Siren's bracelet, he was a dead man.

"No luck?" The Siren's henchman snickered. "Personally, I hope you don't find it. I'd love to rearrange your face, pretty boy."

"Will you shut up?" Nicholas groused. "This isn't helping."

The man bolted out of his chair.

"Spare me the flexing," Nicholas said tiredly. "We both know you're not going to hurt me."

"Yet," the man snarled. "Sooner or later, Siren will get tired of this goose chase you're playing and give me the approval to end you."

"Until then," Nicholas stressed in a bravado he didn't feel, "I'm untouchable."

His aggressor patted his jacket pocket. "For now."

Thinking of another number, he turned his back and called another contact.

"Bruce." He sighed with relief when the phone was answered. "I need a favor—"

"Oh no you don't. You haven't paid me for the last favor you owe me. If you were here right now, I'd have you killed."

"Get in line," Nicholas said dryly. He got up and moved to the opposite side of the room to get a modicum of privacy.

"Look, I know I owe you money. I'm good for it. You know that. But right now, I need to know where Gates is at."

"Uh-uh. I don't know anything anymore. Especially not for free."

Nicholas turned and faced the wall. "Come on," he pleaded. "This is life-and-death."

"Not from where I'm standing."

"Bruce, I'm serious. Gates stole something. From the wrong person," he added. "I need to get it back—or else."

"Or else what?"

"The Siren will come looking for anyone that Gates knows or has come in contact with, whether they have her bracelet or not."

"Wait, Gates lifted jewelry from the Siren?"

"Yes."

Nicholas was tapped on the shoulder. He turned around.

"Time's up. Siren wants to see you."

"I gotta go. Think about what I said," he whispered into the phone. "You aren't safe, either."

"I'll see what I can do," his friend replied noncommittally.

"Yeah, you do that—and fast."

"Give me twenty-four hours," Bruce replied, and hung up.

Nicholas didn't know if he had twenty-four minutes, much less hours.

This time he was taken to a garden. He found the Siren pruning a rosebush.

Oh, great. She's a green thumb in addition to being an assassin.

"How's progress, Mr. Michaux?"

He shifted on his feet. "I'm not going to lie. It's slow. I need more time if you want me to locate this bourgeois bracelet of yours."

Siren smiled and removed one of her gloves. "I thought I was clear in my intent," she said with a baffled expression.

Without warning, she walked over to Nicholas and punched him in the solar plexus, followed by an uppercut to the jaw. With a grunt and then a round of violent coughing, he dropped to his knees.

"I have killed men smarter and cuter than you. Your logistical problems are not my problems, Mr. Michaux."

"I get that." The metallic taste of blood in his mouth wasn't the only thing that made him queasy. He was still having difficulty breathing.

Turning to her employee, she said, "Take him to my office. If he doesn't provide Miss Porter's account number the moment after you've arrived, cut off a finger every minute that I don't have what I want."

"No, wait," Nicholas yelled as he was grabbed by the arm and escorted out. He fought every step of the way. "Don't do this!"

The Siren grinned. "Ah, nothing like motivation," she called after him before returning to gardening.

ALEXA, HER FAMILY and Andrew were in the kitchen when she received a telephone call.

"Excuse me, I have to take this," Alexa replied when her phone rang.

"How's everything going?" Dyan asked when Alexa answered.

"Not bad. We're having a great time."

"I'm sorry to disturb you at your parents' house."

"No worries, Dyan. What's up?"

"We heard back from the forensic accountants. I emailed you the report of findings."

"Hang on a sec," she said, rushing up to her bedroom. Sitting at her desk, she opened her laptop and checked her email. After reviewing the document, Alexa leaned back in her chair.

"Well, this likely won't go well."

"I don't doubt it," Dyan agreed. "Do you want me to tell her?"

"No, I'll do it."

"Given your history, Alexa, do you think that's wise?"

"Probably not," she said truthfully, "but it's my responsibility. Can you ask Miranda to call me? I need to speak with her on a few things."

"Sure. Have you spoken to her lately?"

"No, why?"

"Yesterday, I ran into her coming out of the ladies' room and she looked like she'd been crying."

Alexa furrowed her brow. "She hasn't said anything."

"To me, either. I asked her what was wrong, and she tried to brush it off. I think it has something to do with her new boyfriend."

"Apollo?"

"Yep. Miranda is as pleasant and cheerful as lemonade in the summertime. But lately, she seems distracted."

Alexa could've kicked herself for not noticing. It didn't sit well that one of her employees was in distress, and she wasn't aware of it.

"Would you ask her to call me?"

"Will do."

She hung up with her associate and reread the report. Alexa let out a weary sigh before tossing it aside. She did not relish Sophia's reaction to hearing about Nicholas's hidden agenda. "And Mom talks about me having a conniption."

Her thoughts turned back to Miranda. Alexa couldn't recall one day when she wasn't her best. Grabbing her phone, she texted Dyan and asked her to do a preliminary background check on Apollo Hayes. Something was up with him, but Alexa couldn't say what. His not meeting Miranda's friends and her not meeting his didn't sit well. For Miranda's sake, she'd look him over to make sure he was everything he claimed to be.

"Hey, you okay? Your mother asked me to come up and check on you. She said we're leaving in fifteen minutes."

Alexa glanced over her shoulder to see Andrew standing just outside the doorway.

"Yes." She set her phone down. "Just an issue at work that I need to take care of."

When he remained, Alexa said, "You can come in, Andrew."

He eased into the room, peering around as he walked.

Alexa's bedroom looked like she hadn't been in it since leaving for college. Two nightstands flanked a full-size canopy bed against one wall. There were multicolored lights draped around the top, a white comforter set with yellow and green flowers, and a few throw pillows. Three books were stacked on one nightstand with a lamp and an alarm clock.

Across the room was an alcove with a plush white couch and flat-screen television mounted to the wall. A large built-in with a vast collection of books anchored the space.

French doors led out onto a balcony with white wicker furniture and floral-colored cushions. The walls were white, but there were colorful landscapes and pictures of animals hanging around the room. The space was neat, orderly and composed, just like Alexa.

"Finished scoping out my old room?"

A glimmer of amusement sparkled in his eyes. "Not yet."

Andrew walked over and sat on the love seat. "How long has it been since you've slept in here?"

"Usually just holidays."

"That's cool."

Shutting her laptop, Alexa joined him on the couch. "Yep, one of the duties of an only child. Make yourself available for all family functions."

He laughed. "True." He curled a lock of her hair around his fingers.

"It's nice seeing another piece of the Alexa puzzle."

Her eyebrows shot up. "I'm a puzzle?"

"Yes, indeed," he replied. "And I'm enjoying learning how the pieces fit together."

"I'm hardly as exciting as you make me out to be."

He inched closer, regarding Alexa as if he was studying something intriguing. "You are to me."

Alexa found it hard to breathe under the sheer weight of his gaze. Her heartbeat pounded in her ears. She wondered if he could hear it.

Andrew held out his hand. Alexa didn't hesitate to lock her fingers with his. He kissed the back of her hand. "I have to admit, I'm feeling kinda honored right now."

"Why?"

"Because I'm the only man that's been in your inner sanctum."

"How do you know that?" Alexa tossed back. "I've had a man or two in here before."

"Your family doesn't count. Besides, your mother told me."

Alexa closed her eyes and tried to contain her embarrassment. She and her mother were going to have a talk about boundaries.

When she felt the touch of his fingers along her cheek, her eyes flew open.

She wasn't prepared for her reaction to the desire in Andrew's gaze or the way his hand drifted down to her neck.

His fingers touched the pulse point. "Your heartbeat is elevated."

"You don't say?"

Alexa's voice drifted out like an intimate caress. Their eyes locked briefly before he lowered his head and replaced his fingers with his lips.

Her hands closed around his neck and held his head stationary. Leaning into his touch, Alexa didn't protest when Andrew deepened the kiss.

Andrew's weight pinned her back against the cushions.

Her body hummed with excitement as her hands roamed his back, shoulders and the nape of his neck.

"Lexi," Andrew murmured against her lips, trailing kisses down her throat. "You don't know how incredible you feel."

"About as good as you do right now."

Everywhere Alexa caressed, Andrew's skin felt hot to the touch. At that moment, she wanted him with a passion so consuming that it took her several moments to realize he was saying her name.

"What?" she finally managed to say.

He kissed her a final time and said, "Your mother is calling you."

Alexa didn't think. She just reacted.

"Yes?" she yelled so loud that Andrew scrunched up his face in reaction.

"I'm now deaf in one ear."

"Let's go, you two," her mother bellowed.

Alexa moaned. "We have to go."

He smiled at the genuine frown on her face before kissing the tip of her nose.

"Yes, I know."

"I don't want to," she said frankly.

Andrew buried his face in her neck. "And you think I do?"

Alexa took another moment to enjoy the closeness with Andrew before nudging him.

"We'd better go before she comes looking."

He reluctantly got up and helped Alexa to her feet. After she had adjusted her clothing, Andrew reached up and traced the path she had made to guide the few errant strands away from her face. He continued along her neck and down her shoulder.

Not once had their gazes disengaged. They continued to stare at each other in mutual fascination.

Alexa felt her body swaying closer to Andrew.

When did that happen? she wondered. When had she relaxed her "no relationship" policy so completely?

"We should go before your mom sends up a search party," he warned softly.

"Uh, yeah," she replied, clearing her throat. "I wouldn't put it past her."

Alexa moved past Andrew and headed for the door. She didn't need to turn around to check if he was following. The hair tingling at the back of her neck told her all she needed to know.

When they reached the foyer, everyone was putting on their outerwear.

"Perfect timing," her father said gleefully. "We're ready to go."

"Great, I'll go get our coats," she said quickly and bolted to the hall closet. But truthfully, she needed a few moments to gather the wits scattered around her head.

She placed her hand on her heart and felt the rapid staccato beat hammering against her chest. She blew out an exasperated breath.

Get a hold of yourself, Alexa, she chided.

For the first time since Andrew arrived, Alexa started doubting her bright idea to open a box she couldn't close. Now that she had tasted a sample of the fruit, she wanted the entire bowl.

Retrieving their coats, Alexa turned around to find Zane standing right behind her with an amused expression on his face.

"You say one word, and I'll put you in a choke hold," she snapped before shoving past him.

"What?" he countered sweetly before dissolving into a fit of laughter.

Chapter Twenty-Four

The event ended late, so they hurried home to prepare for the black-tie event across town. When Alexa came downstairs after getting dressed, only Andrew was waiting. She glanced around.

"Where'd everyone go?"

"Since your mother was the event chair, they went on ahead so they wouldn't be too late."

"Oh. Not like I took that long," she muttered, reaching the bottom step.

She finally noticed that Andrew was wearing a black tuxedo with a red bow tie and red silk pocket square. Alexa had to force herself not to gape. He looked more handsome than when she'd seen him in Chamonix, and that was saying something!

Alexa watched him look her over from head to toe before saying, "Lexi, you look breathtaking."

Her face lit up at his praise. It had taken her forever to get dressed, and up until that moment, she had second-guessed every choice. Now she was glad that she had chosen a black satin floor-length gown. It had an hourglass design that was outlined by rhinestones. The arms and low-cut back of the dress were sheer.

"Thank you," Alexa responded as he helped her into a long velvet coat. "You look wonderful, too."

Not releasing her lapels, Andrew backed Alexa up until she was against the wall. Startled, her expression showed her surprise.

"What are you doing?"

"Admiring the view," Andrew quipped before touching her cheek. "You are so beautiful, Alexa King."

She did not get a chance to reply before Andrew kissed her with a heat that could have lit a wet match.

"Drew, we have to go," she whispered against his lips. "Any longer and they'll think we're not coming."

"If the alternative is staying here with you in my arms, I see nothing but upside."

Eventually, he released her coat, but did not let her go. Instead, he rested his forehead against hers.

"Thank you," he whispered against her lips.

"For what?"

"For allowing me to know you better. For a glimpse into your personal life—to *see* you."

Alexa was ready to dissolve into a puddle on her parents' marble floor.

Her line of sight moved from holding his gaze down to his lips. Instead, it lingered on the rapidly beating pulse at his neck.

"Lexi, that's dangerous," he warned.

Her glance traveled back up to his eyes. "I deal with danger every day, remember?"

"Not this kind."

Before she could retort, Andrew held her wrist out of the way before crushing her body against his chest. His mouth claimed hers for a searing kiss. The power of it took Alexa's breath away.

"That wasn't dangerous at all," she murmured against his mouth.

In a flash, Andrew picked Alexa up. Her legs locked around his waist as he backed them up against the closet door. Her gown bunched in yards of silky fabric between them. Before she could react, he kissed a trail from her lips to her neck. He lingered at the spot where her pulse beat out a rapid staccato against her skin.

"Are we just friends, Alexa?"

"Hmm?" she said in a dazed whisper.

Andrew leaned closer. His lips floated just above her skin and hovered over her ear. His warm breath caressed her as he spoke.

"Tell me that you feel nothing but friendship for me. Say you don't want me as much as I want you, Alexa, and I will never mention it again."

She gravitated toward his touch. A small moan escaped her lips.

"Andrew."

Andrew Riker would run away with her heart if she let him. And right now, Alexa wasn't sure she would stop him, and that scared her to death.

WHEN THEY ARRIVED, the party had already begun. They picked up name tags at the entrance, where there was a long-stemmed red rose for each lady. A hostess directed them to their family's table, where she found her aunt and uncle sitting.

"Where's everyone?" Alexa asked as Andrew helped her out of her coat.

"Zane and his date are on the dance floor. Your parents are making the rounds," Ernestine replied. "My, don't both of you look gorgeous."

"So do you," Alexa replied with a kiss on her cheek.

Andrew placed a hand on her back and leaned in. "What do you say, Alexa? Will you dance with me?"

"I'd love to." She beamed at Andrew, allowing him to lead her to the floor.

"This is 'Corcovado,'" she informed him as he swept her into his arms. "It's one of my favorites."

"Mine, too."

Andrew guided her into a bossa nova dance. Alexa laughed as they glided together in unison. "You're full of surprises, Mr. Riker."

"So are you, Miss King."

After the dance, Alexa went to the ladies' room to freshen up. As she was coming out, a woman called after her.

"Alexa King, is that you?"

Turning, Alexa's mouth dropped open. "Andi?"

"Yes," the woman cried and, throwing up her arms, rushed across the room to gather Alexa in a loose bear hug.

"My goodness, it's wonderful to see you!"

When she finally released her, Alexa stared at Oleander Barlowe, her former roommate, with genuine shock.

"How have you been? Honestly, you haven't changed a bit since college," the woman gushed.

"I hope that's not the case," Alexa retorted. "So, what are you doing here?"

"A client of mine invited me. You know me, always working, and stuffy events like these are the perfect place to land new clients."

Same old ambitious Oleander. She would never let a roomful of rich people go to waste, Alexa noted.

Latching arms with Alexa, Oleander said, "So, what have you been up to?"

She grabbed a glass of champagne off a waiter's serving tray as they walked.

"Still working for your dad's company, married with a slew of kids, a minivan and a quaint Cape Cod in the suburbs?"

"Not exactly." Alexa brought her up to speed on life since college.

"No kidding? How fortuitous that we ran into each other."

Setting her empty glass on a high table, Oleander retrieved a business card from her velvet clutch and handed it to Alexa. "Let's keep in touch, I can definitely send some clients your way—if you return the favor, of course." She winked.

"Oh, uh, sure."

"Thanks, love. You always were dependable."

Alexa glanced around for Andrew so she could introduce them. When their eyes connected across the room, her happiness was crushed by his look of surprise and then pain. A second later, Andrew stormed out of the room.

What just happened? she asked herself.

Disentangling herself from Oleander's arm, Alexa excused herself and rushed out of the room to find Andrew.

SLAMMING OUT OF the ballroom, Andrew strode down the corridor and out the back door. It was frigid outside, but it didn't register. His emotions were a jumbled mess of broken promises, betrayal and regret.

There, right in front of him, was Alexa talking to the woman who had smashed his heart to pieces before devouring it like chocolates on Valentine's Day. His worst nightmare had just come true. Now he knew why there was a reason Alexa had reminded him of Olee. They were the best of friends!

Bile rose into his throat, and his palms grew sweaty. He hadn't listened to his gut instinct trying to warn him about Alexa King, and now he was paying for it.

Taking a minute to get his anger under control, Andrew eventually went back inside. When he did, he was brought up short by a woman blocking his path.

"Hello, Andrew."

"Olee."

The one word was laced with a perfect balance of surprise at her audacity and hatred. If Oleander was affected at his tone, she did not show it.

She smiled. "I'm surprised you still remember that nickname you gave me."

"I haven't forgotten anything over the years," he said in a barely controlled voice. "What are you doing here?"

"Isn't it obvious? Hobnobbing with the wealthy benefactors, same as you."

"That's not why I'm here."

Her voice grated on his nerves, making him long to get away. Not willing to bear her presence longer than necessary, Andrew got straight to the point.

"How do you know Alexa King?"

"Alexa?" she shot back with a raised eyebrow. "I could ask you the same question."

Seeing that he was waiting for an answer, Oleander shrugged. "We met in college. We were best friends and roommates. We were inseparable. Can you imagine running into each other again? It's like the years just melted away."

Seeing Andrew frown, Oleander continued. "So, what's your story?"

"We're colleagues," he said, not elaborating.

"Ah. Alexa and I are meeting for lunch in a few days. I have a joint venture I wanted to discuss. It should be very lucrative." She gleamed.

Andrew let out a contemptuous laugh. "You haven't changed a bit, Oleander. Ambition still overrides everything else—except your love of money."

"Neither have you," she shot back. "Still holding grudges. You plan on taking what happened to your grave, I see."

A couple walking by spared the two a curious glance. Andrew took her elbow and guided her down the hall back toward the party.

"I can tell you now that Alexa isn't interested in any proposition you might concoct."

She yanked her arm free of his grasp and stopped walking. "I'd wager that I know Alexa a lot better than you do," Oleander threw back.

His jaw ticked. "Alexa is nothing like you."

Oleander went to slide her hand under his tux jacket. "If you say so," she said smugly. "We couldn't have been besties all those years and not have a few things in common."

Capturing her wrist before she could touch him, Andrew leaned in.

"You know, I don't know what's worse. The fact that you don't even acknowledge your part in our breakup, or the fact that you're still only interested in using people."

Her once-amiable expression darkened. "People in glass houses should steer clear of stones, lover."

Not bothering to respond, Andrew looked at her disgustedly before leaving. When he rounded a corner, he almost collided with Alexa. His hands instantly reached out to steady her.

"Andrew. I've been looking everywhere for you." She sighed with relief. "What's going on? I looked up, and you'd disappeared."

"Did you invite Oleander Barlowe here?"

Alexa was taken aback by his tone. "No. We went to college together. I haven't seen her in years."

"What did she want?"

Alexa frowned. "She asked to meet with me in a few days to catch up and discuss a business venture.

"Andrew, what is going on with you? You're acting strange."

"Don't do it. Olee can't be trusted and has only ever cared about herself."

"That's not true. We used to be best friends in college."

"So does that mean the two of you are cut from the same cloth?"

Alexa took a step back. His accusation hurt. "Why would you ask that?"

"Because I know her," he snapped. "She'll end up betraying your trust. I'm warning you, don't entertain any business proposition she has for you. You'll jeopardize your reputation fooling around with Oleander Barlowe."

Alexa felt her anger rising. "Andrew, I appreciate your concern, but I don't appreciate you implying I can't handle myself where Andi's concerned."

He threw his hands up in frustration. "Are you that naive? She's a professional grifter, Alexa. She won't hesitate to eat you up and spit out the bones."

"And how would *you* know?"

"Because she did it to me!"

The words shot out of Andrew's mouth like a cannonball.

Alexa's eyebrows shot upward. "Andrew, I—"

He held a hand up to stop her. "I don't need your sympathy. You know what, suit yourself, Alexa. You're going to do what you want anyway. It's obvious you don't need me trying to look out for you, right?"

"You're not being fair, Andrew."

"Just admit it. You don't need anything or anyone. You don't *need*."

The color drained from her face. "That's not true."

"Yeah? You could've fooled me."

Chapter Twenty-Five

Andrew stared out the hotel room window. A towel was slung low around his middle. His warm body in proximity to the cold window caused it to fog up, but he was oblivious. There was nothing about his evening that had gone according to plan.

Rubbing a hand over his jaw, Andrew retreated from the window. He padded to the bed and fell back onto the fluffy mattress.

He realized that he had overreacted to Alexa's conversation with Oleander, but at the time was powerless to stop it. He would apologize for his behavior, but the fact that Alexa didn't set him straight only reiterated his point that it was Alexa's pride and fear of commitment keeping them apart. Could he be content waiting for her to accept they were perfect for each other? Should he throw in the towel and walk away? That thought didn't sit well. Andrew had never given up on anything in his life. Especially not something he wanted with a passion that kept him up at night and made him restless.

He cared for Alexa unlike anything he had experienced before. Even his relationship with Oleander paled by comparison, and he had thought himself completely in love with her. Alexa was different. His feelings for her had been way past the level of friendly since before she graduated from Phalanx. He was all in the moment Alexa stared at him with a perfect blend of lust and fascination.

"Come on, Riker. You gotta double your efforts to win her

over." And he would, but it was hard to overcome Alexa's trust issues and the past. She was complex, stubborn and trapped in a cycle of fear like a spider's prey dangling from its web. But regardless of how long it took, he'd help her break free. The first thing he would do is give her space. As much as it would kill him to distance himself from her, it was necessary. Alexa needed to come to terms with not just their relationship, but the past. Their future happiness depended on it.

ALEXA SPENT THE next week at work putting out fire after fire. Several members of her staff were on leave. Either sick or scheduled, it meant they were short-staffed, so Alexa had to fill the gap. She didn't mind. In truth she was glad for the distraction.

It had been two weeks since she had spoken to Andrew. After their argument at the Christmas fundraiser, she returned home to find him gone. He had left a note thanking her parents for their hospitality and wishing everyone happy holidays. Hurt, Alexa had tried to call, but he didn't answer. Unable to deal with the questions from her parents, Alexa pretended that nothing was wrong and Andrew was called away on an unexpected assignment.

She had regretted her words to him, but his behavior had gotten under her skin. Now, he had retreated behind a wall of cool indifference that made her grit her teeth in frustration.

What did you expect? You basically told him you didn't trust him and didn't want a relationship, her inner voice scolded. Plus, pride kept her from setting the record straight on working with Oleander Barlowe. She didn't trust Andi, but she had neglected to tell Andrew that, which in retrospect had only made matters worse. *You got exactly what you wanted, so leave it alone.*

With her relationship with Andrew in tatters, Alexa threw herself into the job. Everyone at work had noticed the change in her mood, and that she had not mentioned Andrew, but no one pressed her on it. Not even Dyan and Miranda.

Her latest assignment was protecting a widowed business-man, Nigel Weatherby, and his young son while they were going to London for a tech conference in Kensington. His company rented out a luxurious seven-bedroom house in Chelsea, an affluent area in central London. It was close to the River Thames, Harrods and Michelin-star dining. In addition to Alexa's team, his nanny accompanied him, as did his assistant. Her principal enjoyed jogging, so they would go out at night after his son went to bed and the house was quiet.

The rental was close to Chelsea Embankment, a road and a walkway along the river's north bank.

While jogging and running weren't two of Alexa's favorites, she did them if it was a client's preference.

They jogged almost two miles in silence before Nigel slowed the pace to cool down. It was cold out, so their walk was brisk.

"So, why does a woman like you get into executive protection?"

She fell into step beside him. "A woman like me?"

"Tall, beautiful and pleasant to be around. From your looks, though, you don't look like you've been in many fights."

"I assure you that I have. It takes more work to avoid physical altercations than to get into them."

"Then you must have a knack for it, because you look like you've been behind a desk all day," Nigel observed. "So, is there a mister bodyguard at home?"

Alexa laughed. The heat from her breath caused a cloud of condensation. Was he flirting? If so, she would firmly shut him down. It was her company policy that employees never got romantically involved with clients. And even if it weren't, Nigel wasn't the one.

Alexa snapped out of her daydream. "No, there's not," she said quickly. "Just a lot of houseplants that keep dying off."

"I know the feeling," he responded. "Luckily for me, I have a live-in housekeeper who keeps on top of all the greenery."

They continued to chat while they walked. Alexa enjoyed his company, and though relaxed, she was alert. After walking a short distance, she spotted two men approaching, so she stepped in front of her client while continually chatting.

"Pardon me? Do you have a light?" one of the men asked.

"No, sorry, I don't," her client replied.

The stranger glanced over at Alexa. "What about you?"

"What about me?"

"Do you have a light?"

"No," she said sweetly. "I don't."

"How about that watch?" he countered, motioning to her client's wrist.

"If you think I'm—"

Alexa rested her hand on her client's forearm and squeezed lightly. He stopped talking, but his anger was still evident in his stance.

She raised both hands. "We don't want any trouble," Alexa said, keeping her eyes on his hands the entire time.

"Too late," the man in front of her replied with a grin before he lunged.

His hand came up, and Alexa saw the knife. Immediately, she grabbed his wrist and pinned his hand against her leg while rotating with him to get him away from her client. Then she struck him under the chin and didn't wait to see him collapse before turning on the other assailant going after her client.

Grabbing the back of his jacket, Alexa yanked him backward and down to the ground, where she delivered an elbow strike to the stomach. Unfortunately, his coat was thick, so she had to hit him twice.

"Let's go," she commanded, pulling her client along as she broke into a run.

Alexa glanced back twice to ensure they weren't being followed.

"We're clear," she announced at the end of the block.

Two men were running from the house to intercept them.

"Miss King," one of them huffed. "We saw you running. Are you both all right?"

"We're fine, thanks," she said, ushering her principal up the walkway and through the front door.

"Thanks to you." Nigel leaned over to catch his breath. "Your quick thinking kept that situation from being much worse."

"That's what we're here for," she countered.

He reached out for the wall. "I feel a little light-headed."

"That's the adrenaline rush. It'll go back to normal soon."

He nodded. "I'm going to go take a shower and then check on my son. Thanks again, Alexa."

"You're welcome. Good night."

ALEXA WAS SURPRISED to find her bed turned down and a fire roaring in the fireplace when she came into the room.

Decorated in taupe and cream with rose-gold accents, the room was relaxing.

After a shower, Alexa donned a pair of fleece pajamas, climbed into bed and snuggled under the thick comforter. Lying in the luxurious bed wrapped up like a burrito, Alexa's thoughts kept drifting to Andrew. He was the one she always called when she had something on her mind, or after a particularly stressful day or a run-in with a bad guy. Speaking to him made her feel better.

When she heard the indicator for a request for a video chat, Alexa's heart thumped wildly in her chest. *Andrew.*

Alexa grabbed it excitedly. Her elation was dashed when she accepted the call and found Dyan's face on the screen instead. "Oh, hey, Dyan," she said with as much excitement as she could muster in the wake of her intense disappointment.

"Wow," Dyan replied. "I've had more excitement coming from bad guys I've had to beat up than you."

"Oh, I'm sorry. It's not you. I just—"

"Thought I was Andrew?"

"What? No," Alexa countered quickly. "I just had a rough

evening. Had a run-in while out with my principal on a late-night jog. Nothing I couldn't handle."

"If that's true, then what caused the rough night?" Dyan countered.

Alexa ignored the knowing grin on her friend's face. Confessing that she missed Andrew with a vengeance and hadn't thought of anything else since he went radio silent wasn't a truth that she was ready to share.

Chapter Twenty-Six

When Alexa scheduled a meeting with Sophia a few days later, she was exhausted. Jet lag and work were starting to take their toll. To make matters worse, she hadn't connected with her family since returning from London. She had called Andrew and was surprised when she got him. At a loss for what to say, she wished him a happy new year. Andrew had thanked her and wished her the same. He was cordial but distant. After hanging up, Alexa's mood tanked for the rest of the day. Later that afternoon, she had a meeting with Sophia.

As usual, Sophia glided into Alexa's office like she owned it.

When she sat down and finally looked at Alexa, she gasped. "Good grief, you look horrible."

"Thank you," Alexa retorted tiredly. "Sophia, we need to talk."

"Presumably that's why I'm here?"

Ignoring the sarcasm, she retrieved a folder from her desk.

"Are you aware of a joint account with Nicholas in Portugal?"

"What?" Sophia sat forward. "I never opened an account with Nico."

Alexa spun the report around and pushed it across her desk.

Sophia read over the pages before tossing them back. Her face was a mottled red. "This is ridiculous. Clearly, it's a mistake."

"So, you're saying that's not your signature?"

"Uh, what part of forgery isn't coming across? No, that's not my signature. Close, but not exact."

"That's not the only suspicious activity Mr. Michaux has been up to while you've been apart. Didn't he tell you that he was in France?"

Sophia shifted in her chair. "Yes. Why?"

"Well, his cell phone records indicate that he's in Portugal. Just outside of Lisbon."

"So he's not where he said he'd be. He could be hanging out with some friends. We did argue. Likely he's just blowing off some steam."

"Is this one of his friends?" Alexa asked, handing Sophia a photograph.

She scanned the picture of a red-haired woman with Nicholas. Her aloof facade started to slip. "None that I know."

"Her name is Eileen English. Her nickname is the Siren, and she's a dangerous woman. She spent several years in jail for fencing stolen items, extortion and kidnapping. She's been brought up on multiple charges in the last few years, but there was never enough evidence for an arrest. We don't know her connection to Nicholas just yet, but—"

"Why are you investigating my boyfriend? Aren't I the one you're supposed to keep tabs on?"

"Yes," Alexa confirmed. "And those around you who could be potential threats."

"We fought. I'd hardly call him a threat," Sophia scoffed. "You're taking this to the extreme, don't you think?"

"This is what we do, Sophia. We look for suspicious activity that could cause problems for those we protect."

"Well, this has been more intrusive than helpful," Sophia complained. "We've been at this for weeks, and nothing has happened. Clearly, whatever threat I was under is no longer an issue, so it looks like I don't need your services anymore."

"Sophia, we don't know if you're out of danger yet. Therefore, ending your protection is unwise."

"I disagree. I'm done with your team snooping into my private life. Whatever outstanding balance you have, send me the bill." Sophia jumped up.

"Wait a minute," Alexa replied, rising. "Sophia, I know you're upset about Nicholas, but that's no reason to be reckless and—"

"Oh, *I'm* reckless?" Sophia sputtered. "That's rich coming from you. I knew this was a mistake from the beginning. You haven't changed one bit."

Digging into her purse, Sophia retrieved a checkbook. She filled one out, signed it and slammed it on Alexa's desk.

"Here. I'm sure this more than covers any owed amount."

Alexa didn't bother to take it. "You can't fire me, Sophia. The contract is with Ruben."

"Trust me. He'll side with me when he realizes there's no way we can continue working together. Have a nice life, Alexa King."

Sophia stormed out of the room, almost slamming the door off its hinges.

Alexa bolted out of her chair. "No amount of money is worth this aggravation!"

"Do I even want to know what that was about?" Dyan called from the doorway. Miranda hovered right behind.

"Same Sophia, different day," Alexa muttered. "Just when you think she couldn't act brattier and more entitled, bam! She exceeds your expectations."

"Should I contact Mr. Tyndale for you, Miss King?"

"No, thanks, Miranda. I'll handle this."

Her assistant nodded, then retreated to her desk.

Dyan sat down.

"Alexa, do you—"

"Don't you dare say you think I'm overreacting," Alexa fumed. "*We* are putting our lives on the line for a woman who doesn't appreciate it. And you know what else?"

"You're going to tell me," Dyan said calmly.

"She doesn't waste an opportunity to undermine our efforts." Alexa paced like a caged panther looking for a way out.

"I'll admit that part of the reason I took Sophia on as a client was because I felt guilty about Shelley and wanted to help their family in any way I could, but this is cruel and unusual punishment, Dyan. I'm done putting my employees' lives on the line for someone who doesn't appreciate or deserve the sacrifices we're all making."

"Alexa, I understand. And of course, this is your call. Whatever you want, you know we'll make it happen."

"Thanks, Dyan," Alexa said, plopping onto the couch. "I appreciate the support—and you letting me rant," she added with a smile. "I hope you know how invaluable you are to me."

"Sure I do, Alexa." Dyan came over and hugged her boss and friend. "I'm here if you need me. Oh, by the way. Have you noticed anything off with Miranda?"

"No, like what?"

Dyan shrugged. "I don't know yet. She's just not acting herself. I have to repeat things several times, and she's been jumpy."

"No, I haven't, but I've been meaning to circle back around regarding Apollo Hayes."

"Don't you think you'd better deal with Sophia first?" Dyan reasoned.

"You're not wrong," Alexa agreed before calling Sophia's business partner, Ruben Tyndale, to explain their latest run-in.

"I'm sorry, Alexa. Truly I am," he said ruefully. "I had hoped that Sophia's animosity would have diminished."

"As did I. I gave Sophia some news about Nicholas that she wasn't expecting, and it set her off. I've had time to think about it, and I can understand her lashing out. Even growing up, she was never good with surprises."

Alexa relayed their findings to Ruben.

"What? I can't believe he'd do that to Sophia," Ruben snarled. "I knew he had bad points, but forging documents and possibly embezzling money from her? That's insane—and criminal."

"Sophia is sure there's an explanation for it. So the first

order of business is to learn more about why he's hanging out with a dangerous criminal, and how it ties into this new bank account—that is, if we're not fired."

"Earlier, it sounded like you were happy to see her go."

"I was," Alexa admitted. "But that wouldn't solve any of Sophia's problems, would it?"

"No, it wouldn't. And for the record, I was never going to let you go, Alexa. She may not know what's best for her right now, but I do. You and your folks stick by her side. At least until we get all of this mess sorted out."

"How long do you plan to hold me hostage?"

The Siren sat across from Nicholas and waited while one of her servants set a dinner plate in front of her. "Flower Duet" from the French composer Léo Delibes's opera *Lakmé* piped through in-ceiling speakers.

She leaned over and smelled the savory aroma of her chef's latest culinary delight. Her face radiated pleasure as she bit into the medium-rare meat perched on her fork. Siren slowly chewed the food and swallowed before washing it down with a sip of red wine.

"That's a rather harsh word, Nicholas. I'd like to think of you as my guest."

"A guest that isn't allowed to leave of their own volition," he tossed back. "And one that you were more than happy to maim if I didn't provide you with a bank account number. That hardly jibes with my definition of the word."

Nicholas sliced the large rib eye steak and took a hefty bite. It was perfect, but he would never tell his captor that.

Siren motioned to the glass decanter between them. "Wine?"

"No, thank you."

He had no plans to drink anything around the Siren because he'd need his wits about him to come up with a plan to get that bracelet back.

Nicholas wondered about Sophia. Their relationship would be over if she somehow learned about the bank account and him helping the Siren clean her money. He was playing a dangerous game, but his deranged captor had to believe he was on board and getting her bracelet back. She had threatened to chop off his fingers if he didn't.

Desperate for cash to fund his business, he'd done Gates Budreau a favor. Gates had a copy made of the eighteenth-century Bellasini bracelet to sell to some unsuspecting rich man as a gift for his wife. He was mortified to discover the man's wife was Sophia's friend. What if she found out he was involved in the bait and switch? Their relationship would be over.

Nicholas had no idea what his friend had done with the original. He felt like killing Gates himself for involving him in his scheme and putting his life at risk, but how could he blame him? If he'd been the one being tortured instead, he would've said just about anything to save himself.

Gates must've been betting that I'd be able to get back the counterfeit bracelet, Nicholas reasoned. *Why else would he say I had it?*

It was a dangerous move trying to trick Siren. After all, she was bound to realize a fake from the real deal. No. It was too dangerous. He needed the original. If not, he had better be on the other side of the world when the Siren found out she had been duped.

Originally, Nicholas had flat-out refused to help, but changed his tune when one of Siren's goons hung him over the tower railing by his ankles.

At least Sophia is safe, he told himself. Nicholas knew that Siren's threats were far from idle, and the last thing he wanted was to endanger Sophia's life.

This is all your fault, he scolded himself.

Nicholas had been desperate to get his business off the ground and had no plans to crawl back to his father for more money or involve Sophia. *Now look at me*, he thought bitterly. *That streak of pride may cost me my life. First, I have to find Gates to see who has the original bracelet, and get it back.*

Nicholas didn't know how, but he would convince her to let

him go under the guise of getting her precious bracelet. He'd see Gates and force him to give up the whereabouts of the original. If his friend resisted, he'd make him see reason. The first thing he would do if he made it out of the Siren's lair alive would be to contact his father. It was time to put pride aside. He would tell his father that his life was in danger, minus all the details, and pray that his father would assign him a security detail to keep him safe until he located Gates. He was not going to die for anyone.

Chapter Twenty-Seven

"We're here, sir."

Nicholas completed the payment on the ride-sharing app and thanked his driver.

He still couldn't believe that the Siren had let him go. Not that he was under any illusions. He was only free so that he could convince Gates to give him the bracelet and return it to her. It was also likely that he was being followed, and that his life would be in jeopardy once she got what she wanted.

He got out of the car and walked up to the black wrought-iron gate. Next, Nicholas entered the six-digit pass code and stepped aside while the gate opened. Then, before it fully extended, he ran up the stamped concrete driveway and rang the doorbell several times. Finally, after another minute, he walked around to the side of the house. Spotting the large stone planter, Nicholas picked up one of the decorative rocks and twisted it. Then, after shaking the house key into his hand, he returned the faux stone hide-a-key to its place. After unlocking the door, he let himself inside the Spanish-style house.

"Gates?"

Nicholas set the key on the credenza just inside the door. The first floor was completely dark, save for a few lights plugged into outlets. Entering the kitchen, he turned on the light and spotted several dishes on the granite counter and a skillet on the stove. He floated his hand over the pan.

"It's still warm," he said aloud. "I know you're here, Gates," he called as he turned on lights around the house.

The interior was painted white with dark brown wood beams on the ceiling. The home was luxuriously decorated, but Nicholas wasn't paying attention to the open floor plan and decor. Instead, he was zeroed in on the sound of a gun being cocked behind him.

"Don't move."

Nicholas held his hands up and said, "I'm unarmed, Gates. Lower your weapon."

"Nico, what are you doing here?"

"I'm here to talk. That's it. Now, can I turn around without being shot?"

"Okay, but no sudden moves."

He turned around to find a gun pointed at his torso. His friend immediately lowered it but didn't set it down. Nicholas's gaze roamed over his friend. He looked like he had been in a car accident. His right arm was in a sling, his face was bluish yellow in some places from bruising, and he had a black eye and swollen lip.

"Jeez, Gates," Nicholas said in dismay. "You look terrible. Siren's thugs did all this?"

His friend bristled. His expression turned fearful. "What do you know about it?"

"Relax, I'm not here to hurt you. I just want information."

"How do I know that? You break into my home—"

"No, I didn't. I used the spare key. Remember you showed me where it was and gave me the gate code?"

He still looked suspicious. "How did you know I was here?"

"It seemed like a logical place for you to go. You told me once that you come here when you want to disappear for a while."

Gates nodded and relaxed. He sat the gun on an end table before limping outside onto the balcony.

Nicholas followed. The setting sun gave them a breathtaking

view of the La Jolla coastline. In addition, his home offered an uninterrupted view of the Pacific Ocean.

Gates gingerly lowered himself to the cushioned sofa. He retrieved a remote from the table and turned on the firepit across from the seating area.

Nicholas sat across from him and leaned back against the plush padding.

"How are you feeling?"

"How do you think?" Gates said bitterly.

"What were you thinking?" Nicholas eyed his friend. "Why would you steal from Siren?"

"Do you honestly think I would've bought that bracelet if I'd known who it belonged to?" Gates snapped. "My contact told me it was in his family for years and was purchased at an estate sale. I had no reason to doubt him. Next thing I know, I'm being picked up at my shop by two of her goons and roughed up because I said I didn't have it anymore."

"Trust me, I know. I've been there."

"She almost killed me, Nico!"

"I'm sorry, Gates. Those same thugs kidnapped me and took me to her villa in Lisbon. The only reason I'm not fish food is that I told her I'd get it back. So I'm going to need that bracelet."

"I wasn't lying, Nico. I don't have it. By the time she darkened my doorstep, I'd already sold it. Who knows where it is now."

"Well, we'd better find out. If I don't, we're both dead."

Gates almost turned apoplectic. "Are you crazy? You brought her men here with you?"

"No," Nicholas assured him. "No one knows I'm here. Her men were tailing me, but I lost them."

Gates was almost hyperventilating. "So you say." He leaned back against the cushions and tried his best to calm down. Wiping his sweaty brow with the back of his hand, he sat forward.

"I'm sorry to bring you into this mess, man. This is not how I expected things to turn out."

"Yeah, well, now we're both screwed." Nicholas stood up

and paced around the terrace. "She wasn't just bluster, Gates. Siren will kill everyone standing in the way of her getting that Bellasini bracelet back." He ran his hand shakily over his jaw. "When I did you a favor to get some quick cash, I had no idea it would risk my life—or put Sophia in danger."

Gates's face turned red with embarrassment. "I thought it was a sure thing. We'd make a profit and go. I had no idea things would go south." Gates broke down in tears. "I'm sorry, man."

He sat down next to his friend and gingerly patted him on the hand.

"Look, if we're going to both get out of this alive, we have to work together," Nicholas reasoned. "And the first step is finding the fence that you sold the bracelet to. Our lives depend on it."

ALEXA STROLLED INTO the office with a decorated box of doughnuts in her hand. She dropped them in the break room and headed to her office.

"Miranda, I've brought your favorite doughnuts in. They're in the break room," Alexa said as she walked past her assistant's desk. Miranda was not there.

Glancing around, Alexa checked her watch. It was after nine. Thinking that she was just away from her desk, Alexa went into her office.

Thirty minutes later, she was working on a briefing when Dyan came in.

"Good morning, Alexa. Where's Miranda? She and I had a meeting fifteen minutes ago. Did you pull her for another assignment?"

"Hey, Dyan. No, I didn't. I came in earlier and she wasn't at her desk. I just assumed she was working on something."

Alexa and Dyan walked out of Alexa's office and over to Miranda's desk. Everything was as pristine as she usually kept it. Right down to the rose-gold monthly planner on her desk with a white pen with a fuzzy tip.

Alexa picked up the desk phone receiver and dialed her assistant's cell phone. When she didn't answer, Alexa tried again.

"Nothing," she said, hanging up. She turned to Dyan. "Do we have an emergency number for Miranda?"

"Hang on." Dyan called Human Resources and got Miranda's emergency contact.

Alexa dialed Miranda's mother.

"Have you spoken to Miranda today?" Alexa inquired after introducing herself.

"No, I haven't. I was starting to get worried myself," her mother replied. "This isn't like Miranda. Normally, I speak to her twice a day. I haven't spoken to her the entire weekend. I'm very worried, Miss King," her mother said tearfully. "This isn't like her."

"Don't worry, Mrs. Travers. We'll check on Miranda immediately. It's possible she is home sick. I'll contact you the moment I find out."

The second she hung up, she turned to Dyan.

"Let's go."

MIRANDA LIVED IN Northwest Washington, DC, right off Sixteenth Street, a historic and prestigious road that runs from the White House to the Maryland border and is home to over fifty churches, synagogues, shrines, temples and embassies.

Located on a quiet street, her house was a single-family redbrick home with a black door and shutters and a small, well-manicured yard and a one-car garage. They didn't see anything unusual, so they walked up the steps and rang the doorbell. Dyan pressed the buzzer several times.

"I don't like this."

"Neither do I," Alexa replied.

Retrieving a lockpick and torque wrench from a tool set in her purse, Alexa quickly unlocked the door while Dyan watched out for curious neighbors.

"You ready?" she asked when the door opened.

Dyan nodded and followed Alexa inside.

The house was barren except for a few broken chairs and a lamp on the floor. Paintings hung on the wall askew, and a plant was knocked over.

"Miranda?" Alexa yelled, retrieving her pistol from her purse. She dropped the bag and her coat on the floor so she wouldn't be hindered.

Also armed, Dyan called out as she cautiously moved around the first floor.

Once they had done a sweep, they took the steps to the second floor. There were three bedrooms, so they split up.

"I don't understand," Dyan replied when they met back up in the hallway. "Miranda never said anything about moving."

"My gut tells me that's not what this is."

Alexa retrieved her cell phone and dialed her office.

"I need a trace on Miranda Travers's cell phone—right now."

Dyan rushed down the steps behind Alexa.

"Text me the location when you have it."

Five minutes later, they were heading through Rock Creek Park toward the C&O Canal.

"Thirteen minutes," Dyan said as she maneuvered through traffic. Luckily, it wasn't rush hour so there weren't the usual delays.

The Chesapeake and Ohio Canal operated from 1831 to 1924 along the Potomac River between Washington, DC, and Cumberland, Maryland, to transport coal using mules on a towpath to pull the boats along the canal. It was now a popular running and cycling path, and picnic area for residents and office employees. There were also boat tours during the summer months.

Alexa was on the phone with a member of her operations team as they directed her to Miranda's location.

Parking the car, the two raced down the walkways on one side of the canal. Scanning the area, it was Dyan who spotted her first and pointed.

"There she is."

The two took off running. Their heels tapped out a rhythmic beat on the concrete as they dashed past several restaurants and down the brick-paved walkway that ran across the canal.

"Miranda!" Alexa yelled.

When she didn't turn around, she called out again.

Slowly, she turned to face them. When she did, Alexa stopped and gasped aloud.

Her assistant looked haggard, like she had not slept in days. Her clothes were disheveled, her eyes bloodshot, and her face puffy like she had been crying for just as long.

"Stop," Miranda croaked out. Her voice sounded like gravel being scraped across cement.

"Miranda, what's wrong?" Dyan called out. "Tell us what's happened. Whatever it is, we can fix it."

"You can't fix this," she cried out. "I'm ruined. My life is over."

Alexa held her hands up and moved forward as slowly as she could without being detected.

"Miranda, please talk to me. I want to help you. We both do," she said, nodding toward Dyan. "But we have to know what's wrong."

"I'm wrong. I messed up, and there's no way out."

She inched closer to the railing.

"No, no, no," Alexa called out. "Nothing you could ever do can't be undone, Miranda. I promise you. Just tell me what's happened."

"He's taken everything from me," she sobbed. "My money, everything in my house—things that can't be replaced. And I allowed him to. I fell for all his lies. I let him in and he destroyed me."

She grasped the railing and peered over the edge. Dyan began speaking to Miranda, which gave Alexa precious time to close the distance between them without being detected.

"You know what we do for a living. We can undo anything he's done, Miranda."

"No, you can't," she lamented, not bothering to look up. "My credit is shot, I'm behind on everything. I may even lose my house over this. I was so blind. I thought Apollo loved me, but I was just like all the others, he said. Gullible. Convenient. Easy."

Miranda said the word with contempt.

"I just want it to be over," she whispered.

Hearing his name caused Alexa to pause. Apollo Hayes. The man she had been suspicious about because of his evasiveness at meeting them. She closed her eyes. She was supposed to have looked into his background and got sidetracked by other things. She had dropped the ball. She had failed Miranda. She fought back tears as she moved closer.

"Listen to me, this is not the way, Miranda. Your parents are frantic with worry. I promised I'd call them the moment we found you to let them know you're okay."

"No! They can't know about this! No one knows about this. I can't tell them I've been duped by Apollo and I've had my life stolen from me. I can't hurt them like that. I won't."

In a split second, Miranda hoisted her leg up over the railing and was trying to pull herself up. Alexa sprang into action. She reached her assistant just in time to grab hold of her coat to keep her from falling into the freezing water below.

"No!" Miranda screamed. "Let me go."

Alexa was half over the railing trying her best to hold on to Miranda. Before she could call out, Dyan had reached her side and was helping to pull their distraught friend back to safety. All three landed in a heap on the ground.

"We've got you," Alexa said, breathless from the exertion, but trying her best not to fall apart. "You're going to be okay, Miranda. I promise you'll be okay," she said as her assistant's body shook with despair. Miranda's sobs zeroed in on Alexa's heart and broke it in two.

Chapter Twenty-Eight

Alexa sat on her living room couch engulfed in a loden-green comforter that she'd taken off her bed. She stared at the fire-place, watching the flames greedily devour the wood log she had stacked there. Her doorbell chimed, interrupting the silence like an unwelcome guest. She didn't even bother to look up. When it echoed around the room a second time, she yelled out, "Just leave it at the door." Annoyed that she had to repeat something that she had specified in the instructions when placing her food order.

The firm knocking was the last straw. She groused as she got up and shuffled toward the front door. Unlocking it, she wrenched it open with enough fire in her eyes to go to battle, her blanket draped around her like a medieval cloak.

"I said leave it!" she stormed, but the rest of her tirade died on her lips as she realized it wasn't the delivery person with her dinner order.

Her eyes bulged with shock, an action she instantly regretted because they were puffy and painful.

"Andrew."

"Hello, Alexa. May I come in?" he asked after a few moments of silence between them.

She nodded and shuffled aside. "Watch your step." Plates and glasses lay over every table in her living room. The floor was littered with empty carryout boxes, along with the plastic or paper bags they had been delivered in.

As if the state of the house wasn't alarming enough, Alexa looked like she hadn't slept or showered in a week. She smoothed her hands over her wrinkled clothes.

He motioned toward the couch. "Do you mind if I sit down?"

Shaking her head, she staggered back to the couch and sat, pulling her blanket around her like a shield. Andrew followed behind, and after removing some magazines and papers from the seat across from her, he sat gingerly on the edge.

She regarded him cautiously. "What are you doing here?"

"I was worried. I haven't spoken to you in weeks. And it's been even longer since I've seen you."

"And now you're worried?" she scoffed. "If memory serves, *you* ghosted me."

"I know. I'm sorry about that. I thought it would be easier for you. Less complicated."

"I thought we were friends. Clearly, I was mistaken."

"Alexa, of course we are. That's why I gave you space. Time to sort things out."

"Well, don't do me any favors," she snapped. "I don't need them. Frankly, I don't know why you're concerned."

"Alexa, no one has seen you for over a week and you haven't been to work. So, yes, that caused me to worry."

"I took some time off."

He glanced around the room. "Yes, I can see that."

"And you can also see that I'm just fine. Who called you? Let me guess. Either Dyan or my parents."

"Both."

"That wasn't necessary." Alexa pulled the blanket closer.

"Alexa—"

She stood. "Thanks for stopping by. You can report back to everybody that I am doing great."

"I'd be happy to, if that were true."

She glared at Andrew with annoyance. "What is it you'd like me to say?"

"How about how you really feel?"

For a second, her face relayed her pain. It was enough to make Andrew feel like he had been gut-punched.

"Please leave," she whispered.

"I'll leave once you level with me, because I know you're not fine."

Something inside Alexa snapped. "Fine, you want to hear the truth? Here it is. I am ripped apart inside! I am devastated!" She started pacing in front of the mantel.

"I can't sleep, and I can barely keep food down. All I can think about is Miranda. Her face. The fact that she was moments away from trying to end her life! She wanted to die, Andrew. And I could've stopped all this. I could have kept her safe and prevented her pain and suffering at the hands of some grifter who saw her as another mark. He took everything from her. And I handed it to him. How does that make me feel? Horrific," she cried, sinking to the floor.

Andrew came over and joined her on the floor in front of the fireplace. He tried to take her hands in his, but she pulled away.

"Listen to me. What happened to Miranda is not your fault."

"Yes, it is. My gut told me that something was off about him. So I was going to have my team investigate him. And I didn't. I was so caught up with Sophia's histrionics that I forgot. I let the ball drop, Andrew, and it almost cost Miranda her life. Everything that's happened was my fault."

"That's not true, Alexa."

"It is! I didn't protect them!" she yelled. "Not Shelley, Tanya or Miranda. I failed them all. They would've been better off without me in their lives."

"You don't mean that."

"Yes, I do. I couldn't even protect my friends. People that I love, Andrew. How in the world am I supposed to protect perfect strangers?"

"By doing the best job you can. By showing up and being present, Alexa. You can't hide from who you are or what you've been called to do. This is a temporary setback. You will find your center again."

She shook her head. "You should go. You're safer not being around me. As a matter of fact, I should just quit the business. I'm no good to anyone."

Andrew touched her cheek. Encouraged when she didn't pull away this time.

"That's just your pain and grief talking. The Alexa King I know has a heart of steel."

"The Alexa King you know is dead. She died from a thousand cuts."

"No, she's in there," he said, pointing to her chest. "You are a guardian to those you love and the ones you protect. And you always will be. No one is better without you. Do you hear me? Not me or anyone else."

"That's not true. You said some hurtful things at the Christmas party and then left me without a thought. You said I didn't need anything or anyone, remember? So spare me the fake concern and just leave."

"I was wrong," he said flatly. "I was hurt, angry, and should never have pulled away. I'm sorry, Alexa. I thought giving you some time was what you needed."

"What I *needed* was you."

When the tears came, Andrew didn't budge. He sat there with Alexa and held her as she cried. After she fell into an exhausted slumber, he picked her up and took her upstairs and put her to bed. Back downstairs, he took a few minutes to contact her parents and Dyan to give them an update.

"Keep us informed," Jake replied in a worried voice. "If she needs anything, you let us know."

"I will, sir."

Dyan had told Andrew that she would continue taking care of things at Dragonfly.

"I've never seen her this lost before. Any progress she had made since Tanya has just been blown out of the water."

"She needs time and space to heal. She'll get there, Dyan."

When he hung up, Andrew sat on the edge of the coffee table

and put his head in his hands. There were so many emotions rushing through him that he couldn't get a handle on just one.

Over the years, Andrew had witnessed many facets of Alexa's emotions. Fear, happiness, desire, anger, love and self-confidence. Never had he seen her bereft of hope. It was devastating. Guilt ate at him for his part in her feeling abandoned.

Angrily, Andrew swiped away the few tears forming in his eyes. He was ready to punch something. If he didn't find a task, he would lose it.

For the next hour, Andrew threw himself into cleaning up Alexa's apartment. When she finally awoke, it was to find him seated in a chair across from her bed. A suitcase at his feet.

"How long have I been out?"

"Two hours."

Sitting up, Alexa leaned back against the headboard. She gingerly tapped at the swollen flesh around her eyes. "I feel like I've been punched a few times."

He went to the bathroom, and returned with a wet washcloth. Sitting next to her, Andrew laid it across her eyes.

"Better?"

She nodded.

After a few minutes, she took it off. She gazed around her now-pristine room.

"You've been busy. And what's with the luggage?"

"You're coming home with me. And before you protest, I'm not taking no for an answer. This isn't a time where you should be by yourself and swimming around in your own head. That's a dangerous place to be, trust me."

"I can't just up and leave everything. Sophia—"

"Dyan has been handling Sophia and everything at Dragonfly for the last week. She'll call you if anything requires your immediate attention."

He touched her cheek before letting his hand drift to her shoulder. He gave it a firm squeeze.

"You need to regroup, Alexa. Let me help you do that."

SHE STUDIED EVERY inch of his face. From the brow furrowed with concern to the firm cut of his jaw. Her heart constricted in her chest. She had missed Andrew. Everything about him. He was her best friend and had grown to mean much more. They needed to work some things out. But for now, Alexa sat in the moment with him and soaked up his strength. She allowed it to wash over her and soothe her crushed soul.

In that split second, Alexa realized that she was tired. She was too tired to think, to feel or to come up with reasons why she should turn Andrew down on his offer. Instead of protesting, she merely nodded in agreement.

ALEXA SPENT THE next week at Phalanx recuperating. James, Esther and Andrew were perfect hosts and went out of their way to ensure that she had everything she needed to rest, relax and heal. She spent most of her days walking along trails or sitting on the porch while Andrew trained the latest group of students.

"You know that I'd be happy to help."

"You are our guest," he clarified. "One that is in need of some downtime."

"And I've had it. You all have been wonderful to me."

He stopped walking and faced her. "Alexa, you must know by now how much you mean to me—and Dad and Esther."

She reached out a gloved hand and touched his face. "The feeling is mutual. I was in such a bad place after what happened with Miranda. I didn't think there was a way I'd find my way back, but then you arrived—you were my anchor."

Andrew pulled Alexa into his arms. "Correction. I *am* your anchor."

He kissed the bridge of her nose. When he stopped there, Alexa realized that he hesitated in deference to her, so she made the next move and kissed him. She felt him hold back for a split second before he was all in.

It was unlike the previous embraces she had shared with Andrew. This one held a lot more than tentative exploration.

It quickly shifted into a heat that threatened to singe Alexa from the inside out.

"Well, that was…" Andrew stopped to search for the right word when they finally came up for air.

"Yeah, it was," she agreed. "This changes some things."

"We're going to be okay," he promised. "We'll figure everything out."

"I know," Alexa said with confidence. "But right now, I feel like I need to cool off."

"You've got a point," he chuckled before sweeping her into his arms.

"Andrew, what are you doing? Put me down!" Alexa shrieked. Her voice echoed off the white-topped trees as he carried her over to a mound of snow.

Wary, Alexa tightened the hold on his neck as she eyed him and the snow suspiciously. "James Andrew Riker II, don't you dare," she warned, inching higher in his arms.

"Oh, I dare," he laughed before depositing her into the flaky heap with a flourish.

She screamed and crawled her way out and got to her feet. She slapped the caked snow off her jeans and winter coat. Alexa's expression promised retribution.

"You're going to pay for that."

"I can think of several ways I'd like to do that," he declared with a wicked grin.

Laughter and taunting were the only sounds heard in the snowy meadow as they engaged in a snowball fight.Andrew gave up after one of her well-thrown missiles hit the tree branches above and dropped a mound of snow on his head.

"Yes!" she exclaimed in victory as she watched him stagger to his feet. "Do you yield, sir?"

"Okay, okay." He howled in laughter while shaking himself vigorously. "I give up. I think I got snow down my shirt."

"Don't expect me to feel sorry for you," she shot back. "Yay, Team King!" Alexa ran around the yard exclaiming victory but tripped on a piece of wood buried under the snow. She yelped in pain as she went down. Andrew was at her side in seconds.

"Lexi, are you okay?"

"Yeah, I'm fine," she assured him. "I just twisted my ankle."

Andrew tried to help her, but she got up alone. Hobbling a bit, Alexa walked around testing her foot.

"You know you don't have to do everything on your own. It's okay to accept help when it's offered."

"You're right," she agreed. "It's been difficult for me, you know? But I'm here, aren't I? So that's proof that I'm trying, right?"

"True," he conceded.

He helped her back to the cabin and had her sit on the kitchen counter while he examined her ankle.

"Looks like it's just a twist. Some ice and elevation should do the trick."

"Thanks for looking at it for me."

"My pleasure."

Andrew pulled a clean dish towel from one of the cabinet drawers and then grabbed a freezer baggie and filled it with ice.

"So, how are your parents?" Andrew finally asked while he wrapped her ankle with the floral towel.

"They're great. Relieved that I'm feeling better and wondering when I'm bringing you back with me to visit."

"Just name it," he replied. "You know I love visiting Washington, DC."

"Be warned. I'm sure Dad will bring up the fact that you caused him to owe Mom twenty bucks."

"Why?"

"After you came to stay, my family had a pool going on if we'd end up together. Dad was doubtful, but Mom never wavered."

His shoulders shook with mirth before he grew serious. "And are we?"

Alexa grasped his hand. "Andrew, I didn't know if I was even capable of having a relationship given my past. But, through it all, you've been patient and allowed me the space to figure things out. I want you to know that I'm grateful for that, Drew. I'm not afraid anymore. I want us to be together. Time isn't promised to any of us, and I don't want to let another day pass without declaring that I care about you, Andrew. Deeply."

He took her face in his hands. "And I care about you— deeply."

Andrew slid her closer to him for a kiss. "Was there an expiration date on that wager?" he murmured against her lips.

Alexa scrunched her face in concentration. "No, I don't think so."

"Good. Then I hope Jake knows that his baby girl caused him to lose."

Alexa poked him in the ribs. "Very funny."

They were still laughing when Alexa got a call.

"It's Dyan," she said after Andrew handed her the phone from her jacket pocket.

"Hi, Dyan. What's up?"

"Hi, Alexa, I'm sorry to disturb you while you're on leave, but we've got a situation."

"Okay. Let's hear it."

"Sophia was abducted."

"What? How was that possible? There should've been two teams guarding her at all times."

"There were, but we were outnumbered. The intel we received was faulty. By the time we arrived at the venue, several teams were waiting. We took on heavy fire. Two of our men didn't make it, Alexa."

Alexa closed her eyes for a moment then slammed her fist on the counter.

"Where was Sophia's last known location?"

"Paris. Not far from her apartment. She was supposed to meet Nicholas Michaux there after her show."

"Why?"

"I don't know, but our advance team said he never showed up."

"I want him found, Dyan. Send the jet to pick me up. After

that, I'm going to Paris. I expect the team to have laid out a tactical plan to get her back by the time I arrive."

"There's one more thing, Alexa."

"This isn't bad enough?"

"We know who kidnapped Sophia. One detained man had the same tattoo as the men in Los Angeles. After some painful coercion, he admitted that everyone that works for the Siren has this tattoo."

"Are you certain?"

"Yes. He refused to tell us where Sophia's been taken. He said he'd be killed if he gave up her location. So we contacted the authorities, and he's been taken into custody. Maybe they'll get him to talk."

"Thanks, Dyan. I'll see you soon."

"We'll get her back, Alexa," her friend said firmly.

"I know we will."

After ending the call, Alexa shoved her phone back into her pocket and hopped off the counter. She landed on one foot before gingerly testing the other out.

She could tell by Andrew's expression that she didn't need to elaborate.

"I have to go pack."

"You can't go after Siren, Alexa. She's extremely dangerous."

"She has my asset, Andrew. Which makes *me* extremely dangerous."

He stopped her. "I'm serious."

"So am I." Alexa stared at him in surprise. "I've never seen you look spooked, Andrew. Have you crossed paths with her before?"

"No. I know her only by reputation. She's bad news, Alexa. Bad, deadly news."

"Precisely why I plan on getting Sophia back before she gets hurt."

"Then I'm going with you."

She resumed walking. "No, you're not. This was my operation, Andrew, and it went south. Sophia is Dragonfly's responsibility. My team didn't keep her safe, which means I'm the one who's going to get her back."

Chapter Twenty-Nine

They were still having a heated discussion when Esther and James arrived.

The elderly couple exchanged glances as they set groceries on the counter.

"What's going on?" James asked when he could get a word in.

"Your son doesn't think I'm competent enough to handle a threat," Alexa snapped as she hobbled over and sat at the kitchen table.

Andrew's expression turned incredulous. "Whoa, I said no such thing. Don't put words in my mouth."

"And don't treat me like I'm a child who needs to be rescued!" she shot back.

He threw his hands up in frustration. "Alexa, where is this coming from? I've never once treated you like you couldn't handle yourself."

"Until now."

Andrew's jaw clenched, and an almost painful silence descended. The couple stood glaring at each other so long that James cleared his throat and would've said something, but Andrew turned to his father and Esther and said, "Excuse us."

Without another word, he swept Alexa up in his arms and carried her upstairs to his room.

"I can walk," she groused.

"You need to rest that ankle."

A few moments later, the door shut firmly behind them.

Esther glanced over at her husband. "Well, I've never seen that before."

"Me, either," James replied with a barely disguised smile.

"It looks like JJ has finally met his match—and so has Alexa King!"

ALEXA SAT AT the foot of Andrew's bed, her arms crossed and looking ready for battle. But it was the first time she had seen his bedroom, so despite her mood, she was curious.

His room was spacious, clean and extremely masculine.

"I can tell by your silence that you're still angry."

Alexa turned back to Andrew. "Yeah, I am."

"That makes two of us," he shot back. "Do you know how much I value who you are and what you've accomplished? I've never seen anyone as smart, capable and adaptive as you are. For you to even suggest that I didn't think you could handle yourself is crazy. I'm only worried about you because things are different now, Alexa."

"How?"

"Because it's not you and me anymore. It's *us*." The word shot out of his mouth like it was ejected from a cannon. "We're together now. In a relationship, and I had hoped both committed to seeing where this thing goes."

Some of Alexa's anger ebbed away. Despite her ankle, she hobbled over to him and touched his shoulder.

"Of course we are."

"Then don't go after Siren alone. Being together is hard enough without one of us going off and getting ourselves killed."

"I won't be by myself, Andrew. I'll have operatives with me and—"

"Do you think that gives me one moment of peace or eases the dread that settled into my gut when you said you were going after that lunatic?"

"Andrew, I don't—"

"I can't lose you, Alexa!"

He said the words like they were ripped out of him by force. Andrew ran his hand over his jaw as he struggled with his emotions.

Alexa was stunned. She remained ramrod straight as if her feet were welded to the floor.

Before she could get her bearings, Andrew grabbed Alexa by the shoulders and kissed her as if she'd just asked him for mouth-to-mouth resuscitation. Something uncoiled deep inside Alexa as if Andrew were breathing life into her body. She clung to him like she never wanted their embrace to end.

"Stay with me," he whispered against her lips.

"Drew, I want to, but I have to leave tomorrow. I don't want to make that any harder. For either of us."

"I just want you by my side. That's all, Lexi."

She knew he was telling the truth. Alexa trusted Andrew 100 percent. With her life, if it ever came to that.

Standing on her tiptoes, Alexa kissed him with a newly acquired possessiveness.

Some of the edginess left him. He squeezed her hand and stepped past her to light a fire in the fireplace. Alexa sat on the bench at the end of his bed and watched him. When Andrew was satisfied that it had taken hold, he extended his hand to Alexa. She didn't hesitate. He sat on the chaise longue by the fireplace and pulled Alexa into his lap. They both stretched out and, releasing a collective sigh, watched the fire.

After a few minutes, Alexa said, "Andrew, we both chose our professions for a reason. I temporarily lost sight of why I do what I do, but you helped guide me back from the edge, and for that I'm forever grateful. We want to protect people and keep them safe. We put our lives on the line every day to achieve that goal. So you must know I will do everything possible to protect my assets—and my team."

He stared at the fire as if hypnotized. "I know."

"But," she added, looking up at him, "I promise that I will also do everything in my power to come home—to you."

He touched her cheek and grazed her bottom lip with his thumb before he kissed her.

"And I promise you that I will always do the same."

Eventually, Alexa fell asleep. Carrying her back to his bed, Andrew took off the shoe on her other foot and eased the covers over her. Kicking off his shoes, he got in the bed next to her, but instead he sat up against the headboard and let out a tortured sigh. Nothing about this scenario sat right with him. Sophia being kidnapped and two of Alexa's operatives getting killed were bad enough. But Alexa was walking into the Siren's lair, and that shook him to his core. Andrew leaned over and moved a lock of hair out of her face. There was nothing that he wouldn't do to keep her safe. He had known it for some time, but now that statement truly hit home.

AFTER BREAKFAST THE following day, Andrew drove Alexa to the airport to meet her plane. One of the men on her team retrieved her luggage while Andrew walked her across the tarmac to the plane's airstairs.

He hugged her goodbye. "Call me the moment you land," he whispered.

"I will."

"If you need anything—"

"I will let you know," she promised.

He nodded, kissed her a final time and moved away.

Dyan was on board, as was the rest of Alexa's team. Once at her seat and buckled in, she glanced out the window to find Andrew still standing there. Waving, Alexa held eye contact until the pilot announced they were ready to take off. Only when she could no longer see Andrew did Alexa settle back against the seat.

After the plane left, Andrew retrieved his cell phone and dialed a number as he walked back to the Jeep.

"Daniel, it's Andrew Riker. I need to call in a favor, buddy."

IT WAS A fourteen-hour flight from Colorado to the Humberto Delgado Airport in Lisbon. After landing, Alexa's group was met and taken to a rented house near Torres Vedras. Alexa's dragonfly pendant she'd given Sophia indicated that she was not being held at the Siren's compound, but in a farmhouse nearby.

To ensure the best possible outcome, Alexa contacted her colleague Alejandro Reyes again. Alejandro had painstakingly cultivated a network of allies from around the world. With his help, Alexa had access to resources to ensure they had the best possible extraction plan with minimal collateral damage.

After their briefing, Alexa's team would move out around two o'clock in the morning to get Sophia back.

Though she was tired, Alexa still called Andrew before bed and brought him up to speed.

"Sounds like you have everything fully mapped out."

Yawning, she settled under the covers and tried her best to remain awake.

"Hey, did I lose you?"

"No," Alexa replied, trying not to yawn again. "I'm here."

"Not for long," Andrew teased. "I'm glad you called, but you need some sleep."

"I know," Alexa murmured.

"Be careful, Alexa."

"We will be. Alejandro's men will be on point tomorrow and lead us in. Of course, we'll have the usual complement of body armor and Marena's tech, so don't worry. We'll be ready."

"Sweet dreams, Lexi," he said softly.

Alexa said good-night and hung up. She thought of Andrew and couldn't help the smile that crossed her face.

She thought of her deceased best friend. "You'd have liked him, Tanya," she said before falling asleep.

ANDREW HUNG UP the phone, but he was wide-awake. He had a meeting scheduled for the next day himself, and if all went well, the Siren would no longer be a threat to Alexa or any members of her team. It was a calculated risk he was taking. One that had the potential to go very wrong, but if it meant Alexa would be safe, it was worth it.

Chapter Thirty

Dyan rechecked the signal. "It's still strong," she confirmed. "She's in the west wing of the house. It looks like a back bedroom based on the map."

"Okay. Let's move out," Alexa announced.

She grabbed her gear and followed the group outside into the cold night air. It was forty-five degrees in Torres Vedras that morning. Clear skies aided in visibility as they loaded into a van. Dropped a good mile from the location to avoid detection, they went the rest of the way on foot.

Every precaution was taken as they approached the house from the woods. They used thermal imaging to determine that the point of entry would be a back window. From there, they would need to ascend to where Sophia was held, retrieve her and exit the building without alerting anyone of their presence.

Dyan and her team would secure the perimeter and hold off anyone advancing to the house.

Getting inside without incident, Alexa followed Alejandro's men upstairs.

The bedroom had minimal furniture, only a twin bed, a chair and a small table on the other side of the room. The full moon illuminated the area with small pockets of light, helping them navigate. Sophia was asleep, so Alexa knelt down and lightly shook her arm.

"Sophia?"

Her eyes flew open in an instant. Fear and confusion were

there in equal measure until her gaze rested on Alexa. She blinked a few times and sat up.

"Alexa?"

"Yes, it's me," she said soothingly. "Come on. We don't have much time."

Sophia nodded before she launched herself into Alexa's arms. Her arms clamped around her neck. "You found me!" she murmured tearfully. "I didn't think you would come."

"Shh. It's okay, but we have to go," Alexa whispered. "Now."

Nodding, Sophia got up and put on her shoes. Her jeans and red shirt were crumpled, but clean. When they were ready, the men motioned for them to follow.

Alexa put Sophia between her and the first man. The other two were behind Alexa, bringing up the rear. They had just reached the top of the stairs when someone opened a door behind them.

Startled, the man yelled, *"Pare!" Stop!* in Portuguese.

"Move," the man behind Alexa commanded. They all rushed down the steps and were met by several of the Siren's men.

Their escorts laid down cover fire and immobilized the assailants while Alexa pulled Sophia behind her to the window.

"Wait, where are we going?" she said frantically.

"Down," Alexa explained.

"On what?" Sophia shrieked.

"We're rappelling down. You'll be okay, Sophia. I'll take the lead, and you follow me."

"No, I won't," she countered quickly. "I can't do this, Alexa. I'm scared of heights."

When a bullet whizzed past Alexa's head, she didn't hesitate to shove Sophia to the floor.

"Sophia, follow me," she commanded. They crawled behind a high-backed chair, and Alexa returned fire.

"Alexa? Are you on the way out?"

"Negative, Dyan. We're pinned down," she whispered, turning toward the earpiece. "The window's no longer an option.

Sophia is scared of heights. We'll be target practice trying to get her out the window. The front door is our only option."

"Then you'd better hurry. We'll have company in two minutes."

"Punch a hole," she replied. "I need a clear path."

"Roger that," the team leader replied. "Sixty seconds."

Alejandro's men were back and crouched by Alexa's side. One checked his watch. They had heard the exchange and got into position.

"Fifteen seconds."

"Get ready to run when I say go," Alexa told Sophia. "And don't stop, no matter what."

"Okay," Sophia replied quietly.

Suddenly, the front door exploded, and many pieces of charred wood flew like projectiles into the foyer and around the first floor. Stunned, Alexa's ears were ringing. Still on the ground, everything appeared in slow motion to her. Men who were close to the blast lay either motionless or screaming and writhing in pain.

Rolling over, she checked on Sophia. There were a few cuts on her face, and she was disoriented by the blast.

"Are you ready?" one of the men crouched beside her asked. "It's time to go."

Alexa nodded before turning to her right.

"We have to move." She grabbed Sophia up by the arm.

The five of them sprinted for the gaping hole that seconds earlier was a well-guarded barrier.

Alexa ran ahead with Sophia in the middle, where it was the safest. They had to jump over a few bodies, inside and outdoors, but they met no opposition.

Dyan and her team were waiting near the tree line. Alexa glanced over her shoulder to see the blaze had spread to the second floor.

"Let's go," their team lead called out.

Everyone took off for the waiting van and piled inside. Watching the scenery whiz by, Alexa instructed everyone to check for injuries. Sophia had not said anything during the ride, for which she was grateful. Sometimes she was a bit irritable and nauseous coming down from an adrenaline rush, so she appreciated the quiet.

When they arrived at the safe house, Alexa felt better but tired. Dyan took Sophia upstairs while she debriefed her team. Afterward, Alexa went to her room and showered.

She was too tired to talk, so she grabbed her phone and texted her friend first.

Hey, on a mission. I just wanted to say your dragonfly pendant worked like a charm. The signal remained strong, and we had no incidents. Sophia is safe.

Glad to hear it, Dr. Marena Dash-McKendrick replied. Where are you?

Lisbon.

It's early there, isn't it?

Yep. Haven't gone to sleep yet. I just wanted to say thanks for the tech. I'll call when I get back to DC. Say hello to Coulter for me.

Will do. Talk to you soon, Alexa. Stay safe.

Always am.

Next, Alexa texted Andrew.

Hey, Drew. Op went well. Exhausted.

Good to hear from you. How's Sophia?

Better than I expected. I'll talk to her later after I've slept a few hours. Right now, I'm running on fumes.

I hear you. I'm glad you're all safe. Get some rest, sweetheart. Call me later today.

Will do. How are your dad and Esther?

Well. I'm in the field, so I'll tell them you asked about them when I get back.

Oh? I didn't know you were on assignment.

I know. This just came up. I'll tell you about it later.

Okay. I miss you.

Miss you, too, Lexi.

Alexa set her phone on the nightstand and got under the covers. She was thankful for the dark curtains that would be blocking the sun once it rose.

Closing her eyes, she thought about Andrew. Alexa felt more at peace than she had in a long time. He was the balm that her heart had needed to heal and come to terms with the pain of the past. Shelley and Tanya were losses Alexa never thought she would recover from, and the incident with Miranda, while still fresh, was easing now that Miranda was doing better. Her team was working on locating Apollo Hayes so that he could be brought to justice for his crimes. Whatever it took, she would make Miranda whole again.

Now Alexa wasn't in it alone. This time, she had an ally. She had Andrew.

Despite her initial apprehensions about opening up to someone new, Andrew was constant and dependable, and cared about her in a way that allowed her to drop her guard and be herself.

Suddenly, a sense of dread came out of nowhere, causing her uneasiness. As did the next thought that popped into her head. *Dropping your guard is usually when something goes wrong.*

"LET ME GET this straight. You two stroll in here with some sob story and expect me to violate my client's trust and anonymity to ask for a bracelet back that Gates sold me weeks ago?"

"More like borrow," Nicholas added.

"How long do you expect me to be in business doing stupid stuff like that?"

"Look at me, man," Gates demanded. "This isn't a game. Our lives are at stake. You bought a stolen Bellasini—"

"Something I do all the time," his associate added.

"But not belonging to the Siren," Nicholas shot back.

The man was thoughtful. "Yeah, that was unexpected."

Gates shifted on his crutches. "Gee, you think?"

"If I help you, what's in it for me?"

"How about your life? You're delusional if you think she'll let us live if we don't give her what she wants. And how long do you think Gates and I will hold out before dropping your name?" Nicholas added.

"And trust me, she has spies and connections everywhere. Who knows, we could be under surveillance right now."

Gates's contact gasped. A look of terror on his face as his gaze zeroed in on the front door of his shop.

"Hey, how'd I know it belonged to her?" he stammered. "In our line of work, it doesn't pay to ask too many questions."

"Then you'll help us track it down?"

Nicholas's cell phone rang. He excused himself and went to answer it.

"Do you have my property yet?"

He paled and shot Gates a worried look. "Not yet. We've run into a few problems and—"

"Your problems don't concern me, Nico. However, you should know that some of my men are babysitting your girlfriend."

"What? Wait, that's not what we discussed," Nicholas roared into the phone. "Where is she?"

"Call it added collateral to ensure you give me what I want—Sophia in exchange for my bracelet."

"How do I know you haven't killed her already? I want to talk to her."

"You're in no position to demand anything. But if you and Gates keep stringing me along, I'll be forced to start mailing your beloved back to you. One lovely piece at a time."

She hung up before he could respond.

Nicholas shoved his phone in his pocket and stomped across the room. Then, grabbing two fists of that man's shirt, he hauled him up so they were eye-to-eye.

"Whoa, what are you doing?" the man sputtered. "Let go of me!"

"Nico, put him down." Gates hobbled over to his friend but didn't get close enough to risk a fall. "What's going on?"

"That psychopath has my girlfriend!" Nicholas thundered before glaring down at the store owner. "Your time is up. You find that bracelet, or I swear, I'll kill you myself."

"Okay," the man cried out. "I promise I'll get it back, but it will take some time. I'll need at least forty-eight hours."

Nicholas shoved him away. "You have twenty-four."

Chapter Thirty-One

"Where is she?" the Siren stormed as she threw a tray with her afternoon tea across the room. It hit the wall and shattered. The tea dripped haphazardly down the wood paneling. "When I checked in earlier, you told me everything was under control."

The man sitting across from her shifted on his feet. "It was, but then we had a situation."

"*Your* men are the incompetent fools that couldn't hold on to one tiresome hostage. So I think *you* should be responsible for this excessive lapse in judgment."

"I lost several good men in that break-in, boss," he said defensively.

Siren reclined in her chair, her feet propped up on a small footstool as a servant handed her a new cup of tea. "Well, they can't be that good—they're dead."

The man blanched. "I'm sorry. I won't let you down again, I promise."

"I should hope not. I won't be as forgiving the next time."

Bowing, he rushed out of the room with the remainder of his men in tow. Sipping her tea, Siren turned to one of the employees standing off to her right.

"I don't think he showed the proper amount of remorse. Go explain it to him."

"Yes, Siren. Right away," the man agreed before signaling for a few men to follow.

"MR. RIKER? MR. LIVINGSTON will see you now."

Andrew stood and followed the woman down a dim hallway. She knocked once and opened the office door. Andrew followed her inside.

A large, well-dressed man was sitting at his desk. The room was elegantly furnished with dark wood paneling. Though it was a long and narrow room, no expense was spared. The oval desk was placed at the end of the space. The window behind it was dressed in floor-to-ceiling black silk drapes.

Above the desk was a large circular wrought-iron chandelier with rows of hanging teardrop oval crystals. Built-in bookcases flanked the desk with recessed can lighting in the paneled ceilings.

To Andrew, it was a luxurious yet claustrophobic space that seemed better suited to be a library than an office of one of the wealthiest landowners in the world.

Randolph Livingston's family was one of the top procurers of stolen art that grossed about six billion worldwide, but Randolph's father began investing in legal businesses decades prior. Eventually, his branch of the Livingstons turned to real estate and managed to triple the size of their fortune. So when his father retired and Randolph took over the company, he made significant gains in keeping their operation legitimate.

"Mr. Riker, it's a pleasure to meet you." He extended his hand. "Though I must say a surprise."

"Thank you, sir. Likewise."

"Please, have a seat."

Andrew unbuttoned his suit jacket and sat opposite the desk in the patterned brown leather chair.

"I won't take up too much of your time."

"When one of my business partners asked for the meeting, I must say, I was intrigued as to why. He said that you worked for him on several occasions."

"Yes, I provided security for him on a few overseas trips to precarious destinations."

"Well, you must be exceptional, because Arthur had nothing but praise when I inquired about you. So, what can I do for you, Mr. Riker?"

Andrew opened the briefcase at his side and retrieved a folder. He slid it across Randolph's desk.

"I found something that I thought would interest you."

Mr. Livingston sighed before he picked it up. "If this is another investment request—" he began.

"No, but it is something valuable to you."

He reclined in his chair to hoist his feet up on the desk. The chair creaked in protest. When Randolph opened the thick folder and started flipping through the pages, he gasped in shock.

The color drained from his face and, after a few moments, was replaced with splotches of red that disappeared below the collar of his crisp white shirt.

"Is this accurate?"

"Yes, sir."

The older man rose from his chair as fast as his large frame could. He eyed Andrew shrewdly. "Why are *you* bringing this to me?"

"Because I now have a vested interest."

"Do you know how long I've had my men on this? And you stroll in here with information I've been trying for years to get?"

Andrew shrugged. "I have a lot of assets at my disposal."

"And I don't?" Randolph stood up and walked over to the window. He stared out at the cold, rainy day. Then, with a loud sigh, he turned around.

Andrew noted that he looked years older.

"I don't care what it takes or how many resources you need. I want you to deliver the Siren to me—alive."

ALEXA WAS EXHAUSTED but upbeat as she sprinted down the sidewalk and into her condominium's front door. She retrieved the key from an inside pocket on her exercise pants, unlocked the door and stepped inside.

A few minutes later, Alexa was enjoying the first sip of her favorite smoothie when her doorbell rang.

Disappointed, Alexa set her drink on the counter and strode to the door. Staring through her peephole, she looked surprised.

"Okay," she whispered, and opened it.

"Sophia. This is a surprise."

"Hi, Alexa," she said, standing awkwardly in the hallway. "I hope I'm not disturbing you. Oh, are you about to go out? If so, I can—"

"No, you're fine," Alexa assured her. "I just got home from a run. Come in." She stepped aside and let her enter. Alexa hadn't even been aware that Sophia knew where she lived much less would ever come by to visit.

Taking her coat, she hung it on the freestanding coatrack by the front door. Something told Alexa that she wouldn't be staying long enough to hang it in the closet.

"Would you like something to drink? Hot chocolate, coffee or tea? Unless you want something cold?"

"No, thank you. I'm fine," Sophia replied congenially.

Motioning to the couch, Alexa said, "Have a seat. I'll be right back."

Going into the kitchen to retrieve her smoothie, she took a moment to compose herself. Sophia was not her usual brash, hurried self, which had Alexa feeling wary. When she returned, she sat on the couch next to Sophia.

"This is a surprise," Alexa remarked while sipping her drink. "What brings you to Washington, DC?"

"You."

"Come again?"

Sophia looked like she was in physical pain. She shifted a few seconds and wrung her hands nervously before she finally got to the point.

"My actions placed my team in danger, and I was kidnapped because I didn't listen to anyone when you all were just trying to keep me safe, and I'm sorry," she got out in a rush.

Alexa's mouth dropped open in shock. Whatever she had been expecting to hear from the younger woman, it wasn't this.

When Alexa didn't immediately reply, Sophia bolted off the couch and began to pace. Tears streaming down her face.

"I've been angry at you for so long, Alexa, that it's been hard to bury the pain and forgive." She took a deep breath. "I was the annoying little sister who was always trying to hang with my big sister and her friends. And then, after the attack, everything changed. I felt like I had a huge part of my childhood ripped from me and I was forced to grow up overnight. We all had to care for Shelley and be there for her. And then weeks turned into months, which turned into years. And I just felt lost—and angry." Sophia glanced at Alexa. "I took that anger out on you, and it wasn't fair. I finally see that."

Alexa was floored by Sophia's acknowledgment. She had not realized that she was holding the smoothie container so tight that her fingers were going numb. She set it down.

For years Alexa had dreamt of a reconciliation with the Porter family. Eventually, she had lost hope of it ever happening. But Sophia was here bearing her soul and explaining how the incident had changed her life, too. Some of the hurt Alexa had carried with her began to lift.

"Sophia, I honestly don't know what to say. I—"

Her client rushed to her side and grabbed her hands. "Please say you'll forgive me for lashing out at you about Shelley, for getting kidnapped, and that you won't terminate Ruben's contract."

"Of course I forgive you, Sophia. I'm not ending Ruben's contract, and I don't want you blaming yourself for being abducted. That wasn't your fault."

"None of this makes sense," Sophia replied with frustration and sat down again. "There were no demands when they grabbed me. I overheard one of the men holding me talking on his cell phone. He said they were supposed to babysit me while the Siren waited for Nicholas to get her bracelet."

"Did he mention details?"

"No. Just that it was priceless to her, and that she'd do any-thing to get it back."

"She was using you for collateral," Alexa surmised.

Sophia jumped up. "See, this is why you have to help him, Alexa."

Alexa stared at Sophia in shock.

"What?"

"It's obvious he's in over his head. Nico tends not to focus on the big-picture items. He gets lost in the weeds on things sometimes. Whatever he's doing for the Siren, it's obvious that it's dangerous and needs an extraction."

"An extraction?" Now it was Alexa's turn to start pacing around her living room.

"First off, I'm not in the spy business, Sophia. The only people we *extract* are the clients we've been hired to protect. And if we're doing our job properly, this isn't even something we'd need to worry about."

"Alexa, I want to hire you to protect Nicholas."

"Sophia—"

"I'm serious. Granted, he annoys me more times than not, he's fickle and doesn't have a head for business, but I love him, Alexa. I don't want him to end up dead, courtesy of some lu-natic woman robbing and killing people to get what she wants. Please, Alexa."

Alexa didn't know what to make of this new development with Sophia, but she was just grateful that they could finally stop being at odds with each other. That they would be able to finally heal the wounds of the past.

She sat sideways to face Sophia.

"I can't, but I have someone in mind for the job."

"You do? Who?"

"Andrew Riker. He trained me a few years ago. He's the best regarding strategy, tactical, protection and weapons—besides his dad."

Sophia launched herself at Alexa.

"Thank you," she cried.

"It's okay." Alexa patted her back while trying to sit them both upright. "I'll set everything up with Andrew. Nicholas will be in good hands, I promise."

Nodding, Sophia went to stand up, but Alexa stopped her.

"Wait, before you go." Alexa took a deep breath and forged ahead before she got cold feet. "I wanted to ask you how Shelley is doing. I've hesitated to ask because I didn't want to cause you any pain. And I've also been too chicken to inquire," Alexa confessed.

"It's okay, Alexa. I think it's time to talk about it anyway. Shelley has good and bad days." Sophia sighed. "But she is taking care of herself. She is a gardener and landscape designer. Shelley says that she feels most herself when working with the soil and in nature."

"She always loved it," Alexa added. "I'm glad she's doing something that brings her joy."

"It's been hard for her, Alexa. Mom hovering all the time hasn't helped." Sophia's expression turned sad. "What happened put such a drain on our family. I thought my parents would divorce from the strain. But they didn't. It seems like we all turned a corner. Each in our way."

"You don't know how happy I am to hear that Shelley is— doing well. I know it's not perfect, but she's dealing with what happened on her terms. In her way. Shelley is a survivor."

Sophia glanced at Alexa and smiled. "And so are you."

Chapter Thirty-Two

"Are you sure this is gonna work?"

"Relax, Gates. We have a plan. We stick to it, and we'll be good."

"I don't know if breaking in is the best way to go about this. Why not level with the guy and make him a counteroffer?"

"Do you have sixty-three thousand dollars to give this dude in exchange for the Siren's bracelet? Because I don't."

"I'm sure he doesn't know its true value." Gates rubbed his bearded jaw. "Maybe we could lowball him?"

"Neither one of us has the cash to be waving under his nose nor the time to barter. Have you forgotten about Sophia? The clock is ticking, Gates. I put her in danger, now I have to make this right, and the fastest way to do that is to steal the Bellasini. Now, are you going to help me or not?"

Gates shifted on his feet so long that Nicholas glared at him.

"Okay, okay. Yes, I'm going to help. I almost died once because of this stupid bracelet. I'm not about to make it easy for the Siren to do it again."

"Good." Nicholas lightly punched Gates in the arm. When he instantly grimaced, he apologized.

"Sorry, man. Now, let's get back to work. Shine a light on the lock, please."

Gates reached into the bag he was holding and retrieved a penlight. He turned it on and aimed the beam just above the lock.

"You sure you don't want me to do that?"

Nicholas looked up. "Have you suddenly discovered how to pick a lock with one hand?"

Gates grimaced. "Sorry, I forgot. I'm nervous." His gaze darted behind them and to the left and right.

It took Nicholas several tries, but eventually, the back door opened. Dousing the light, Gates handed his friend the bag and followed him inside.

Several night-lights were plugged into the outlets as they walked through the kitchen and down the hallway, so they didn't need flashlights.

Nicholas turned to Gates and whispered, "Where did your contact tell us to go?"

His friend retrieved a piece of paper out of his pocket. He leaned against the wall for support. Gates beamed the light on the makeshift map and instructions by taking the flashlight out of his bag.

Suddenly, rapid beeping was heard throughout the first floor.

"He's got an alarm." Nicholas scanned the area for the keypad. Then, spotting it, he rushed to the front door. "What's the code to disarm it?"

"Hang on. I'm looking," Gates called out.

"We've got forty-five seconds left. Hurry it up."

Frantically, Nicholas was watching the time count down. "Gates," he called over his shoulder. "Ten seconds."

When his buddy didn't reply, he yelled, "Gates!"

"Five, two, six, one."

Punching the keypad, Nicholas entered the numbers and the disarm button. The beeping ceased, and the pad turned green. He blew a breath out in relief.

Gates came up behind Nicholas. "Man, I just aged about three years." He headed for the steps. "He keeps the valuables in a guest room safe."

Nicholas hurried up the stairs while Gates took his time. Once he'd made the second landing, he turned right and headed down the hallway.

"First door on the left," Gates called up the stairs.

Scanning the room with a penlight, Nicholas spotted a bronze statue on the desk.

"That should be the Greek Spartan King Leonidas," Gates called from the doorway.

"It is. Now what?"

"Rotate the arm with the spear forty-five degrees and then back to its original position. Behind that painting is a wall safe. Key in five, four, six, six. It spells lion."

Nicholas shook his head. "This guy isn't that original."

He did as Gates instructed, and the safe opened without incident. Nicholas grabbed the bracelet and ignored the cash, loose diamonds and other jewelry pieces. Next, he closed the safe and pushed the painting back in place.

"Let's get out of here," Nicholas remarked while placing the Bellasini in a small velvet box.

"You're not going anywhere," a male voice declared.

Nicholas and Gates turned around to find a man holding a pistol blocking their path.

He was tall and was wearing a double-breasted gray suit with a purple silk tie and black dress shoes. He looked like he was going out for a night on the town instead of standing there pointing a gun at them. He was graying at the temples, but everywhere else his hair was black. His face was mottled red with anger.

"Give me one reason I shouldn't kill you both where you stand."

Gates opened his mouth to speak, but Nicholas said, "The Siren."

The man was visibly shaken but didn't lower the gun. Instead, he moved across the room to stand behind his desk. He dropped into the chair heavily but kept the gun trained on Nicholas and Gates. He motioned for them to sit on the couch.

"What does she have to do with this?"

Nicholas shrugged. "Well, she wants the bracelet back that you stole and won't stop until she gets it."

The color drained from his face. "I didn't steal anything. I purchased that bracelet—"

"From the man that stole it from her," Nicholas replied. "Do you think she'll care that you have a receipt?"

"I don't believe you." He motioned toward Gates. "Don't tell me he works for the Siren?"

"No, I'm the guy who had the misfortune of standing next to her when she discovered her eighteenth-century Bellasini bracelet had been stolen," Gates chimed in. "But I was lucky. The guy who gave up your broker's name, not so much."

"What?" The man began to sweat. His gaze darted frantically between them.

"This isn't what I signed up for. I have a wife and kids." He reengaged the safety before setting the gun on the desk. "Take it and leave."

With Nicholas on his heels, Gates hurried on crutches as quickly as he could.

When they returned to the car, Nicholas started the engine but didn't immediately pull off. Instead, he leaned his head on the steering wheel.

Gates placed a hand on his shoulder. "Nico, are you okay?"

He ran a hand over his face. "That was close," he exclaimed. His voice shook with emotion. "We could've been killed, Gates."

"Tell me something I don't know. And for me, it's been twice!"

HOURS LATER, NICHOLAS let himself into the loft-style condominium he shared with Sophia. Located near Canal Saint-Martin in the tenth arrondissement, it was in one of the hipper areas in Paris. Sophia had picked it because there were many artisanal boulangeries, or bakeries, coffee shops and fashion designer boutiques nearby.

He loved the exposed wood beams, cherrywood floors, open floor plan and floor-to-ceiling windows in every room.

Opening the door, Nicholas trudged inside, dragging his

luggage behind him. After he closed and locked the door, he turned on the hall light to illuminate the way into the kitchen so he could get a glass of water.

He strolled into the dark living room. Groping at the wall, he found the light switch and flicked it on.

"Jeez," he yelled at the sight of a man sitting in a chair by the window. The glass he was holding crashed to the floor.

"Who are you? What are you doing in my apartment?" Nicholas said, overly loud.

"Waiting for you."

"I see that, but who are you? Did the Siren send you?"

Before the stranger could answer, Nicholas ran out of the room. Moments later, he returned with a butcher knife in his hand.

"Start talking," he said, brandishing the meat cleaver in front of him.

"I'm Andrew Riker. Your new guardian angel."

"My what?"

"I've been hired to protect you."

Andrew was about to stand, but Nicholas held the knife out and backed up. "Uh-uh. Not yet. By whom?"

"Your girlfriend, Sophia. She thinks you need safeguarding. Considering the company you've been keeping lately, she's not wrong."

Now that Nicholas was less rattled, he stepped around the broken glass and water and went to sit on the edge of the couch. He ran a shaky hand through his hair.

"I can't take too many more surprises," he muttered. "Start talking, and hurry to the part where I don't call the police or run for my life."

"Trust me. You wouldn't reach the phone—or the door."

Nicholas set the knife down on the coffee table and stared at Andrew. "And that's supposed to help ease my mind?"

"Sophia knows everything, Nicholas. So now would be a good time to disclose how you got caught up with one of Europe's most notorious criminals."

"Look, I don't mean to be rude— Wait, why am I apologizing? You're the one breaking and entering. So why don't *you* start talking?"

Andrew stood up and began walking around the room. He picked up pictures and other decorative items as he went. "As I said, I was hired by your girlfriend because she found out that you got yourself kidnapped. She also knows that you've been working with the Siren to launder money through a joint account you opened in her name without her consent, which makes it illegal. Alexa King, currently protecting said girlfriend, has extensive information on your whereabouts concerning the Siren. We also know that you connected with a friend of yours, Gates Budreau, who dabbles in stolen goods. Sophia was recently kidnapped and extracted by Alexa's team, which I'm sure you knew by your facial expression. So we can conclude that she was taken to use as collateral to blackmail you into continuing to help the Siren. And by the looks of your buddy Gates, you've been much more helpful than he has. How am I doing so far?"

"On target," Nicholas replied grudgingly. He got up and went into the kitchen. Upon return, he carried a wastebasket, a roll of paper towels, and a small broom and dustpan. Kneeling, he began cleaning the mess.

"Gates asked me to do a favor and give a fake bracelet to a guy who purchased it for his wife," Nicholas explained while sweeping. "My job was to deliver it to the man and collect the payment while the original Bellasini bracelet was sold to a fence, or broker if you will, that Gates knew. But then he sold it to a collector."

"So the collector has it?"

Nicholas hedged. "Not exactly."

"Then what exactly? And I'd be truthful if I were you. Your life depends on my knowing all the facts."

He dumped the glass shards into the trash can. "Gates and I broke into his house to steal it. He caught us, but we convinced him we were working for the Siren and his life was in danger, so he gave it to us without a fuss."

Andrew nodded. "Anything else?"

"No, that about covers it."

"Nobody is safe until she gets that bracelet back."

"I know that. The Siren almost killed Gates over it, and I think she did kill a few of her men over losing it in the first place. Trust me, the last thing I want to do is keep this death trap, but I need to ensure that once she gets it, there are no more threats, kidnappings or retaliation against me, Sophia or Gates."

Andrew picked up his phone and dialed a number.

Nicholas glared at him. "What are you doing? I just came clean about the entire mess, and now is the ideal time you want to be making a phone call?"

"It's a perfect time," Andrew countered. "Sophia is well protected at Dragonfly, and I'm calling in a team to keep you and Gates safe while I go strike a deal with the Siren. Then we'll rendezvous with Alexa when I return."

"I don't think that's wise, dude. I don't know you that well, but you seem like a nice enough guy. I'd hate for you to do something that may get you killed."

"Thank you, Nicholas. I appreciate that, but this is what I do for a living, so relax."

With that, Andrew stepped away to make his phone call.

"Don't worry, man, relax," he mimicked Andrew's voice. "Yeah, I'm sure that's what the Siren's men said before they went headfirst over the Pearl Tower."

Chapter Thirty-Three

Andrew arrived in Lisbon without incident. A man was holding his name on a sign at Baggage Claim.

"I'm Andrew Riker," he announced as he walked up.

The man nodded. "Follow me."

His guide didn't bother with the pleasantries, which suited Andrew just fine. He didn't want to be here any more than the man wanted to be escorting him around Lisbon.

"Two necessary evils," Andrew said under his breath.

Once they were in the sedan and on their way, Andrew glanced at his watch. He was supposed to check in with Alexa in two hours. He wasn't looking forward to that conversation. Leaning against the plush leather seat, Andrew folded his arms across his chest and closed his eyes. He was tired, hungry and worried about his next conversation with Alexa. She would be livid.

She knew nothing about his plan to make a deal with the Siren. Andrew knew her reputation. She was deadly and wouldn't hesitate to dispose of anyone in her path. But he had a mission to complete, and there was no going back. Soon he'd tell Alexa of his plans, and then all hell would break loose. She'd be angry at him for keeping his operation from her, but it couldn't be helped. He'd sought out Randolph Livingston because of his resources. Andrew couldn't risk Alexa falling prey to the Siren's machinations. Most of them proved deadly, and if anything happened to Alexa…

Andrew stopped. He couldn't even finish his thought. She was too important to him to lose—end of story.

The driver didn't bother announcing that they'd arrived. Instead, he merely drove up the circular driveway and parked the car.

A man immediately stepped up and opened the door.

"Good evening, sir. Welcome to the Hotel Beleza."

Andrew got out of the car and buttoned his suit jacket. "Thank you."

The porter glanced at the trunk.

"Do you have any luggage, sir?"

"No, I don't. I'm just here for a meeting."

"Understood. If you step inside, a staff member can assist you."

Andrew stopped short when he reached the other side of the glass doors.

He could understand why the hotel was named "Beauty." The furnishings were decorated in warm tones of cream and gold. The furniture was cream with Tuscan brown wood for the arms and legs of the sofas and chairs and the tables throughout the reception area. The chandeliers were crystal, and the light bounced off the delicate gold chargers on the tables holding potted plants.

"Good evening, sir. How may I help you?"

"My name is Andrew Riker. I have a meeting with—"

"Of course, Mr. Riker. Please follow me."

The woman took him down a long hallway and through large French doors into a greenhouse. Andrew glanced around at the tropical plants.

He spotted a woman sitting on a stone bench. She was wearing a flowing kimono-style cardigan with a peacock feather design and form-fitting black pants. There was a small table next to her with a tea service and a tray of finger sandwiches and bite-size desserts. Siren was sipping tea when Andrew approached.

"Don't you just love teatime? It's so relaxing and civilized."

"Siren, I presume?"

"Yes." She set her cup down and observed him with mild interest. "What can I do for you, Mr. Riker? Do be seated. I don't like anyone standing over me."

He lowered himself in the chair next to her tea set. He waved away the proffered tea.

"It's what I can do for you that counts," he replied. He reached into his pocket, and out of nowhere, several men appeared with weapons drawn.

"Nice and slow, Mr. Riker. My men don't like sudden movements."

"So I see." Andrew retrieved his cell phone and flipped through several pages before handing it to the Siren.

"You arranged for this meeting to show me what?" she laughed. "A selfie?"

"In a manner of speaking. This picture was taken yesterday."

When she saw the image, the Siren's expression turned from amusement to menacing in seconds. "This is a dangerous game you're playing, Mr. Riker. I don't take kindly to anyone dangling my property over my head like a carrot. Especially someone I don't know."

Andrew retrieved his phone. "From what I've heard, you enjoy a good negotiation. So do I, provided it doesn't end in death."

The Siren tossed her head back and let out a boisterous laugh. "I like you, Riker. You have a sense of humor. That's an asset. Still, it takes extreme guts or stupidity to come here yourself."

He allowed himself a slight smirk. "Who says I'm alone?"

She nodded and then turned to her bodyguard. He retrieved a card from his pocket and handed it to Andrew.

"This is my address. I want my Bellasini in my hand no later than Friday."

"That's in three days."

"Not beyond you, I would think, considering you just showed me a picture of it." The Siren set her cup down and stood. "Don't keep me waiting, Mr. Riker. My patience is not inexhaustible."

Before Andrew could respond, she and her men swept past him and out of the door.

"Three days, huh." He needed to brief Alexa and then arrange to drop off the Siren's bracelet. A moment of discomfort washed over him as he anticipated her reaction to him seeking a known killer out to make a deal.

Andrew retrieved his cell phone from his pocket and made a call.

"It's me," he said, striding out the door and down the hall toward the lobby. "There's been a change in plans. Let the captain know that we're heading to Washington, DC." Ending the call, Andrew got back into the sedan and left.

The Siren observed Andrew's car drive away.

She tapped the headrest in front of her and the driver eased the black sedan out of its parking space and down the long driveway.

"I want someone monitoring Mr. Riker at all times," she told the man sitting next to her. "He's adorable, but I don't trust him. I want him watched 24/7. If he sneezes, I want to know about it. Is that clear?"

"Of course," her bodyguard replied. "I'll see to it personally."

The Siren settled against the buttery soft leather seat and gazed at the lights whizzing by her window. She suddenly looked much older than her forty-five years. Grasping at her head, she pulled the pearl Kanzashi hairpins from the tightly wound bun. Her red hair unraveled and cascaded down her shoulders. She tapped the elegant pin against her thigh. "Fair warning," she said almost as an afterthought. "I'm holding you responsible if anything goes wrong."

Her bodyguard swallowed loudly. "Understood."

ALEXA STROLLED THROUGH the glass doors and into the lobby of the Salamander hotel in Washington, DC, and headed straight for Check-In. It was almost eight o'clock at night, and the reception area was buzzing with patrons. Oblivious to the comings and goings and the people chatting away in the elegantly furnished reception area, there was only one thing on Alexa's mind. Andrew.

She had missed him with an intensity that was overwhelming at times and brought her to a major decision. Talking to Andrew on the phone and sharing texts between missions wasn't enough. Tonight, Alexa would show Andrew that she was ready to take their relationship to the next level. She wanted him— all of him.

Alexa had spared no expense getting ready for their date night. She had spent most of the day at a spa getting pampered. There wasn't one inch of her body that hadn't been massaged, buffed and well-oiled. She had also treated herself to a manicure, pedicure, waxing and hairdo. Alexa was so relaxed, she had fallen asleep twice during her services.

"Hello, Miss King," one of the staff replied warmly. "Welcome back. I'll be with you in just a moment."

She waited patiently while the staff member finished up with a customer.

It was cold and overcast outside with a few indications that they might get some snow. Alexa took a few moments to remove her black leather gloves and loosen her black velvet wrap. Her excitement was practically bubbling over. Alexa's foot tapped an absent-minded tune on the marble floor while she waiting for Benny to finish helping a guest.

Benny finally glanced up to give Alexa his full attention. "Wow, you look amazing, Miss King! How can I be of service?"

Alexa smiled at the compliment. "Thank you, Benny. And it's nice to see you again."

"The pleasure is all mine, Miss King," he said warmly. Suddenly, he glanced around. "Are you on duty?"

"Not today," Alexa said with a grin. "I'm meeting my boyfriend here for dinner."

Benny's mouth dropped before he could catch himself. "Pardon me, Miss King, but did you say—"

"Yes, I did." Her smile was as bright as a solar flare as she provided Andrew's name.

Recovering from the shock, Benny checked for his room number and gave it to Alexa. "You know, in all the years I've known you, I've never heard you say that before?"

"Times change, Benny." She winked before heading for the elevator, her strappy black heels clicking on the floor as she walked.

On the ride up in the elevator, Alexa tried to quell her nervous energy. Now that she had decided to make love with Andrew, all the pent-up desire had her pulled as taut as a bowstring. She checked her pulse while waiting to arrive at his floor.

You need to calm down, she mused. *Even your heart rate is elevated.*

When she got there, she knocked twice and nervously shifted her weight from her left to right foot while she waited.

Tonight, everything will change. No going back now, King. You've got this.

Andrew opened the door. Alexa watched the happy smile he was wearing skid off his face. It was replaced with jaw-dropping surprise that made Alexa's insides warm with delight.

When she came inside and Andrew eased the black velvet wrap coat off her shoulders, he let out an audible gasp.

Alexa was wearing a wine velvet Bardot neckline dress. The off-the-shoulder, long-sleeve creation sinfully hugged her body from top to bottom and landed just below her knees. Andrew's gaze drifted lower, taking in her toned legs, and finally to the black crisscross-strap open-toed heels before trailing back up her body. Her hair was smoothed into a chignon bun at the nape of her neck and she wore long dangling gold earrings. Her makeup was minimal, except for the matte wine-colored lipstick.

When his heated gaze connected with hers, Alexa felt like every nerve ending in her body had fired at the same time. She had to stifle a giggle when he almost dropped her coat to the floor when he took it off.

"Alexa...you are. Wow. Truly breathtaking," Andrew finally managed to get out.

When she leaned in to hug him, his cologne wafted into her nostrils. Closing her eyes, Alexa let herself enjoy the feel of being in his arms after so long apart.

"Thank you," she murmured against his ear. "You look amazing, too."

Andrew had chosen a black suit with a dark gray shirt, black tie and a black-and-gray silk pocket square.

They drifted apart from the hug just enough to kiss. The passionate embrace only stoked the tension circling around them.

Eventually, they moved apart so that Andrew could hang up Alexa's wrap. It gave Alexa time to glance around.

The opulent one-bedroom suite had beige walls and a sizable cream-colored sofa with seafoam-and-gold-patterned pillows. The carpet was also the same color scheme. The glass-and-gold coffee table across from a built-in entertainment unit held a flat-screen television. In the corner by the window were a wooden desk and a fabric chair in the same green color.

In the middle of the floor was an elegantly decorated table with long white taper candles, fresh flowers and covered dinner serving sets.

"I hope you don't mind dining in instead of going to a restaurant," Andrew said as he held out the chair for her and then turned on some soft music. "I found myself not wanting to share you tonight."

Alexa's face pinkened with the hint of a blush. "I'm glad you did. Everything is perfect, Drew."

The personal chef Andrew hired had prepared rack of lamb with an herb crust and plum sauce, along with herb-roasted potatoes and roasted asparagus.

They chatted while they ate, each content to enjoy the other's company.

"Ready for dessert?" he asked some time later when they were done.

Leaning back, Alexa rubbed her stomach. "I'm too full right now."

"I know the perfect thing to help you settle your meal." Andrew stood and helped Alexa up. He led her away from the table and drew her into his arms to dance.

"I'd forgotten how well we dance together," she replied as they moved in time to the lazy jazz tune drifting around the room.

"I haven't. I'll take any excuse I can to get you into my arms, Miss King."

Alexa closed her eyes and leaned her head on his shoulders. "All you have to do is ask, Mr. Riker."

"I've missed you, Lexi," Andrew said seriously. "So much."

"I've missed you, too, Andrew."

He spun her around and then dipped her. Andrew continued to lean over until he kissed her lips. "Have I mentioned how incredibly sexy you are?" he asked when he pulled her upright.

"I'd rather you show me, Drew."

Before he could respond, Alexa's hand drifted up between them and unbuttoned his suit jacket and eased it down his broad shoulders before tossing it on the chair. Next, she ran her hands across his chest and then up to his head to pull him down for another kiss before leading him over to the couch. When she guided him down, she straddled his lap.

"What are you doing?" he breathed against her lips as his hands came up to either side of her waist.

"Something we should've done a long time ago."

"Alexa," he said raggedly. The shred of control that Andrew was trying his best to exert was splintering by the minute. "I need to talk to you."

She began to unbutton his shirt. Next, she kissed a trail down his firm chest. She leaned forward and playfully bit his bottom lip. "It can wait until morning."

Andrew grasped Alexa's wrists to halt her progress before easing her off his lap.

"I'm afraid this can't. Alexa, I went to see the Siren."

Chapter Thirty-Four

"You what?"

A bucket of cold water couldn't have had a faster effect on squelching Alexa's libido.

Andrew repeated himself.

She smoothed her dress down. "I heard what you said. What I'm not clear on is what possessed you to do that?"

"The centuries-old gem bracelet stolen from the Siren was worth about sixty-three thousand dollars."

"That's a hefty price tag. But what does that have to do with us right now?"

"She kidnapped Sophia to use as an incentive for Nicholas to return it. Plus, a husband of one of Sophia's friends purchased a replica of the stolen piece. He bought it from Gates Budreau, a fence, or dealer in stolen goods, and friend of Nicholas. Gates talked him into delivering the fake to the man. Unfortunately, Nicholas didn't know about the original being stolen from the Siren until she had him kidnapped and brought to Torre de Pérolas."

"So, when did you find all this out?"

"After Sophia hired me to protect Nicholas, I insisted on full disclosure. So he told me everything, including him and his friend Gates breaking into the house of the guy that purchased the original."

"He did *what*?"

"Yeah. Luckily for them, Nicholas is quick on his toes and

convinced the guy the Siren sent him. That was all he needed to hear, and he gave up the bracelet."

"So where is it now?"

"I have it."

Alexa frowned. "Why?"

"That's what I went to see her about. I struck a deal that I'd give her the bracelet in exchange for her not coming after anyone else."

Andrew watched as Alexa's expression changed from avid interest to growing anger.

"You went to see the Siren without telling me about your plan first?"

"Yes."

"Andrew, why would you deliberately keep this from me? You know how dangerous she is—everyone knows—and yet you felt it was a good idea to negotiate with her or try to make deals with a known killer? The police have tried to get something to stick to the Siren for years, but she never directly gets her hands dirty. Instead, she uses her minions for all the scare tactics and shakedowns. Did you know they call her Lady Teflon?"

"That's exactly why I did it, Alexa. I wanted you as far away from the Siren as possible. This woman kidnaps, kills or has people beaten within an inch of their lives for the slightest provocation. I wasn't going to risk you getting on her radar."

"Oh, *you* weren't going to risk it?" Alexa snapped before jumping up from the couch. "How could you go behind my back? I deserved to know what you were planning. This affects my protectee, too."

"I had a call to make. Nicholas is under my protection, and I did what was necessary to keep him safe. Telling you beforehand had no upside."

Andrew regretted his word choice the second it left his lips. He closed his eyes and prepared himself for the retaliation, which was swift.

She sucked in a breath. Her eyes narrowed. "What did you just say to me?"

"Alexa, I—"

She held up her hand. "Uh-uh. Don't backpedal now, Drew. You said it, and you meant it. And for the record, I don't need you swooping in with your shiny red cape to save the day. I'm not some weakling who can't take care of herself."

"I never said that."

"I have a global company specializing in close protection and security," she continued as though he hadn't said anything. "Which qualifies me to fight my own battles—and those of my clients," she snapped.

Too angry to sit still, Andrew also bounded off the couch. They faced each other like it was a cage match.

"I'm aware of your credentials, Alexa. I'm the one who trained you, remember?"

"And you think that qualifies you to protect me when I don't need it?"

"No, but my being your boyfriend does. And before you try to disagree, you should know I stand by my decision. Nicholas and Gates are in danger every second they have that bracelet. I'm glad that Sophia had the foresight to ask me to protect him because at the rate those two were going, they'd eventually be found by the Siren's detail and killed. Sophia was captured once, Alexa. How long would it have been before she was retaken?"

Alexa was about to turn away, but he stopped her.

"Do you think I would stand by and risk that happening? If Sophia was in danger, I knew that would entail you putting yourself in harm's way to keep her safe—that wasn't a scenario I was willing to risk."

"I risk my life every day, Andrew. You know that. I don't interfere in your ops. You had no right injecting yourself into mine. When I need a guardian, I'll ask for one."

AGITATED, ANDREW PACED the floor. "So, you're not going to try to see this from my side? You're going to ignore that I did what I had to because I care about you?"

"That doesn't give you the right to try to coddle me, Andrew."

"I will always protect you, Alexa, no matter what—and that's with or without your permission. You do that for the people you love."

Alexa stopped for a moment. She was stunned at Andrew's declaration, but then she shook her head. "That's not love, Andrew. That's control. And if you think I'm giving anyone control over me, you're mistaken."

Andrew crossed his arms over his chest. "And there it is. I knew sooner or later that we'd get to the crux of the matter. This argument isn't about me keeping you in the dark about the Siren or your accusation that I'm trying to control you. It's about *your* need to control everything that happens in and around you because you're scared of feeling helpless."

Alexa recoiled as if she'd been struck. "That's not true."

"Isn't it?"

"No. It's about being in a relationship with someone you can communicate with and trust—someone that has your back."

"When have I not had your back, Alexa?" Andrew roared. "Everything I have done since we met was my attempt to protect and keep you safe. I had every intention of telling you about my meeting, and yes, I was dreading it because I knew you'd be upset, but I did it anyway. And before we made love," he added. "Because I never want anything standing between us."

"Really? Well, if that were the case," she shot back, "you would've told me about it before it happened, not after."

She brushed past him and went to the closet to get her coat.

"Where are you going?"

"Isn't it obvious? I'm leaving."

"Just like that? We haven't resolved anything, and you're just going to up and leave?"

"Yes, because if I stay, I'll say something that I can't take back."

"Alexa, if you head out that door, I can't guarantee I'll be here when you get back."

She wrapped her coat around her like a shield before she

turned around. Their angry gazes connected from across the room.

"Goodbye, Andrew."

STORMING OUT OF his suite, Alexa was so angry that she was shaking. Once at the elevator lobby, she jammed her gloved finger on the down button and waited impatiently for it to arrive. She glanced over her shoulder a few times, but the corridor was empty. By the time she'd reached her car, she still hadn't calmed down.

Alexa drove straight from the hotel to her parents' house. When she entered the house, she found her parents in the family room playing cards.

Her mother glanced up in surprise. "Alexa? Hi, honey. What a wonderful surprise," Margot said. "Wow, you look beautiful! How'd your date with Andrew go?" She glanced at her watch. "Ended a bit early, didn't it?"

"Thanks, and yes, it did. Sorry to just pop in unannounced."

"Nonsense," her father replied. "This is your home, too, sweetheart. You know you're welcome anytime."

"Thanks." She plopped onto the couch, removed her heels and put her feet on the ottoman. "I didn't feel like going home."

Margot studied her daughter for a few moments before she said, "Alexa, what's wrong?"

"It's Andrew," she confessed, not bothering to deny there was a problem. "He and I just had a huge fight. Huge."

Her parents turned around in their chairs and gave their daughter their undivided attention.

"About what?" her father inquired.

Reaching for the unfinished bowl of chocolate-drizzled popcorn, she stopped.

"Hold that thought. I'm going to wash my hands." Alexa rushed from the room.

Jake turned to his wife in question.

"Don't ask me," she replied as if he'd spoken aloud.

"I guess we'll find out soon enough."

Alexa returned and resumed her seat. She picked up the bowl and dived into the chocolaty treat.

While she ate, she recapped her argument with Andrew. Then, when she was done, she turned to her parents.

"Well?"

"Well, what?" her mother countered.

"Was I wrong to get angry at his high-handedness?"

"Alexa, we're not getting into the middle of your disagreement with Andrew."

"Mom, I'm merely asking if you think I overreacted or if what I said was founded."

"I'm going to agree with your mother on this," Jake chimed in. "We'll leave you to work around your impasse with your boyfriend. But I will say that he has a point, honey."

Alexa stopped munching. "Dad?"

"Ever since the Great Falls park incident, you have been hypersensitive in a few areas."

"Your father is trying to say yes," her mother added. "You have a problem when you think you're not in control of a situation. I'm not saying I agree with how Andrew went about meeting with what's-her-name, but I agree with him wanting to keep you safe."

"I don't need him for that," she said grudgingly.

"Alexa, you are in a relationship now," Jake pointed out. "He cares about you. Andrew wanting to protect you is ingrained in him whether you want it to be or not. And the same for you. You'd protect him if the need arose, wouldn't you?"

"Dad, of course I would. But I don't need him keeping information from me."

"Of course you don't," he agreed. "And I agree with you on that. I'm merely pointing out that his motives didn't sound like he believed you incapable of protecting yourself."

She mulled over her parents' words while they returned to their game. Finally, when they were done and getting ready for bed, Alexa said, "Do you mind if I stay here tonight? I'm wiped out."

"Of course not." Margot went over to hug and kiss her daughter. "We'll see you in the morning."

"Good night, kiddo." Jake also did the same. "Turn everything off before you come up."

"Okay, Dad. Good night."

Alexa retrieved her bowl and resumed eating while she stared at the dwindling fire in the hearth. She was exhausted, and her mind was a jumble. Their fight was the first since becoming a couple, and it was a bad one. And considering that she had walked out on Andrew, possibly a game changer.

Pulling a throw blanket from the back of the couch, Alexa stretched out on the sofa and stared at the glowing embers in the fireplace. She pondered what Andrew and her parents had said about her need to control her surroundings. Her past was still tainting her view of the present. Deep down, Alexa knew they were right and that it was a problem she would have to acknowledge.

The fight with Andrew replayed in her mind's eye. The realization that she could lose him caused her stomach to ball up in knots and her heart to hammer in her chest. Alexa curled up into a ball. "My God, what have I done?"

Chapter Thirty-Five

"Sweetheart, wake up."

Feeling a gentle nudge on her shoulder, Alexa opened her eyes.

"Good morning, Lex," her mother replied, sitting on the coffee table adjacent to the sofa.

"What time is it?" Alexa murmured.

"It's a little after ten."

"Seriously? I can't believe I slept so long." She sat up and stretched. "Or that I didn't make it upstairs."

"Your dad made breakfast this morning. We saved you a plate."

Standing, Alexa folded up the blanket and laid it on the couch. "Thanks, Mom. I'm going to go up, shower and get dressed."

When she got upstairs, Alexa peered in the mirror in her bathroom. She wrinkled her face at her bloodshot and puffy eyes. "You look horrible," she said aloud.

Later, Alexa assessed the clothes she'd left in her closet. First, she retrieved a pair of jeans and a red wool turtleneck sweater. Next, she searched a few shoeboxes and found navy blue sneakers. Brushing her hair into a top bun, Alexa was almost done when her cell phone rang. Picking it up from her bed, she was disappointed that it was Dyan, not Andrew.

"Hey, Dyan. What's up?"

"What's wrong?" Her friend and employee sounded worried.

"Nothing," Alexa answered.

"Mmm, okay. I'm sorry to bother you on your day off, but Sophia is in an uproar. She spoke with Nicholas yesterday, and he was freaking out because he can't reach Andrew."

"What do you mean he can't reach him?"

"He said Andrew had an appointment and his team came in to guard Nicholas. Andrew was supposed to check in after the meeting, but that was yesterday, and there's still no word."

"He's here in DC. I met up with him yesterday, and we—"

"Fought?" Dyan asked.

Alexa sat on the edge of the bed. "Why would you say that?"

"Because you sound out of sorts."

"Yes, we did," she confessed. "And it was big."

"So where is he now?"

"I don't know." She got up and started throwing on clothes. "Andrew was at his hotel last night, and I haven't heard from him today. Hang on."

Alexa placed Dyan on hold and called Andrew's phone number. It rang several times before going to voice mail. Then, ending the call, she transferred back to Dyan.

"He's not answering, but his cell phone isn't turned off."

"Maybe he's in Portugal? Nico told Sophia about the Bellasini bracelet and Andrew's deal to return it to the Siren. The deadline was today."

"He wouldn't have left without saying goodbye," Alexa countered.

"Yeah, but you just said you had a huge fight. Maybe he did."

"Regardless of what happened, Andrew wouldn't do that. I'm going back to the hotel. In the meantime, I want his cell phone tracked and an update from his team on his flight plan."

"I'm on it," Dyan replied, and hung up.

Running down the stairs, Alexa went into the kitchen.

"I've got to go," she said. "Andrew missed a check-in with his team. He'd never do that, so I'm going to find him."

"I'll go with you," her father replied.

"No need, Dad, I'll be fine. I'll let you know if I need anything."

Margot hugged her daughter. "Be careful, Lex."

"Always, Mom."

THE SALAMANDER TURNED up nothing. Andrew had not checked out yet and no one had seen him leave that morning. One of the managers escorted Alexa to his room. There were no signs of a forced entry, and nothing seemed out of place. He was just gone.

Alexa went home. As she was parking, she received a call from Dyan.

"Hey, what do you have?"

"GPS shows that Andrew's cell phone is at your condo, Alexa."

She took a moment to lean against the steering wheel in relief. Andrew was safe and waiting for her at her place.

"Thanks for tracking him down, Dyan."

"My pleasure, Alexa. Can you—"

"Yes, I'll have him call Nicholas and his team," she agreed.

Ending the call, Alexa took the elevator upstairs. Turning the key in the lock, she realized that the bolt wasn't engaged. Opening the door, Alexa wasn't prepared for the scene inside.

Andrew was fighting for his life against three men. He was thrown into her entertainment center and crashed to the floor in a heap. Pictures and books that were on it followed him to the floor.

"Andrew!"

Alexa didn't think. She just reacted. Dropping her purse, she ran across the room and attacked the first man she reached.

Punching him in the gut, Alexa followed through with an uppercut. He stumbled but did not go down, so she grabbed a statue from her end table and whacked him. Then, she rushed to jump in front of Andrew, not bothering to watch the attacker go down.

While he struggled to his feet, Alexa bought him time by blocking a punch from the closest man. He brandished a Taser, but she knocked that out of his hand with a well-placed kick.

She recovered and swept his legs out from under him before delivering an elbow strike to his midsection.

Andrew hit his opponent in the nose, breaking it. The man screamed and dropped to his knees, blood gushing through his hands.

She turned to check on Andrew. "Are you okay?"

He wiped a trickle of blood from his mouth. "I've been better."

Before they could catch their breath, three additional men burst through Alexa's front door.

She didn't wait for them to get close to Andrew. Instead, she ran across the room and launched herself at the group. The first to recover, she delivered a blow to the carotid artery in one man's neck, rendering him unconscious. The second rushed past her. Before she could pursue him, another assailant grabbed her and shoved her into the wall and then the glass foyer table. It collapsed under her weight.

"Alexa!" she heard Andrew call out.

Breathing heavily, she scrambled to her feet. Two men held Andrew down. She went to move, but she was grabbed from behind. An arm snaked around her neck. While she struggled, she watched the third man rush up and stab Andrew.

"No!" she screamed as Andrew doubled over in a heap.

Alexa balled up her fist and hit the man holding her in the groin. Then, as he dropped to his knees, she delivered an uppercut to his jaw.

"Andrew," she yelled out, and ran to his side. She stopped halfway when she saw one of the men hold up a weapon. She heard a muffled sound and then felt something pierce the skin on her neck.

Reaching up, Alexa retrieved a dart. She stared at it, but her vision grew blurry, and her steps faltered.

"No," she said in a voice that sounded foreign to her ears. Dropping to her knees, she struggled to move, but it was fruitless. Her body would not cooperate. The last thing Alexa saw was Andrew's still body sprawled out on her hardwood floor.

"ALEXA? LEX, WAKE UP!"

The darkness slowly receded. Her name was being called repeatedly, but it sounded to her like it was through a far-off tunnel.

"Is it raining?" she slurred.

Eventually, the haze cleared, and her parents and cousin, Zane, loomed overhead. Her face was wet to the touch. She glanced down and saw a washcloth in her mother's hand.

"Andrew?" Alexa bolted upright, her head spinning in protest of the sudden movement.

"Easy," her cousin warned. "Go slow, Alexa."

Zane helped Alexa to her feet. She weaved a few times as he lowered her on the couch.

"Drink this." Her father held a glass of water in front of her lips.

After taking several sips of the cool liquid, her throat felt better, but her body ached like she had been in a cage fight.

Gazing around the room, the events were beginning to return. Broken vases, a ruined entertainment center, glass everywhere, and several turned-over plants and pictures. Everywhere she looked relayed the remnants of the fight.

She checked her watch. Twelve hours had elapsed.

Alexa shook her head and instantly regretted it when pain grabbed a hold of her.

"That can't be right." She turned to her father.

"Dad, where's Andrew?"

Jake looked worried.

"He's not here, sweetheart. When we arrived, you were on the floor unconscious, and your apartment was empty."

Her worst nightmare realized, panic coursed through her, trying its best to incapacitate her, but Alexa tamped it down. She'd fall to pieces later. Andrew needed her now.

"They took him." She jumped to her feet but then swayed. Everyone reached out to steady her.

"I have to find him."

"Who's they? And you can't go anywhere just yet," her father reasoned.

Margot returned with a first aid kit she had found in Alexa's bathroom. Taking a Band-Aid and ointment out of the case, she bandaged her daughter's head.

"We need to take you to the hospital," her mother reasoned. "Who knows what those goons injected into you."

"She's not wrong," Zane replied while sweeping up debris and dumping it into the trash can he had retrieved from Alexa's kitchen while Jake assisted.

"There's no time," she said dismissively before turning to her father. "The Siren took him, and I'm going to get him back. But first, I need to go to Andrew's suite at the Salamander. I need the Bellasini. That's why he was taken."

"What?" Jake replied.

She got up. "I'll explain when I get back."

"No, you'll explain now, and we're all going with you," her mother countered.

"We don't have time," Alexa said tersely. "Plus, it will be dangerous, Mom. I'm not putting my family at risk."

"We're not asking," her father remarked.

"Fine," Alexa agreed. "Wait here."

She hurried up the stairs. When she returned, Alexa was wearing all-black tactical clothing with a backpack in her hand.

"Let's go."

While Jake drove, Alexa explained.

"Andrew has a centuries-old bracelet that was stolen from the Siren. A woman that is a criminal and killer. Sophia Porter's boyfriend, Nicholas, and his friend Gates were involved in its disappearance. Andrew promised to get it back in exchange for her leaving us all alone. Unfortunately, he didn't make the deadline, and now he's been taken for collateral."

When they arrived at the hotel, Benny escorted them to Andrew's room. Her family helped search.

"I found it," Margot exclaimed, coming out of the bedroom.

She held it up in the light. The sapphires, rubies and emeralds shone brilliantly.

Margot laid it against her skin. "Wow, this thing is something."

"Yes, and right now, it's the only thing keeping Andrew alive."

Alexa's phone rang. Not recognizing the number, she answered it anyway.

"Hello?"

"Hello, Alexa. I won't bother introducing myself. You have something I want, and I have something you want. I propose we make an exchange. Unless you don't want your boyfriend back?"

It took everything in her to remain calm. "Of course I want Andrew back—unharmed."

Her family stopped and zeroed in on the conversation.

"And I want my bracelet. So do we have a deal?"

"We do."

"And the girl, of course."

"I don't understand."

"Sure you do. Bring my bracelet and Miss Porter."

"I will do no such thing," Alexa said vehemently. "I'm not about to deliver my client to you."

"You will if you want to see Andrew again—alive, that is."

Chapter Thirty-Six

Terror ripped through Alexa, but she fought to remain calm.

"I'm doing what you asked. You wanted your bracelet, and I'm delivering it to you. Sophia has nothing to do with this."

"Oh, but she does, Miss King. She's the love of Nicholas Michaux's life and, therefore, essential to me. Besides, I have a bone to pick with Nico. He made me wait and caused me great inconvenience. So now, either bring the girl to me, or I start killing people, starting with your beloved parents, Jake and Margot. They have a lovely house, by the way. It's your call, Alexa."

Alexa's hand tightened on the cell phone. She glanced over at her father. "If you harm anyone I love," she whispered, "I promise I'll kill you."

"Aw, brave words. And while I appreciate your spunk, time is ticking, Miss King. You have the power to save everyone or kill them all. I don't care which you choose. I'm fine either way. I'm sure you'll be able to find the Pearl Tower. So don't keep me waiting."

"I want to speak with Andrew. I need to hear that he's still alive."

"Can't you just take my word for it?"

"No."

There was some shuffling on the Siren's line before she heard the one voice that mattered most.

"Hey, Lexi."

She closed her eyes and said a silent prayer. Andrew sounded tired, but it was still wonderful to hear his voice. "Drew," she breathed. "How are you?"

"Suffering from a minor knife wound, but I'll survive. Are you okay?"

She fought back tears. "I'm fine. Promise me that you'll keep yourself alive until I get there."

"No," he replied firmly. "Don't give her what she wants, Alexa. Stop worrying about me. I'll be fine."

There was a shuffle, and then she heard, "No, he won't unless you give me what I want. If you don't, your lover will die."

"He's injured and needs medical attention."

"You aren't in a position to demand anything."

"Yes, I am. I don't care how many threats you make. If anything happens to Andrew, the deal is off."

There was a long silence before the Siren said, "Fair enough. I suppose a dead hostage isn't much of an incentive, is it?"

She hung up before Alexa could respond.

Placing her phone back in her pocket, Alexa and her family rushed back to the car. Her father drove while Alexa gazed out the passenger window, struggling to pull herself together while she filled them in on the conversation.

"None of you can go home. It's not safe. She knows where you live and likely has her men watching the house." Tears flowed down her face, and her hands shook so badly that she crossed them.

"Don't worry about us," her father replied. "Getting Andrew back safely is the priority."

"I can't lose him," she said softly.

Jake squeezed her hand. "Everything will be okay, sweetheart."

"No, it won't. The last time Andrew and I were together, we fought, and I told him I didn't want to see him again. I didn't mean it," she cried. "I would give anything to take back what I said."

"Andrew knows that, sweetheart."

"How do you know, Dad?" she said tearfully.

"Because he knows your heart."

"Love is powerful and can heal all things," Margot replied from the back seat. She squeezed her daughter's shoulder. "It can survive even the most difficult of tests."

"I do love him," Alexa finally admitted. "I've wasted so much time being afraid, and now Andrew might die without knowing that."

"Alexa, you will save Andrew and defeat this crazy woman," Zane chimed in. "I know it."

She spun around. "How do you know?"

Zane flashed her a reassuring smile. "Because you're the best at what you do, Alexa. Trust that."

When they arrived at her condo, Alexa called her office to make arrangements for her team. Next, she phoned her friends Alejandro and Marena for help, along with Andrew's father, James, to bring him up to speed on the situation.

"I'll meet you in Lisbon," he stated.

There was no way that Alexa would try to talk James out of being involved in helping his son. So instead, she thanked him for the help and got to work.

THIRTY MINUTES LATER, Jake pulled up at Ronald Reagan Washington National Airport. He retrieved her bags while Alexa said goodbye to her mother and cousin.

"Promise me that you'll go somewhere safe."

"They will," her cousin promised.

"Be careful, Alexa."

"I will, Mom."

Margot hugged her tight. "Okay. Then go get your man."

Alexa smiled and kissed her on the cheek. "That's the plan."

Zane enveloped her in a fierce hug. "I'm so proud of you. Now, go sweep the floor with this psychopath!"

"I will."

Jake was waiting behind them.

"You call me if you need anything, Lex," he said gruffly. "You hear me?"

Alexa went into his arms. "I will, Dad. I promise."

Taking her luggage, she waved goodbye to her family and headed to the jet. When she got on board, the flight attendant took her bags while Alexa spoke briefly to the captain. Then she trudged to her seat. However, she stopped short when she saw Dyan, her driver, Valerie, her assistant, Miranda, and Sophia waiting.

"What's going on? Why are you all here?"

"We're here to help," Dyan replied.

"You are helping by keeping Sophia safe," Alexa remarked sternly. She turned to her assistant. "Miranda, you should be at home resting."

"I'm fine, Alexa. And after all you've done for me there's no way I'm not helping, too."

"I heard about the Siren taking Andrew and her demands," Sophia chimed in. "I'm going with you."

"No, you're not," Alexa countered. "It's too dangerous to have you anywhere near her, Sophia. She wants to use you to make Nicholas suffer. I'm not giving you over to her—even to save Andrew. You're under my protection, which supersedes everything else."

"This is Andrew's life at stake, Alexa," Sophia countered.

"I'm aware, but I still won't risk your safety. He wouldn't want me to."

Sophia sat forward. "Well, it's not your call to make."

Alexa's eyebrows shot up. "The last time I checked, I'm still the CEO of Dragonfly. And my decision is final."

Sophia turned to Dyan and smiled. "Tell her."

"Alexa, Ruben canceled his contract. As a result, Sophia is no longer under Dragonfly's protection."

Alexa glared at Sophia. "What did you do?"

"I overheard you speaking with Dyan. That's how I learned the Siren demanded that you bring me, and you said no. I can't allow you to sacrifice the man you love for me. I've been horrible to you for years, Alexa. I've blamed you for things that weren't your fault. This is my chance to make amends for how I've treated you. You've lost a lot, too, and I won't be the cause of more heartbreak for you."

The captain announced that they had been cleared for departure. Seeing the resolute expressions of her staff and Sophia, Alexa shook her head and took a seat.

Exhaustion poured over her like rainwater, so Alexa took a quick nap before briefing her team on their operational plan. When she awoke, Dyan was on her computer, Sophia was watching something on her phone, and Miranda and Valerie were talking.

Realizing that she hadn't eaten all day, Alexa buzzed the flight attendant and requested some food.

Once she had slaked her hunger, she opened her laptop and got everyone's attention to go over the plan.

"We have three teams on the ground—Dragonfly's operatives, Andrew's men, and James and his officers. But I'll have operational control. While I'm meeting with the Siren, all teams will move in to surround the main house. James's men will cut the tower's main power and access to the backup generators while our team takes out their transportation. His men will move in and will be responsible for ensuring we retrieve Andrew and get back out safely."

"And what will I be doing?" Sophia inquired.

"Staying safe with the backup team."

"That's not going to work. You heard the Siren's demands. She wants you to deliver me as well, Alexa."

"Sophia—"

"Look, I've listened to your plan, and I think it's lacking one major thing."

Alexa looked up. "What's that?"

"Leverage."

"We have it. The Bellasini is what she wants most. We keep that until everyone is out safely, and then I hand it over."

"That's not enough," Sophia persisted. "We need another carrot to dangle over her head, and that's where I can help."

"How?" Dyan queried.

"We hit her where it hurts—her wallet. Remember those accounts she forced Nicholas to open in his and my name so she could launder her money? Well, thanks to Nico, I've got access to them. We transfer those funds and use them as leverage to secure our safety."

Alexa shook her head and grinned. "Sophia, that's genius."

"Thank you." She beamed. "I'm sure her millions are worth more to her than that bracelet."

"Okay, ladies," Alexa said excitedly. "Let's go to work."

Chapter Thirty-Seven

When they arrived at the Humberto Delgado Airport in Lisbon several hours later, Alexa felt secure that their plan would succeed. And thanks to Sophia, they had a wild card that the Siren would not anticipate.

A black Mercedes-Benz Sprinter van was waiting to escort them to their rental villa about forty minutes from the Siren's compound.

Their rental home was a majestic two-story casa of white stone with bright lights and mature trees and flowers. It was dark, and she was tired, so Alexa didn't pay too much attention to the exterior.

There were guards strategically placed outside. Several stepped up to retrieve their luggage when they left the van.

"Good evening, Miss King," a matronly woman said as they walked into the entryway. It was bright, with white walls and dark brown baseboards and doors. The tan and brown tiles were in a checkerboard pattern, and there was a grandfather clock and a table with two armchairs nearby. Tapestries and paintings were strategically placed around the space, as were statues, planters and mirrors.

The steps to the second floor looked centuries old, as did the wrought-iron railing.

"Welcome to Casa Encantada. My name is Senhora D'Sousa."

"Olá," Alexa replied, and then switched to English. She introduced Sophia and her staff.

"Everything is in order. We have light refreshments in each bedroom, and every room has an en suite bathroom."

"Thank you, Senhora D'Sousa."

They followed the housekeeper upstairs. The older woman was short and shapely, and wore her salt-and-pepper hair pulled back into a chignon. She wore a navy blue dress with white trim and comfortable black shoes. She reminded Alexa of her aunt Ernestine.

Alexa walked in and glanced around the charming room.

One of the men set her bags at the foot of the bed and left. Across the room was a sofa and coffee table with a food tray and a glass water bottle. Though exhausted, Alexa nibbled on some nuts and dried fruit and drank a small glass of water. Next, she took a quick shower. Then, not up to putting her clothes away, she only retrieved a pair of cotton pajamas and socks.

After dressing, Alexa climbed into the bed and turned off the light. She turned on her side and stared out the window. For the first time all day, Alexa was alone, and it was quiet. She took a moment to think about Andrew. Her heart ached at what he must be going through. Her newfound love expanded in her chest and fueled her desire to rescue him. She would do whatever it took and bring all her expertise and resources to bear to save the man she loved and to keep Sophia safe.

"Please hang in there, Drew. I'm coming," she murmured before falling asleep.

ANDREW TRIED SEVERAL times to find a comfortable position in which to sleep. His stab wound in his midsection was giving him a hard time. True to her word, the Siren had sent a doctor in to assess his injury. He was happy to hear that it wasn't fatal, but it required stitches.

He couldn't forgive himself for being so careless. But after his fight with Alexa, he hadn't slept well, tossing and turning all night before finally giving up on sleep. By daybreak, Andrew had decided to see Alexa and sort everything out. She had said goodbye, but it didn't occur to him for one minute that their relationship was in danger of being over.

He arrived at her condo, and when she didn't answer, he turned to leave but heard a noise inside. Bracing the door, Andrew rotated the knob as quietly as he could and inched the door open.

Seeing two men moving around Alexa's apartment made him furious. He was then flooded with fear. Was she there? Was she hurt?

That thought prompted him to action. He barreled into Alexa's living room and began pounding on the intruders. Unfortunately, when a third man arrived, they were able to do him harm. When he looked up and saw Alexa rush into the mix, his first reaction was that he would kill her for being so reckless. The second was that he'd never seen her more beautiful. Watching her defend him made his heart swell with love and pride. Andrew had known before that he was in love with Alexa, but seeing her take on those men to keep him safe was his undoing. He fell even harder.

"Good night, my love," he whispered, and closed his eyes.

ALEXA FOUND JAMES sitting in the dining room when she came down for breakfast the next day. She rushed right over and into his arms when she spotted him.

"I'm so glad you're here," she murmured against his chest.

"Where else would I be but here helping you bring JJ home?" he said, hugging her tightly.

"I'm sorry I couldn't stop them from taking Andrew."

"Uh-uh. None of that, Alexa. I know you did everything you could to defend him. So don't despair, kiddo. We are going to get him back. Our plan will work."

They were moving out that evening, so the entire team gathered to go over the plan until everyone was briefed and ready to go.

When Sophia saw Nicholas enter the room, she ran over and flung herself into his arms. He caught her and held her tight.

"Are you okay?" he whispered into her hair.

"Yes," Sophia confirmed. "I'm fine."

"I'm sorry," Nicholas confessed. "For all of it. When I heard you'd been taken…" He stopped and struggled to speak for a few seconds. "My entire world turned dark."

"I know," she agreed. "I'm sorry, too, Nico."

Nicholas leaned down and kissed Sophia with a passion that relayed his feelings as clear as if he'd spoken them aloud.

He searched her face. "Are you ready?"

"Yes," Sophia said with conviction. "Let's take her down."

ALEXA'S TEAM MOVED out at two o'clock in the morning. Valerie drove one of the four black armored Mercedes-AMG G 63 SUVs that Alejandro Reyes supplied while the other teams were spread out between the other three and the Mercedes-Benz Sprinter vans. Everyone was dressed in black tactical gear with body armor, except Alexa.

"Are you okay?" she asked Sophia.

"Yes," she replied confidently. "I'm good."

A few moments later, she turned to Alexa. "But, if—"

"It won't," she replied, reading Sophia's mind. "You're going to be fine. We all are."

Per their usual procedure, the teams were dropped a mile off and continued the rest of the way on foot. All except Alexa's vehicle, which continued up to the house. Equipped with night-vision goggles, the groups splintered off when they reached the Siren's compound. Each team with a specific job to do.

Adjusting her communication device in her ear, Alexa said, "We've arrived. Bluebird and I are heading in."

"Roger that, Guardian. We're in position and awaiting your signal."

Valerie drove up to the door and stopped. Men immediately headed toward the car. Each took one side and swept it for explosives. Then, satisfied, they opened the back door.

"Watch yourself," Alexa warned Valerie.

"I will. You, too."

Opening the door, one of the Siren's men stepped aside to let Alexa and Sophia get out.

"Your driver can park around the—"

"She stays right where she is," Alexa said firmly. "I don't plan on being long."

He didn't reply but turned and headed to the house. Alexa and Sophia followed behind.

As they entered, they were patted down before being led to meet the Siren. Sophia was carrying a laptop bag that was searched as well. The man checked Alexa's pockets, but they only produced a penlight, lip balm, a key chain and the velvet bag holding the Siren's bracelet.

"They're clean," the man announced.

"This way," another replied.

Alexa took a mental note of every window, exit and person they passed.

They were led down the floating staircase into the Siren's dojo. She spotted the woman sitting across the room on a raised dais. Her red hair was braided into a single plait that rested on one shoulder. She was wearing black leather pants and a black top, and a red-and-black open-front cardigan that fell just above her ankles.

"You must be Alexa."

"Siren," Alexa replied.

"I see you brought the girl after all."

"Where's Andrew?"

The Siren waved to one of the men across the room, who left and returned with Andrew in tow. Alexa noted that he was disheveled and moved with difficulty because his hands were bound behind his back. By the thin line of his lips and gray pallor, Alexa suspected his injury was causing him pain.

He was given a chair to sit on between Alexa and the Siren.

"As you can see, I kept my end of the bargain. Now, where is my property?"

Alexa reached into her jacket and retrieved the velvet bag. She handed it to the closest man, who took it to his boss.

When she opened the pouch, her eyes lit up with excitement as she studied the bracelet. Then, satisfied, she nodded to one of her employees, who went over and cut the ties binding Andrew's hands.

Andrew sagged in relief and rubbed his wrists.

"Now, the girl."

"What about another trade, Siren?"

The older woman was intrigued. "I'm listening."

"Let Andrew and Sophia go in exchange for me."

"No," Andrew said, getting up. "You have what you wanted. Let Alexa and Sophia go and keep me."

Alexa shook her head. "Andrew and Sophia go."

"I have a counteroffer. How about I kill all of you and be done with it?"

"You could, but then you'd lose millions of newly laundered dollars—or did you forget that?"

The amused smile slid off the Siren's face like oil on a slick surface.

"Looks like you did forget." Alexa turned to Sophia and nodded.

Sophia walked over to a table, opened her laptop bag and retrieved her computer.

"Wait, what is she doing? Why wasn't she checked?" the Siren demanded.

"She was," one of her men replied. "She's not carrying any weapons."

Sophia logged in to her bank account and set up a transfer. Then logged in to the following account and repeated the action. Finally, she spun the PC around to face the Siren.

"If they don't leave, I hit this button, and your money goes poof."

The Siren's face remained calm. "Foolish girl, you can't press anything if you're dead."

"That's true, but if I don't text the branch manager an abort code in fifteen minutes, he will complete the transfer for me." Sophia smiled triumphantly. "What's it going to be, Siren?"

The Siren's expression turned furious. She let out a roar of anger, threw off her cardigan and charged at Sophia.

Alexa tapped her ear as she moved to intercept her foe. "Ten minutes," she whispered.

"Roger that," came the reply over her earpiece.

"Alexa," Andrew called out. He went to move, but one of the Siren's men grabbed his shoulder and forcefully shoved him into the seat, causing him to grimace in pain.

Placing herself in front of Sophia, Alexa evaded several of the Siren's hits, but one caught her square on the jaw, and she struggled to maintain her balance. When the Siren tried to sweep Alexa's legs out from under her, she nimbly avoided the move and countered with several body strikes, knocking the Siren to the ground.

Several of her men rushed to defend her, but she ordered them to stop.

"She's mine," the Siren announced, spitting out blood.

The two continued sparring, with neither gaining the advantage.

"She's tiring," Andrew called from across the room.

"Shut up," the man guarding him warned.

Andrew switched to German to instruct Alexa on a defensive move.

"Danke," Alexa called out before implementing his suggestions.

She began hitting the Siren with combination moves that she couldn't defend.

Finally, realizing that Alexa was gaining the advantage in hand-to-hand combat, the Siren took it to the mat and tried to best Alexa with jujitsu. She tried a rear choke hold, but Alexa was trained on how to break it, and her response was automatic.

Tucking her head, Alexa grabbed the Siren's arm and pulled it down hard. Then, quickly, she wrapped her leg behind the Siren's calf, dropped her base, and spun around before pushing against her blocked leg. The Siren immediately lost balance and crashed to the floor. Alexa mounted her and delivered several blows.

Eventually, the Siren was able to push Alexa off and make it to the side wall. She retrieved a katana sword from its sheath.

Alexa yanked another of the ancient swords from the wall in the nick of time to defend herself against the Siren's attack.

Steel collided with steel as the two women fought. Each moved around the dojo mat with skilled precision as they engaged each other in battle. The Siren had more skill and thus the advantage in using the katana, but Alexa was calmer, providing her an edge.

Suddenly, a loud pop sounded, and the room went pitch-black.

"What's going on?" the Siren called out.

"I don't know, boss."

"Then go find out, you imbecile," she snapped.

Alexa silently dropped her sword and got low to the ground. "Sophia?"

The younger woman flicked her miniature flashlight on and off once like Alexa instructed and remained quiet.

They heard a man moan, and then a loud thud.

"Andrew?" Alexa exclaimed, trying to determine the direction of the sound.

"I'm okay. One down," Andrew confirmed, breathing heavily. "Who knows how many more to go."

Suddenly, an arm snaked around Alexa's neck.

"I can play in the dark, too," the Siren whispered in Alexa's ear.

Bending over, Alexa flipped her and followed through with a hit to her solar plexus when she landed on the mat.

Gunshots rang out in the distance.

She retrieved her penlight from her pocket, turned it on and moved it in a sweeping motion around the room. "Andrew, Sophia, we've got to move."

"Okay," Andrew replied.

Alexa turned and flashed the light on the other side of the dojo.

"Sophia?"

"I'm here."

Seconds later, one of the men grabbed Sophia around the waist. Remaining calm, she fished her lipstick out of her pocket. Sophia twisted the barrel to the left and right before touching it to the man's arm around her neck.

He started shaking violently and then dropped to the floor.

Free, Sophia turned off the mini Taser, grabbed her bag and headed to the steps.

"Not so fast." The Siren slammed into Alexa, knocking her to the ground.

"Andrew, you two get out of here," she called out. "You'll have help."

As if on cue, the lights were restored, and James and his team rushed down the stairs.

The Siren used the distraction to pin Alexa to the ground. Then she retrieved a knife from her boot and slashed Alexa's arm. Next, she raised it to her face.

"I'm going to leave you with something you'll always re-member," she threatened.

Grabbing the Siren's wrists, Alexa struggled to get the blade away from her face. When she was successful, Alexa placed her knee to her opponent's chest and launched the Siren over her head, giving herself time to get up.

Finding her sword, the Siren swung wide and would have seriously injured Alexa had she not jumped back.

Spotting her sword, Alexa dived to get it. When she got to her feet, she brandished it to keep the Siren at bay.

The clashing of steel against steel was deafening.

"Eileen, stop!"

The loud, deep voice boomed from across the room. Startled, the Siren whipped around. When she saw the man standing there, the color drained from her face, and her sword clattered to the floor.

"Dad?"

James was helping his son while his men disarmed the Siren's remaining bodyguards. When Andrew glanced up and saw who it was, he smiled.

"Good to see you again, Mr. Livingston."

"Likewise, Riker. Though I have to admit that you look terrible."

"Thank you," Andrew said tiredly.

"A member of your team contacted me with the coordinates. Thank you for that. You held up your end of our deal and found her. I'll do the same."

The Siren glanced at Andrew and then at her father. "What do you mean?"

Randolph regarded his daughter. "It's time we end this, Eileen."

Her face contorted with anger. "Stop calling me that," she said vehemently. "My name is Siren."

"You are Eileen Livingston, my daughter. And it's time you came home."

"I'm not going anywhere with you. And it's English. I'm using Mom's maiden name now," she spat. "And you can't just barge in here, throw your weight around and interfere with my plans. How'd you even find me?"

He didn't respond. Instead, Randolph touched her wrist.

She yanked her arm away. "What are you doing?"

"That's your mother's bracelet. I gave it to her before she died."

The Siren jutted her chin out. "And she gave it to me. It's all I have left of her."

"That's not true," her father replied. "There are many things I have saved that belonged to her that now belong to you. But this—" he pointed to her hand "—was always your favorite, so I knew if it went missing, you'd move heaven and earth to get it back."

She backed up several paces. "You had it stolen?"

"Yes," Randolph replied. "It was the only way I could find

you, to draw you out. I'm just sorry men had to die in your quest to get it back."

"You tricked me?" Her eyes grew bright with tears. She glared at Andrew. "You led him to me," she spat. "This is your fault." She tried to lunge at Andrew, but Alexa blocked her path.

"Don't try it," Alexa warned.

"Your reign of terror ends now, Eileen. You're coming with me, and I'll get you the help you need."

"No, I'm not. And stop calling me that. I'm a grown woman. If you think I'm going to give up my life of independence to be under your thumb again, you're mistaken, Father," she said as if the word were a curse. "I have a very lucrative business that I built from nothing. I worked hard to get where I am."

"No, you killed and intimidated people to get where you are. You're sick, and you need help," he said gently. "Please, let me help you."

The Siren continued to back up. "No." Her voice shook, and she looked confused. "You're just trying to trip me up. I ran away from that mausoleum for a reason, and I'm not returning."

Randolph signaled his men. The Siren spun around to look for her bodyguards, but they were gone. She ran to grab her sword, but they beat her to it.

"Don't touch me," she yelled when two men took her by the arms and ushered her up the stairs. "No, you can't do this. I'm the Siren. Do you hear me? I promise I'll kill every last one of you when I get the chance. I'm the Siren!"

The echoes of her screaming eventually faded away.

Randolph sank into a chair. He sighed loudly. "I'm sorry for all the trouble my daughter has caused. Unfortunately, she has a delusional disorder, just as her mother did. I took Eileen to the top mental health professionals. Her treatments worked for a while, but she refused to continue her sessions. Then, while I was on a business trip, Eileen got free of my staff and ran away."

His eyes were saturated with pain. "You can't imagine the helplessness of having a child run away and not being able to find them. I had my men searching everywhere, but my efforts were useless. By the time I heard about the Siren—" His voice was racked with grief. "I was too late to help my wife before she…died, but I have found a facility that can provide Eileen with the help she needs. One where I can visit her and help in the healing process."

"What about the people hurt or that died because of her?" Alexa asked.

"She isn't well enough to face prosecution, Miss King. And honestly, with my legal team, it's unlikely that she would. But this is my cross to bear, and I will do whatever it takes to ensure my daughter isn't a threat to anyone again."

Randolph got up and left with his men, looking decades older than when he first arrived.

Alexa held Andrew's hand. "It's over."

He squeezed it back. "Thanks to you."

"It was a group effort." She smiled and then grimaced at the cut on her lip. "Andrew, about the things I said—"

"Forgiven," he finished for her. "I went to your condo that morning to apologize and humbly ask you to reconsider leaving me. Alexa, I never meant for you to feel like I doubt how capable you are of protecting yourself, me or whomever you're hired to guard. You're my world, Alexa. You have been since you stepped into my life. And I will do anything to keep you safe from harm. It's who I am. I'm just sorry I went about it in a way that caused you to doubt my true intentions."

Alexa shook her head. "Forgiven. And you should know that I went back to the hotel that morning to tell you I was sorry for what I said. I'm truly grateful to you, Andrew, for how you've protected, cared about and supported my endeavors since we met. Because of your hard work, dedication and commitment, I found a career that I love and a passion for serving others in a way that keeps them safe."

"And *you* whole."

She smiled. "And me whole." She laced her fingers through his. "I'm not scared anymore. I know what we have is real.

You were right. We can't live in a bubble worrying about losing those closest to us. I can finally let go of my past and direct that energy to my future."

He touched her cheek. "Our future," he corrected.

Alexa beamed with happiness. "Our future."

Andrew lowered his head and kissed her. Alexa's hands came up to rest on either side of his face. A few moments later, she pulled back.

"Do you know the first stop on our new journey?"

He grinned lasciviously. "Do tell."

"The hospital," she said lovingly.

Andrew chuckled and wrapped his arm around her waist.

"Lead the way, Miss King."

Chapter Thirty-Eight

"Here, is this better?"

Alexa took a pillow from the couch and adjusted it behind Andrew's head.

"Much." He sighed happily. "You know, I don't think I ever told you how proud I am of you. You were willing to let me die to save Sophia. That shows that you take your job seriously."

She burst out laughing. "Well, I'm glad you approve. Though I had no intention of letting you die, Mr. Riker. In truth, I would've been devastated if something had happened to you."

"Because you realized you loved me?"

"Yes, after our fight and you were taken, it hit me square between my eyes that I loved you and didn't want to lose you."

Andrew touched her cheek. "You are never going to lose me, Lexi."

She settled next to him on the couch. "You can't promise that, Andrew. None of us is in control. Our lives could be over in the blink of an eye."

"True, but when you love someone, you give it your best shot and do what you can to keep each other safe."

She leaned in and kissed him. "I love you, too. But honestly, Drew, because of what we do for a living, sometimes it does worry me." She snuggled closer, careful not to lean on him too heavily.

They watched the fire blazing in the hearth in silence for

a few minutes before Andrew said, "You know I'm not made of glass, right?"

"I know, but the doctor said it'll be another week before you can get your stitches out. And until then, no strenuous activity—of any kind."

Andrew leaned over and kissed Alexa's lips, then a trail down her neck.

She immediately gravitated toward his touch. "You're not playing fair." Her words drifted out of her mouth like a soft caress.

"You know, there are a few things that I can think of that are not necessarily categorized as strenuous."

"No, sir," she laughed, pulling back. "You promised you'd be back to one hundred percent before the next group of trainees arrived. I love you, Andrew Riker, but those sparring sessions with overeager students can be a bit much."

"And I will," Andrew said, chuckling, before picking up her hand and kissing her palm. "And on that note, lunchtime is over. Back to work we go."

"Ugh," she protested. "I'd much rather be snuggling on the couch here with you."

"That prospect is just as exciting for me, but you know if we're late, Dad will come looking for us."

Alexa bolted off the sofa. "You've got a point. Let's go. Phalanx is calling."

They rode the ATV from the guest cabin back to the main building for their next class. Alexa enjoyed helping Andrew and his father with the training sessions. She had taken a leave of absence from fieldwork at Dragonfly to stay in Pagosa Springs for an extended period until Andrew was fully recovered. She was still acting CEO and conducted most of her business by video conference while Dyan handled meetings with new clients and Alexa's duties as the principal chief protection officer.

"There you two are," James said when they returned to the training room. "I thought I would have to send up a flare signal."

"You know Alexa wouldn't miss jujitsu training. She loves grappling with the students."

"I'd rather be grappling with you," she whispered in Andrew's ear.

His gaze could have scorched a block of ice.

"Anytime you want to try those nonstrenuous activities, just let me know."

She laughed and playfully pushed him away. Then, after taking off her coat, Alexa warmed up to prepare for their next class. When the students trickled in a few minutes later, Andrew took the lead, instructing the students on which grappling techniques they'd learn during the class.

While he explained, Alexa used a volunteer to execute the motions that Andrew relayed. Unfortunately, the student didn't understand the technique at one point, so Andrew stepped in to demonstrate.

"Be careful," Alexa warned.

"Always am." He winked.

As Andrew explained, he placed his hands on Alexa to show the trainees how their bodies should rotate in and out of a position. Next, he demonstrated how to flip an opponent using the attacker's body weight, not their own.

He flipped Alexa, and she landed on the mat.

"Sorry, my love," he said sweetly as she lay there staring up at the ceiling.

"No problem, my love," she responded with a saucy grin.

Rolling over, Alexa pushed herself up.

"You dropped something, Miss King," one of the students remarked.

"Oh?" Alexa was wearing a karate uniform called a gi, which didn't have pockets. "Thank you," she said, automatically looking down.

There was a black velvet ring box sitting on the mat. She

stared at it for a few more seconds before gazing, bewildered, at Andrew.

"What in the world?" she said as she knelt to retrieve the box. When she opened it, all the air left Alexa's lungs. She remained frozen in her spot, speechless as she stared at the square-cut diamond engagement ring with stair-step diamonds flanking the main one.

When she looked up, Andrew was down on one knee in front of her. Her hand covered her heart as she stared at him through unshed tears.

"Alexa Yvonne King, I have loved you since I carried you back after getting shot in the chest during training."

The group let out a collective gasp, each looking around worriedly.

"I had a bulletproof vest on," Alexa said, trying to ease the horrified students' minds.

"You are intelligent, caring, funny and sexy," he continued. "Plus, you truly make me the best version of myself. I would be elated to spend the rest of my life loving, working with and coming home to you. Will you do me the honor of becoming my wife?"

Alexa leaned forward. "James Andrew Riker II, I have admittedly been stubborn and have run from relationships, but you have shown me that love can be constant, and I don't have to fear it, nor does it have to end in sorrow or tragedy. Because of you, I know that love is patient, kind, understanding and long-lasting. Being vulnerable enough to give another person a chance to share your life is the greatest gift of all. I love you, Drew, and yes, I will marry you, and I can't wait to be your wife."

Beaming proudly, Andrew leaned over and kissed Alexa. She wrapped her arms around him and cried tears of joy as she returned the kiss. Everyone clapped as he placed the ring on the third finger of her left hand. Alexa peered at the brilliant diamond ring for several moments, in awe at the surprise proposal. Then she spotted her family standing off to the side.

Alexa was so shocked that she yelped before rushing over to greet her parents, cousin, aunt and uncle. Next, James and Esther stepped up to offer their congratulations. James dismissed the class early so their families could return to the house and honor the newly engaged couple.

While they were celebrating, Alexa received a video call from Sophia. She and Nicholas wished her and Andrew congratulations.

"Thank you and Andrew for protecting us both," Nicholas stated. "And for keeping us, you know, from being dead."

Alexa's eyebrows rose. "Oh, you're welcome, Nico."

"You know, we worked so well together that anytime you and Andrew need operatives, Nico and I would be happy to lend a hand."

"Wow," Alexa said with genuine surprise. "If the need arises, we'll let you know."

"Cool. I have a special engagement gift for you, Alexa." Sophia grinned. "Just a moment."

She and Nicholas moved out of the way, and another woman moved into view.

Alexa was stupefied. "Oh my gosh. Shelley?"

"Yes," her old friend confirmed. "It's wonderful to see you, Alexa."

"Likewise," she said between tears. "I can't believe it's you. You look amazing," she cried.

"So do you. Sophia's told me so much about your life now. I'm so happy for you."

"Sophia has kept me in the loop, too. I'm glad you're living life to the fullest, Shelley."

They chatted for a few more minutes before Shelley had to go, but she promised to keep in touch.

"I'd love to as well," Alexa confirmed.

When they ended the call, Alexa found her fiancé and wrapped her arms around his middle. She told him about her video call with the Porters.

"Thank you," she said sincerely. "This was a perfect proposal, and I love you so much."

"I love you, too, soon-to-be Mrs. Riker."

"I love the sound of that."

* * * * *

COMING SOON!

We really hope you enjoyed reading this book.
If you're looking for more romance
be sure to head to the shops when
new books are available on

Thursday 15th February

To see which titles are coming soon, please visit
millsandboon.co.uk/nextmonth

MILLS & BOON